Syn

R.L. Canning

authorHOUSE

AuthorHouse™
1663 Liberty Drive
Bloomington, IN 47403
www.authorhouse.com
Phone: 1 (800) 839-8640

© *2017 R.L. Canning. All rights reserved.*

No part of this book may be reproduced, stored in a retrieval system, or transmitted by any means without the written permission of the author.

Published by AuthorHouse 02/01/2017

ISBN: 978-1-5246-6980-5 (sc)
ISBN: 978-1-5246-6982-9 (hc)
ISBN: 978-1-5246-6981-2 (e)

Library of Congress Control Number: 2017901453

Print information available on the last page.

Any people depicted in stock imagery provided by Thinkstock are models, and such images are being used for illustrative purposes only.
Certain stock imagery © Thinkstock.

This book is printed on acid-free paper.

Because of the dynamic nature of the Internet, any web addresses or links contained in this book may have changed since publication and may no longer be valid. The views expressed in this work are solely those of the author and do not necessarily reflect the views of the publisher, and the publisher hereby disclaims any responsibility for them.

To Kirby H for all your help and support over the years.

Special thanks to:
Krissy VanAlstyne,
Kiki Von Waou,
Amy Louise of OrganiChaos for all your patience and beautiful artwork, and all my friends for your kind words that helped keep me writing.
Cover by Christian Corkery

CHAPTER 1

"Hello?"

"Hey, man, it's Pete. You up?"

Looking down the bed at his nicely formed tent, Holden said to himself with a snicker, "Hello there. You're up early." Answering Pete, he said, "Yeah, some of me is." He laughed at his own inside joke. "What do you want?"

"Jeff and Andrew are coming into town around three. We're going for a late lunch and then a late night. You in?"

"Uh … yeah. What time is it?" Holden asked, glancing over to the clock on his nightstand. It was flashing 12:00. "Fuck," he said, annoyed at the power outage and the fact he was too lazy to get a battery backup. He didn't wait for Pete to answer. "Yeah, call me when they get there."

"Will do," Pete agreed.

After hanging up the phone, Holden rolled over a couple of times but couldn't fall back asleep, not knowing the time. "Fuck," he said again as he got out of bed. Wearing only his boxer shorts, he walked into the living room and sat on his couch. He turned on the TV, and, after scrolling through the guide for a third time, decided that *Sanford and Son* was the only thing worth watching.

He opened the lid to his laptop to check what had happened in the world while he was asleep. Messages received: 0; e-mails: 0. *Oh, to be popular,* he thought. Checking the clock, he saw it was nine o'clock, so he decided to lie down on the couch and watch TV before taking his morning nap.

The phone rang again. "Hello?"

"Hey, man, you ready? We're going out in half an hour."

"Half an hour? I thought you said threeish," Holden said in horror.

"Dude, it is three."

"What? Fuck. All right, the boys are in town? I need a shower; I'll stop by when I'm done."

"Sounds good," Pete acknowledged.

Holden was amazed he'd slept so long. Not believing it, he verified the time on his laptop. The TV was now showing a cooking show; the chef was explaining how to make the perfect chicken Kiev. "Yeah, right," Holden said as he clicked off the TV. He leaned over to the laptop once again to plug in the speakers located in the bathroom. He stared at the screen for a moment, trying to decide what to listen to from his extensive playlist. He finally decided on some rock to shake off his late morning, early afternoon nap. Zeppelin was the obvious choice. "I has got to get the Led out," he said aloud in a horrible British accent.

The speakers came alive with Robert Plant's distinctive a cappella wail.

"Ah, 'Black Dog'. Almost perfect." His fingers slid the volume control to the max. "Now it's perfect," he mused.

After the shower, he quickly got dressed by throwing on the first things in his dresser and sliding on his favourite Chuck Taylor's. Pete's house was only five blocks away, but Holden still felt the need for his MP3 player. He used Billy Talent as his walking music.

Ding dong. Ding dong. Holden pressed the doorbell over and over again. He let out a chuckle as the song "Close to you" popped into his head. He heard his friend shout to him from an open upstairs window. Holden slowly opened the door and saw his buddy Andrew standing at the top of the stairs. Before Holden could even say hello, Andrew yelled, "Heads up, asshole!" and a can of beer came flying down the stairs at him.

Instinctively, he caught the beverage, cracked it open, and had his first sip before he even took off his shoes. He knew right then that it was going to be a very long night. "Damn nice to see you, Andrew," Holden said sincerely.

He walked up the stairs and saw the boys wrapped up in an intense game of Guitar Hero. He sat down and took another drink of beer. "So, what brings you guys into town?"

"Jeff has a job interview at a law firm, and I thought I'd come for the road trip," Andrew said.

"Law firm, eh? Look at you, growing up so fast," Holden said and laughed. The four had been friends since elementary school and had just finished their last year of college. Upon graduation, Jeff and Andrew had gone back to their home town of Muskoka for the summer, while Holden had moved from his school in Oshawa to Toronto. Pete, who had gone to college with Andrew and Jeff in Toronto, elected to find work in the city. This would be the first weekend they'd hung out together since graduation.

Holden was happy to finally be living in Toronto after spending the last two years alone in Oshawa, taking a sports administration course. He now had an entry-level job with a local roller hockey team. Pete had taken law enforcement and been recruited by the Metro Toronto Police; he was going to leave in a couple of weeks for his training. Jeff, with his legal assistant course under his belt, hoped to get a job with the prestigious law firm he had an interview with the next day. Andrew had taken office administration and had a job lined up at a resort in Muskoka, starting Labour Day weekend. It was possibly one of the last times the four would be able to get together for the foreseeable future.

"Damn nice to see you guys," Holden said again.

"Aw, do you need a hug?" Pete asked sarcastically as he continued to kick Jeff's ass at Guitar Hero. The other two guys gave him a courtesy chuckle.

Several beers went downrange before Pete finally decided he was hungry. The group finished their drinks and headed out the door. Although it was suppertime, the restaurant they picked was fairly empty, and they got their seats right away. Their waitress was a beautiful young blonde who wore a shirt that was at least one size too small, accentuating her rather large breasts. The boys couldn't have been happier.

They ordered their first round of drinks and then browsed through the menu. Holden hoped to order chicken Kiev; he didn't understand why, but he was craving it. Finding it under entrées, he threw the menu on the table as the first round showed up. He looked around the restaurant and noticed that every waitress was blonde and very ample. He wondered if they had walked into Hooters by accident. Nope, they hadn't, he determined. Apparently the restaurant just had a fantastic recruiting program, and no one was hired over the phone.

The waitress flirted with the table as she took their order. Jeff was obviously in love with her, so Andrew, being the friend that he was, made small talk with her. He casually mentioned the fact that they were from out of town and only in Toronto for a few days. She took the bait and asked them where they were from and what special occasion brought them to the city. Andrew threw his arm around Jeff and loudly exclaimed they were there because Jeff had an interview at a law firm to become a lawyer. Jeff, the shyest of the bunch, blushed and quietly corrected his friend. Andrew cut him off, making him take the promotion and all the attention that comes with such a job, whether he liked it or not. Obviously impressed, the waitress focused most of her flirting on Jeff. The meals came and went, as did several more beers. Jeff slowly came out of his shell, his confidence boosted by the waitress's flirting. Of course, the liquid courage didn't hurt.

Before the bill showed up, they came up with a plan for the rest of the night. Andrew, the ladies' man of the group—at least in his own mind—said that he'd heard a new "ballet" opened up in town. He wanted to stop in and say hi to the ladies. All the guys knew he was referring to a new strip club. It was like teasing kids with candy; once the seed of naked women was planted in their brains, there was no stopping them. They jumped at the idea, and they were off.

Jeff was still obviously worked up from the flirtation of the waitress, Misty or Mimi or whatever the hell her name was, and almost ran to the strip club. As the boys rounded a corner, they saw the big, flashing, pink neon sign: "Fantasia". Pete opened the door, and Jeff almost ploughed him over to get inside.

The doorman stopped them. Despite the fact they were college graduates, the doorman still had the nerve to ask for their IDs. Pete huffed in mock discontent at the inconvenience, getting a laugh out of the group.

They quickly took their seats on perverts row, so they wouldn't miss a thing. Girl after girl came on stage, all shapes and sizes. The odd girl came up and, as sexily as she could, asked each one of them if they would like a dance. They decided their beers and the floor show were good enough for the time being.

It was now eight o'clock, and the evening crew was starting to filter in. After becoming bored with the generic girls on stage with their *thump, thump, thump* hip-hop music, Holden glanced around at the girls walking in. He always found the girls in their street clothes much sexier than those scantily clad in stripper outfits.

"Holy shit!" he yelled. He turned around and slapped Jeff across the chest, almost knocking him out of his chair.

"What the fuck?" Jeff asked, confused.

"Look!"

"Oh my God" was all Jeff said.

The other two guys cheered when they noticed the waitress from the restaurant walking in, carrying a bag.

"You think she dances here?" Jeff finally muttered.

They all agreed it wasn't out of the realm of possibility, but also that there was a chance she was only waitressing here as well.

Only a minute later, out popped the waitress. She was wearing big plastic high heels, white knee-highs, a very short plaid skirt with slits to the waistband on both sides, and a tiny white blouse with only one button done up. Her red lace bra shone through her blouse under the black lights.

Holden turned to Jeff. "I think the chances of her dancing here have greatly improved." Jeff nodded in agreement.

Andrew leaned forward, shouting for the group to give him money. Pete and Holden knew what he was up to, so they freely coughed up some dough. After collecting the cash, Andrew frantically waved the money into the air.

The waitress recognized them, and a big smile lit up her face. She pranced over to them, her tits bouncing freely with every step. Definitely hot. She leaned into Andrew, and he whispered something into her ear.

She smirked at Jeff and gave him a wink. He was now speechless and blushing. He gave her a wave back. She slowly and seductively walked over to him, gently held his hand, and led him to the back room. Jeff was only too happy to follow her.

Holden slid over into Jeff's chair. "One down and three to go," he said with a laugh.

Andrew was the next to go when a beautiful French girl wearing a corset and thigh-highs approached him, leaving only Pete and Holden on the row.

Even with the crew change, the girls all appeared the same; the music was the same generic dance club music. Holden definitely liked the odd beat but thought it was too much. He wondered why they didn't break it up with different genres of music.

His train of thought was interrupted as Led Zeppelin's Black Dog came blaring over the sound system. The DJ paused the song after the opening line and said, "Ladies and gentlemen, get ready to beg for forgiveness because taking the stage next is Syn." The rock started again the second the DJ stopped talking.

Holden's attention was fully on the stage when the most gorgeous woman he had ever seen walked up the stairs. He first saw her very long, curly black hair. Her big brown eyes felt as sweet and innocent as the best girl next door, but her devilish smile told a different tale. She had a well-tanned complexion that was accented by her dark hair. She had on a black mesh shirt with holes big enough to reveal her black plastic bra. The bra had a white trim and a skull half covering a broken heart and crossbones on her left breast. She had her thumbs through holes in the sleeves of her shirt, somewhat hiding her hands except for the very tips of her fingers, which were adorned with black-painted fingernails. She was also wearing black cotton boy-cut panties, complete with white trim and the skull design on her left cheek. *Syn* was written in the heart. Black, knee-high, fishnet socks and a pair of Converse Chuck Taylor high tops with the tops turned down completed the outfit.

She walked around the stage, making eye contact with every guy in the place. Her movements were very graceful and in perfect rhythm to the music. Holden couldn't take his eyes off her. He thought she was very sexy.

Pete elbowed Holden, acknowledging Holden's lifelong weakness for punk rock girls. Holden ignored him because he was in a trance, watching Syn's every move. Besides the style, he wondered what made her different, what made her amazing. He tried to convince himself that he was being silly and that she was a dancer like all the others. Only the music was different. That was it. He told himself that he hadn't fallen instantly in love with her, that he only loved the song.

Despite his objections, he still couldn't stop watching her. Her dancing and crowd interactions was like no other because she obviously really enjoyed what she did. As she worked her way visually through the crowd, she finally met Holden's steel-grey eyes. She stumbled and stopped dead as their eyes locked on each other.

Syn had many admirers, guys who came back night after night to see her. She flirted with each and every one, knowing she needed them to make a living. But once she saw Holden, she knew he was different. Not only were his eyes glued to her, watching every movement, but she saw something deeper. He had wavy blond hair and was wearing a button-up, short-sleeved plaid shirt that clung to his muscular chest. What made him different, she thought, was his smile. His jaw was defined and strong, but he had an innocent, sheepish quality about him. She knew he was waiting to see her naked, but she also knew he wasn't like the other perverts in the place.

She regained her composure once she realized she was still on stage, and got back into the groove of the music. But her eyes were still focused on Holden's, giving him her sexiest, baddest smile.

The first song ended, and the familiar guitar intro of Marilyn Manson's "I Put a Spell on You" started up. *Fuck, she has style, I'll give her that,* Holden thought. The second song was when a dancer typically began to shed clothing. Holden was nervous. It was the first time he had ever felt like that in a strip club.

Pete noticed Holden's anxiety and tried to make fun of him, but Holden blocked him out. As a matter of fact, Holden managed to block out the entire crowd, as if Syn were dancing only for him. She did a spin around the famous brass pole and continued to twirl to centre stage. Her right foot kicked her ass, then slammed to the stage, bringing her twirl to a halt. She was standing directly in front of Holden with her feet apart. She stared down with an intensity like no other. Her smile faded, and her eyes burned into him. She reached down, to the bottom of her mesh shirt, and slowly pulled it over her head.

Holden was so fucking hard, he was worried that if he had to stand up too fast, there wouldn't be enough blood flow to his brain to keep him stable.

With a toss, her shirt went sliding towards the stairs of the stage. She kept an eye on the garment, ensuring it landed a safe distance away from her. Her body remained still as she snapped her head back towards Holden. She reached around to unclasp her bikini top, forcing her elbows as far back as possible to show off her perfectly formed tits. The top loosely fell open as she bent at her waist. Her head almost touched the floor as she glanced at the table behind her. She ran her hand up her leg and over her pussy. She then put both her hands on the floor. Her head tilted up so their eyes met again, and she gave Holden a quick smile.

Then the intensity was back as she began to very slowly rise. Her top fell to the ground and her hands reached behind her neck. Her forearms buried themselves in her tits, showing off a star tattoo on her right elbow. Holden thought her bare stomach was very hot. She wasn't as skinny as the other girls, but she was also nowhere near chubby. She had more mass, giving her very sexy curves as well as a unique softness.

Holden wanted her badly. He told himself not to be stupid; she was a professional, and he knew he couldn't fall for her. He realized she must have seen his puppy-dog eyes and was playing with him, expecting him to pay for dances after.

She spun around, showing Holden her perfect ass, and dropped her arms to the cheers of the crowd on the other side of the stage. She reached her hands back, dug her fingers deep into her ass cheeks, and squeezed. With a flip of her hair, she looked back at Holden and gave him another wink. She moved around the stage again, walked to the pole, and shimmied to the top. In a show of true athleticism, she used her arms to extend her body fully parallel to the floor. Everyone's jaws dropped.

Even more amazingly, she just let go of the pole, dropping to the ground. The crowd thought she had fallen. Holden began to stand to help her until he saw her twist in the air. She landed in a push-up position. With one pump she pushed herself up so she was standing. The audience applauded her exceptional dancing skills, but she ignored the accolades and carried on with her routine.

Putting one foot behind her until she was resting on her toes, she used that foot as a pivot and began to spin as she slowly spiralled to the floor, ending up on her side with her back once again to Holden. He found it very frustrating because he wanted to see her face and her tits, but he appreciated the game she was playing. It added excitement to the night, and having a hot, naked girl flirt with him, regardless of the reason, was always an ego boost.

The guys across from Holden were getting a good show as they cheered. All Holden could see were her hands moving over her body. He recognized the last verse in the song; her second set was almost over. Holden didn't want to see it end, but he knew the third set was for all the marbles. He hoped to have the opportunity to finally see this goddess naked.

She collected her things, left the stage, and disappeared into the changing room. "Syn will be right back for her last dance," the DJ announced.

Fuck, I don't want to wait that long, Holden thought.

On the upside, he had time to finish his beer and order another. Andrew and Jeff were still in the back room. Holden noted the two vacant chairs and turned to Pete. "They must be having a good time," he shouted. Pete nodded in agreement, not trying to speak over the blasting music.

As the filler song ended, the lights went out, except for two red spotlights. The music started and the DJ came across the speakers once again. "Syn is back for her last song of the set, but don't get too close. There is no absolution for this Syn."

Syn gave the DJ a mock glare of discontent. She had changed into a long, elegant black dress slit up to her waist, and fishnet gloves that went to her elbow, but she was still wearing her Chuck Taylors and fishnet knee-highs. Holden laughed to himself. *Yup,* he thought. *I never go anywhere without mine either.*

As she stood at centre stage, the two spotlights went to black. The sound of a church bell rang. With the first ring, the red spotlights flashed. With the next ring, white spotlights flashed. The pattern continued for four more rings. During the flashes, Holden could tell Syn was focused on him. He could feel her passion. *Fuck*, he thought, wanting her so badly.

Instruments joined the bells for "Hell's Bells". The full set of lights came on, matching the beat of the music. Syn again walked slowly around the stage, every movement in rhythm with the music. She made it appear effortless but so intense. She was like no other dancer he had ever seen.

She dropped to her knees and crawled over to him, her long, black, curly hair hanging down. Holden wanted to reach out and grab it, pull her to the ground, and fuck her right there on stage. He tried to control himself as she moved his beer out of the way. She reached up to his short blond hair and pulled him towards her. She slid her cheek down his, bit his ear, and whispered "Hi, I'm Syn." Then she pushed Holden back in his chair and said something else. Holden couldn't quite make it out. She continued her routine.

"What did she say?" Holden frantically asked Pete.

"Dunno" was all he replied.

Fuck, what did she say? Holden asked himself.

Holden tried to let it go. He took a sip of his beer and sat back, pretending to be relaxed as Syn slowly slipped out of her dress. She was making eye contact with him as the gown fell to the stage. During the break, she hadn't put her bikini top on, so her tits were now fully exposed to him. She could see the lust in his eyes as she slid her hands behind her neck, playing with her hair. He knew she was intentionally letting him get a good look at her. Holden's eyes stayed focused on hers as she gave her own hair a pull, forcing her head to tilt towards the ceiling as if she could read Holden's mind.

Holden took the opportunity to sneak a peek. Her tits were perfect and natural. They were no bigger than a B cup, which was slightly bigger than Holden's preference, but he was quite all right with it. She gave him a knowing glance as if she had caught a kid in the cookie jar.

She turned away, and he noticed that she was still wearing her boy-cut panties that accentuated her ass perfectly.

She turned her side to Holden and dropped to her knees. She lay back on her elbows, leaning her head back until it touched the stage. Her toned legs showed great definition under the stage lights. Her stomach was very hard and flat, and her tits were firm and perky. The way she was positioned was by far the sexiest pose a woman could do in any circumstance, Holden was definitely hooked.

She slid her legs out straight, then pulled her knees to her chest. She moved her arms to her waist and slipped her thumbs into the waistband of her panties. The crowd, anticipating her getting naked, erupted once again. Holden could tell that she really thrived on the crowd's cheers.

Her intensity level increased, and with a quick move she ripped her panties off her ass, past her knees, and over her shoes, and gave them a toss towards the stairs. She gently opened her legs, giving some guys at a table by the stairs a nice show. Her hand moved to her breast, momentarily covering them. She slid it down her ribs and over her stomach to her pussy. Holden couldn't exactly see what she was doing, but the guys at the table seemed to be enjoying the show.

Her hand slowly made its way back up her body to her lips. The finger that had just been inside her disappeared into her mouth. She tilted her head so she was staring right at Holden as she ever so slowly stuck out her tongue to give her finger a long lick. Then she slid it back into her mouth, sucking off all the flavour. She leaned to her side with her knees slightly bent, as if she'd rolled over in bed. Their eyes were locked. She rested her head on her hand as they had a staredown. Neither of them wanted to be the first to break eye contact. The music continued to play in the background, but neither of them were paying attention to it.

Holden wasn't sure how long she lay there, but before they knew it the song was over. Without hesitation, she stood up and walked off the stage. Another song played, meaning another girl would soon be onstage, but Holden knew none of the others would compare to Syn.

Holden felt abandoned. *What in God's name was I thinking, getting worked up like that over a stripper?* he thought.

Just as he was about to turn to Pete to comment on the absence of their friends, Holden heard a door slam over the club's loud music. He looked up and saw Syn. She appeared pissed off as she stormed through the crowd with her head down. Holden wondered what had happened. He hoped she wasn't in trouble. Then he saw what the problem was. Apparently it was him.

She charged over to him and grabbed him up by his collar. Not giving him a chance to fully get to his feet, she dragged him as he stumbled along to one of the armchairs that lined the walls of Fantasia. All he heard from Pete, as he was being dragged away to what he thought was certain death or at least a hefty ass-kicking, was "Bye."

She threw Holden into the chair, put her arms on the armrests, and slammed her knees between his legs and the chair. She pulled the back of Holden's hair so his neck was exposed and his eyes met hers. "What the fuck is your story?" she asked.

"What?" Holden questioned.

"You, asshole. You know what I mean. What's with you?"

"I, uh, don't know what you mean."

"Yes, you do. The way you stared at me, you threw me off my routine."

"Sorry?"

"No, you're not! And honestly, neither am I. Come on, you're buying a dance. You owe me." The aggression in her voice turned to a gentle sweetness he wasn't expecting.

"All right, but I should warn you, I have two left feet," Holden said as he was dragged into the VIP rooms. Holden saw Jeff and Andrew with their dancers, and they were obviously enjoying themselves. Andrew gave Holden a thumbs up as he saw him walk by.

Syn picked the room she liked and told Holden to have a seat. She sat on his lap. "Hi, I'm Syn," she said with a smile.

"Yeah, I think I heard that before," Holden said playfully. "I'm Holden."

"Holden?"

"Yeah, you know, from—"

"*Catcher in the Rye*," she said. "I loved that book in high school."

"Yeah, apparently so did my parents," Holden said, laughing.

She extended her hand and said she was very pleased to meet him. Holden happily accepted her hand and shared her sentiments.

"Sorry I'm sitting on your lap," she added. "I find it so hard to talk in here over the music."

"Oh, it's OK, I guess," Holden said as if he were put off.

She laughed and slapped his arm. "Poor guy, I'm sure you'll live."

Several songs played, during which the pair only made casual conversation. Then she said she it was time for her to dance for him. Holden said, "It's lucky we're in the right place, then," trying in vain to make a joke. Syn said that she found it hard to dance in the booths, because she couldn't pick the music and she hated most of the music the other girls selected.

The next song started. She never broke eye contact as she slowly took off her clothes, getting as close to Holden as possible. Her bra fell to the ground from beneath her mesh shirt, which she kept on. Last to go were her panties. As she reached for them, Holden commented on how awesome they were. She jokingly said she could leave them on if he wanted. Holden said he could live without them and asked her to continue. She smiled and stood up, bending over at the waist as far as she could, her ass tightening.

It is so beautiful, he thought. It was also close; he wanted to lean in and bite it, but he refrained.

She slowly pulled the panties down over her perfectly shaped cheeks and dropped them to the floor, pausing momentarily to let Holden see her pussy. It was shaved and, by the looks of it, very wet. She turned around, seeking acknowledgement. All Holden said was that it appeared like she enjoyed her job. He had a sexy smirk as he said it. With an equally sexy smirk of her own, she replied, "Some days more than others."

She fell into his lap, pushing her back into Holden's strong chest. Holden left his arms on the armrests. She reached down and pulled them to her stomach, cuddling deeper into him and resting her head on his shoulder. The scents of her shampoo and perfume filled the air. He thought she smelt fantastic. He pressed his cheek against hers. She let out a very sexy sound, a small moan of satisfaction. Holden hugged her tighter. He thought if they weren't in a strip club, it would be a very romantic embrace.

Syn breathed deeply into his ear. She felt less like a girl dancing for a customer and more like a woman in her lover's arms. She gently kissed his earlobe. She was straddling his leg, and he knew she had to be feeling his hard cock through his jeans. She started slowly moving her hips, grinding into his leg. Holden squeezed her stomach, and his hand wandered all over her midsection. She ground into him harder. He could feel her thigh against his hard cock.

And she could feel his large member against her. She wanted to pull it out; she wanted to feel him inside her. She was amazed at how carried away this stranger was making her. She knew this wasn't an average night for her and by no means was Holden an average customer. She clamped her hands on his legs and squeezed tightly. Holden's fingernails dragged her sides. A loud moan emerged from her, and the sound snapped her back to reality.

Worried one of the staff might see her getting carried away, she stood up, composed herself, and continued with a more traditional dance. She glanced up and down Holden's tall, well-toned body. She had been able tell as he watched her stage show that he was in good shape, but it took being close to him to feel the muscles under his clothing. What got her attention was the bulge in his pants. She smiled and put her forefinger to her mouth, biting it and giving Holden an oh-so-innocent expression.

Holden melted. She appeared so hot with her sweet facade. He wanted to throw her into the chair and fuck her hard. Again, he resisted and decided to just enjoy the rest of the show.

Her hands slid over her tits and down her stomach to massage her pubic area. She put a leg up on the chair between Holden's legs. One hand continued to work over her clit while the other extended to his face and traced his jawline to his mouth. Holden parted his lips to accept her fingers. She tapped his nose and waggled a finger, saying, "No, no, no."

Rejected, Holden fell back into his chair, giving her a sad look. She smiled and spun around. Bending at the knees, she leaned back and tipped her head into his crotch. Her hair draped over his lap. Her hands rested on her knees, and she shook her head as if she were continuing to tell him no. She turned her body so she knelt with her mouth mere inches away from his throbbing cock.

Holden wasn't sure how much more he could take. He peeked down and caught a light glimmering off her cheek. He was seeking ways to ease the pressure, so he focuses hard at the sparkle. It was a piercing. He was surprised he hadn't noticed it before. He asked her if she had any others that she might have taken out for work. She showed him the keeper she had in her eyebrow.

Holden confessed that piercings and tattoos were his weakness. He told her that he had four himself. "Where?" she asked.

"Well, I have one nipple and three elsewhere."

With the "elsewhere", she checked out Holden's bulge, bit her lip, and nodded towards it as if to ask, *There?*

"Yeah," Holden confirmed.

"Can I see it?"

"I guess. I could send you a picture to your email if you want."

"No, now! I want to see it now," she demanded.

"Well, I don't mind showing you, but I know enough about strip clubs to know that whipping my cock out would get me one hell of a beating," Holden said with a laugh.

Syn agreed it was a predicament. She got up and peeked out the door of the booth. "OK, coast clear. Hurry, honey."

"Seriously?"

"Yes! Now hurry," she said impatiently.

"Um, OK, but remember you asked, if the cops come," Holden said chuckling. He proceeded to unzip and pull out his very hard cock. He was happy that she was seeing it in its best possible condition – erect. He smiled at Syn; he couldn't believe he was pulling his cock out in a strip joint.

Her eyes widened. "Wow," she whispered. "I want to suck that so bad."

Holden laughed, and he could feel his cheeks get warm with embarrassment. "Stop it. You're making me blush."

"No, seriously, that is very impressive." She added, "The piercings are cool too." They both laughed as they examined his penis and the ladder of piercings that descended down his shaft.

"Well, if it were big, I wouldn't have had to decorate it. Did you see that the top bead is the Superman logo? I call it my little man of steel."

"Don't sell yourself ... ahem, short. It's not that small at all."

"Um, well, thanks. Can I put it away now?"

Laughing, she said, "Of course."

Zipping up quickly, Holden blurted out, "So ... wanna get married?"

"Sure, but the minister has to be Elvis and the bridesmaid Marilyn Monroe," she shot back.

"Elvis? Marilyn? Where do you think we are, Vegas? Seriously though, I do have two tickets to the theatre tomorrow night, and my friend cancelled at the last minute. Would like to come with me? That is, if you're not working."

"You're in luck. I have tomorrow off. What show?"

"*The Phantom of the Opera* at the Pantages Theatre."

"I have always wanted to see that, sure. I don't have anything to wear though."

"No problem. I was going to go pick something up for myself tomorrow. We can go shopping together. What time do you want me to pick you up?"

"Meet me at my favourite coffee shop, the corner of Yonge and College, at, say, two? Where were you going to go shopping?" she asked.

"It's a surprise. I'll see you at two, if you don't stand me up," Holden joked.

"I wouldn't dream of it. Call me Paige, by the way. You can text me if you get lost," she said and whispered her number into his ear. "Don't stand *me* up, Holden. It was nice meeting you."

She gathered her clothes and disappeared out the door. Holden had no idea what time it was or how long he had been in the booth with Syn. He wasn't even sure if his friends were still around. He questioned what had just happened, thinking he was only setting himself up to get hurt. He paused at the entrance to the VIP rooms when he realized he hadn't paid her. He wondered if she too had forgotten. That couldn't be it; she was a professional. Had she stolen his wallet? Nope, still in his back pocket.

He figured he would see her before he left and could pay her then. He looked around and saw his friends across the bar. His cock was still fully erect, and he assumed it was painfully obvious to all who was paying attention. He took his seat. "So, how was it?" Pete asked, knowing Holden had been twitterpated with Syn.

"Great, thanks." Holden said. The others laughed. Holden ignored their remarks as he frantically punched her number into his cell phone. He glanced up at Pete with a cocky smile and said, "Save contact. And you, Jeff? How was your night?"

Jeff turned to the group with a beaming smile. "You're not the only one with a date," he boasted.

"That a boy," Andrew said.

After they finished their beers, they headed for the door. Holden paused and told the boys he had to say goodbye to Syn. He found her and said, "I think I forgot to pay you for your hard work."

She smiled. "First one's free. You want any more, you have to come back to me." She winked, turned, and walked away.

Holden joined up with his friends as they climbed into a cab. They sat in silence, thinking all in all it had been a great night out with the boys.

CHAPTER 2

As Holden got off the subway, he checked his phone for the time. The digital display read 1:45. He had fifteen minutes to spare. College Avenue, where the coffee shop was located, was two blocks away; he figured he would get there in plenty of time. All he could think about was his upcoming date with Paige, but he tried to remain guarded. He didn't want to be too disappointed if she wasn't there. He tried to shake the negativity from his head, but it persisted. *She was just being nice. In her line of work, she must have hundreds of guys hit on her. It's her job to make each one feel special.* He decided that at the coffee shop, he would wait until two thirty. That was respectable. He had her phone number – that is, if it was indeed her real number.

Holden reached the corner and peered down the street. As he had feared, there was no coffee shop to be seen. He walked up and down the block, thinking maybe he had missed it in his haste. He was about to give up, and then he saw a small sign on a door that could easily be overlooked. It was above a short set of stairs that led down into a basement. Holden followed the stairs and hesitantly opened the door. It was a coffee shop all right.

Because he was early, he didn't spend a lot of time searching for Paige. He ordered his coffee with the plan of sitting down, checking his social media, and waiting patiently for his date. After getting his order, he turned to found a suitable place to sit.

Instead what caught his eye was a very beautiful woman sitting alone, a backpack resting against her chair at a small table for two. She was wearing a white tank top, black bra straps exposed on her soft shoulders. She was also wearing three-quarter-length cargo pants, ankle socks, a pair of black Puma shoes with white trim, and dark-rimmed glasses.

Is that Syn? he wondered.

The woman at the table didn't notice him. Her head was buried in a book, and she was listening to something on an MP3 player. Holden tried to get a better view without getting caught staring. "It can't be her," he told himself. He remembered Syn being beautiful, but this girl was breathtaking. He thought about walking a little closer to see for sure.

Then inspiration struck. He decided to send her a text to tell her that he was there. He hit Send, and the girl reached into her backpack and pulled out a beeping cell phone. With a tilt of her head, her long, curly hair fell over her shoulder. He saw a star tattoo on her elbow, confirming without doubt that this goddess was Syn, and she was there to meet him.

Paige read the text as Holden approached her table. She smiled and her legs became tingly with nerves. Unbeknown to Holden, she had shown up at the coffee shop an hour early to wait for him, not wanting to risk missing the man who had made her emotions run wild the night before. She had been thinking about him all night. Now that he was close, her nerves were overwhelming her.

Before she could panic, Holden was standing at the table. "Excuse me. I can't seem to find a seat. Mind if I share your table?" he asked.

Paige glanced around the near-empty shop. She chuckled at his weak pickup line and invited him to take a seat. She was trying her best to hide her giddiness, fighting back a smile.

Holden put down his drink. He took a seat as Paige gathered up her things to make room for him. "Whatcha readin'?" he asked.

Paige peeked over the top of her dark-rimmed glasses and blushed ever so slightly. She showed him the cover of the book. "*Catcher in the Rye*. For some reason I was inspired to reread it." She felt embarrassed at her confession. *What must he think? I know. He thinks I'm a psycho stalker; that's what he thinks.*

Holden was very flattered that he had influenced her like that. "I hear that's a good book," he said. They both laughed.

"Yeah, a freak last night made me think of it, so I picked up a copy for old times' sake," she said, taking a sip of her coffee to hide her embarrassment.

"A freak, eh? He sounds like a very smart guy to me," Holden joked. "I wasn't sure if you were going to make it. You were up late last night," he added.

She leaned forward, grabbed his collar, and pulled him towards her. She put her lips to his ear. "I couldn't wait to see you today. I woke up at nine to get ready," she confessed.

"Well, it was worth it. You look fantastic," he said, not knowing what else to say. He was still trying to process her words.

"Thanks," she replied with a smirk.

They drank their coffees and made small talk for the next hour. Holden felt he could have talked to her all afternoon, but he subtly suggested they should get going. "Oh, goodness, yes," she agreed. "Sorry, I didn't realize how long we've been here."

They gathered their things. In unison, they stood and slung their backpacks over their shoulders, causing them to smile at one another. When they left the shop, Holden guided her into a right turn and headed towards Kensington Market. He thought it was a lucky coincidence that her favourite coffee shop and his favourite place to buy clothes were within a few blocks of each other.

The market was a great little area hidden in the heart of Toronto. It had everything from groceries to vintage clothing, which was why it was one of Holden's favourite places to go shopping.

"You're trying to find theatre clothing here?" Paige asked.

Holden smiled at her, gave her a wink and diverted into the first shop. The counter was at the right of the entrance. A young Goth girl welcomed them before she went back to reading her magazine. The shop had all kinds of old clothes: seventies-style tuxedos, band uniforms, suits, Victorian dresses, and much more.

Paige left Holden's side and wandered around the women's section while Holden took his time browsing through the menswear, occasionally pulling out fun clothes to show Paige. She was doing the same with her findings. There were great things in the shop, but nothing stood out to either of them, so they left and continued down the street.

They went through three or four more shops before Holden found his perfect outfit. He took Paige's hand and pulled her towards his new treasure. The pièce de résistance was a maroon seventies tux with tails highlighted in pink trim, matching ruffled shirt, bow tie, and cummerbund. He loved it. Paige wholeheartedly agreed.

Holden went to try it on. When he exited the change room, both the clerk and Paige were waiting for him. Paige couldn't control her laughter. "That's awesome; you *have* to get it," she exclaimed. "And I found this while you were changing." She threw him a black cane with a silver skull handle.

"So, ladies, what do you think?" Holden leaned on the cane, folding one leg over the other in a classic Charlie Chaplin pose. Paige, still laughing, thought the cane was the perfect touch, and the clerk agreed. "I don't look stupid?" he asked.

"Very," Paige said, "but in the best possible way ever."

"Sold. How much?" Holden asked, turning to the clerk.

The clerk thumbed through the items. "OK, the tux and the cane will be thirty dollars."

Paige and Holden both commented on the remarkable price. "One down. Now let's get you something equally awesome," Holden said to Paige.

"Agreed!" Paige said, giving a big nod.

They thanked the clerk for her assistance. Holden grabbed his bags, and they left to continue their hunt. Exploring a few more shops, they carried on with their search for perfection while keeping in mind which shop had the best plan B.

The second-to-last shop on the block had Paige's newest wardrobe addition. The dress was low cut and full length in Victorian style, maroon with pink lace trim that complemented Holden's tux perfectly. It was as if the two garments had been made together. Like Holden's tux, her dress was a perfect fit, except she looked much better in hers than Holden felt he did in his.

Exiting the change room, Paige felt very elegant, as if she were in a fairy tale. Despite the elegance, she was also a bit self-conscious – until she saw Holden's expression. He gazed at her as if she were a real princess. Her heart melted. She had never felt more beautiful. She performed a twirl to show off the flow of her new dress for Holden's benefit.

Holden wanted to hug her. He forced himself to remember that this was their first date and they weren't that familiar yet, so he held back. She noticed his intent and reached out, putting her arms around his shoulders. Holden responded by putting his arms around her waist. Pulling her close, he caught the scent of her perfume, which instantly reminded him of the intensity of the night before.

She whispered, "So … I look good?"

"Yeah, you look amazing."

"I think so too," she replied with a smile. "I'll take it." She leaned in and kissed his cheek.

After the transaction was complete, they left the store. Paige suggested that they go to her place to change, since her apartment wasn't too far from the coffee shop. As time was becoming a factor, Holden agreed. Paige led him by his hand down the maze of streets to her place. It was located over a restaurant, and small. "Must be easy to get takeout," Holden joked.

"Yeah, that place is going to make me fat," she replied.

They climbed the stairs to her door; she fumbled with her keys until she finally managed to get the door unlocked. Over her shoulder, she said, "Ignore the mess. I think my roommate is at work, so make yourself at home."

"No problem. You should see my place," he said.

The door swung open, and he realized she wasn't kidding about the mess. Her place was an older two-bedroom apartment that had the feel of a typical college student's room. The living room area was to his left; the couch was old and torn, with clothes thrown over the back. The table wasn't much different, except instead of clothes, it had dirty dishes and papers covering the top.

Immediately to the right was a bedroom. Paige threw her backpack on the ground behind the couch, then headed into the bedroom. She stopped in the doorway, turned around, and said, "You can change in here. My roommate won't be home for hours. I'll be out in a minute." With that, she lifted her tank top, showing Holden her bare back.

"Tease," Holden yelled.

She used the heel of her foot to close the door. "Whatever do you mean?" she yelled back through the closed door. Her question had a playful tone, and Holden knew it was definitely rhetorical.

He snooped around the apartment a bit more. He found their tiny kitchen on the other side of Paige's bedroom. The countertop held more papers, dirty plates, and cookware. Hanging above it were wine glasses dangling upside down by their stems. The small fridge and stove were retro in style and golden in colour. The stove had a pot of something sitting on the cold element. The kitchen held a small, rickety table and a lone chair. The table was another throwback that could have been bought from the market they were at earlier. It had a white top with brown swirls, and long steel legs. The chair had green upholstery and the same steel legs. It reminded him of a similar one his parents had had in his childhood home. On the table was a small laptop with a half a bottle of water beside it and nothing else. The floor had shoes and clothes tossed everywhere, making it as difficult to negotiate as a minefield.

At the very back of the apartment was the second bedroom. To the right of the bedroom door was another door, which Holden assumed led to the bathroom. He took a peek through the open door. The room was a disaster. The mess made Holden smile a bit.

Overall the apartment had a nice smell and a very comfortable feel about it. Holden took some time to look at the pictures on the wall. Most of them were collages of Paige and another woman he assumed was her roommate, with different friends at various parties and landmarks around the city.

Holden heard a bang and a thump from Paige's room. He turned to see what was going on. "I'm all right," Paige yelled. She was laughing. Holden couldn't help but laugh as well.

He found a spot by the living room table to put his bags. He undressed. It felt weird to be getting undressed in a stranger's house, especially while fearing her roommate could come home at any time.

Holden reached into a bag and pulled out his new tux. As he dressed, he got excited for the evening. All went well until he got to the bow tie. "Damn, it's not a clip-on," he cursed to himself. The clerk could have at least mentioned the demonstration bow tie wasn't the same as the bow tie he rented before throwing it in the bag with everything else. He had no idea how to tie a bow tie. He threw his old clothes into his bag and slipped on his black leather chucks. He was all ready to go except for the damned bow tie.

He saw the computer on the kitchen table and wondered if Paige had an Internet connection. Maybe he could search "how to tie a bow tie". But he wasn't overly worried about it. He made himself comfortable on her couch and turned on the television.

Paige heard the noise and yelled, "Are you ready?"

"Sort of. Don't suppose you know how to tie a bow tie, do you?"

"I'll be ready in a minute. I'll see what I can do."

Holden found a game show. His feeble attempt at answering the trivia questions made him feel pretty stupid. He knew only a few of the answers. He thought, *definitely not smarter than a fifth grader.*

He heard a rustling at her door and turned in time to see it swing open. His jaw dropped. Paige stood in the doorway, striking modelling poses. "What do you think?"

Holden was speechless. The long pink dress clung to her perfect body, and the low-cut neckline highlighted her cleavage. The waist was cinched tight as if she was wearing a corset. The bottom of the dress had pink lace trim and a subtle maroon strip. It even had a small train trailing behind her. The sleeves and collar were trimmed with pink lace as well.

In Holden's opinion, what pulled the entire outfit together and accentuated her beauty was her long, black, curly hair hanging over her shoulders. She had accessorized her hair with two white diamond clips that sparkled in the dim light of the room. She had also added a pair of black elbow-length fishnet gloves that were fingerless, having only loops for her middle fingers to hold them in place. Holden had the urge to jump over the couch, push her into the bedroom, pull the dress up over her ass, and fuck her.

Still doing her modelling poses, she pulled up her dress to show him her legs. She had changed into a pair of fishnet nylons and the black Chuck Taylors she had worn the night before.

"I think I love you," Holden said, in awe of her beauty.

"Um, thanks? So you approve then?"

"Oh, very much so. Hey! We have matching shoes," he said, positioning his leg so she could see his footwear.

"Nice. Now come over here and let's see what I can do about that bow tie."

Doubting her skills, he walked to her anyway. She turned him around, reached her arms around his neck, and moved in nice and close to him. He felt her tits pressing into his back and could once again smell her hair. Between her smell and her touch, he got hard. Tight polyester pants were not ideal for hiding an erection.

It took her only a minute and she had him tied up. Leaving her arms on his shoulders, she told him to turn around. When he did, their faces were only an inch apart. Holding Holden as close as she was, Paige wanted to take him on the back of the couch. But, like Holden, she knew this was their first date, and she didn't want to come on to strong. Instead, she gathered her emotions and settled for staring endlessly into his eyes.

With her beauty and the sweet scents filling the air, Holden was experiencing sensory overload. He really wanted to kiss her. She read his eyes, and throwing her inhibitions aside, she leaned in slightly, Holden met her halfway. Their lips touched. It was their first real kiss.

Holden didn't want to rush things, but he certainly wasn't going to stop. Their lips spread ever so slightly as the kiss became deeper and more passionate. It was a kiss neither were willing to end.

When they finally did pull apart, Paige said she had to fix her lipstick. Holden followed her into the bedroom and sat on the edge of her bed as she reapplied her lipstick. Her bed was covered in the clothes she had been wearing earlier. Her dresser was cluttered with various make-ups and perfumes. On the floor were more clothes and shoes in separate piles. There were also piles of panties and socks. Holden assumed the piles were for clean and dirty. The mess made the small room appear very full.

Holden took a peek at her clothes and shoes. Messy as they were, he could tell she had style. *I'll keep her,* he thought.

At the head of the bed was a window that had various knick-knacks on the ledge. At the foot of the bed was a wardrobe closet with more stuff atop it. The walls were covered in band posters and held a shelf with a radio and a stack of CDs. A big nail had medals, necklaces, and bracelets hanging from it. All in all, it was typical of the college girls' rooms he had seen.

After Paige finished her make-up, she smiled at Holden and said, "Let's go."

They ran down the stairs. Holden had his backpack in tow, and Paige was careful not to trip over her train so she didn't hurt or embarrass herself. She asked, "So, where we going for dinner?"

Holden looked at his watch. It was already six. They only had an hour until they had to be at the theatre. "Nothing fancy," he said. "Sorry."

"Oh, all dressed up with nowhere to go."

Holden glanced at her and smiled.

They walked down the street until they arrived at a fast food place. Holden reached for the door and held it open for Paige. "After you, ma'am," he said, putting his hand on her back to escort her through the door. As they didn't have much time or money, it was pretty much the only choice for them.

At the counter, they were met with very different stares. Some people were impressed and others pointed and laughed. Holden was happy to be noticed, mostly because of the gorgeous girl on his arm. Paige seemed a little more uncomfortable, despite being used to the stares of strangers. At work she was in control; at the restaurant she felt vulnerable.

Holden noticed the unease in her eyes. He moved closer to her, put his arm around her waist, and reassured her that she looked incredible. He was the one that was out of place. She laughed. With her confidence back, she approached the counter and ordered. Taking their tray, Holden led Paige to a table in a far back corner of the restaurant, away from the gawkers so they could have some privacy.

Paige told Holden she had to go powder her nose, trying to be as prim and proper as the era her dress was intended for. Holden happily excused her. *It's all coming together,* he thought. She was no sooner out of sight than he went to work. He knew she would be a while sorting her dress out. He put his backpack on the vacant table next to theirs, along with their food trays. Reaching into his bag, he pulled out a white tablecloth, two candles with holders, a lighter, a plastic flower arrangement, two paper plates, and plastic glasses. Holden removed the food from its packaging and spread it out on the plates; he also disposed of the empty cartons.

As Paige turned the corner, she paused and let out a gasp. She stared hard at the table arrangement and then turned to Holden. Her smile beamed, her eyes lit up wide, and her hands covered her mouth. "Oh my God, that is the sweetest thing anyone has ever done for me!" she exclaimed.

Holden walked to her, took her by the hand, and escorted her to her seat. As she sat, Holden held on to her hand, gazed into her eyes, and kissed her fingers. He finally let go of her hand and took his seat as Paige reached for a fry.

"*Stop!*"

She jumped, dropping the fry. She looked at him quizzically, wondering what she'd done wrong.

Holden reached into his backpack and pulled out two cloth napkins. He handed her one and placed the other on his lap. "I wouldn't want anything to get on that pretty dress of yours," he said.

"Oh yes, we can't have that, now, can we?"

The rest of dinner consisted of small talk and constant glances from passers-by. Holden overheard an elderly woman say to her husband, "Oh honey, isn't that sweet?" The sentiment made the young couple smile.

Once dinner was finished, Holden glanced at his watch. "Shit, we have to get going." He blew out the candles, tossed the garbage, and stashed the other item in his backpack.

As they walked through the door, Paige reached down and took Holden's hand in hers. She was nervous, but he had been so good to her all day, she couldn't resist feeling his warm skin against hers.

Holden, when he felt her hand touch his, became nervous as well. The calm, cool demeanour he had tried to maintain all day was about to go out the window. His legs became weak, and the butterflies in his stomach were in an uproar. *Relax. Play it cool*, he thought.

He knew they didn't have time to walk, so he hailed a cab. In true Toronto fashion, one wasn't too far away. Assisting Paige into the car, he made sure her long dress wouldn't get caught in the door as he closed it. He walked around and took the seat next to her.

The cab pulled up in front of the theatre. It barely had time to stop before a young kid with black, spiked hair, wearing a red suit jacket, opened Paige's door. They were overwhelmed by the bright lights of the theatre that hung over the sidewalk. Paige, feeding into the atmosphere, extended her hand to the valet. He gladly accepted it and assisted her out of the car. Holden met up with them.

The valet was obviously quite taken with Paige. He couldn't keep his eyes off her, and he blushed when she gave him her hand. As Holden joined Paige, the valet checked out the pair and commented on their retro attire. Holden, pretending he was accustomed to such treatment, nonchalantly reached into his pocket and tipped the valet.

The couple turned towards the large oak doors of the theatre, which were carved with intricate detail. As they approached, the doorman, who was also dressed in a tuxedo, smiled and swung open the seemingly heavy door so they could easily pass through.

Holden held out his elbow, and Paige gladly slid her arm into his. He knew everyone's eyes would be on them. He couldn't have been prouder to walk in with someone so beautiful. Paige's hesitation at the restaurant had all but vanished under the lavish treatment they were receiving.

Holden whispered that he was going to check his bag, Paige looked at her watch and reminded him that they had ten minutes before they had to be seated. She was going to stand in the queue for the bar. Once his bag was checked, Holden found Paige in the line. They each got a glass of wine in lieu of beer, which, under normal circumstances, they would have preferred. They sat quietly, drinking their wine and commenting on the theatre and the other patrons. They were truly overwhelmed with all the glitz and glamour and were also impressed that all of the employees dressed in black tie, as did most of the patrons.

The lobby lights dimmed twice, indicating it was time for everyone to find their seats. Holden jumped off his stool, grabbed Paige by the hand, and helped her jump down from hers. Tickets in hand, they found the door closest to their seats and showed the usher their stubs. They got a smile of approval from the usher as she escorted them their seats.

The seats were well situated in the first section, in the middle of the row. In order to get to their seats, they had to pass several seated theatregoers. En route, they could tell their outfits were again being met with very mixed reactions. Neither Holden nor Paige really cared what the others thought. They were happy and they were together; no one else in the theatre mattered to them. Holden felt like the king of the world, and Paige definitely felt like his queen.

The curtain opened to an auction scene. Paige didn't know much about *The Phantom of the Opera*, so she was caught off guard when lot 667 came up – the chandelier. She almost jumped out of her seat when the orchestra played the overture. Holden too got goose bumps, especially when an overexcited Paige tightly gripped his hand.

The time past very quickly, and before they knew it, it was intermission. They headed back into the lobby for another glass of wine. As they talked about the performance, Paige had a very distinct glitter in her eye. Holden's adrenaline had him all pumped up as well. They took their last sips of their wine, and as if on cue, the lights flashed. Again the couple headed to their seats.

After the final curtain, they quickly retrieved Holden's backpack and went out into the cool Toronto night. A string of yellow cabs lined the sidewalk in front of the theatre. It was almost midnight. Paige asked Holden what he wanted to do. Holden suggested a nightcap at a local pub, then asked her what she had in mind. Paige again looked at her watch and said it was getting late and she didn't have much money, but she had some beer at her place if he wanted to go there for a drink. Holden took less than two seconds to think about her offer. He hailed another cab. Paige gave the cabbie her address. The cabbie picked up the radio and told the dispatcher his destination.

Paige snuggled up to Holden as she took his hand in hers. Her big brown eyes melted Holden as she spoke. "Thank you for such a great day. I've had so much fun."

"It's not over yet – or is it?" Holden said with a sly smile and a wink.

"We'll see," Paige said coyly. "I just wanted you to know how much fun I had."

"Yeah, I've had a great day too, even if it does end now," Holden said, squeezing his arm tighter around her.

The cab pulled up in front of Paige's door. Holden paid the cabbie by throwing a fistful of cash at him. He scrambled out of the car to catch up to Paige, who was already through the front door and up the stairs.

As she got to her door, she again fumbled with the lock. "Shhh, I don't know if Melissa is sleeping." Once through the door, they saw no evident signs that her roommate was home.

Paige told Holden she was going to go change, and for him to make himself comfortable. Holden took a seat on their couch, flipped on the TV, and tried to find something to watch, He wasn't interested in infomercials, so it was a challenging task. He clicked past endless channels of paid programming before he finally found a rerun of *Family Guy*. He did his best to ignore the rustling in Paige's room until he heard the door open. He turned in her direction.

She had changed into an old, slightly worn, tight white T-shirt that clung to her perfect tits, and a pair of baggy grey sweatpants. She flashed Holden a smile as she made her way to the kitchen. Holden kept his eyes on her the entire way. The pants had faded writing on the ass, which of course was designed to draw attention to that particular feature. In Holden's mind, it was perfect, because the cotton fabric definitely accentuated her magnificent ass. He felt himself getting hard. *Not yet. I don't want to get ahead of myself. It was a beautiful night with a beautiful girl. I'll have a couple of drinks and call it a night, nothing else*, he thought as he fought the direction of the blood flow. He didn't want to move too fast since he didn't want to ruin the chance to see her again.

Holden heard the familiar sound of bottles being opened. Paige quickly reappeared, holding a couple of beers. He was sitting in one corner of the couch, and Paige nestled in the other corner.

She handed Holden his drink; she couldn't believe that one guy could be so great. She wanted to rip his tux off him with her teeth, but she was hesitant. If he was indeed genuine, she wanted to take her time and do things right. She also wanted to maintain her guard in case he was playing her to get into her pants.

Getting her mind off of all the possible scenarios, she decided to simply relax and see how the night progressed. "Oh, *Family Guy*, I love that show." They sat quietly drinking and watching TV. After a short time, Paige broke the silence. "I can't believe you're still wearing that. It has to be uncomfortable."

Holden smiled at her concern. He reached down and untied his bow tie. "There, that better?" he asked.

"I think you could do more," she replied with a coy smile.

Holden dismissed her comment, and they went back to sipping beer and watching TV.

At half past the hour, Holden flipped to the guide channel. Paige saw a movie she liked and encouraged him to select it. After Holden found the channel, Paige suggested popcorn. Without waiting for his response, she jumped up and made her way to the kitchen.

Holden stood up and walked over to his bag. He told her that he was going to go into her room to change while the popcorn was popping. As he changed, the smell of popcorn filled the tiny apartment.

Holden joined Paige again in the living room. He was wearing the same clothes he had been when they first met up in the coffee shop. He was surprised to see that Paige had turned off all the lights. The only illumination was from the TV and what had to be twenty candles throughout the apartment. Their glow cast shadows on the ceiling and in the corners, which made the room appear a bit eerie.

Holden took his spot on the couch as the introduction to the movie was beginning. After putting the bowl of popcorn on the table, Paige lay down on the couch with her head in Holden's lap and stretched the rest of her body out. Holden, trying to get comfortable, put his feet on the coffee table and placed his hand around her shoulder. They snuggled in to watch the movie.

Halfway through, they were both yawning like crazy. Paige said, "Well, it's getting late."

Taking her remark as a hint, Holden looked at his watch. "Yeah, you're right. I guess I should be going. Thanks for the—"

"Not so fast," she said. She shifted; her head was still in his lap as she put her hand on the back of his neck and pulled him in so they could kiss. Holden didn't hesitate for a second, jumping on the opportunity while he could. He put his hand on her head and played with her hair, gently pulling it as he stroked it. Her kiss tasted sweet.

Wrapped up in the moment, he pulled her hair harder than he intended. The extra force caused her to let out a soft moan, and her hand squeezed tight on his thigh. The positive reaction made Holden pull harder still, this time in more control of the force. She opened her lips slightly. Her eyes rolled back in her head as she let out a louder moan and a very soft "Fuck."

Holden repositioned himself so he was lying beside her. He finally let go of her hair and kissed her again. Paige was getting worked up. The fatigue she had felt earlier disappeared. Her body was alive and Holden was moving too slowly. She appreciated the restraint he was showing, but she decided he needed encouragement.

Paige put her hands around his back and pulled him on top of her. Very ungracefully, he lost his balance, and instead of a smooth transition, he fell on top of her, landing only an inch away from her face. He was worried his body was crushing her. He gazed deep into her beautiful eyes, and the light from the candles lit up her face. He felt as if he were looking at a porcelain doll. He paused, taking in her beauty. "Hi," he said.

"Hi," she responded with a big smile. "Thank you for tonight. It was the best I've had in a while."

"It's not over yet," he whispered with a devilish grin of his own. He shyly bit his bottom lip. Her hand moved off his back to his head and pulled him towards her. Holden met her kiss and returned her tight embrace. He could feel her tits against his chest. This time he wasn't able to keep his erection under control, which didn't go unnoticed by Paige. She slid her hand down his side and past his waist to his cock. She grabbed it hard through his shorts and gave it a gentle squeeze. The unexpected sensation made Holden moan.

"I love your cock," she said matter-of-factly.

Holden fought back a laugh as he thought, *Well, he's awfully fond of you too*. Now that she had touched his no-no spot, he decided that she was fair game. His hands began to tremble as his brain told them his intent. He didn't understand why he was getting so nervous. He had been with a lot of girls before and never felt this nervous – well, not since his first time. He was concerned that she had such an emotional grip on him so fast. He was setting himself up for heartbreak.

Paige too, throwing caution to the wind, was concerned that she was setting herself up to get hurt. But every ounce of her being told her that what she was doing was right, so she decided to take the chance.

Holden, no longer thinking about the possible heartbreak, focused on the beautiful girl who lay beneath him with her hand on his cock. He moved his hand over her tank top, slightly grazing her tit as he made his way down to the waistband of her pants, pausing when he felt skin. Her legs opened as she interlocked them with his. Her hand moved to his back, and she dug her nails deep into his flesh. Holden felt her hips move as she positioned herself so his cock was pushed up against her pussy. Holden only got harder at the sensation and at the thought that he was soon going to be inside her. *Can this really be happening? Is she really going to let me fuck her?*

His hand slid under her soft cotton tank top and up her body, feeling her stomach and ribs along the way. He slowed down to feel every inch of her and, more importantly, so she could feel his hands on her, making the anticipation build. His touch sent shivers up her body. She wanted him to take hold of her, touch her, feel her. The anticipation was killing her. She knew it was only a matter of time before she felt his strong, smooth hands on her breasts, so she decided to enjoy the moment as it was. She just wished he would hurry things up a bit.

Holden was hoping his slow, deliberate movements would drive her to the point of begging. Her kisses moved to his neck and ear. Her breath caressed his skin. It was too much for him to take. His plan was backfiring.

He unsuccessfully tried to refocus on what he was doing. His hips moved in unison with hers as his cock ached to penetrate her. His hand gently traced each rib. Her hand roughly groped him, scratching his back and grabbing his ass to push his cock harder against her. Holden reached his left hand up to caress her face. He played with her earlobe, trying to further build the anticipation. His right hand slowly continued its journey up her body, rib by rib; he was so close to her tits that he wanted to pounce on her with both hands. But he fought every urge that coursed through his body. Sensing Paige wanted him just as badly, he knew the fight was futile.

To keep her off guard, he ran his finger down her ribs with unexpected force. As he did, she let out a gasp and jolted forward into him. Trying to overload her senses, he used his left hand to get a handful of her gorgeous, curly locks and pulled her against the couch. Her head tilted until her neck was fully exposed. Holden cupped one breast; it felt so soft in his hand. Her long nipple was fully erect against his palm.

Paige's heart raced as Holden forced her head back. The tenderness he had displayed disappeared in that moment. The pain startled her so much that she didn't feel his hand on her tit right away. As she caught her breath, she felt his fingers kneading her. She felt his heart beating through her own chest as his breathing increased. She had never wanted anyone more than she wanted him at that moment.

They moved their hips faster. Holden was becoming concerned he would get overstimulated and end things too quickly. He continued to caress her breast, which fit perfectly in his hand. He applied alternating pressure on his fingertips and the heel of his palm, trying not to get into a rhythm. He wanted to keep her guessing where and how she was going to be touched next.

In a fluid motion, Holden leaned into her, using his chest to put pressure on her other breast as he gently bit her neck. Her legs squeezed hard around his as she tried to force his cock into her through their pants.

Holden moved his hand all around her nipple, which was still very erect. He took a moment to tease it. Then he slid the same finger around her soft flesh.

Playing Holden's game, Paige suddenly rolled over, throwing Holden to the floor. "I'm going to bed now," she proclaimed.

Damn, did I do something wrong? Did I go too far? Holden wondered as she stepped over him and walked into her bedroom.

At the door, she reached down, pulled her tank top off, and threw it to the floor. She looked back at Holden and used her left hand to barely cover her breasts. She said, "You coming or what?"

Holden felt like a cartoon action figure; he imagined himself up so fast, he almost knocked her down as he passed her and jumped onto her bed. In actuality, he stood up quietly, composed himself, and walked over to her.

She continued into her bedroom with her arms hanging by her sides. She had made it only about three steps before he caught up to her. As his fingers touched her back, she turned to him. The only light they had to navigate by was that of the TV and the still-flickering candles. Paige reached around his waist as his arms went around her bare shoulders, slamming the door shut with her free hand. Her room suddenly became very dark. It took Holden several second for his eyes to adapt.

Confident the door was secure, Paige walked forward, pushing Holden back. He went cautiously, blindly trusting her to guide him through the maze of clutter on the floor. He almost lost his balance when the backs of his legs hit the bed. Paige quickly caught him and kept him standing. He felt her hands tugging at the bottom of his T-shirt. In a quick movement, she had it over his head.

Happy with her success, she put her hands on his hips and turned him so he had his back to her. She pressed her body against his so her tits rubbed against his muscular back. Her hands ran all over his chest, finding his nipple rings. She let out an "Oooh" and fondled them. Holden reached back and put his hands on her waist. Her arms wrapped around his as she continued to rub his chest. Her cheek pressed against his back as her hot breath warmed his cool skin. Holden wanted her badly, but she was definitely in control now.

Her hands moved lower and lower until she sneaked her arms under his and patted him as if she were frisking him. When her hands finally found his erection, she tapped it a couple of times. "Oh, what do we have here?" she asked, trying to sound like a cop who had found a weapon on a suspect.

Before he had a chance to reply, her hands busily opened up his belt and the button on his shorts. She placed her thumbs in the waistband of his boxers and pulled them to the floor, bending at the knees as she guided them down. She held them in place, allowing Holden to step out of them. She then dropped to her knees and bit his ass, immediately kissing it better.

Her hands worked up his legs. Holden felt a shiver. He didn't know if it was from the coolness of the room or the fact that her hands were approaching his cock. He just stood there, letting her do her thing.

Paige's fingers slid between his thighs and around his hips until they found his waist. He could feel her trying to reach for his cock with her fingers while keeping her palms firmly on his waist. She was so close, millimetres from his shaft. He wanted to pull those hands onto him until they were full of cock, but he didn't. He couldn't believe how horny he was. He was truly concerned that he would come before anything had a chance to happen.

Paige's thumbs buried themselves deep into his ass cheeks as she forced him to spin around. As he spun, his cock accidentally slapped her across the face. Holden apologized. She put her hand on the side of his cock and playfully slapped it back. "Bad," she said, giggling. She then grabbed hold of it with a more serious expression on her face. "Mm, this is what I've been waiting for," she murmured as she leaned forward.

Her breath, which had been tantalizing other parts of his body throughout the evening, was now teasing his cock. Her grip was firm but pleasant. Her lips touched the head of his cock, and she kissed down his shaft, her hand wandered up his length, stopping at each piercing, gently pulling and prodding them. Her kisses became faster and harder before she moved her hand to his bag, giving it a squeeze. Her kisses stopped as she opened her mouth and slid her soft lips around his cock.

Paige tasted the pre-come that was already oozing out of him. She cleaned it off with a flicker of her tongue. *Oh God, don't come now*, Holden chanted to himself over and over again, knowing he only had one chance to make a good first impression.

Her hand squeezed and fondled his balls as her lips and tongue continued to work his shaft. Just when he was about to reach the point of no return, she suddenly stopped everything. She stood on tiptoes and kissed him. Holden was all too eager to kiss her back. She stopped, and he felt both her hands thrusting against his chest, knocking him onto the bed. "Get comfortable. I'm going to get some light in here."

He heard rustling. Several seconds later, the room came alive with a flickering candle. It cast shadows over her body, accentuating her breasts and belly button. Holden had failed to notice that she had taken off her pants in the darkness. She was standing before him wearing only her panties. He couldn't tell exactly what colour they were because of the yellow cast of the flame, but he could see they were a G-string.

He stared at her perfect body. Although he had seen it before, this wasn't her alter ego Syn he was looking at. This was Paige. As sexy as Syn was, she wasn't as beautiful, intense, or passionate as Paige.

Paige slowly walked towards Holden. She couldn't keep her eyes off his sculpted body. Despite being cold, the cotton sheets of her unmade bed felt very comfortable and inviting. He was confident they were about to get much warmer.

She watched as Holden lowered his hand to his cock and touched it, stroking it up and down, waiting for her to take over. She wanted to wait for him to finish himself. She ran her hands over her tits and down to her pussy. As one last tease, she turned around, letting him get a glimpse of her round ass; the G-string was hidden perfectly in the crack.

She turned around again and took the last two steps to the bed. She started low, by his feet, and crawled over his body. Her tits rubbed against his legs and her face slid against his cock. Her nipple tickled the head, making him jump.

She finally made her way up so they were face-to-face. She straddled him, and his cock rubbed against her soaked pussy. He could feel the heat and moisture radiating through the thin layer of the G-string, which was the only thing preventing him from penetrating her.

She pressed her chest against his, kissing him and running her hands through his hair as her hips ground into him again. Her smooth, bare legs squeezed his hips. Holden scratched down her back; she arched in self-defence. She pushed her hands against his chest and in two short bounces was sitting up right. She bit her lower lip, as Holden often did, and her eyes widened like a kid at Christmas.

With a big smile, she peered into Holden's eyes. "Fuck me."

Being one to follow orders, Holden rolled over, forcing her onto the bed. A soft moan was all that came out of her. "Now it's payback," Holden said.

Paige ate up the submissive role. She reached up for the wire headboard of her bed, giving Holden complete access to every part of her. His heart was racing faster than before. He was no longer worried about premature ejaculation because he was more worried about a heart attack. *What a way to go though*, he thought.

Holden kissed her lips and her cheek. He rested his body against hers, pressing her tits into him as she had done earlier. He bit her neck and ear and whispered how beautiful she was, how hot she was. He promised he was going to fuck her like no one else ever had.

After getting a positive response from Paige, Holden kept moving. Using his left hand for support, he leaned to one side so he could get a better view of her. His right hand explored her body, first caressing every part of her gorgeous breasts, then pressing firmer in spots. He soon bent forward to bite one of her erect nipples. With her eyes closed, she didn't see what he was about to do. She bucked a bit; her legs moved, searching for something to wrap around. Her moans and movements told Holden that she was enjoying his touch.

He slid his hands down her hard stomach, past the waistband on her panties, until he ever so lightly brought the tips of his fingers over her so his hand was cupping her pussy. He could feel that her panties were not only getting hot but were very wet. He couldn't believe that he'd got her so horny.

Holden was normally very confident sexually, but with Paige it was different. She had him feeling nervous and very much like a virgin. He knew that, being a dancer, she got a lot of advances from a lot of different men each night. She was definitely no stranger to sex. He was worried he wouldn't be able to please her. Her panties told a different story.

Using the same technique as he had earlier with her tits, he applied different pressures to her sensitive pussy in an attempt to keep her guessing. His left hand played with her hair and her ear. Her hips tried to get him to press harder against her eager cunt. Holden resisted, to make her want him even more. Her hips moved faster, and he knew she was ready.

He positioned himself between her legs. He carefully removed her G-string as if he were unwrapping a fragile present. As her foot slid through the floss, he held it. He kissed her toes and stared at her glistening pussy. Her free leg moved, bending at the knee; she spread as wide as she could. Holden kissed her ankle, her calf, her knee pit, and her inner thigh until he got to her freshly shaved mound. Unable to get over the pure lust he was feeling, he hoped to give her the best orgasm of her life.

He flicked her clit with his tongue. Paige's body tightened. "Fuck yes, lick me hard," she moaned as her hips thrust. So far so good. He took one long, deep lick of her entire pussy. Her juices splashed on his cheeks and dripped off his tongue. She was so wet and she tasted so good, he wanted to spend hours licking her.

In an effort to get deeper inside her, he put both his hands on the back of her knees and pushed them towards her chest. She let go of the headboard and rubbed her tits, squeezing and pulling them as his tongue worked. *She likes it rough*, he noted. He extended his tongue, getting as deep as he could. *Oh, to be Gene Simmons right now.*

He could feel her orgasm building; her entire body shook. She almost poked his eye out when she shifted one hand from her breast to her clit. She frantically rubbed herself as he continued to eat her out. In vain, Holden tried to match the pace of her hand, but she was moving too fast to keep up with.

"Fuuuck!" she screamed. Her body continued to tighten and convulse with every lick of his tongue. Her pussy felt like a tsunami as she ejaculated. Holden swallowed as much as he could. What he couldn't, covered his face and her sheets. Proud of his accomplishment, he lapped up every drop until she begged him to stop.

She grabbed a handful of his hair and pulled him up to her. He tried to reach down to play with her, in hopes of keeping her orgasm going, but she stopped him. "Oh no, no, too sensitive," she said brokenly. Holden lay beside her, and she kissed him. She could taste herself on his face. She licked up as much as she could. "Sorry for the mess," she said sarcastically.

"Yeah, be more careful next time, will ya?"

"Oh, you think there'll be a next time?" Paige toyed with him. "I guess it's my turn now, you bad boy," she said, sliding down his body. Without hesitation, she took his cock in her mouth. Her tongue flicked his piercings as his cock thrust in and out of her mouth. He lay back and enjoyed her head. Following her example, he gripped the headboard behind him. Her firm lips felt great on his cock.

Holden froze as he heard the apartment door unlock and people enter. Paige stopped sucking to listen, and she heard her roommate yell, "Hey, hon, you home?"

"Yeah, I'm in here," Paige yelled back.

"You left the TV on and the candles lit again."

"Oh. Sorry about that. I was in a bit of a hurry," Paige said, laughing.

"You're going to burn the damn place down some day. How was the date?"

"Still going good. I'll talk to you in the morning," Paige said trying to end the conversation.

"Wait, I have something to tell you," her roommate said as she burst through the door. Paige was still holding Holden's cock inches away from her freshly fucked mouth. She rolled on her side so she could see her roommate. She used her fingers to wipe the saliva and pre-come from the corners of her lips.

Her roommate was unfazed as she sat on the bed. "Oh my God, you'll never believe what happened to me tonight."

"Mel, can't you see I'm busy?"

"Oh, right, sorry," Mel said. She turned to Holden. "Hi, nice cock." Then she refocused on Paige.

"Isn't it, though?" Paige agreed. "Look. It's pierced."

Holden, not sure how to feel about the situation, just let Paige do her thing.

"Get out!" Mel said excitedly as she leaned in to see. Paige moved his cock around, giving her roommate a better view of his hardware.

He didn't know if it was the beer or the extreme comfort level he shared with Paige, but Holden decided he didn't mind the interruption. Maybe Paige would invite Mel to stay.

"That is awesome," Mel said. She poked a piercing and then ran her fingers down the three barbells.

Here we go, Holden thought, anticipating a ménage à trois.

Paige squeaked, "Awesome eh?"

"Very weird. What do they feel like?" Mel asked as if Holden weren't even there.

"I don't know yet, but I'll tell you in the morning."

"Well, keep it down. Oh, I came in to tell you I picked up too. That's what I wanted to say before I got distracted." As quickly as she had appeared, Mel left the room. She paused at the door to issue Holden the standard don't-hurt-my-friend speech and then told them to have fun.

As the door closed, Paige turned to Holden. "Sorry about that. Now, where we?"

"I believe you were seconds from making me come."

"Well, don't want to miss that, do we?" His cock disappeared again into her warm mouth. In the background, he heard Mel's bedroom door slam.

One of Paige's hands ran over Holden's chest; the other groped his balls. She felt his cock twitch and his body stiffened. She took him deep, her tongue ring flicking the base of his cock.

That was it. "I'm going to—" was all he was able to get out before he exploded in her mouth.

She didn't move an inch. Holden's intense orgasm lasted for what seemed like a minute, and Paige took all of his come, letting it slide down her throat. Her lips massaged the base of his cock, making sure she got every last drop. Confident that he was finished, she slid her lips up his shaft and let his cock fall out of her mouth. She gave the head a lick. Then she collapsed on his chest, her eyes still fixed on his now-flaccid cock. "Wow, that was a lot of come."

Embarrassed, Holden said, "Sorry. I tried to warn you."

She turned around and her hair fell onto his cock. It felt very soft against his skin. She reached a hand down to his penis, pushing her finger into the tip and pulling it away. A long string of come hung from her finger. Keeping an eye on him, she moved her finger to her tongue. She licked her finger and said with a smile, "It's OK. I love come."

"You really are the perfect woman, aren't you?" Holden said with a wink.

Paige lay her head on Holden's chest as they both caught their breaths. They started to laugh at the same time when they heard the faint sound of screams coming from the back bedroom. "Sounds like your roommate is having fun."

"Yup, she's a screamer all right."

"For Christmas last year, my dad got me a sweater," Holden said randomly.

"Oh yeah?"

"Yeah. This year I hope he gets me a screamer."

"Oh, that's bad!" She slapped Holden's leg.

Several minutes passed as they lay holding each other. Paige was getting cold, so she pulled up a blanket and covered them. Holden adjusted himself so they were facing each other. Paige rested her head on Holden's arm and fondled his ear and neck. Her body moved around as she was still sensitive from her last orgasm. He knew it wouldn't take much to get her heated up again.

He kissed her, casually played with her tits, then slid his hand down to her wet pussy. Not much encouragement was needed to open her legs. Holden gently ran circles around her clit, applying more and more pressure until he was pressing hard on her magic button. Her second orgasm built quickly, but Holden decided he wasn't going to be that nice. He stopped dead.

It took her a couple of seconds to regain her senses. "Don't stop," she begged.

"Oh, I won't. just warming up."

She let out a noise of acceptance. Holden repositioned himself between her legs; he craved the taste of her again. His tongue worked her already sensitive clit as he slowly slid a finger inside her. She was so soaked that it was easy, so he added another finger. He let them work inside her, touching as much of her as he could. Her hips gyrated as she tried to fuck his fingers, working in unison with his tongue. She was obviously enjoying the sensation. He occasionally stopped licking her to blow on her pussy. The shock of the cold air on her hot cunt kept her senses guessing.

Again, he could feel her orgasm mounting, so he stopped. He heard a disgruntled snort from Paige. He smiled and reassured her that her time was coming.

Holden thought back to a video he'd once seen, a training video. The guy in the video had claimed any girl could be made to squirt by following his simple instructions. Kneeling or standing beside the girl was the best position. He instructed viewers to insert two fingers in the girl with the pointer and pinkie fingers fully extended, pointing down her ass. The end position was supposed to replicate the horns of rock seen at concerts. The heel of the palm pressed on the clit, with the pressure being adjusted by the girl as necessary.

Holden had tried the technique before. Although he hadn't succeeded in getting the girl to squirt, her orgasms were definitely intense. Searching for a memorable closing move, he decided to try this on Paige.

He started slowly, and immediately she responded. She grabbed the headboard, her body flailing around. He used one hand to massage her chest, occasionally rolling her nipples between his forefinger and thumb. He rubbed her pussy harder and faster.

Paige closed her eyes; she knew she was losing control. As Holden worked inside her, she felt her body spasm. The urge to piss was overwhelming, and she was scared she was going pee all over Holden. She wanted to tell him to stop, but she couldn't formulate a coherent sentence. She felt her hands let go of the headboard as she lost muscle control in her hands. Her legs twitched violently. Never has she experienced such a sensation before. She made strange noises and screams, unable to stop herself.

Holden felt her body react. He knew her orgasm was imminent. He reached up from her chest and put his hand to her throat, lightly choking her. She flailed at the hand on her throat, and he knew she couldn't take any more. He let her go and quickly pulled his fingers out of her. A stream of water shot a couple of feet down the bed. Paige let out a very long, loud scream of pleasure. Holden watched the water squirt and wished he could have drunk every drop of it, as she had done for him.

She convulsed violently, like she was having a grand mal. Her eyes rolled back in her head. She tried to reach out for Holden, but she didn't have control of her body yet. She giggled uncontrollably and squirmed into the foetal position. Holden put his hand on her shoulder, and his touch set off another series of convulsions. She rolled onto her back as her legs thrashed. She barely got out the words "Fuuuck meee!"

Holden lay down beside her. Every touch made her convulse again. "What … the … fuck," she gasped. Unable to think straight, she could barely utter a syllable.

Holden laughed. He was very proud of himself. *Thank you, video instructor guy. You're the best,* he thought.

He found the blanket that had covered them earlier and pulled it over them. He took her in his strong arms. He held her tightly in hopes she would get her shaking under control, but having his naked body next to hers only seemed to exacerbate the situation. He held her for what seemed like hours until she regained her mental faculties. She put her arms around him and gave him a kiss as she managed to squeak out a goodnight.

Morning came. Holden woke up with a huge hard-on. *Not again,* he thought, but he couldn't blame himself when he looked at Paige's naked body, half-covered by the sheets. Holden wanted to wake her up to fuck her, but she had had a busy night, and he knew there would be other opportunities. Quietly he got out of bed, found his boxers and T-shirt, and decided to watch TV so she could sleep in.

He strolled out of the bedroom to the kitchen, poured a glass of orange juice, and sat on the couch. Remote in hand, he flipped through the channels before settling on a sports highlight show.

Paige's roommate's door swung open quickly, startling Holden. Mel stumbled into the living room, wearing only an open white bathrobe. Her hair was a sure sign of the rough night she'd had. Holden wasn't sure she saw him, because she left her robe open. He whispered a hello so he didn't scare her and wake Paige or the other guest.

Mel had the same idea about breakfast Holden had had, except she added two aspirins to her orange juice. Robe still open, she sat on the chair beside the couch, but not in the traditional fashion. She squatted, opening the robe further and revealing a small strip of hair on her pussy. Holden figured she had implants, not that he was about to complain.

Trying not to stare, he met her eyes and said hello again. She raised her head, and he was amazed to see she was the waitress Jeff had been lusting after. He couldn't wait to tell him. Then he wondered if Jeff was her date, asleep in the next room. She took a sip of juice.

"Mornin'," Holden said.

Making as few movements as possible, she replied, "Sounded like you two had fun last night."

"Yeah, it was OK," Holden said with a big smile. "Your night sounded pretty good as well."

"It better have been great; I'd hate to feel this shitty for nothing." Her eyes widened. "Oh my God, I came in on you two last night, didn't I?"

"Yup, you did," Holden said, holding back his laughter.

"Your cock is pierced, isn't it?"

"Yup."

She put her hand to her head and gave it a shake. "I touched it, didn't I?"

"Yup."

"I'm *so* sorry," she said, obviously embarrassed.

"Think nothing of it," Holden responded nonchalantly.

As if to save Mel from awkwardness, Paige emerged from her bedroom, wearing the same sweatpants and tank top she'd worn the night before. She threw Holden his pants, then floated into the kitchen. She also poured herself a glass of orange juice before sitting next to her roommate. "Nice to see you, dear – all of you," she said, trying to adjust Mel's housecoat in vain.

Although Paige and Holden hadn't drunk much the night before, he felt there was no excuse for Paige being as mobile and alert as she was. He felt like hell, and he knew Paige hadn't had more sleep than he had.

"Holden, have you formally met my roommate Mel?" she asked.

"Sort of, from the restaurant and the club. Hi," he said to Mel, extending his hand, Mel painfully reached out and gave his hand a shake.

"Don't be rude," Paige said, slapping Mel on the back of the head. It had to have caused her pain, but Mel just made a disgruntled sound.

Holden thought back to the night they met, trying to remember Mel's stage name. *Sunshine? Yup, Sunshine, that's it.*

Mel had left her bedroom door open, and her companion was moving around the room. He climbed out of bed and, with his back to the living room, bent over to put on his pants. Holden couldn't turn away, appreciating the great ass the guy had. It made him a little concerned. Paige was sitting there, as well as another beautiful, naked girl, and yet he kept staring at a guy's ass.

Mel's guest didn't bother putting on a shirt. He came into the living room. Holden was more than relieved when he realized that "he" was a girl. *Thank God*, he thought. She was startled to see Holden, but not enough to cover up. Holden thought the day was starting out as the best day of his life.

Mel's date leaned in and kissed Mel's neck while whispering something to her. Mel slammed down her glass, stood up, grabbed the other girl by the hand, and headed for her bedroom. "Nice meeting you," she yelled over her shoulder and slammed the door, not waiting for a response from Holden.

Holden realized he was rock hard. Paige joined him on the couch. He put his arm around her as she snuggled into him. The moans and screams began from Mel's room, so Paige turned up the TV. To no avail: Mel was just way into her new friend.

Paige and Holden watched TV for a couple of hours before she checked the time and said, "I'm sorry, Holden, but I have to start getting ready for work."

"Yeah, I should get going too," he said. As if on cue, his cell phone rang. The call display read *Pete*, and a picture of him passed out on a lawn flashed to the screen. "Dude, I have something awesome to tell you. I'll call you later," Holden said, skipping the traditional phone etiquette.

Paige stared disapprovingly. Holden tried to figure out what was wrong. He recalled what he had said to Pete. "No, no, *no*. The awesome news is that your roommate is the waitress my friend has a *huge* crush on."

"Sure, sure," she said, laughing. "You go brag to all your friends about your conquest. I'm going to go get ready for work."

"Will I see you again?" Holden asked hopefully.

With an expression of pure focus and purpose, she walked over to him, took him by the collar, and slammed him against the wall. "You're fucking right you will."

Smiling and reassured, Holden bit her neck. One of the symptoms of his move the previous night was that the feelings could be recalled hours later. Her knees went weak, and Holden had to catch her before she fell to the floor. "Damn you," she said. "Go. We'll get together next weekend if that's OK with you." She handed him his jeans and backpack as she shoved him out the door so he wouldn't distract her from getting ready.

Holden bounced down the stairs without a care in the world. His heart and mind were racing with possibilities. *Don't get too far ahead of yourself. It was only one date – one amazing date*, he thought. He opened the door to the street; the sunshine hit him in the face. *Yup, a beautiful day.*

CHAPTER 3

Shortly after Holden rang the buzzer to Paige's apartment, he heard a loud *thump, thump, thump* down the stairs. The steps sounded like they were coming from a person twice her weight.

When she swung open the door, Holden was once again stunned by her beauty. She was wearing her hair in a ponytail tied up with elastic bands, complete with bright red bobbles. She was also wearing a white, low-cut, cherry-print summer dress that hung to mid-thigh. To complete her outfit, she wore big Doc Martin boots with white knee-high socks underneath.

As he fantasized about spinning her around and pressing her face against the red bricks of her building so he could lift her skirt and fuck her against the wall, he realized he was getting hard. To avoid the potential embarrassment of getting caught with a hard-on, Holden made small talk on the way to the subway station. They talked about the weather and what she had done during the last week since they had seen each other. He had a decent idea, since they had spoken to each other every night on the phone, but he enjoyed listening to her and watching her facial reactions as she spoke.

During a recent conversation, they had decided that if the weather was good on the weekend, they would go for a walk in the park along Lake Ontario. The park was only a couple of subway stops away. Paige had to work that night, so they figured they would rather spend their time in the park than on the busy city streets.

Holden loved taking the subway. They were both people watchers, and the TTC gave them ample opportunity to see strange people. As they made their way down the tunnel, they passed the usual people begging for change or sleeping in corners. They saw a guy playing the saxophone, so they stopped and listened to him for a minute. They agreed he was quite good. Holden tossed him some change before they moved on to the platform to wait for their train.

They were met with a gust of wind that indicated their train would soon be there. The familiar sound of chimes filled the nearly empty platform as the doors of the subway car slid open. The pair climbed aboard and found seats. During the ride, Paige entertained Holden with funny stories from work, about patrons and co-workers. Holden listened intently as she spoke. He could have listened to her all day because she was very upbeat and positive.

He casually scanned the train and noticed the stares Paige was getting from pretty much everyone else. It filled him with a sense of pride knowing that everyone wanted her, yet she chose to spend her time with him.

Station after station flew by. The PA finally announced that their stop was coming up next, so they stood and huddled by the doors, waiting for the train to come to a stop. Once it was safe, the chimes sounded again and the doors opened. Paige and Holden jumped out and headed for the surface.

The park was not very far from the subway station, so the walk did not take long. There they found a series of paved trails. Neither of them was familiar with the park, so they found a map posted on a sign and decided on the route they wanted to take. Though he was nervous, Holden cautiously reached for Paige's hand. They had held hands at the theatre, but this was a whole new date. He didn't want to rush things. His hand touched hers, and she clutched it tightly.

Holden was starting to feel really comfortable around her, but he was still hesitant. He didn't want to throw his heart out too soon only to have Paige stomp all over it. Yet she was making it very hard for him not to fall madly in love with her.

The warm summer sun kissed their skin as the gentle breeze brought the smell of the surrounding trees, the lake, and Paige's perfume to

Holden's nose. He inhaled, eagerly taking in the scents. Along the trail they had to dodge inline skaters, joggers, and dog walkers, but even with all of that, the park wasn't as busy as they had thought it was going to be on such a beautiful day.

Paige spotted a swing set and her big brown eyes lit up. She ran over to it, dragging Holden behind her. They were all alone on the set as they sat down and casually dangled in the wind. They had an amazing view of the lake and were happy that no one else was around to invade their privacy. They didn't really talk, just absorbed the moment and the view.

Finally, they started a very light conversation, which quickly turned to more substantial topics like family and childhood memories. Paige told Holden how her parents had divorced at a young age. Her mom remarried shortly after the divorce. Paige's real dad wasn't in the picture after that, but her stepdad was very supportive and filled the role of male figurehead. Her stepdad had always put an emphasis on schooling and pushed her to go university. He was disappointed that she had completed two years of a business degree but then left to dance full-time. Her relationship with her stepdad had been rocky ever since because he couldn't understand the lifestyle. He told her that she was living a life of sin and throwing her life away. She wanted to go back to school after she figured out what she really wanted to do with her life, but in the meantime she really enjoyed dancing and was making excellent money.

There was a brief pause in the conversation as they got off the swings and continued walking. They found a more secluded patch of grass that still had a view of the lake. They lay down together, and she rested her head on his stomach and looked up at him. He got lost in her eyes.

Since she had already opened up about her family, he asked her more personal questions about other relationships. Eventually the topic turned to first loves and first times. Holden asked Paige when and how she lost her virginity.

"Well, there isn't much of a story. I was 18 and we were about to finish our last semester of school. My boyfriend and I had been together for almost a year, and we were heading off to separate universities. He said a long-distance relationship probably wouldn't work out. I agreed.

We were lying in bed and knew that that night might be our last time together. We were both virgins.

"After some time lying there talking, I worked up the nerve to ask him to have sex with me. We loved each other, and I didn't want to go away to school, get drunk, and lose my virginity to a complete stranger. I had always been the one telling him to wait; he was all for it. He agreed that for a first time, it was important to be with someone you love, because you always remember the first time. He said he wasn't going to forget me anyway, so it only made sense.

"We started kissing and touching each other ... Don't get me wrong, we had fooled around a lot together, but that night it all seemed new. He was more awkward than normal. He stood and took his clothes off. He had a beautiful cock that was very hard. I got nervous knowing it was soon going to penetrate me. He leaned over and undressed me, then stood at the side of the bed, staring at me.

"I didn't know what to do. I spread my legs. He fumbled over me and reached down to his cock. After a few attempts, he finally got inside me. It hurt at first. I wasn't sure if he was doing it right, but I couldn't ask. It was his first time too, so he didn't know if he was doing it right either.

"He was only inside me for what seemed like seconds. Then I saw that familiar expression. We weren't kissing, and he wasn't touching me. I think he was too focused on fucking me to think about the other stuff. I just watched him. I was trying not to think about the uncomfortable feeling inside me.

"He tensed up and pulled out of me fast. I could feel his come shooting all over me like a fire hose. He stopped and stared me uncomfortably. Then he got dressed, gave me a big kiss, and walked out. I didn't see him again for a very long time. It was odd. Even though we had been together for so long, the way he left made me feel a bit dirty."

"Wow, that was awful. At least it was with someone you loved."

"Yeah, at least we had that ... but when I saw him again, he made me feel so bad."

"How so?"

"Well, when he came back from school, he had a new girlfriend. She was beautiful. She was like a Barbie doll. Back then I was such a tomboy, it made me feel awkward seeing them together. To top it off, he looked at me – well, through me – and said it was nice to be dating a real girl for a change. You have no idea how much it hurt. I didn't know why he was so mean. We'd parted on good terms. The only thing I could think of was that he was embarrassed about his performance and he was trying to make me feel bad for it. But whatever, I got over it."

"I'd say you're gorgeous. Has he seen you lately?"

"No. Fuck him. He's an asshole. OK, you, tell me about your first time," Paige ordered.

"Mine? Well, it's not as dramatic. It was my sixteenth birthday. I was talking to a girl on the phone, and she asked what I was doing to celebrate. When I told her nothing, she said she was sad that I was alone for my birthday. She had her dad drive her to my place. I jokingly asked her what she'd brought me. I was kidding, of course, but she said, 'Nothing.'

"The conversation turned to sex. She asked if I had ever done it before. I told her I'd fooled around before, but never actually had sex. She walked over, grabbed my hand, and led me to my bedroom. My parents were both at work and her dad wasn't coming to pick her up for a while, so we had lots of time.

"We went into the bedroom, and she pushed me onto the bed and stripped for me. She obviously knew what she was doing. I, on the other hand, had no clue. It was the first time I had ever seen a girl completely naked. I almost came in my clothes."

Paige laughed.

"She asked if I was going to get naked," Holden continued, "so I stood up and ungracefully undressed. While I was doing that, she took my spot on the bed and put her hands between her legs and played with herself. It was beautiful. I was excited to think I was about to fuck her. I was also nervous. Of course I had fantasized about sex, but it was about to become a reality.

"I got naked, lay on top of her, and didn't bother with foreplay because, well, I had *no* clue where anything was or how to work any of it. I tried getting my cock inside her; I couldn't find the hole anywhere. She got frustrated but she still giggled a bit, trying to put me at ease. I'm sure she could tell I was really nervous.

"She eventually guided me inside her and— Well, like your first time, I only lasted about two seconds. I wasn't wearing a condom, but I came inside her anyway. I didn't think to pull out and I didn't want the feeling to stop. She understandably got mad at me, and all I could think of was to say sorry. I rolled off of her, got dressed and lay beside her again. I tried kissing her, but I had no idea what post-sex protocol was.

"Satisfied my present was delivered, she got dressed and called her dad. We kissed when he got there, and well, we never really talked about it again. It was a mess. Still, I was happy to finally get the first time over with. I assure you, I've gotten much better since then!"

"Sure, sure, that's what they all say," Paige said.

They sat quietly for a bit. Holden asked, "So, besides the money, what made you get into dancing?"

"Do you really want to hear the story?"

"If you want to tell me, I'm definitely interested."

"Well ... OK, but remember, you asked."

"Oh, this has to be good," Holden said with an air of curiosity in his voice.

Paige smiled. "It was the summer after my last semester of university. Like I said, I was a tomboy all through school. Yes, me. I honestly was," she insisted, seeing Holden's doubtful expression. He couldn't imagine such a beautiful, feminine woman as being a tomboy, but he didn't say anything. "All my friends were guys; I never got along with girls growing up. One of our friends had just turned 19. He was the last one of our group to become legal, so we took him to a strip club.

"We started off in the afternoon at my best friend's apartment. We drank a lot of beer, smoked a joint, and headed out to the bar. I thought the dancers were hot and was amazed at the attention they got, not only from the guys in the audience but from all my friends. I was jealous. No guy had ever looked at me like that.

"We thought it would be a nice idea to get the birthday boy a lap dance. We picked out the one we all agreed was the hottest girl in the bar, and she came over and led him into a back room. I was curious about what happened back there. My best friend took my questions as a cue to get me a dancer of my own. I objected at first until this beautiful young girl came over and ran her fingers through my hair, grazing my ear. She leaned in and whispered, 'Hi, I'm Sunshine. I hear you'd like to go for a dance.' I couldn't refuse. She wasn't what I expected strippers to be, and I actually found myself getting aroused by her.

"She led me by the hand to the back room. She paraded me past the open booths. My friend was stunned to see me there. The friends who bought me the dance were disappointed she wasn't going to dance at the table so they could watch. *Sucks to be them*, I thought.

"I sat down in the chair, not sure how to act. She sat on my lap. We chatted about why I was there, and she totally put me at ease. The next song started to play, and I watched her get naked. It was the first time I really looked at another girl naked. I'd seen them at the gym and in sports, but I'd never really looked. Now, here was this girl and her vagina was inches from my face.

"She told me I could touch her anywhere I wanted. I was hesitant at first so she took my hands and put them to her tits. I felt them and compared them to my own. Hers were definitely bigger, and they felt great. Her back was pressed into my chest as she asked me if I liked them. I of course told her I did, and she asked if she could feel mine. Before I could answer her, she spun around and straddled me.

"I could see her legs spread. Her clit was about pressed against my jeans. At the same time, I could feel her hands all over my chest. I was getting really turned on.

"She told me how much she liked my tits and how firm they were. Before I knew it, she had reached up my shirt and felt me under my bra. I'd only had a couple of guys touch me like that. I was surprised to have a girl feel me up, and I was even more surprised how gentle she was. She was much more tender than any of the guys I'd been with. I really liked her.

"I asked her about her life story, how she started to dance, and so on. She told me it was to put herself through school because the money was great. I asked her about drugs and drinking and all the stereotypical things you hear about strippers. She said that those things definitely existed in the profession, but they weren't as rampant as everyone thought. Most of the girls were shy and quiet when they weren't at work. They were simply trying to make money.

"I asked her how taking off her clothes and being worshipped by so many guys made her feel. She said it was hard to get over at first. She'd been nervous and uncomfortable. But the other dancers made her feel comfortable, and the guys' cheering definitely helped motivate her. I asked her what it was like dancing for some gross guy and letting him touch her. She said that she tried to find a happy place and go through the motions to get it over with as fast as possible. Standing just out of reach didn't hurt either. But she also said most guys were respectful and not that bad to dance for.

"In no time, our song was over. She got dressed and suggested that I think about becoming a dancer. I laughed and said that there was no way I could do something like that; I wasn't in the same league as the girls working there. She said she thought I was hot, but I didn't think much of it at the time.

"I went back to my friends' table. They applauded as Sunshine and I emerged from the back room. After asking them if they'd like a dance too, she gave me a kiss on the cheek. I was surprised how hot she made me. The guys of course wanted a play-by-play account of my dance. I told them to mind their own business and drank my beer.

"After several hours and several beers, we decided to continue drinking back at the apartment. On my way out, I heard 'Wait!' We all turned around and saw Sunshine running towards us. She grabbed me and slid her hand in my front pocket, not so discreetly copping a feel. She whispered in my ear, 'In case you have any more questions.'

"After we were in the cab, I pulled out what she put in my pocket. She'd slipped me her phone number. My friends were impressed and jealous.

"When we got home, I took my normal spot on the couch next to my best friend. One of the guys sat in an old armchair at the end of the couch, and the other in a love seat across the room. Trying to be funny, one of the guys put on a porn flick.

"In a moment of drunken weakness, I told the guys that Sunshine had said I should become a stripper. They roared with laughter, saying I was too much of a tomboy and could never pull it off. I told them that I thought I could, and my best friend told me to prove it. He turned off the porn and put on some music. 'Strip for us if you think you're so good,' he said.

"Well, I don't know if it was the pot or the beer, but I stood up, moved my hips to the beat. The four guys had their eyes glued on me. It was a sensation I had never felt before. It was very empowering. I first thought all I would do was tease them and chicken out, but the more I kept going, the more I wanted to keep going.

"I put my hands under my shirt and lifted it, showing them my stomach and ribs. The guys were dead silent. They were on the edge of their seats. I lowered my shirt just long enough to undo the top button of my jeans. I pulled them down below my panty line and then raised my shirt again – higher this time, giving them a peek of the bottom of my bra. I tried to dance like the dancers I'd seen that night. It wasn't working, but the guys seemed to appreciate my effort anyway." Paige laughed.

"I turned around and bent over, letting them look at my ass. They still sat quietly, obviously wondering how far I would go. I was getting really worked up. Before I knew it, I had my shirt up over my head. I heard a gasp from one of the guys as he saw my muscular back. We had all been friends since childhood, but I don't think any of them had seen me as a girl until that night.

"The gasp was all I needed to push me over the edge. Still with my back to them, I unzipped my fly and pulled off my jeans. I turned around, stepped out, and kicked the jeans up at my friend. He didn't move. They hit him in the face, then fell to the floor.

"I kept trying to move to the music, but it got harder the more worked up I got. I let my hands run all over my body. I slipped them under my bra and pushed it up over my tits. The only thing covering them now was my hands. I wanted them to see me – oh God, how badly I wanted them to see me! I moved my hands to my back and unfastened my bra. I heard one of the guys say, 'Oh God.' I could tell they were all getting hard, hard for me, and it was an incredible feeling. At that point, I could have made them do anything.

"I continued to play with my tits. I rubbed a hand over my waist and pussy. I turned around again and pulled my panties up into the crack of my ass, giving myself a camel toe. I was positive that my white cotton panties were so wet they were see-through. With the panties up my ass like a thong, I played with my ass cheeks, spreading them apart, bending over, and looking at my friends through my legs. Over the fifteen years I had known these guys, none of them had noticed me sexually before. Now I certainly had the attention of all four.

"I turned around and rubbed my tits again. I ran my hands through my hair, which was blonde at the time. Reached over my head made my tits seem really firm and perky. I caught a glimpse of myself in a mirror; my tits looked fantastic and I looked fantastic. Seeing myself gave me even more confidence.

"I took my fingers out of my hair and slid them down my body to my panties. I pulled the waistband down, forcing the cloth out of my ass and off my soaked pussy. I dropped them to the ground, picked them up, and gave them a long sniff, copying a move I'd seen a girl do on stage. That was it for the guys. I could see their smiles.

"I kept dancing, completely naked. I tried to move so they could see all of my body. Apparently it was too much for my best friend to take. Out of the corner of my eye, I saw him fidgeting with his jeans. I thought I knew what he was going to do. I could no longer focus on dancing; I just wanted to see his cock.

"Well, that's exactly what I saw. He pulled out his cock, and it was so big and hard. He rubbed it while he stared at me, and I touched myself. That was all the motivation the other three needed. In seconds all the guys had their cocks in their hands, and I felt like I had to touch them all. I dropped to my knees and crawled over to my friend. I took his cock in my hand and gently rubbed it, making eye contact with the other guys. I eventually leaned in and took his cock in my mouth. I sucked him like it was the last cock on the planet, like a porn star.

"Of course it wasn't the last cock, as I found out when I felt pressure on my hips. A dick pushed into me. I hadn't noticed that the guys had all moved around me. One was on his back. He slid under me until I felt his tongue working over my clit. I reached out and gripped his cock. His mouth felt great on my pussy, so it was the least I could do for him.

"The fourth guy was kneeling patiently, waiting for one of my holes to fuck. I rubbed his cock too. Then it dawned on me: I was taking four cocks at once. I felt so very dirty yet so alive. My pussy was aching with pleasure, which they all noticed because my moans were getting louder. They all reacted. The cock in my pussy fucked me harder and faster, the guy licking me fell into rhythm with the cock fucking me, and the vibrations on the cock in my mouth were driving that rod nuts. I almost ripped off the two erections in my hands as my orgasm grew to the point of release.

"At the same time I started to orgasm, I felt the cock in my mouth explode. I had never tasted come before, but I swallowed every last drop. Now I associate the taste of come with that night. Even the smell of it almost makes me orgasm. I can't get enough of it."

Holden sat silently. He reflected on what her last sentence possibly meant for him. Without saying anything, he let her continue.

"Once my friend finished coming in my mouth, he graciously got out of the way, making room for the guy under me to move in so I could suck him off. I was still giving the other guy a hand job. I had the taste of come in my mouth, and I wanted more.

"I sucked the cock with renewed vigour and jerked off the other one intensely. I felt the guy in my pussy tremble. The cock thrust deep inside me, and I could feel his come explode. That new sensation set me off and I felt as if I was going to orgasm again. I had never had multiple orgasms before, not even by myself.

"The guy finally pulled out of me while he was still coming. I felt it land all over my back and ass. Then I felt his hand rub it into my skin. I couldn't do anything but continue sucking the cock in front of me. The guy barely had time to stop coming before the guy getting the hand job took his place. I heard someone say something about sloppy seconds. I felt his cock plunge deep inside my pussy, then slide completely out. I wanted to be fucked. I was going to encourage him to fuck me, but I felt the tip of his cock putting pressure on my ass. I had *never* had anything in my ass before, I wasn't sure what to expect, but since it was a night of new experiences, I didn't stop him.

"His cock, the largest of the four, slid into my ass inch by inch. I tensed at first, but I quickly realized that tensing wasn't helping. I tried to relax by focusing my attention on the cock in my mouth. The cock behind me slid all the way in and slowly worked me. It felt great.

"Seeing that I was comfortable with him fucking my ass, he fucked me faster and faster until I finally orgasmed again, an orgasm more intense then I had ever felt before. The cock in my mouth blew. Since I was already gasping for air from my own orgasm, I couldn't take his come. I let it fall out of my mouth as I jerked him off, milking out all the jizz. It sprayed hard against my face – so much come, I was almost drowning in it. I was glad I hadn't let him shoot it all in my mouth.

"I think the sight of me being glazed like a whore in a porn video, and knowing he was the first in my tight virgin ass, made the guy fucking me release inside me. I felt his large cock twitch and the come filling me up.

"After his cock slipped free of me, I rolled over onto my back, my legs still spread. The guys were all lying on the floor next to me. I was spent. 'So, you guys still don't think I could become a dancer?' I asked them.

"'You have our vote' was the unanimous decision.

"I woke up naked in the middle of the floor. One of the guys had moved to the couch, one was on the love seat, and two were on the floor next to me. They were all still naked. Sobering up, I could feel that the come had dried on my face, making it hard to see. I thought I would really regret what I'd done, but seeing all those cocks and remembering them all hard for me turned me on.

"My friends and I have never talked about that day, and we've gone our separate ways. We only talk about once a year or so. I called Sunshine the next day, and the rest is history. Oh my God, you must think I'm the biggest slut."

"Quite the contrary," Holden said, trying to reassure her. He was now lying on his stomach like she was. She was completely oblivious to the fact that he had a raging hard-on. "Sunshine, as in your roommate Sunshine?"

"Yup, one and the same. Coincidentally, that day was the same day I saw my ex. He had already put my femininity into question, so I thought I had something to prove before the night even started."

"That is crazy, I want to hear more Syn and Sunshine stories another time. Seriously, I thought that story was *so* hot. It's too bad your ex was such an ass, but at least something good came out of it. You became who you are now, and I think you are amazing."

"Aw, thank you. But really, what could you be thinking about me except I'm some slutty stripper?"

Laughing, Holden replied, "Trust me, I don't think that at all. I think it is awesome you're so open sexually. I'm very flattered you're willing to tell me such a personal story – and I'd be lying if I said it didn't turn me on."

"You're just saying that, but thank you. I'm sure I'll never hear from you again," she said reluctantly.

"Oh, you're going to hear from me again. I would rather be with a girl who's been with a thousand guys than a virgin."

"What?"

"Yeah, really. I figure if a girl was holding onto her their virginity like it was gold, one of two things will happen when they finally lose it. Either she is never going to feel comfortable during sex, so it will always be the same boring thing over and over. Or she will love it, wonder what she has been missing, and eventually cheat on you. If you date a girl who is sexually free and has had many experiences, then by the time she settles down with you, she knows exactly what she wants and she's chosen you."

"I never thought of it that way before. I haven't been with *that* many guys."

"No, no, I wasn't saying that you were with a lot of guys. I like that you're willing to try new experiences. I have experimented myself."

"Oh yeah? Like what?"

"I have never told another living soul this story. You have to promise you won't judge me or repeat it to anyone."

"After what I told you, how could I judge you?"

"Wait for it. Promise me."

"I promise."

"OK. It happened one night in college. The boys and I went out to a strip club. Unfortunately, it wasn't the one you were working at, or maybe we could have met months ago. Anyway, after several lap dances we all got horned up and headed home. I thought I was being all sneaky and quiet when I stumbled through the residence door. I was sure I hadn't wake up my roomie. I turned on the TV and there was soft-core porn on. I took it as sign. In my state of liquid courage, I decided to masturbate.

"I stripped right down to nothing. Then I took my rock-hard cock in my hand and stroked it. I'm not sure if I passed out for a minute or if I was too drunk to realize it, but next thing I knew, my roommate was sitting on the edge of my bed, watching me jerk off. Startled, I tried to cover up. He said, "No, no, it's OK," as he interlocked his fingers with mine on my cock. I yanked my hand away and tried to speak—to tell him to stop or to fuck off—but I realized his hand was still on my cock. His grip was much tighter than mine, and he was stroking me.

"He could see the anxiety in my face. He told me to just watch the TV and imagine that the girl on the screen was the one jerking me off. In my drunken haze, I turned my head and let him continue. I kept denying it to myself, but it felt amazing – so firm, so hard, yet so wrong.

"He changed position and wrapped his mouth firmly around my cock. He sucked me off like no girl has. His mouth expertly slid up and down my hard shaft. His tongue toyed with every inch of me. Holding my balls in his palm, he rolled them around, never missing a beat while he continued to suck me.

"I fought the urge to release in his mouth. I stopped watching the TV and focused completely on not coming – and on the fact that another man had his lips on my cock.

"As he continued to fondle my sac, his fingers grazed my asshole a couple of times. It felt odd, a good kind of odd. I guess, since I didn't jump or push his hand away, he assumed I'd given him a green light. As he continued to take me deep into his mouth, his hand slowly left my balls. A finger made small circles around my asshole, getting deeper with every circle until he penetrated me.

"Then I jumped. Like you said in your story, nothing had ever been inside me like that before. I'm embarrassed to admit it, but the massaging my prostate felt *great*. I let him finger me for about ten seconds, and that was all I could take. I let out an "Oh my God!" His mouth slid off my cock. His free hand grabbed my shaft and gave me a couple of very firm tugs. His finger slammed deep into my ass, as deep inside as it could possibly go. I came hard, with so much pressure that I even managed to hit myself in the face. I have never made so much come before. He didn't stop. He jerked me off hard until every last twitch of come was out of me.

"I lay there breathless and motionless. Random thoughts ran through my head. I questioned my sexuality. I wondered if I was gay or bi. I wasn't sure, but what I did know was that I wasn't attracted to him. I didn't find his body sexy, but I loved the way he touched me.

"He was still kneeling beside me, gazing at his handiwork splashed across my stomach, chest, and face. 'My, my, what a mess. Let's get you cleaned up,' he said.

"I went to stand up, meaning to get a towel. He forced me down and licked my come off of me. I was still drunk and paralyzed with ecstasy. I didn't know if I liked what he was doing, but I let him continue. Everything else had been great, after all.

"His tongue slowly worked its way up my neck. His hot breath started my blood flowing again, and he noticed I was getting hard. 'Wow, so soon?' he said with a smile. He licked the come off of my face. He stood and moved up beside my head. His cock, which was longer and thicker than mine, was inches away from my face. I knew what he wanted, but I wasn't sure if I was ready for it yet. I wasn't sure if I wanted to feel it in my hand, let alone my mouth.

"He finally got tired of waiting for me. He took my hand and guided it to his cock. I didn't fight him; instead I wrapped my fingers around it. I was shy at first, until he gave me the advice to do the same to him as I would do to myself while masturbating. I slowly stroked his cock. It didn't feel weird at all, and he was definitely getting into it. I beat him off just as hard and as fast as he'd done to me. I wanted to make him come; it was my personal goal.

"I saw the tip of his long cock glisten with pre-come. He felt it too. He cleaned off the tip with his finger. The come formed a string that he extended to my mouth. I amazed myself. I didn't fight or say no; I went with the flow. Leaning my head back, I opened my mouth and stuck out my tongue. His finger slid across it.

"I was very hard again. I was no longer questioning my sexuality; I just went with it. I knew I loved women, but this was too great to pass up.

"I finally worked up the courage. I leaned forward and took his beautiful cock in my mouth. I sucked him, clumsily at first. I'd never even thought about sucking a guy off before, let alone proper technique. I remembered his advice about doing it the way I liked it to be done to me. I took him as deep as I could without gagging. He moaned and thrust his hips, fucking my mouth.

"His hand slid down and grazed past my cock. That slight touch almost made me come again. He went straight for my asshole. He fingered me deep and fast. I moved my hips to fuck his finger as his cock worked away inside my mouth.

"Unexpectedly he pulled out and moved my hand. I wondered if I had done something wrong, I didn't think he was about to come.

"He soon answered my question with an action: he pulled his finger out of me and put it behind my knee. He shuffled down the bed. I let out a faint no. He kept saying it was OK and to trust him. I let out another, less convincing no. All I heard from him was 'shhh'.

"He was now between my legs. He leaned his body onto mine. I thought he was going to reassure me, which he did. But while he was talking to me, he positioned his cock so the tip was already starting to ease into me. I didn't fight him or resist, I just clenched my fingers into the bed as he slid his large cock slowly inside me. I could feel it getting deeper and deeper. I was amazed my ass could take a cock, let alone stretch big enough for his. It didn't even hurt – he was so slow and careful, very gentle. The amount of lube he used was probably a factor as well. As much as I was embarrassed by the fact I had a cock inside me, it felt *so* good. I was getting harder.

"Once he was fully inside me, he gave my ass time to expand to fit his girth. Then he fucked me. He went slowly at first, working up harder and deeper. He wouldn't let me touch myself, telling me it wasn't time. Pre-come was oozing from me. He occasionally took a taste of it, using his finger as a spoon. He fucked me harder and harder as the girl on the TV moaned, satisfying her own man's cock. He moaned too, heavily. I told him to fuck me harder, and he told me he was going to come. His fingers wrapped around my cock and almost ripped it off. His body tensed, his cock slammed deep inside me, and with that mighty thrust

I could feel his come shoot inside me. The pressure was enough for me, and I came in his hand.

"He extended his come-soaked hand to my mouth. I couldn't believe it. Was he really going to feed me my own come? He was serious. I ate it all off of him. I could still feel his cock twitching inside me.

"He eventually pulled out, and I came again. This time it was like a fountain. I didn't think I could have any left in me, yet I was coming and I couldn't stop. I almost went into convulsions. I lost *all* control. It was amazing.

"Then suddenly he was off the bed and walking away. I asked him what would happen the next day. He glanced back and asked me what I was talking about. He told me I was drunk and it had all been my imagination.

"We never mentioned that night again, nor have I been with another man. But I have gained a whole new respect for anal sex."

Paige looked at Holden for several seconds before she grabbed his shirt and pulled him to her. She started kissing him, then stopped. "Sorry, and wow, did that really happen?"

"I swear to God."

"That is so hot. Thank you for telling me."

"So you don't think less of me?"

"Not at all. I would never have imagined. Despite the tattoos and piercings, no offense, but you seem pretty conservative."

"Well, yeah, that's just the tip of the iceberg. I'm open for almost anything."

"Sounds like we might have a lot in common," Paige said.

"Yeah. The bad part is, the more adventurous I get, the more adventurous I have to be the next time."

"Me too. That's why I keep dancing. I was hoping dancing would duplicate the intensity of that night with my friends. Sometimes it comes close, when the bar is full and the crowd is cheering, but really, it hasn't been the same."

"Have you ever escorted?"

"No. I've thought about it. But though I know there can be a distance between love and sex, I think that's a boundary I'm not willing to push.

I do fantasize about being paid for sex and being used, but I think that will have to remain a fantasy."

"Cool. For the record, I haven't escorted either. Not because I think it's morally wrong, but – well, I have a hard enough time giving sex away for free, let alone trying to get someone to pay for it." They both laughed. "So why the name Syn?"

"Well, I got the idea from my stepdad, that argument we had. He said I was off to live a life of sin. That word stuck in my head. To me, it means so many things. It symbolizes everything that is wrong if you're religious. Being an atheist, I use it as an anti-statement. I think you can let strangers enjoy seeing your naked body, profit from it, even be sexually explorative, and still be a good person. That's why I spell it with a Y instead of an I."

"Wow, all that in a name? I just thought it was cool."

"See, you learn something new every day!"

Holden turned to Paige. "Is it just me, or have we learned way more about each other than we should have on a second date?"

"I know. I don't know why I got into all that. I normally gloss over details. But Holden, excuse the pun, you have a hold on me. You better not hurt me."

She shimmied up his body and kissed him. Her hand found the back of his head. Her kiss was very passionate and deep. Holden put his arms around her waist and squeezed. Having her in his arms felt familiar, as if they had been together for years. It was a feeling he didn't want to let go of.

Their embrace must have lasted for an hour. Before they knew it, the sun was setting over the lake. She took a quick glance at her watch. "We don't have much time. I have to be at work in a couple of hours," she said with genuine disappointment. "Let go sit on the swings again." They got up, and Holden tried to hide his erection.

No one else was in sight. They took seats and swung hand in hand until Paige jumped off. She used her dancing talents to clench the chains of Holden's swing and pulled herself face-to-face with him. She put her legs through the chains on either side of him and lowered herself until she was sitting on his lap. He hugged her. They kissed again, and it was pure and raw. The fact that her relatively short skirt was over his lap, leaving nothing between them except maybe panties, didn't escape Holden.

Their hands ran all over each other. The swing gently swung in no particular direction. Holden could tell she was thinking about what she was going to say for a while before she finally worked up the nerve. "Your story made me fucking hot. I like you so much. I want to fuck you, and I want to feel your piercings inside me."

Holden didn't need much more incentive. He reached down to his shorts. As he fumbled to unzip, he had Paige look around for any unsuspecting voyeurs. She pulled herself up the chains, high enough that her waist was above his head. Her skirt blew up, and he could see that she wasn't wearing any panties after all. That made him even more excited.

He pulled out his cock. She leaned over to take a peek. Reassured that neither of them would get caught in the jagged metal of Holden's zipper, she slowly lowered herself, positioning his cock to match her wet pussy. She slid down, taking all of him inside her. At the very end she let go of the chains and slammed down on him. Holden was startled and thought he must have let out a strange sound, because Paige asked him if he was OK. Holden quickly reassured her and they hugged tightly.

They didn't immediately start fucking. They swung back and forth, feeling each other with every pump of their legs. It was gradual at first but amazing. She was happy to have such a memorable first time with an amazing guy.

Their eyes locked on to each other. Her dress covered his waist. If anyone were to walk by, they would appear to be just another young couple in love and sharing a ride on a swing. A passer-by wouldn't notice the naughty act that was taking place.

Holden's cock gently worked inside her, easing in and out as they swung. "Do you like the piercings, or do they hurt?"

"Mm hm, I like them. They don't hurt at all," she said in a cute-little-girl voice.

Their swinging got faster until they were both pumping very hard. Her pussy slid on his cock. Their eyes were still locked. They were so fixated on each other that they missed the strain they were putting on a children's swing. Then came a loud *bang* as the chains broke and sent them crashing to the ground.

They never separated in the fall. Their embrace remained tight as they landed on the sand. Paige crashed hard on his cock, forcing him to penetrate her deeply. He was scared he'd ruptured something inside of her, and she was concerned that she'd hurt him in the fall. After a quick assessment, they decided they were both OK and kept on fucking. Paige stayed on top and fucked him fast and hard. The adrenaline from the fall made their hearts race.

She leaned over so he could see down her dress. Her tits freely jiggled with the momentum. She whispered, "Come for me. I want to feel you come."

Holden wanted to wait for her, but it was soon out of his hands. She was fucking him hard, and her breathing got deeper and more sporadic. He knew she was about to come too. He squeezed her hand and shouted, "I'm going to come!"

"Fuck me!" she screamed even louder, not as a direction but more in satisfaction as she felt his come fill her pussy. Her hot liquid rushed against his cock, fighting the juices of his orgasm. She collapsed on him.

Her boots dug into him as she squeezed her legs closed, holding his cock in place. If his cock slid out of her, their fluids were going to gush all over his shorts. Since he didn't have a change of clothes or anything to cover up the mess, that would be a very bad thing.

With her thighs firmly in place, they rolled over. He was now on top of her. He used his powerful arms to push them up so they were kneeling face-to-face. Her arms and legs were tight around him as he stood. He lifted her skirt out of the way as she eased her grasp and parted from him. As expected, once the cork was free, their collective come rushed out of her. She let out a pleasured moan at the unusual sensation. Holden had to catch her as her knees buckled.

They checked each other over for evidence of their act. Holden had a small, wet stain on his shorts, but it wasn't obvious against the camouflage pattern. Paige adjusted her dress, which had become twisted. There was a wet spot between her feet. She looked at Holden with an expression of pure satisfaction and a devilish smile. Holden wanted to jump her again.

Instead, he extended his hand. She reached for it, and he pulled her into him. "Hi," he said.

Paige bit her bottom lip and managed, "Hi."

Holden gave her a kiss. Again they wrapped their arms around each other, running hands wildly all over. Their kiss was long and passionate. At least Holden thought it was passionate, right up until he caught Paige peeking at her watch. "Fuck, I really have to get ready for work. And thanks to you, I need a shower," she said with a wink.

She took his hand, and they walked towards the subway station. For the entire train ride, Holden was paranoid that everyone could see the sex stain on his shorts. Paige fidgeted in her seat as she felt their come drip out of her.

They finally got to her place. Holden stopped at the door as she dug her keys out. "I'll see you later?" she said with anticipation.

"You better believe it," he replied.

Satisfied, she spun around and ran up the stairs. Her quick departure made Holden smile. He smiled even bigger when he heard her singing as she ran. He turned towards the street and gazed up at the night sky. *What a beautiful night for a walk*, he thought.

CHAPTER 4

A couple of weeks had passed since Holden and Paige last saw each other. They were finding it difficult to arrange their schedules to meet, since Paige worked nights and Holden was working days. They did, however, talk on the phone and online regularly.

Holden's phone rang. "Hello?"

"Holden, it's Paige. How are you doing?"

"Good, thanks. What's up?"

"I got an offer to go dance in North Bay this weekend. I've never been there before, and I really don't want to go alone."

"Oh yeah?"

Paige laughed at Holden's attempt to make her spell it out. "Yeah. What are you doing this weekend?"

"Let me check my schedule." Not even letting a second pass, he remarked, "Yup, I seem to be free."

"Well, would you like to go with me? The club will pay for gas and a motel."

"What kind of a club is it? Will you be safe? What will be expected of you?"

"I talked to one of the girls who's been up there. It's about the same as here as far as their touching policy. She said it's a clean, safe place, and the owner/manager is a good girl to work for. I would feel more comfortable with you there. That is, if you're up for it."

"Sure. What time do you have to be there?"

"I have to start around eight on Friday night. It's about a four-hour drive. I'd like to get there in time to see where the club is, eat dinner, and settle into the motel. Would it be possible to leave by two-ish?"

"I work Friday, but I'm sure I can duck out early. They'll understand."

"Thanks, Holden. You're a lifesaver."

"Anything for you, pretty lady. See you Friday."

After Paige's call on Wednesday, all Holden could think about was their weekend away together. He was excited and nervous. He knew she'd be working, and he didn't know his way around North Bay at all. He didn't know what he was going to do to kill time. He did know that he couldn't afford to hang out at a club all weekend.

Friday finally arrived. Holden sneaked out of work at noon so he could get packed and be ready to go on time. He drove over to Paige's apartment, and as luck would have it, he managed to find a parking spot right in front of her building. He chalked his luck up to the fact that it was a Friday afternoon. Most of the city seemed to evacuate to their cottages in Muskoka on Fridays.

Holden walked up to Paige's door and rang the bell. He soon heard the familiar *thump, thump, thump* down the stairs. The door swung open, and Paige clumsily fell through with her luggage in tow. Holden grabbed her bags and helped her to the car. "You know it's only a couple of days, eh?" he said, poking fun at her.

"Well, I do have to look my best."

"Fair enough. Ready?"

"Yup. This your car?"

Holden had forgotten that she had never seen his car before. He rarely drove it in the city; the public transit system and his inline skates were more convenient. "Yeah, that's her."

"It's awesome."

"Thanks," Holden said, glowing with pride.

His car was a classic 1984 BMW 633 CSI. It was his pride and joy. He popped the trunk and packed her things away. After confirming that Paige had everything she needed, they jumped into the car and headed out of the city.

The drive was going to be long. Holden eagerly anticipated having all that time with Paige. The weather was perfect; it was a great afternoon for a road trip. As expected, the traffic heading north was crazy but they had the CD player cranked. They made the best of the situation as they sang and played air guitar.

Paige was gorgeous. She was wearing fishnet thigh-highs, Chuck Taylors, a plaid skirt, and a white blouse. She hadn't done anything special with her hair after she got out of the shower; she'd left it a bit wet, causing her natural curls to hang freely over her shoulders. Holden tried his best to keep his eyes off her and on the road. As she rocked out in the passenger seat, he found it hard not to watch her. She was so fun and full of life. He was happy just to be near her.

At one point she looked out the window, holding his hand as she took in the scenery. They got stuck in yet another traffic jam. Holden glanced over at her and knew it was going to be impossible to keep his eyes on the road. Her free hand was running all over her body. She undid a couple of buttons on her blouse, exposing the red lace bra that had only been hinted at beneath her white top. She let go of his hand to caress both her tits. She put her left foot on the dashboard and the other out the open window. Her skirt rode up almost far enough to show off her pussy, exposing the tops of her fishnets.

Holden was getting hard watching the unexpected show. He wanted to ask her what she was doing, but decided simply to enjoy her antics. She wasn't paying attention to him at all now. Her hands found her knees. They slowly slid up her legs to play with the bows at the tops of her thigh-highs, then continued up her inner thighs. She pulled at her skirt, giving Holden a peek at her sheer black panties. She was still staring out the window, and it became clear to Holden that the show wasn't for him. He didn't care why she was doing it; he was happy that she was.

One hand rubbed her pussy, and the other reached up to her tits. Her hips moved as she got more and more into her show. Holden's cock was fully hard and becoming uncomfortable. His jeans were tight, and they created a lot of resistance for his little man of steel. Luckily the traffic wasn't going anywhere, because he didn't want to stop watching the show.

She firmly rubbed her clit. The soft moans that came from her lips were almost unbearable to Holden. Her hand reached under her bra to caress her bare breast. Holden couldn't see everything that was going on, but the knowing that it was good enough for him.

Unfortunately, the traffic started to move. He had to split his attention between Paige and the road. She stopped what she was doing and flipped the bird out of the window. She brought her feet down to the floor mat and started to laugh.

Holden turned to Paige, very confused. "What was all that about?"

Paige laughed almost uncontrollably. "That trucker beside me has been staring at me for the last hour, so I thought I would fuck with him."

"All that was for a trucker?"

"Yeah, my bad," she said with a devilish smile.

"Wow. If that's how you fuck with people, you can fuck with me any time."

"Sorry! I hope I didn't bother you," she said, biting her lip holding back another smile. Her gaze ever so slowly fell to Holden's jeans. She could see the bulge that was now very prominent. She reached over and gave it a pat, like a person might pat the top of a pet's head. "I'll make it up to you. I promise."

Holden gave her a smile and continued to drive. His hard-on wasn't as easy to pacify. It stayed attentive for the next hour.

The miles passed in more casual conversation, rocking out, and comfortable silence. Finally, the traffic opened up a bit. Holden got the car running perfectly at 150 kilometres per hour, which allowed them to make up time as they passed Barrie.

Paige checked at her watch. It had a skull and crossbones covering the face, and a band with the same print. To see the time, she simply flipped up the skull on the face.

"I'm hungry," Holden said. They were almost half an hour out of Muskoka. He would soon need gas too. He told her he had the perfect surprise for her.

"Oh, I like surprises," she said.

"It's not a big one, so don't get too excited."

The minutes continued to pass. There was now a nice mix of city and country scenery. The traffic thinned as they passed more and more exits. The sun shone with not a cloud in the sky. More songs played; more conversations passed.

Finally, Holden saw what he was waiting for: a big green exit sign that said *Severn Bridge*. He decelerated and took the exit. Paige was surprised by the sudden turn. "Where are we going?"

"Just for a side trip. Trust me," Holden said.

They continued down the road, past twists and turns, until Holden finally let Paige in on his little secret. He was going to take her for a tour of his home town.

He pointed out his old house, other family members' houses, and the homes of neighbours he didn't like. He showed her everything. Paige took in the sights. She didn't say much, but he was happy to share his memories with her while he had the opportunity.

Eventually she broke the silence. "I knew you were from the district of Muskoka, but I assumed you were from a town there."

"Nope, I'm as backwoods as they come. Still love me?"

He took the back roads to the highway and headed north to find something to eat. Instead of driving into a town, they found a small restaurant on the highway. Holden knew Paige, in her sexy little outfit, wasn't going to stand out because the community was used to all the antics of vacationers in the summer. He downshifted the powerful BMW engine and guided the car onto a driveway. Gravel crunched under the tires as he pulled into a parking spot.

Paige took a minute to gather her things, so Holden seized the opportunity to open the passenger door for his beautiful girl. Like a lady, she swung both her legs out so she didn't give the locals the same view the lucky trucker had got earlier. Taking Holden's extended hand, she pulled herself out of the car.

As they walked into the diner, Holden placed his arm around her waist. He opened the door to a *bing bong* sound, which alerted the staff to the arrival of new patrons. They barely got a glance as they found their seat. The waitress came over and took their drink order while dropping off the menus. They decided on burgers.

While the couple waited for their food, they looked around at the other diners – mostly locals, with an odd tourist thrown in. The radio was playing horrible elevator-type music. It was hard to tell what song they were ruining, but whatever it was, they succeeded. Holden and Paige shared knowing glances and nods towards some particularly strange customers. Their attention snapped to each other as a new song played. This one they recognized: it was a very poor cover of a song they'd been listening to in the car.

Smiling, Holden stood up and once again extended his hand. Paige was confused. "Care to dance m'lady?" he asked. She frowned at him as if he were crazy. He stayed put, not willing to take no for an answer.

"You *are* crazy," Paige confirmed as she grabbed his hand and stood up. He pressed his body against hers and put his hands around her waist. They swayed to the music, ignoring the disapproving stares. Paige giggled through the entire dance; Holden fought back his urge to laugh as well. Time seemed to stand still as they shuffled back and forth in that dirty old diner on the side of the highway. Their dance didn't end until the food arrived.

They parted and retook their seats. One or two spectators applauded. Holden wasn't sure if they were applauding the dance or its conclusion. The only person whose opinion Holden cared about was sitting across the table from him, sinking her teeth into a hamburger.

Dinner was over rather quickly and they got back onto the road. North Bay was an hour away, and they were both anxious to get there.

The BMW sparked to life. Holden hit the gas, and six cylinders threw them back into their seats. He accelerated to match the flow of traffic whizzing past them. Paige flipped up the skull on her watch; it read five o'clock. The sunny skies were misleading, burning as brightly as if it were only early afternoon. She relaxed, happy in the knowledge that even with their detours, they were making good time.

As they got closer to North Bay, Paige became more nervous about dancing in a strange town. She felt better having Holden with her.

The towns on their route faded away. The sights turned into rare hamlets surrounded by wilderness. They remarked how beautiful it was. It made Holden a bit homesick. Paige unfastened her seat belt and snuggled up next to him, putting her head on his shoulder and wrapping her arm around his. He could smell her hair. It reminded him of their walk in the park, and that aroused him. Her hand rubbed his leg, creeping further and further up his thigh. Her head rolled on his shoulder as she pressed her breast into his arm.

Holden took his right hand off the steering wheel and put it around her shoulders. Her body slid down so her head was in his lap. He caressed her hip as the car rocketed down the highway. It didn't take her long to notice the erection under his jeans. She pressed her cheek into the bulge and moved her head around. "My, my, what are we going to do about this?"

"I can't do anything; I'm driving. I guess it's on its own."

"Good, safety first. You drive. Don't mind me."

She repositioned herself so that she could undo his belt and zipper. Once she had them completely open, she slid her cold hand into his boxers and pulled out his cock. Her hand softly slid over his entire length a couple of times before she opened her sensual lips and took his cock into her mouth. The warmth of her saliva was a nice change from her cold hands, which were still wrapped around the base of his cock. Her fingertips teased his testicles as her head bobbed.

Holden took the opportunity to pull up her skirt. Between trying to keep his eyes on the road, sneaking peeks at her perfect body, and watching her give head, he had his hands full. He slid a hand under her panties. His fingers carefully teased her ass and pussy. He could feel she was wet. But he couldn't get his fingers deep inside her – she was just out of reach.

Paige was focused on his cock. He kept playing around with her ass. She was so soft. He wanted to touch her for as long as he possibly could.

They passed car after car. Holden occasionally looked at the vacationers. *If only they knew*, he thought. He was sure at least some of them could tell.

Paige's tongue danced around the tip of his cock, lapping up precome. Her fingers were more aggressive as they dug into his balls. She occasionally let out moans that he felt vibrate through his cock. The feeling was incredible. She had his entire cock in her mouth.

His fingers were barely in her ass when he felt that oh-so-familiar feeling. "Oh fuck, Paige, I'm going to come," he warned her. He didn't hear her response, but he did feel vibrations on his cock that trembled through his piercings. That was all he needed. His fingers slid out of her ass. He quickly clutched the steering wheel as he unloaded in her mouth.

She swallowed a couple of times, trying to keep up with the large load. After he was done, she continued to suck his cock, squeezing out all of his come. Finished, she pulled up his boxers and jeans. She tried in vain to zip him up and buckle his belt but had to give up, leaving him to deal with it later. She readjusted her skirt and cuddled up next to him. She kissed his neck and bit his ear. After several minutes, she whispered, "Thanks for not killing us. And don't worry, it's all gone," referring to the semen that had just filled her mouth.

"That's the last thing I was worried about."

"Thanks for coming."

"Um, it was my pleasure?"

Paige laughed. "No, not that! I meant to North Bay with me."

"Oh. I was confused because, well, I could do *that* any time you wanted," Holden said.

"No doubt," she said, slapping Holden's leg.

The rest of the drive went by rather quickly. Soon they saw a sign that read *Welcome to North Bay.* Paige pulled out directions she had written out on a napkin. "OK, it's on this highway, not too far into town. The place is called Bottom's Up."

"Bottom's Up?" Holden asked.

"Hey, I didn't name it."

"Fair enough."

"I think we're coming up on it. Yup, there it is. And there's our motel right across the street," Paige said excitedly.

"Convenient."

"Ain't it, though?"

"So, what do you want to do first?" Holden asked.

"I think we should go in and check it out. Find out about the motel and what time the club wants me."

"OK."

He turned off the highway and into the club's parking lot. It was about six thirty; if they still wanted her for eight, the couple had plenty of time to settle in at the motel.

Holden held the door of the bar open for Paige and followed her in. The place had all of the look, feel, and smell of a typical strip joint.

Only the neon lights of beer advertisements and the black lights that lined the stage illuminated the darkness inside.

Paige approached the bar and asked to see the manager. The manager turned out to be an older yet very attractive woman. She flashed Paige a warm smile as she shook her hand. Paige introduced her to Holden. The manager shook Holden's hand and gave him a stern warning: "I don't care if boyfriends come in to watch, especially if they're from out of town like yourself. But I tell you Syn is single while she is working in my establishment. If you have a problem with that, stay out. I won't tolerate any trouble."

"Yes, ma'am. I promise I won't cause any trouble."

"Yeah, I've heard that before. But for now, it's nice to meet you," she said with a cordial snarl.

"Likewise," Holden responded.

Paige went with the manager to sort out the last of the details, as well as get the key to their motel room. She reappeared, and the two left the club to check in to their accommodations.

The room wasn't anything special, but it was better than Holden had expected. Paige quickly unpacked, undressed, and jumped in the shower. Holden loved watching her take off her clothes. Knowing that in a couple of hours she would be doing it in front of strangers got his blood flowing. While she walked around the room naked, Holden couldn't keep his eyes off her.

While she showered, Holden unpacked the last of her things, spreading the outfit she planned to wear onto the bed. He heard her turn off the faucet. After several minutes, the bathroom door opened. She stood in the doorway, wearing only her towel. In a mock disgruntled voice she said, "I can't believe I had to be in there all by myself. Who knows what could have happened to me? I thought you were supposed to protect me."

"Ah, yes, but who's going to protect you from me?" he said.

Before he had a chance to move, she charged over and jumped him. Her force knocked them both onto the bed. The towel fell to the floor during her short run. Her pussy was just above his belt buckle. Her tits hung down against his shirt. Between kisses, she said, "Next time, eh?

You owe me!" Then she caught a glimpse of the alarm clock. "Fuck, I have to get ready!"

Holden changed gears quickly from the idea of a potential quickie and flipped on the TV. Paige grabbed her make-up bag and outfit and once again disappeared into the bathroom. He sampled the few channels that were available, finally settling on a sitcom.

It didn't take Paige long to change. She made an amazing transformation from Paige to Syn. It was the first time he had seen Syn since the night they met. He had forgotten how completely different she appeared. He must have been staring a bit too hard because she asked him if everything was all right. "Oh yeah, everything is fine. It's just that you look so beautiful."

"Don't I normally?" she asked, trying to trap him.

"You know what I mean," he said, not falling for her game.

She gave him a smile with a subtle wink as a reply. "OK, I'm ready to go. You going to come in for a beer tonight?"

"I don't know. Do you want me to?" he asked hesitantly.

"Of course. I would love to see you tonight."

"In that case, I might have a beer when I drop you off, but I won't stay long. Feel free to text me whenever you get time."

Pouting, she said, "Oh, you're not staying?"

"No, I don't want to cramp your style. Do your thing, and I'll be waiting for you when the place closes."

"Fine! I'll text you lots. For the record, I wouldn't mind if you wanted to stay longer, but I understand." She crawled onto the bed and gave him a kiss on the cheek. "We should go."

"Fine!" Holden mimicked.

The bar was only across the street, but the street was a four-lane highway. He didn't feel comfortable letting her walk by herself, dressed the way she was. So they jumped in the car and did the two-second drive. Paige disappeared into the girls' changing room once they got inside, taking all her stuff with her. Holden found the darkest corner and took a seat by himself. Before he had a chance to get comfortable, the waitress was there to take his drink order, and on the waitress's heels was a dancer.

"Care for a dance?" she asked.

Holden used a line he loved to use at strip clubs: "No, sorry, I can't dance. I have two left feet." More often than not it got a laugh, but sometimes the dancer just walked away.

This girl gave a polite chuckle and then stood there staring at him.

"No, thank you. I'm just going to have a drink, watch the floor show, and then take off," he said, politely rejecting the mostly naked lady's offer.

"Suit yourself. Have a good night," the dancer said, obviously very offended.

"Yeah, you too."

His beer finally showed up. He leaned back in his chair and watched the girl onstage start her show. Normally he wouldn't have been caught dead alone in a strip club, but he kept reminding himself that he was there for Paige. He also took comfort in the fact that he was in a strange city and no one would possibly know him. The bar was relatively slow, with only a few old guys scattered around.

Paige emerged from the changing room. She walked up to the bar and ordered a drink. After she got it, she spotted Holden sitting in the dank corner. Drink in hand, she confidently strutted over to him and sat down in the seat closest to him. She told him what the changing room looked like and about the girls she had met in the short time she was there. The girls hadn't been too talkative, but dancers rarely warmed up to a new girl right away. It was like that in all the clubs.

Holden asked if she was going to be OK. She reassured him that she would be fine. He reminded her that if she needed anything or if she got into trouble, she should call him. She patted him on the head and told him she was a big girl; she could take care of herself.

Holden downed the last sip of his beer and told her he would get going. She asked him what he would do the rest of the night. He said he was going to do a little sightseeing in North Bay, get something to eat, and head back to the motel to watch TV.

Before he left, he asked Paige if she wanted anything when she got off work. "Only you" was her perfect answer.

"How about food or drinks?"

"No, I'll be fine. I'll get something to eat here, and I know I'll have enough to drink."

"OK. Be careful. Have a good night."

"You too."

Holden left the bar and headed for his car. He felt bad for leaving her there alone, but he knew she was a professional and she'd be fine.

He no sooner got the car started than he felt a vibration coming from his pocket. He pulled out his cell. The screen read *New message*. He clicked on the envelope icon, and up came a photo of Paige with the words *I miss you already. Thanks for coming here with me.*

He texted back, *It's my pleasure. Thanks for inviting me. See you at two.* He hit Send and went on with his drive.

The town was bigger than he expected. It was situated alongside a beautiful lake. He took some time driving around to enjoy at the sights. He also took a walk along the boardwalk, eventually stopping at a lakeside pub to have dinner and a pint. The town was quite pleasant and he enjoyed his evening, even thought he was alone. The waitress was beautiful and quick-witted, which made his dinner that much more enjoyable. He was willing to sit by the lake, drink beer, and chat with the waitress all night, but he wasn't sure how to get back to the motel. He also couldn't forget that he was driving.

He took a different route back; he wanted to see if he could find his way. He passed a liquor store and figured that taking back a couple of drinks for the room probably wasn't a bad idea. He bought a twelve-pack and a bottle of wine for them to share before bed.

As he was leaving the liquor store, he saw a flower shop. On impulse, he stopped in and bought Paige flowers. He laughed at the proximity of the two stores. "Definitely cuts down on travel time when you need to say you're sorry for a night of drinking!"

Purchases complete, he managed to find his way to the motel. He parked and strolled up to their room. The only thing left to do was wait until two. To make sure he didn't fall asleep on Paige, he set the room's alarm clock and his cell phone alarm for 1:30 a.m.

As he hit Set, his phone came alive again, vibrating in his hand. It was a new message from Paige that simply said, *Thinking of you.*

He replied, *Me too. I hope you're having fun.*

GTG back to work.

Feeling happy she was thinking about him, he cracked a beer and leaned back in the bed to watch whatever cheesy movie was on. He woke up a short time later to a *beep, beep, beep* from his cell phone. He couldn't believe he'd dozed off.

Just as he was getting his bearings, the alarm clock screamed – a very loud, piercing sound. "Guess no one will sleep through that!" He turned off both alarms and checked the screen of his cell phone. Three new messages. "Damn," he said. He hoped she wasn't mad at him for not writing her back.

Thinking of you.
Thinking of you.
I love you.

The last one really caught his attention. He smiled at the thought, but he figured she was drunk. He grabbed his car keys and the flowers and made the very short trek to the bar. He walked in discreetly, trying not to attract any attention, but Paige saw him immediately. "Holden!" she yelled across the room. She ran over and jumped into his arms, wrapping her legs around his waist. "I missed you, baby," she said, giving him a kiss on the cheek. "You want a dance, big boy?"

"Maybe later," Holden said.

Paige knew what he meant. "Deal," she said with an exaggerated nod.

Holden put Paige down and they walked up to the bar. She stood behind him with her hands around his waist. Then she whispered, "Go sit down. This one is on me for being so nice to me."

Holden resisted at first, but she insisted. So as not to offend her, he turned and found the same table he'd sat at earlier. After getting the drinks, she walked as sexily as she could over to him. Her eyes stayed focused on his. When she got to the table, she didn't sit in the chair beside him. Instead she knelt on his chair, pressed her tits into his face, and placed their drinks on the small table top. "I missed you so much. Did you get my texts?"

"Yeah, sorry. I dozed off," Holden admitted.

"Oh yeah? What did you think of them?"

"They were very sweet."

"And …?" Paige asked with a hint of frustration.

"You love me?"

"Yes, I do." She leaned in to give Holden a kiss.

"Oh you, you have to be drunk."

"Nope. I've been drinking water all night. I don't like to get drunk in strange places or around people I don't know."

"Sounds reasonable. So you're completely sober?"

"Yup." She looked down at him with her big brown eyes, biting her lip in that very sexy way that she did. He could tell she was waiting for him to say the words back to her. He met her gaze, happily holding her in his arms. He told her he loved her too. She let out a little shriek of joy and clapped her hands. She gave him another kiss and walked away.

She approached another dancer, and Holden watched them talk, Paige pointed in Holden's direction. They both clapped their hands and laughed. He wondered what he had gotten himself into, but he was happy to now have the attention of almost all the dancers in the place. He and Paige had only been together for a few weeks, but those few weeks had been awesome. He really did believe that he loved her. He thought about her, what he'd just said. He also thought about how much more difficult delivering the news he was saving for the drive home was going to be.

His beer wasn't even finished when the lights came on and the doorman began ushering people out. Paige told the doorman that Holden was her ride, so he allowed him to stay with the other boyfriends as they waited for the girls to change. The guys made idle chit-chat and cracked a few jokes as they finished their drinks.

Paige came out wearing jeans and a T-shirt – a shirt Holden recognized immediately. It was his retro Space Invaders shirt. She saw the expression on his face when he recognized it. "I didn't think you'd mind. I love this shirt. Besides, I look much better in it than you do."

Paige was anticipating getting out of the bar. He could see that she really wanted to go, so he took a final sip of beer, put the bottle on the counter, and escorted her to the door. She told him he could have finished his beer if he wanted, but he couldn't wait to get her back to the room. He had been missing her all night and he couldn't have cared less about the others in the bar. He also sympathized with her. After working a long shift, she undoubtedly wanted to get some sleep.

Paige was happy that Holden had made her a priority. Rarely had any guy done that for her.

As they left the bar, Paige smiled at the other girls who were making their way out of the dressing room. She proudly took Holden's hand and led him outside. Once they got to the car, Holden went to open her door. She stopped him and pushed him against the car. "Fuck, I have wanted to do this all night." She kissed him – the most intense, powerful kiss of their young relationship. She was groping at him, hugging him, and pulling at his clothes.

"Gear down there, big rig," Holden said. He unlocked the car and opened the passenger door for her.

She was about to sit, but she saw the flowers at the last minute. "For me?" she exclaimed. Holden nodded. She picked them up and tore into the paper covering them. "They're beautiful!" She dropped them into the front seat and kissed him again.

She finally stopped and told him she wanted to get back to the room; she was exhausted and needed a shower. Holden asked if she was hungry. She said that a pizza wasn't a bad idea, but her focus was on having a long, hot shower to rinse the grime of the club off of her. Holden agreed to the plan.

They made it back to their room. Holden swiped the magnetic card to get access to their room. As he turned on the lights, she gasped. "Oh my God, Holden, you're amazing."

"I promise one day I'll do it up right for you. For now, this will have to do."

He had gone to the dollar store and bought a couple of candles and some flower petals. Taking the risk of burning down the place, he lit the candles before he left to pick her up. He had spread the flower petals all over the bed. There was an assortment of Chinese food containers on the table. She almost began to cry. "Thank you" was all she was able to say.

"Don't worry about it. It was the least I could do. After all, you worked hard all night and I sat on my ass. I would have had a hot bath waiting for you, but, well, I personally wouldn't bathe in a motel tub," he said with a laugh.

"Yeah, that would have been gross," she agreed. "OK, I'm going to go shower if that's all right. Then we'll eat?"

"Works for me."

As she had earlier, she got undressed by the bed before walking into the bathroom. Holden listened for the sound of the faucets being turned on. He could hear the shower curtain open and close, and the sound of water splashing against the tub. Confident that she was now in the shower and couldn't hear the bathroom door being opened, he decided to take her up on her offer from earlier. He undressed, walked into the bathroom, and pulled back the curtain.

Paige let out a scream, obviously startled by Holden's latest surprise. She regained her composure and invited him in. Her body was already lathered in soap, causing her tits to glisten. Her normally curly hair lay flat against her back. Her bare pussy had goose bumps from being exposed to the cool air. She smiled as she looked up and down his body.

Holden was freezing. He felt lucky his cock maintained its erection and didn't shrivel up to become an inny, as its first instinct told it to do.

Paige's hands were soapy from shampoo. She had intended to use it to rinse the smell of the bar out of her hair. Instead, she found his member. She moved her hands around it as if she were washing his hair. Slowly, she stroked it. The lubrication from the soap and water felt great against his skin. His head was already very sensitive, and he almost jumped through the roof as her hands grazed it.

He picked up the bar of soap and lathered his hands before running them all over her body. He began with her neck and back. Once he was confident those were clean, he focused his attention on her tits. She continued rubbing his cock as he lathered up her chest. He skipped the rest of her body to go directly to her vagina and ass. He had to pull her closer to him so that he could reach around her. They were close; he could feel his cock against her skin as she continued to wash it. *It must have been very dirty*, he thought.

She worked harder and faster. Matching her momentum with his hand, he cleaned her clit. She put one of her feet on the edge of the tub, letting Holden get in nice and deep. His fingers disappeared inside of her; his palm was firm against her swollen clit. Their hands brushed as they frantically scrubbed one another. Their bodies were so close, only their hands separated them. He thought about how close he was to being inside her, yet so far away.

As they kissed, he could feel her hips moving against the palm of his hand. He applied more resistance. The grip she had on his cock got firmer. Holden moaned. He moved his fingers in a come-here motion, tickling her G spot.

"I'm coming!" she screamed. Her body tightened and moved involuntarily, almost ripping off Holden's cock in the process. The unexpected force on his cock set him off. He pressed up against her body as he squirted all over her pussy.

When they were both done with their orgasms, they held each other in their soapy, wet arms. He grabbed her ass and pulled her more tightly into him. They could feel his come smearing between their bodies.

She finally slid her hand off his cock. She could see his come covering it. He expected her to rinse it off in the water flow. Instead, she looked into his eyes and brought the come to her lips. She used her tongue to clean her hand. They held each other close again, their chins resting on each other's shoulders. No words were spoken.

They finally parted, cleaned themselves properly, and left the shower. Holden only needed one towel to dry himself off. Paige used three: one to dry her hair, one to dry her body, and the other to wrap around herself. Together they went to the table, Holden pulled out Paige's chair for her. "Not going to eat?" she asked.

"In a second. I have to get something first."

He walked over to the fridge and pulled out two chilled wine glasses and a bottle of wine. He popped the cork and poured them each a glass, then sat down with her to enjoy their late-night dinner.

As she brought her glass to her lips, the towel fell off her head and onto the floor. She barely gave it a thought. Holden watched her. Her wet locks freely hung over her bare shoulders. She didn't have any make-up on and was wearing only a towel. She appeared more vulnerable than he had ever seen her before.

When they were done eating, it was time for bed. He crawled into bed first. Paige blew out the candles and turned off all the lights except for the one on the bedside table. She stood at the end of the bed, picked up the towel that had fallen off her head, and tossed it into the bathroom. With the motion, the towel she was wearing came undone and almost fell open. Quickly, she saved it. "Uh oh," she said. She opened and closed the towel, teasing Holden with peeks of her naked body, careful not to show off any of her naughty bits. Her lips formed a very evil grin that was amplified by the shadows cast by the dim light.

Holden was enjoying her show. She looked very cute, and he couldn't help but laugh at her antics. Finally the expression on her face turned from happy and playful to very focused. She let the towel fall to the floor and stood at the foot of the bed, letting him examine her body. Holden immediately got hard.

Paige rubbed her hands all over her body. She turned around to pick up her towel, letting Holden get a good view of her bare ass and pussy. She spun around like a ballerina and gracefully tossed the towel into the bathroom. She ran her fingers through her hair. "Well, it's late. We should get some sleep." She slid her hands down her body again. This time they found her pussy. Her eyes were glued on Holden's.

He didn't want her to have all the fun, so he stroked himself. Their gazes never broke from each other. No words were spoken as they mutually masturbated.

Just as Holden was about to throw her to the bed, she put her knees on the mattress and crawled up to him. Her face made it as far as his waist. Her hands left her pussy and went for his cock. She stroked him, and without any hesitation her mouth found its mark. He could feel her tongue flickering as she took him deep.

Eager to satisfy her, he took her leg and pulled it towards him. Getting the hint, she let his cock fall out of her mouth as she shuffled over. He guided her leg over his head. Once her knee had settled on either side of his face, she moved her cunt into position over his mouth and went back to sucking his dick.

Holden didn't wait to dip his tongue deep inside Paige. It was hard for him to concentrate on licking her as her mouth moved masterfully over his cock. His pride kicked in. There was no way he was going to let her get him off without first giving her an orgasm. She'd had one earlier, so it shouldn't be that hard for him to get her back in the mood.

His hands reached around the outside of her legs, gripping her ass and pulling her cheeks apart, allowing his tongue to get just a little bit deeper inside her. He kept his eyes open so that he could see all of her. He tried to read her body to see if she was enjoying what she was doing, but it was difficult. His cock was twitching. Her tongue moved up and down his shaft, playing with each bead on his piercings as her hand massaged his balls.

Eager to take his mind off his mounting orgasm, he tried something new. His tongue left her pussy and moved up to tease her ass. At first he gave her button light flickers, progressing to small circles. She responded better than he had expected. She moved her hips, lowering her ass to his mouth and giving him a very clear sign that she enjoyed the new game.

Her ass was so tight that it was difficult for his tongue to penetrate her too deeply, but he was in deeply enough to stimulate her. His tongue danced, delivering long strokes over her pussy and teasing her asshole. She followed his cue and slid a finger into her mouth, next to his cock. The sensation was new to Holden. It only lasted a second before she slid her finger out of her mouth and into Holden's ass.

The second he felt the pressure in his ass, he squeezed her ass firmly, making her emit a moan. He wasn't sure if the moan indicated pain or pleasure, but either way, Holden was sure she was OK. He moved his mouth alongside her pussy lips and gave her a small bite on her thigh. He shifted awkwardly so he could get a finger inside her. Her mouth went back to his cock, violently taking it in as his finger worked her. Her finger jerked sporadically inside him. It made him want to come badly, but he held out as long as he could. He tried to get her off faster by burying his tongue deep in her pussy. Her hips ground hard into his face and his finger.

Her teeth accidentally dug into his cock, which helped him hold out a bit longer. He let out a small ouch and a flinch. She gave him an apology, muffled by his cock. Her hand slid up his body as she started to rub her clit, she knew he couldn't reach it himself.

Holden did his part. He sank his fingers as deep inside her ass as he could get, while simultaneously using his tongue to apply more pressure to her pussy. Rubbing her own clit got Paige to the point of orgasm faster than he would have been able to do on his own. He appreciated the assistance because he knew he wasn't going to be able last much longer, and he didn't want to make her wait for her release. If she was almost to the point of orgasm, his coming would break her flow, and they would have to start all over again.

Then her finger thrust hard inside his ass, causing him to orgasm without warning. He didn't realize until his own orgasm subsided that it had been her own orgasm that had caused her to thrust as hard as she did. His face was soaked with her juices. He licked as much out of her as he could before she had to move. "Oh my God, it's so sensitive," she said as she rolled over and collapsed.

Holden lay with his head by her knees. Her head still on his waist, inches from his flaccid cock. Her finger scooped up his come, which was still leaking from him. She brought it to her sensual lips. "Wow," she said. "It's been a long time since I've had so many orgasms in one day."

Feeling proud of himself, he tried to remain realistic and remember his own limitations. "That last one was all you; I was just along for the ride," he said, giving her due credit.

"We both came, and that's all that matters."

"Indeed."

They both fell asleep in their inverted positions. At some point in the night Paige moved, making Holden jump. She crawled out of bed and went into the bathroom. She left the door open and the light on. Holden's heart raced from the late-night scare. He watched her brush her teeth. He was still naked, lying on top of the covers.

After spitting and rinsing, Paige joined him in bed and patted his cock, which was resting on his hip bone. "Good boy," she said and snuggled up next to him, pulling the blankets over them. She gave his cheek a kiss. "Thanks again for coming with me."

Holden laughed. "I believe you've said that already."

"I know, but this time I meant the other way."

Holden laughed again.

"No seriously, I know I said it, but I'm really happy you're here."

"I'm happy I'm here too. I love spending time with you."

"Me too."

Holden reached up and turned off the lights. Within seconds they were both asleep, naked, intertwined in each other's arms and legs.

Not sure of the time, Holden woke up to the sound of running water. He rolled over to say good morning to Paige, but she was gone. The water running was her shower. *Damn early risers*, he thought. He checked at the alarm clock: 11:45 a.m. *Up at the crack of noon. Still too damn early.*

He rolled over and tried to go back to sleep. The thought of joining her in the shower crossed his mind, but he was still tired and his cock hurt from the sex the night before. He had no sooner closed his eyes than Paige dived on the bed, waking him up. "Get up, lazybones," she said.

He thought she was way too chipper, considering the night before. "Why are you in such a good mood?" he asked as he tried to bury his head under the covers.

"Like you don't know." She pulled the blankets off him and gave him a big kiss. He was wide awake now, but he wasn't going to make it easy for her. "Get up! let's go to lunch."

"Fine, let's do everything *you* want to do," he mocked.

"Damn right. Oh, nice – shake it, baby," she added as she watched him crawl out of the bed naked.

Once they were both ready, they jumped in the car. Paige asked where they were going, so he told her about the restaurant he'd found the night before. They pulled up, and even though it was the lunch hour, the restaurant was fairly empty. They had no problem finding a seat on the deck.

They had an amazing view. The sky was a clear blue, and the sun was shining, making them nice and warm. There was no wind, so the lake was as smooth as glass. Paige was in awe as she took in the view.

The waitress came right over to take their order. It was the same girl who had waited on Holden the night before. "Oh, it's *you* again," she said with fake disappointment.

Holden smiled, flattered. "Well, you know, I can't stay away."

Paige stared disapprovingly at Holden. Her jealousy made Holden smile.

After they ordered, Paige gave Holden shit for flirting. He told her it wasn't a big deal; the waitress was being friendly because he had been sitting alone the night before, waiting for Paige. "You told her about me?" Paige asked doubtfully.

"Of course I did. Why wouldn't I?"

Paige let it go. She was content that he had told the pretty waitress about her. The next time the waitress came around, Paige relaxed and joked with her as well.

After their great lunch, they realized that the time had passed too fast. Paige was working the supper-to-close shift and had to get to work. She had her outfit in a bag so she could change at the club. They paid the bill and generously tipped the waitress. She even told Paige she might go see her dance later that night. Holden got lost in a fantasy of Paige lap dancing for her, but he tried to hide his thoughts as best he could.

The traffic was light, so Holden was able to get Paige to the bar in plenty of time to change, have a drink, and start her shift. He didn't go in with her this time because he knew she was safe and had met the other girls now. He told her he was going to catch a movie. She gave him a kiss and cheerfully bounced out of the car.

Holden turned around and was pulling away when his cell phone vibrated again. *Miss you already* was the text. It made Holden smile. He texted back *Miss you too*.

Syn scanned the crowd, finding guys she recognized from the night before. One customer stood out: a smiling, warm, and very friendly face. It was the waitress. Syn joined her on pervert's row.

"Hi, I'm Amy."

"Hi, Amy. I'm Syn."

Amy asked her when she was going to dance onstage. Syn looked at her watch and said she wasn't up for another hour or so. The day crew was still cycling through their last sets. "So, you have time for a drink and a private dance?" Amy nervously asked.

"With you? Definitely," Syn said in a flirty tone.

Amy caught the tone and gave her a smile. They went to the bar to get some drinks. When they got back, they sipped and talked for a long time. Finally Amy asked when Syn was going to take her into the back room. "Oh, I thought you were kidding," Syn said.

"Not at all," Amy said very seriously.

Syn stood up and led her new friend into the back room. Since a song had just began, they used the extra minutes to talk. Syn treated Amy like every other customer. She placed a small towel on Amy's knee. Then she sat on Amy's lap as they talked.

The DJ announced the next dancer, and the song played. That was Syn's cue to start dancing. She stood up and moved her body to the music, receiving oohs and aahs from Amy. After several seconds, Syn slowly undressed, much to the joy of her customer.

After losing her very short dress, she leaned back into Amy. She pretended she was having trouble with her bra. Syn tilted her head so her mouth was pressed against Amy's ear. "Can you help me out? I seem to be having a problem."

Amy slid her hands up Syn's bare back. It was hard to find the clasp when Syn was pressed so close. After a couple of attempts, she finally got it open.

"Thank you," Syn whispered. She stood and turned so that Amy could see her bra fall to the ground. Amy stared at Syn's perky tits.

It was time for the last article of clothing to come off. Syn hooked her thumbs into the waistband of her thong. She turned her back on Amy as she bent over to slide the thong down her ass, past her legs, and around her ankles to the floor.

Syn again took a seat on Amy's lap, this time between her legs. She could feel Amy's much larger tits pressing against her back. "Nice tits," she said, much as Sunshine had said to her a long time ago.

"I was thinking the same about yours," Amy said. She reached around and massaged Syn's breasts.

Syn spun around. "May I?" she asked, hopefully.

"Absolutely," Amy eagerly responded. Syn slid her hands under Amy's shirt, then under her bra, and played with Amy's ample breasts. Syn started grinding her pussy into the towel that was still resting on Amy's leg.

Amy was obviously getting into the act. She slid her hand down Syn's ribs to her stomach. Before Syn realized it, Amy had her hand between Syn's legs. A finger slipped inside her. Stunned at first, Syn was also more than a little turned on. She let the fingering continue longer than she should have before she jumped up and got her clothes. "Oh no. That's a no-no. Sorry, honey," Syn said, trying to hide her obvious pleasure.

Amy stared at her. She brought the finger that had just penetrated Syn to her lips. "Sorry," she said, feigning remorse as she tasted Syn.

Syn had already gotten her money for one dance. She grabbed her drink and told Amy she'd see her around. She was anxious to get away from Amy because she was worried she would do something very inappropriate with the waitress, something that might get her fired or hurt Holden. She ran into the dancers' changing room to regroup. After texting Holden about what had happened, she took a drink of water and went back into the bar.

Waiting for her was Amy, standing right outside the door. "I hope I didn't do anything wrong," she said.

"No, no. It was just … unexpected, and it's against the rules here."

"But you were OK with it?"

Syn formed her trademark mischievous smile. "I won't say anything this time. Don't let it happen again," she scolded in a very unconvincing manner.

"All right. I was worried after you took off. Here, this is for you," Amy said as she handed Syn a small piece of paper. She turned around and left without giving Syn a chance to read it.

Syn was sorry she hadn't had more of a chance to talk to Amy. She unfolded the note and read it. It was Amy's phone number and a short note:

> *Syn—*
> *It was nice meeting you. I know you're leaving town tomorrow, but I really want to fuck you. I know you have a boyfriend. If that's what it would take to get with you, I would gladly let him join us.*
> *Love, Amy xoxox*

Paige was very flattered. She definitely intended to show the note to Holden later. But for now, she had to get her mind back on work. She put the note in her purse and continued to try to find potential customers.

After the movie, Holden decided to stop in and see Paige at work. The late show got out at one o'clock, so there was only an hour before Paige was off work anyway.

He walked up to the bar, and the bartender recognized him and got him a beer. They were having a conversation when he felt fingers run over the back of his neck. The sensation sent shivers down his spine. Excitedly, he turned around to see Paige. She smiled and went through introductions, pretending she was a stranger picking up a hot guy at the bar. Holden thought it was a fun game, so he played along with it.

They continued their banter. He wasn't sure where it was heading, but he was hoping it would end up in a lap dance. Then Paige violently spun around and stumbled, almost falling over. Holden wasn't sure what had happened until he heard another female voice.

"Are you that whore Syn?"

Holden looked around Paige to see a tall brunette wearing khaki pants and a grey hoodie. Her hair was a mess and she had an expression of pure hatred in her eyes.

Paige didn't have a chance to answer before Holden shoved himself between the two girls. He knew Paige would be pissed at his interference, and that it might get them in trouble with the manager, but at that moment he didn't care. He remembered his promise, but he certainly wasn't going to let his girlfriend get hurt. "What the fuck?" Holden shouted at the stranger.

"This whore was fucking around with my girlfriend, that's what the fuck."

"What?" Holden asked again.

"Tonight, that slut was fucking around with my girlfriend. She felt Amy up and she let Amy stick a finger in her cunt. *Whore!*" she shouted at Paige.

Holden turned to Paige, who was being held back by a staff member. She looked at Holden with a glimmer of acknowledgement in her eyes. He pieced the brunette's comment together with Paige's text.

He told the angry woman to relax. He then said that she should keep her girlfriend out of strip clubs and tell her to stop assaulting the girls if she was that jealous. The last words barely escaped his lips before he felt a burning sensation on his cheek. It caused him to take a step backwards, but he managed to maintain his balance. The brunette had just hit him.

Holden grabbed Paige, who was rushing in the girl's direction. He told her he was fine and not to make it worse.

Paige settled down, taking her cue from Holden. She decided to talk out the disagreement instead of compounding it with a fight.

Holden struggled with the urge to hit the angry woman back, though he knew that was the worst possible thing he could do. He focused on not giving her another opportunity to hit him. Before Holden had time to decide what his next move was going to be, two burly bouncers took a hold of the brunette and dragged her out of the bar, kicking and screaming.

Holden again turned to Paige to make sure she was all right. Of course they had the full attention of the packed bar. Paige took one glimpse of his swollen face, and her own face flushed. She started to cry. "Oh my God, Holden, you OK?"

"Yeah, I'm fine. Why?"

"You're bleeding."

"Nah, it was just a punch to the face, not a big deal."

"Yeah, you are, badly. Let me see."

As Paige got closer, he could feel warm liquid running down his face. Adrenaline had caused him not to notice it before. *Son of a bitch, she cut me*, he thought.

Paige said, "It's deep. You should really have it checked out."

"Yeah, you're right. Get me that hot little nurse I saw running around here. No, seriously, I'm fine. How are you?"

"I just got pushed. You didn't have to do that for me, you know."

"I know you can take care of yourself, but I wasn't about to sit back and watch you fight."

By that time the manager was standing next to him. "What did I tell you the first night you were here?" she demanded.

"I'm sorry, ma'am, but I didn't do anything. I was running interference between Paige and that girl," Holden pleaded.

"I don't care. You have to get out, both of you, and have yourselves looked at."

"I'm fine," he said. He was upset that he might have cost Paige the job.

"These things happen. I know what happened, and I know you weren't the aggressor, but I can't have this shit go on in my bar."

The bartender handed Holden a clean rag for his face. He put it on his cheek to stop the bleeding, and felt the sting of his injury.

"Go home. Come back in at noon tomorrow to get paid, and we'll talk about you staying," the manager said with a smile.

"Thank you and sorry," Paige said sheepishly. She turned her attention to Holden and started fussing over him again. He assured her he was fine. "Do you want to go to emerg?" she asked.

"Hell no. It's not that bad. Let's get back to our room."

Before they left, Holden had the bouncers take a look around the parking lot to ensure that the psycho bitch wasn't waiting for them. Confident they were safe, they got in their car and went back to the motel.

They took a long, hot shower together. Paige carefully inspected his injury. When they were out of the shower, Paige went down to the receptionist and got gauze and medical tape from a first aid kit. After she had fixed Holden up, they crawled into bed.

Paige was still visibly upset that she had gotten Holden hurt. He tried to tell her it wasn't a big deal, but she kept cursing her job. He had gone out of his way to help her, and to pay him back, she'd got him hurt. Again, Holden tried to reassure her, but nothing helped.

He finally asked her what exactly had happened. She told him the entire story about Amy the waitress, the lap dance, their momentary encounter, and the note, which she produced. He tried to make her feel better with a joke. "Hey, wait a minute! Does this mean the threesome is out of the question?"

"I'm sorry," she said again. She was crying, still upset from the situation, not from his joke.

"Paige, honey, it's OK, really. I play roller hockey and I box. I've been punched in the face before and I survived. I'll be fine, I promise." He put his arms around her.

"Yeah, but this time it's my fault. It's not worth it."

Holden didn't say anything. He held her tightly, hugged her, and let her cry on his shoulder. They fell asleep in their embrace.

Holden didn't sleep well that night because the throbbing in his face kept waking him, but he wasn't about to tell Paige that. The alarm went off at eleven. Paige was still upset, thinking about what happened the night before. She was also impressed that, even after a punch to a face, Holden had remained calm.

At noon they went to the bar. Paige told the manager she couldn't dance that day. The manager agreed that it probably was for the best, and recommended taking Holden to the hospital for stitches. She graciously paid for three days even though Paige had only worked for two. It was easy to tell the manager liked them both. They could also tell she was sincere when she invited Paige back. She even said Holden was more than welcome.

Paige took the money and politely thanked her for the opportunity to work there. After she gave hugs to a couple of the other dancers, they were out the door. The car was already packed, so all they had to do was start the long drive home.

The drive south was much more subdued than the drive north. The radio played the same rock they had listened to on the way up, but this time they weren't singing along. They were tired and just wanted to get home.

Paige occasionally asked if everything was OK. Holden was happy to reassure her as often as she needed. He told her he was fine but tired. He played with her hair and smiled at her so she would know he wasn't mad at her.

When he turned his face towards her, she got a horrified expression that turned to a smile. "Oh my God, that is so bad. I'm so sorry," she said, reaching out to touch his bandage.

Holden laughed. "Trust me, it's all good. No worries, honey."

Paige snuggled up against him. He put his arm around her and continued driving; he had a lot on his mind.

Halfway home, they stopped at a very popular hamburger place for a bite to eat. It was so popular that the management had had to install a second parking lot and a pedestrian walkway over the highway. They sat in relative silence, making occasional witty remarks about the other diners.

As they walked back to the car, Paige could tell Holden was distant. She was nervous, still believing that that incident at the club could ruin their relationship. She didn't want to say anything again, but it was eating away at her.

Thoughts were weighing heavy on Holden's mind as well. He wasn't sure how he was going to bring up the inevitable and unpleasant conversation haunting him. He finally got his break when Paige broke the uncomfortable silence.

"Holden, I can't stand it anymore. What's going on? I can tell something is bothering you."

"We need to talk."

"Oh God," Paige said. She curled up into a ball in her seat, fighting back her urge to cry.

"You know I'm falling in love with you. I love spending time with you. This weekend was great, but …"

"But what? I'm sorry, Holden. Please don't," she cried.

His heart was breaking, but he knew he had to tell her. "This is so hard, but … I got another job offer. It's for director of operations for the Vancouver Witch Doctors. I have to move to BC."

"*What*? When do you move?"

"At the end of this season. I have to be there after Christmas to get things ready for the new season."

"So it has nothing to do with last night, and you're not breaking up with me?"

"No! I told you last night was nothing. I'd take a punch to the head for you any day. But as far as the breaking up goes, a long-distance relationship would be almost impossible." Sadness radiated in his voice.

Paige was so happy she hadn't blown things with the fight that she stopped crying and almost began to smile. The news that he would be leaving her really hadn't sunk in yet. She gave him a kiss on the cheek. "I love you."

"I love you too," he said with confidence, knowing that he really did. The weekend had proved it.

Finally, a look of realization crossed her face. "Wait. You have to move to BC in just over two months?"

"Yes. Well, a bit longer than a couple of months. More like 3 and a half months, maybe even four."

"Ok, but still, that's not a lot of time. What about us?"

CHAPTER 5

The gravel crunched under the tires as they pulled in to Paige's parents' driveway. Holden's legs went numb with nerves. Paige could tell he was a bit anxious, so she gave him a reassuring smile. "It will be OK. I promise they won't bite."

"It's not biting that I'm worried about."

He opened her door, then went to get their things out of the trunk. It was the circumstances of the meeting that gave him the most anxiety. He would have preferred to meet them for dinner on a casual evening rather than showing up at their house for an entire weekend. Especially after the bombshell he had dropped on Paige only a couple of weeks before.

Holden was very busy at work. The play-offs had just begun and his team were contenders. It was the worst possible time for him to go away, but he knew it was important to Paige for him to meet her parents before the move. Since it was important to her, it was important to him.

They approached the door. He took a deep breath as Paige turned the knob. "Hi, I'm home," she yelled as she barged through the door. Holden fumbled with the bags as he followed her into the house.

Her mom came running down the hallway. "Honey!" she screamed. She embraced Paige and gave her a kiss on the cheek.

Paige's stepfather wasn't too far behind his wife. Seeing Holden, he extended his hand. Holden gladly shook it. "Hello, sir. I'm Holden."

"Please, my name is Ben and this lovely woman is my wife Mary. Now, don't just stand there. Come in, come in. Here, let me give you a hand with those bags." Holden held out a suitcase, and they both remarked on how much Paige had packed for a weekend. Holden went to shake Mary's hand but she elected for the less formal hug before Holden followed Ben into Paige's room. They dropped off the bulk of the luggage before her dad showed Holden to his room. Paige had warned Holden on the drive that they would be sleeping in separate rooms. Her parents were more traditional and didn't feel comfortable with the younger couple sharing a room – not because they weren't married, but because their relationship was only a couple of months old.

Holden completely understood. He felt that it was a very natural parental concern. His parents would have done the same thing. He looked around the room he would be occupying for the next two nights. It was small, but the single bed appeared very comfortable, and he had plenty of space to put his things.

He joined Paige and her mom in the living room. Paige was sitting on the couch, talking a mile a minute as she filled her mom in on everything that had gone on since the last time they talked. Paige's father came out of the kitchen with two beers. He handed Holden one. "I think we'll need these," he said, laughing at his own joke. He sat at the dining room table; Holden took a seat opposite, and they got into their own conversation.

Holden and Paige had arrived after dinner, and the nightly ritual in that household was to go for a long after-dinner walk. Holden was anxious to see Paige's home town and hear stories of a young Paige. They started off in a group, but her parents quickly picked up the pace. Paige and Holden struggled to keep up at first; however, they soon found their rhythm.

Her parents told him stories about Paige growing up. Some embarrassed her, while others made them swell with pride as they spoke. They told him about their other daughter and a bit about what they did for their livings. They surprised Paige with the news that her sister was also coming home for the weekend. Paige got giddy with excitement. She held Holden's hand and told him more about her sister;

it was obvious that she loved her very much. Her parents mentioned that Paige's aunt and uncle had been invited to supper the next day.

When all the stories were done, the sun was setting. Paige and Holden dropped back, and she wrapped her arm around his. She pointed out sights of childhood memories as they walked. Her parents held hands. Holden and Paige thought it was cute. As the last of the sun disappeared over the horizon, they rounded the corner and were back at the house.

After cleaning up, they gathered downstairs in the TV room. Her parents had a beautiful set-up that included a big-screen TV, surround sound, Blu-ray player, and three large leather sofas arranged perfectly so they all had the best possible view of the screen. Holden was in love. He knew he wanted a room like this in his own house – when he could afford it.

He wasn't sure of the movie they were going to watch, but he and Paige staked out a prime couch, grabbed a blanket, and lay down together in anticipation. Her mom brought in a big bowl of popcorn and drinks for the four of them. Her dad sparked up the theatre system by pushing one button on the remote. The lights dimmed, and the system came to life.

The opening credits rolled. The bass shook the room. Holden made a very quiet comment to Paige about how great the vibrations would be during sex. She agreed.

Halfway through the movie, they had put a couple of drinks away, the popcorn was gone, and her parents were fading fast. Holden discreetly kissed Paige's neck and whispered naughty things in her ear. He could feel her ass pressing against him and grinding, which gave him an erection. He was sure she could feel it.

He squeezed Paige tightly, and she fidgeted. He was worried she would draw too much attention to them, but those thoughts faded fast when he realized her hand was going for his crotch. He whispered that it was a bad idea; her parents were right next to them. She didn't seem to care. Her hand slid down his pants and wrapped tightly around his member. With tiny movements, she rubbed him.

He wanted to reciprocate, but he was too nervous, afraid her parents would catch them. That wasn't the impression he wanted to make. But there was only so much he could do. Her cold hands felt great against his warm skin as she stroked him.

The movie was an action flick. Her dad had been eager to show off the capabilities of the system, and the only true way was with lots of explosions. The sound from the TV was enough to mask Holden's involuntary moans. He tried to pull away, as Paige had him on the brink of orgasm, but she refused to let him go. She thought it would be funny if she kept tugging on him.

His cock twitched. He gave her a big squeeze, and she could feel his hot come soak her hand. He trembled with pleasure and closed his eyes to take in the moment.

He reopened them when her dad cleared his throat. Holden's eyes went huge seeing him sitting on the edge of their couch. His daughter's hand, hidden under the blanket, was covered in come and still firmly holding Holden's penis.

Holden froze. Ben stared long and hard at him. Paige too was frozen. After a long moment, her dad said, "Well, I guess we're off to bed. Can we get you guys anything before we hit the sack?"

"Um, no, I think we're good," Paige replied.

Holden kept his eyes glued to Ben's face. He glanced back at Holden with a "caught you" look; it seemed a little angry. He ushered his wife out of the room. Before he left, he said, "Just hit off on the remote. It will take care of everything." Then he gave Holden a smirk and a wink before disappearing out the door.

"Whew," Holden sighed.

Paige laughed as she pulled her hand out of his pants. "Oh yeah, Dad's cool. He knows what's what."

"Cool," Holden echoed.

Paige examined the mess on her hand. She brought it to her mouth and licked a string off before it had a chance to drip on the carpet. She stopped as she realized what she had just done out of habit. She looked at Holden, then seductively finished cleaning off the mess with her tongue.

Holden wanted to pay her back by fucking her into an orgasm of her own, but he knew, as cool as her dad was, that would be pushing their luck.

The movie ended, so they tidied up the basement and headed upstairs. Paige's room was the first down the hall. Holden stopped to give her a kiss before he made his way down to his own room. He lay in bed, thinking about the next day. He was nervous about meeting the entire family, but since the meeting with her parents had gone well, he was cautiously optimistic.

He woke to the smell of bacon and the sound of voices talking. He put on jeans and a T-shirt and strolled into the kitchen. "Good morning, sleepyhead," Paige's mom said to him.

"Good morning," he replied, realizing the voices he had heard were actually from a TV talk show.

"Would you like a coffee?"

"Oh, very much so, please."

She handed Holden a coffee as Paige walked through the front door. She had already gone for a jog. "About time you woke up," she said, laughing at him. "I hope my parents were hospitable while I was out."

"Well, what can I say? The bed was insanely comfortable and yeah, your mom's been terrific in the five minutes I've been up."

"I was going to wake you up for a run, but I figured you needed your sleep."

"You saying I need beauty sleep?"

"Damn, these potatoes are bad," Paige's mom interrupted. Paige and Holden looked at her. "I'm going to have to run to the store to get more."

"No, no, Mom. If they're not a big hurry, I'll shower and Holden and I will run to the store for you. Make a list of everything you need."

"Thanks, dear. Holden, you don't mind?"

"Of course not. Paige offered to give me a grand tour today anyway."

Paige walked down the hallway. Once she was hidden from her mother's view, she coughed to get Holden's attention. He watched her take off her sweat-soaked T-shirt and running shorts. She wasn't wearing any panties underneath. He smiled and shook his head as she ran her fingers up her leg, over her pussy and to her lips. She blew him a kiss and went into the bathroom, locking the door behind her.

Her dad came in just as Paige disappeared. He had apparently been outside mowing the lawn, which surprised Holden because he hadn't heard the mower running. Holden was amazed at all the activity he had missed out on. He sipped his coffee as they made casual conversation about current events, TV programs they liked, and what his family members did for their livings.

Paige quickly showered and dressed. Before he knew it, she was ready to go. She beautiful wearing only a pair of old, grey sweatpants, a plain white T-shirt, a black ball cap, and minimal make-up. Holden had never seen her go casual in public before, but it was a style she could really pull off.

He laughed when she put on her black Chuck Taylors that didn't go with her ensemble, but matched the ones he was wearing. She took the list from her mom and gave her a kiss on the cheek while Holden knocked back the last drops of his coffee. He put the mug in the dishwasher and followed Paige out the front door.

Holden started the car. Paige slipped in a CD she'd found in her room and gave Holden directions. The music was good, very retro. Some of the songs embarrassed her, but Holden was a gentleman. He only teased her for the entire drive.

The directions didn't seem to be taking them to a grocery store. Holden asked where it was, and she told him she had other things she wanted to show him first. He saw her elementary school, her high school, the place she first smoked pot, her friends' places, her ex's house, and some of her other favourite sights.

Finally, she said she had a very special spot to show him. She directed him to a winding dirt road that led up a hill. With the tree canopy partially covering the road, he wasn't sure if his car was going to be able to squeeze through the overgrown brush or not. Paige reassured him that it wasn't much farther so Holden continued on, despite the horrific sounds the branches made as they scraped along his vehicle.

Out of nowhere, the trees parted and they were in the open, overlooking the town and lake. Holden thought it truly was an amazing spot. Paige told him stories of drunken parties and make-out sessions she'd had there.

He parked the car and got out to walk around. The clearing was small, only enough room to park about five cars. It included a small campfire area. Judging by the empty beer bottles and condom wrappers lying around, it was still a popular spot with the local teens.

They sat down on a log beside the fire pit. They didn't say much as they were busy taking in the scenery. Holden didn't want to talk; he could tell Paige was reminiscing internally. He was happy that she had shared her spot with him.

Finally she stood up. Without saying anything, she reached for his hand and they walked towards the car. He thought she had had enough and that they were going to head back to town. But as they got to the front of the car, Paige pulled his hand, spinning Holden around. She pushed him onto the hood. She grabbed at him, pulling his shirt up and running her hands over his hard stomach. The angle made his abs flex; she remarked how tight they felt and how great they felt. She pulled at his belt buckle, and after successfully unbuckling him, she didn't bother to unzip the fly. Aggressively, she yanked his pants over his hips. She giggled as his cock flapped around.

Holden thought it was never a compliment when a woman laughed at a man's junk. However, he didn't mind because after the giggling stopped, she took it in her mouth. He loved the view of the lake, the forest, the town far down below, and the hottest girl he had ever dated working over his knob.

Her hands caressed his stomach as her mouth moved around his shaft and head. She was sucking him as though she hadn't seen a penis in a year. He didn't know what had gotten into her. Maybe it was memories of an old boyfriend, or that being home made her feel like a high school girl again. Perhaps making out in that spot felt dangerous and forbidden, as if she were getting away with something. He didn't care why, he was just happy it was happening. It felt amazing.

He leaned back on the hood. The engine was still hot, but he ignored it as he soaked in the sun and the fantastic oral he was receiving.

Paige wasn't satisfied with having him in her mouth. She pushed him further back on the car. "Pull your pants the rest of the way down," she commanded. Holden obliged. She hoisted herself onto the car, took his member in her hand, and held it in place as she lowered herself onto it. She didn't kiss him, talk to him, or even look at him. Her hands pressed against his six-pack as he lay back, using his hands to support his head.

Paige ground her body onto his cock harder and faster than she ever had. Confident that no one was within earshot, she let out sounds like nothing he'd heard before. The trip home had apparently been good for her.

She bounced, using the flex of the thin metal of the hood as a springboard. She made her pussy contract tightly around his length as she moved her hips. She was all over the place, like a woman possessed. Holden knew he was nothing more than a tool, which he was very all right with. He did his best to help her, but she had him pinned down so hard that he could barely move.

He felt how wet she was. Her juices were dripping down his balls and onto the hood. He wanted to know what had got into her head and inspired the passion; he hoped to figure it out later.

Her cunt tightened. Her hips thrust forward as she slammed down hard on him, letting out one incredibly loud scream. Holden felt the fluids pouring out of her. "Come *now!*" she ordered. Holden was always one to follow commands, so he released his sperm deep inside her. She moaned as she felt the squirting pressure.

She leaned forward and kissed him passionately. The change in position released everything that was inside her in one sudden flow all over Holden's waist and car. "I love you."

"I love you too," Holden said.

"Come on. They'll be waiting for us, and we still have to hit the grocery store."

She did a ballerina dismount, clearing the fender of the car and landing on her feet. Just like that, the switch was off. Whatever had been possessing Paige seconds ago was gone. They got dressed and drove down the hill to complete their task and save supper.

As they walked into the house, the smell of turkey filled the air. Holden was impressed that Paige's mom had gone to so much trouble. Paige's sister was already home and her aunt and uncle were expected any minute.

Paige immediately disappeared into the bathroom, undoubtedly to tidy herself up a bit. Holden was left to introduce himself to her sister. She was as pretty as Paige, but she seemed a bit more timid and introverted. He could see the familiar mischievous sparkle in her eye, however. She and Holden clicked right away, though he did most of the talking because of her shyness. Her mom and dad teased her a bit, which made her want to talk even less. Holden thought it was cute.

In the middle of a sentence, he saw her eyes widen and a smile grow across her lips. "Paige!" she screamed. They ran to each other and hugged. Paige was obviously just as excited to see her baby sister as her sister was to see her. The three women chatted.

Paige's dad reappeared and, without speaking, handed Holden another beer. He shook his head in the direction of the women. When the powwow broke up, Paige motion to Holden, and they set the dining room table.

Paige began hinting that she had a surprise for Holden later on. He was curious, but he played it off at first. However, the more she hinted, the more he wanted to know. He asked her several times, but she didn't budge.

The doorbell rang, and Paige's aunt and uncle walked in. She ran over to see them, with Holden close behind. Introductions were made. Holden slipped away to finish setting the table as Paige's family reunited. Paige soon joined him and gave him a kiss on the cheek, saying it was sweet of him to help out.

Judging by the smell in the house, the turkey was about ready. The family made their way to the table. Paige's mom poured wine. Holden took a seat next to Paige. Her sister sat on the other side of Holden, her parents on each end, and her aunt and uncle across the table.

Holden didn't know what their family traditions were, so he waited to see if someone was going to say grace. He was relieved to see that they just dug in. Paige's mom told him not to be shy. She splattered mashed potatoes on his plate, giving the table a good laugh. Everyone took their portions and began eating and drinking.

With every sip of wine, the conversation loosened up, turning from superficial topics to ones more substantial. Paige's little sister kept staring at Holden. He thought the attention was cute. Involved in conversation with Paige's family, he didn't notice when Paige excused herself quietly from the table. He was surprised when she sneaked up behind him and put her arms around him. She said loudly, "Isn't he the best?"

He put his hands behind his back as she spoke. She put her hands in his. She discreetly placed something in his palm and whispered, "A little present for you."

Holden took the gift and tried to maintain the same discretion she had displayed. Although he was curious as to what he now held in his lap, he had to wait for the perfect time to peek.

The opportunity came more quickly than he had anticipated. Paige's aunt knocked over her wine glass. Everyone scurried to clean it up, so Holden took a peek at what was in his hand. It was a tiny silver object with two apparent settings: an on/off switch and a small slide labelled "min/max". A remote control?

Holden was curious. He hit the switch and was very surprised to see Paige's reaction. She was bent over the table, helping with the clean-up effort, and almost jumped through the roof as she let out a little screech. She turned to Holden and gave him a dirty look followed by a big smile. He sent back a quizzical glance. He still had no idea what he was holding, nor did he know what was up with Paige's unusual reaction. Her mom asked Paige if she was all right, and Paige brushed off the incident.

No one was paying Holden any attention. He played with the min/max setting, sliding it up to max. Paige fell into her seat. He watched her eyes roll back in her head. Her hands clamped firmly onto the table. Everyone stopped and watched her. Holden laughed as he hit the off button. His outburst drew attention away from Paige, and he had to excuse himself from the table.

Paige gave him another evil glance with her trademark mischievous smile. It took him a while, but he finally realized what it was she had given him. It was a remote control for some sort of sex toy Paige was wearing. He smiled, knowing the power he held. He slid it safely into his front pocket for later use.

They finished up dinner, and Paige's dad went into the kitchen to get dessert. Holden used the break to put his hand in his pocket. He slid the setting to low and flipped the device on. Paige jumped again. Her movements were better controlled this time, but her eyes still said it all. They flickered as she fidgeted in her seat. She was trying to be as discreet as possible, but after a couple of minutes her movements became more pronounced. It was obvious to Holden that the harder she tried to hold back her pleasure, the closer to orgasm she got.

When he thought she couldn't take any more, he hit the off button and she let out a sigh of relief. Just then, her dad brought out a chocolate cake, which drew comments from everyone at the table. As they were about to cut the first slice, Paige stood up. "Mom, Dad, everyone, I have something to tell you."

Her family all glared at Holden.

"No, I'm not pregnant!" she said with a laugh.

A collective sigh could be heard. Her stepdad, who was still holding a knife, said, "Oh, good. I guess I don't have to kill you." Everyone laughed. Holden wasn't as sure it was a joke as the others were.

Paige continued, "Holden got a job with a professional roller hockey team. It's a promotion from what he does now." The family congratulated him and started asking him questions. Paige interrupted them. "He will be director of operations, which means he'll be in charge of running the team administratively. He will be the youngest director in the league. The bad news is, the team is in Vancouver, BC."

The table fell silent. People cautiously exchanged glances.

Paige jumped again. Holden had decided to break the awkward silence by hitting the On button and quickly turning it off again. Paige shot him a look.

"So what does this mean, Paige?" her mom asked.

"Well, Holden asked me to move with him, and I said I would." She paused for the family's reaction.

"Where are you going to work? What are you going to do out there?" her stepdad asked.

"I'm going to go back to school. I applied to the university there, and Holden called his boss and asked him to make calls. They pulled some strings and got me in for the winter semester. They accepted all my other credits. I'll work in Holden's office part-time to help out with the bills."

"How are you going to afford school and rent if you're only working part-time?" her stepdad asked in a very sombre tone.

Paige began to answer, but Holden interrupted. "Sir, Paige has money saved up from dancing. The team is paying me very well, and she only has a year left to get her degree. I don't mind helping her out. Once she graduates, she can support me." This got a laugh from the family.

"Will you still dance?" her sister asked. Everyone, especially her stepdad, sat up to hear the answer.

"This is the part you're going to love, Dad. I'm going to start a new life out there, a new me. I have retired from dancing. I mean, it's still a possibility should we need extra cash—"

Holden cut her off again. "But it's a very last resort. We want her to concentrate on getting her degree."

"When do you leave?" Paige's mom asked.

"At the end of the season. We'll be driving out in October, after Thanksgiving. The team doesn't need him until after Christmas, but we're excited to get settled before school and work start."

The table fell silent. Paige and Holden glanced at each other as the news slowly sank in. Holden reached into his pocket, but Paige shot him the dirtiest look. He smiled as he brought his hands back up onto the table.

Paige's sister was the first to break the silence. "That's cool. Can I come visit?"

"Of course you can; you all can. The team arranged for us to get a two-bedroom condo with a view of the ocean," Paige said.

They talked among themselves, each person trying to see how everyone else felt before sharing his or her own feelings.

Paige's stepdad was the first to express his opinion. "You two haven't known each other that long, and it's a very big move. But it sounds like you've done your homework. Your mother and I are very proud that you're going back to school, Paige, and you know I've never liked you dancing. I guess all I can say is best of luck. If you need anything, you call us. Your room will always be yours. And you, young man, treat my little girl right. Vancouver is only a quick plane ride away."

The threat wasn't lost on Holden. He said, "Yes, sir, I will. And it isn't too far at all. I hope you come and visit often. Especially when I have to go away for work, I don't want her to be alone."

The rest of the family shared in their excitement. They drank more wine and ate dessert. As everyone calmed down, Holden reached into his pocket and hit the on button. He used his thumb to fluctuate the speed with the slide.

Paige quietly ate her cake as the vibrator strapped to her clit revved. She subtly moved her hips around again, trying not to get caught. Holden gave her three quick bursts on high speed. She put her head down and then very quickly pushed herself away from the table. "You guys go watch TV. Holden and I will clear the table."

"We can't ask you to do that. Holden's our guest," her mom objected.

"It's no problem, really," he said.

"I'll help," Paige's little sister volunteered.

"No!" Paige and Holden exclaimed at once.

"We'll be fine. Go watch TV with everyone else," Paige finished.

Holden grabbed a stack of plates and Paige picked up a handful of glasses. Holden left the remote setting on low as they tidied up. Paige awkwardly walked into the kitchen, Holden following her. The kitchen was completely closed off when the door was shut, except for a window to the dining room that appeared like it had never been opened before. Paige peeked through to see if the coast was clear. Holden assumed it was, because she turned around fast, grasped him by the shirt, and pulled him in close. "I love you," she said before she kissed him with all the intensity of the kiss they had shared up on the hill.

Holden slowly turned up the remote. Paige reacted positively, groping at his fly. "No, we can't, not with everyone in the next room," Holden objected.

"Fuck me *now*!" she demanded.

She turned to peek out the window again. He took her up on her offer. She didn't see him pull his cock out of his jeans, and he surprised her when he took her by the waist and pulled down her pants just far enough to give him the access he needed.

As Paige maintained watch, Holden slid his throbbing cock into her soaked pussy. He could feel the toy that was attached to her panties still vibrating away, and with every thrust it vibrated on his balls. The relief of telling her parents their plans, the fact they could be caught at any second, and the three-hour build-up over dinner combined into one passionate act.

Paige reached one hand between her legs and rubbed her clit as he pounded away behind her. She took a clean dish towel off the counter and stuffed it into her mouth to muffle her screams as she lost control. Holden was pretty close to coming hard inside her. He wanted to wait; he knew she was close because her movements became more jerky and her muscles spasmed as she masturbated. Holden heard her screams into the dish towel. He couldn't control himself. He shot a hot load deep into her, thrusting his shaft as far into her as he possibly could. He felt her pussy contract around him; it was so tight he couldn't pull out of her.

The vibrator kept humming along as Paige fought to remain standing. They stayed in that position for a minute or two. Paige finally spit the towel out, and Holden slid his flaccid cock out of her. She pulled up her pants and he put his man of steel away. Paige turned around and put her arms around him, and they kissed again.

"Oh gross!"

They spun around to see her sister standing in the doorway. "Um, how long have you been there?" Paige asked.

"Just got here. Why?"

"No reason," Holden said, laughing. They were relieved to know they weren't busted.

Paige and Holden left the kitchen to gather more dishes. After everything was either in the dishwasher or soaking in the sink, they joined her family to watch another movie.

The next day, they woke up early and packed the car. Her parents were obviously sad to see Paige go, and even though he had just met them, Holden felt a bit empty leaving their warm and inviting house. Her family wished Holden luck with his new career, he thanked them for their hospitality, and then they were off.

Paige and Holden shared their excitement and relief during the drive home. He was excited for the move and the prospect of a new life with Paige and the Vancouver Witch Doctors.

CHAPTER 6

After their dinner with Paige's family, the rest of the autumn passed in a rapid blur. The couple had their respective farewell parties, and then professional movers packed their lives into the back of a truck, ready to follow them on their trek to British Columbia.

Neither Paige nor Holden had ever driven across the country before. They were very excited for the opportunity to see new things and explore as much of the countryside as possible. The movers told them not to expect their furniture for at least two weeks. Since Holden had a very loose check-in time with his new employers, and the organization was going to pay for accommodations anyway, they decided to take their time.

The drive through northern Ontario seemed to go on forever. It was very beautiful, with lots of windy roads, hills, and of course Lake Superior shadowing them for most of the drive. Along the way, they were able to stop at a couple of tourist trading posts attached to gas stations. The stops broke up the long drive and gave them an excuse to stretch their legs. The first night they decided to stay in Thunder Bay. Despite Paige offering several times, Holden drove the nearly fourteen hours himself.

When they finally pulled in to the parking lot of what seemed like the only hotel with a vacancy sign, they gathered their bags and went into the lobby to secure lodgings. Their room was small, but more than adequate for its intended use. They threw their bags on one of the two double beds and quickly headed out for a bite to eat.

Bellies full and a long drive to Winnipeg on the horizon, they crawled into their warm bed, acknowledging the fact it was their first night living together. They cuddled up close, embraced each other tightly, and quickly fell asleep.

They woke to the ringing of their telephone, a scheduled wake-up call Holden had requested when they checked in. They showered together, got dressed, paid the bill, packed the car, and were off on the next stage of their journey.

The drive began in thick woods on a hilly road, with Lake Superior peeking through the trees at every opportunity. They passed several touristy stores, and Paige wanted to stop and browse through all of them. Although Holden wanted to get to the next destination, he was happy to take an occasional break to stretch his legs. Seeing how excited Paige was made him interested to see what each shop had to offer.

Eventually they grew weary of the drive and anxiously anticipated their stop in Winnipeg. The road levelled out and became straighter; they were clearing the Canadian Shield and heading into the prairies. They knew Winnipeg couldn't be much farther.

The sky opened up as the trees and rocks all ended in what seemed to be a distinct line marking the border between Ontario and Manitoba. The lights of Winnipeg were on the horizon, and the two let out sighs of relief. It was easy to find a room in Winnipeg. They elected to splurge for one with a Jacuzzi. Too tired to think about going out again, they ordered room service and a movie.

The room was grander than they expected. Paige wasted no time running water for the tub as Holden waited for room service. Just as Paige stepped out of her last stitch of clothing, there was a knock at the door, followed by a meek voice: "Room service."

Paige dived into the tub, sinking as low as possible. Holden looked back to see if she was ready for him to open the door. She gave him a quick nod. He let in the hotel worker, signed the bill, and locked up after. He brought Paige's meal over to her and poured each of them a glass of white wine before he slowly removed all his clothes. Paige, sipping her wine, made catcalls and playfully splashed water at him.

Holden jumped into the tub and let out a shriek as his naked body made contact with the unexpectedly hot water. "How can you stand that?"

"It's great once you're in, you big baby."

Holden slowly lowered his body into what he called "the Syn soup", and Paige couldn't help but laugh. Finally in the boiling broth, he reached for his glass of wine and his meal. Paige had already begun to eat hers. Holden held up his wine glass. "To us and our second night." Paige smiled widely as she raised her glass.

Holden hit Play on the remote, and the movie began. After they were done eating, Paige moved around so she was sitting between Holden's legs. He put his strong arms around her and held her tightly as they soaked.

Halfway through the movie, the water had cooled and their fingers were shrivelling, so they elected to move to the bed. Holden jumped out of the tub and grabbed two towels, one for him and the other for Paige. He wrapped the oversized towel around her as she stepped out of the tub. Shivering, she was happy to have the warmth. After drying themselves off, they decided not to put on any clothes. They found heat and comfort under the blankets, taking every opportunity to sneak a touch of each other's body.

They both fell asleep to the movie, letting it play over and over again as they slept. Once again, the phone rang to wake them up, and they quickly gathered their things and hit the road. Their plan was to push on to Banff, where they had reservations.

The dew was still on the car as they started that day's journey. They soon realized where the prairies' reputation came from. The horizon stretched on forever. Golden wheat danced in the wind, and the blue sky was tarnished only by a sporadic whisper of cloud. Paige and Holden were amazed at how flat the landscape was. The lack of towns and highway stands made the trip go by faster than on previous days.

When they hit the rare cities, they took the opportunity to tour around and see what each province had to offer. Manitoba was soon in their rear-view mirror, and the Land of Living Skies filled their windshield. After touring Regina for an hour, they elected to move on so they could honour their reservations in Banff.

Before long, the foothills of the Rockies made an appearance on the horizon. The Calgary skyline was impressive, especially after the endless hours of nothingness they had endured. Paige asked if they could stop in Calgary for supper. Holden was only too happy to oblige – he too was looking forward to seeing the city.

At the city limits, they searched for signs to indicate the downtown core. They followed the bulk of the traffic towards a tower that resembled the CN Tower in Toronto. As Holden negotiated traffic, Paige kept a keen eye out for a restaurant they might be interested in. She finally spotted one, and Holden steered the car into a spot fairly close to the entrance. Both of them were famished from their long drive.

The hostess seated them in what she described as the best seat in the house. It was a booth next to a picture window that had a view of the mountains, including a ski jump from the 1988 Olympics. The waitress was friendly and talked with the young couple. Learning they were en route to Banff for the night, she warned them that driving through the Rockies the first time could be intimidating, especially after dark.

The pair enjoyed their dinner as a fire crackled in the background. The view as the sun set over the mountains made the scene even more impressive. The peaks cast shadows over the city as the sun disappeared. The lights of the ski hill illuminated the side of the mountain. The bill came, and Holden threw down his credit card. He was cringing at the thought of crawling back into the car. It had already had been a very long trip. Fortunately, it was their last night of travel. However, he knew that because their condo would not be ready for several more days, Banff wasn't going to be the last hotel they slept in before they were in their new home.

The drive from Calgary to Banff was short, and at night seemed pretty unadventurous. The hotel they had reserved was very nice but not nearly as grand as the one they had stayed in the night before. Their room was on the second floor, and the entrance was on the outside of the building. They immediately fell into bed.

Neither had a good sleep. They were as excited as kids the night before Christmas because they knew that tomorrow, they would be home. As on every morning of the trip, the phone rang to wake them up.

And as on every morning of the trip, they woke up, showered, packed, and left the room.

Unlike other mornings, they were awestruck when they opened the door. The view they had missed the night before was incredible. It overlooked the heart of the Rockies. Snow-covered mountains engulfed the tiny hotel hidden away among the majestic mountains. The vision was unreal; pictures and descriptions could not do it justice.

Holden and Paige felt small and lost. All around them were the tallest trees and mountains the pair had ever seen. They stopped on the walkway and took in the view for as long as possible. They didn't realize they had climbed as high in altitude as they had.

With altitude came dropping temperatures. Before long, Paige was feeling the effect of the cold and urged Holden to keep moving. Taking one last look around, Holden picked up the bags and they walked to their car.

They had barely turned out of the parking lot when they stopped at the first of many spectacular sights. There was a very large elk eating out of a flowerpot on the sidewalk. Paige struggled to take photos as Holden manoeuvred the car as close as he dared. Satisfied, Paige cued Holden to drive on. They hunted for signs to point them west, and before long, they were off for the last leg of their journey.

Around every corner and over every hill was a new, more spectacular view. Holden found it difficult to concentrate. He wanted to stop every kilometre to take in the sights, but they knew that wasn't possible. The traffic on the narrow highway was heavy, and the RVs and transport trucks sharing the road made some of the passages treacherous. Paige would get really excited and yell for Holden to stop, but the roadway wouldn't permit it.

On one occasion, Paige told Holden that there was a grizzly bear walking alongside the road. He knew something had to be going on, as all the cars were bottlenecking. Paige strained to get a shot but managed only a blur that resembled a bear; regardless, she was proud of it. She kept trying to show Holden her prize photo, but he could only laugh at her attempts to distract him. She leaned over and gave him a kiss on the cheek.

She got more excited as they went deeper into the mountains. Every few kilometres there was a new animal on the road: mountain goats, elk, moose, and bears. Neither had ever seen so much wildlife in their lives. Holden thought back to the warning the waitress had given them. He was very thankful they hadn't ventured any farther into the Rockies at night than they did.

Road signs counted down the distance to Vancouver. The sky opened again as the towering mountain range appeared to shrink into the ocean. The houses and buildings became more frequent, and the road improved greatly. They knew they had hit the outskirts of a city. The next sign read *Vancouver 10 km*. They felt their anticipation grow. Although the beautiful natural sights had been replaced by city structures, they were just as excited by these. Paige pointed out unique buildings and stores she'd like to shop in. As traffic congested, Holden had to concentrate more on the road ahead and missed many of the areas that interested Paige.

Their furniture wouldn't arrive for a few more days, but they still wanted to see their new home. From the pictures they'd been sent, it was a beautiful condo with a view of the mountains and the ocean, on the tenth floor of a twelve-storey building. They both loved city life and looked forward to having a place with a view of so much of their new city.

Paige connected the GPS Holden had bought for the trip. To this point, the navigation had been easy: point the car west. Finding their place was going to prove much harder. Holden thought the electronic help was needed.

Paige typed in their new address. The GPS acquired the satellites and announced the appropriate turns to take. The default voice was female and English, with an ever-so-slight accent. Paige had never used a GPS before, so she played with the settings. The one that caught her interest the most was the voice setting. She cycled through the choices; they laughed at the more bizarre options. The funniest was the Yoda setting. "Turn right ahead you must not," was one of the directions Yoda issued. This confused Holden, who scrambled to read signs. He eventually elected to go straight, mostly because he had passed the road and it was too late to turn.

Their apartment wasn't that hard to find, especially with the aid of a GPS. They parked the car and explored the outside of the building. It was very nice and in what seemed to be a good neighbourhood. The mountains appeared to be right in their backyard. They couldn't wait to see inside but knew they had to — Holden hadn't yet picked up the keys.

They typed *hotels* into the GPS, and one showed up a few blocks away. They decided that would be the best choice, since they could tour the neighbourhood from there and see what it was like at night.

After they got settled in their temporary home, Holden made some phone calls to let his bosses know he was in town and make dinner plans with them. They were happy to hear from him. One of the guys he would be working with had been on Holden's course at university, and was the main reason Holden had landed such a key position. Although they'd stayed in close touch after school, they hadn't seen each other since graduation. Holden was excited to be reuniting with his friend.

Paige was nervous about meeting all the new people and wanted to make a good impression for Holden. He reassured her that his friend was laid-back, maybe even more so than his friends in Toronto. The man would love her no matter what.

As for the other two guys accompanying them, Holden wasn't sure what to expect. His friend, Mike, said they would meet Paige and Holden at a restaurant up the block from the hotel at six. Because the drive from Banff to Vancouver had taken less than nine hours, Holden and Paige had made it into town in the late-afternoon, which gave them an hour, maybe two to sleep and shower before their rendezvous.

Watching Paige undress down to her boy-cut panties and sports bra made Holden wish that they hadn't vowed not to have sex again until they moved in to their new place. The vow had been hard enough to keep on the trip. The missed opportunities to fuck in new places had been fine with him because they were both so tired from the drive. Now that they were in Vancouver, though, Holden was feeling particularly horny.

Paige glanced over at Holden as he stripped to his boxers. She could see the outline of his cock beneath the thin cotton. She badly wanted to crawl to him and plead for him to use it on her. She wanted to reach into the elastic waistband and pull out his thick member, feel it in her fingers as she jerked it off inches from her face. She wanted to make him nice and hard, then lean back on the bed to allow him to feed his man of steel into her willing pussy. She yearned for the piercings to hit her just right, as they often had before. But she resisted. *Damn vow.*

Yet it had been her idea. She wanted their first night as a real couple to be something special.

She lay in bed and gently caressed her panties. Hitting her clit, she touched harder and a little more carelessly. Then, scared she would set Holden off, she sprang out of bed. "I need a shower. I feel gross."

"OK, honey," Holden said. He watched her pull her sports bra over her head, tossing it on the floor near their suitcase. Her thumbs hooked into her panties and pulled down. She used her foot to close the bathroom door.

Holden couldn't hold back. Once he heard the water running, he reached into his boxers and grabbed his thick cock. His fingers firmly gripped the shaft, and he pulled on himself. He was more aggressive than normal; the trip had him very worked up. He couldn't fuck his beautiful girlfriend, and he didn't have any privacy to take care of himself. He knew his time was limited, and he was going to take full advantage of it.

He pictured Paige as she had been moments before she went to the shower. He closed his eyes and imagined her hand gripping him. Her scent was still alive in the room, making a visual that much easier. She knelt beside him. His arms were behind his head. She told him to relax and let her take care of it. Her fingers caressed him just as he liked. She wasn't trying to take it slow – she had one thing on her mind, and that was to get him off. She jerked him faster and faster, and before he knew it, he was coming with so much force that he felt come splash up on his own chin.

When he opened his eyes, there was no Paige. The shower was still running. A huge puddle of come oozed on his hand and stomach, with the odd drop across his chest.

As happy as he was to have relieved himself, he now had the tedious task of cleaning up. He stood, trying not to drip anywhere. He made it to the sink outside the bathroom door and used a wet facecloth to clean himself. Satisfied there was no evidence remaining, he put his boxers back on and crawled into bed.

Paige closed the door behind her. Her panties found their way into a corner. She turned on the water and was almost giddy to see the showerhead was the massage-wand style. She turned up the hot water and stepped in. She rinsed herself off for a minute or two, then couldn't wait any longer. Her pussy ached for attention. She too was feeling the effects of the vow and the lack of privacy.

She let the water cascade off her shoulders, splashing onto her very sensitive breasts. She leaned her shoulder into the shower wall to stabilize herself. Her hand moved to her crotch. She ran her fingers over her pubic area and took note it was time for another waxing. She quickly put that thought out of her mind. Her fingers continued to graze her mound, teasing her. Almost at the point of losing control, she rubbed her clit, her forefinger pressed up hard against the magic button. It built the urge for an orgasm, but wasn't enough to finish the job.

She knew what would. She reached up to the showerhead and adjusted the flow to high-pressure pulsations. She spread her legs as wide as she possibly could without slipping, then positioned the water to hit her clitoris just right.

Her free hand groped at her breasts. She elected to skip the flicking of her nipples that she liked so much and went right to sinking her fingers into the tender flesh. The hot, pulsating water was too much for her in that position. She had to lie down.

She put one leg on the edge of the tub and the heel of her other foot on the opposite corner. She pushed the nozzle hard against herself. The water hurt at first, but the sensation it gave her made the temporary pain worth it. The showerhead was big enough that water was forced inside her. The weird sensation of hot water penetrating her, combined with the amount of unpredictable force riddling her pussy, brought her to the brink of orgasm.

To fully finish herself off, she needed more penetration. She adjusted the water to the maximum focused stream and positioned the wand so that all the hot water filled her pussy. Having water touch every part of her vagina and then flow out of her was foreign to her. She reminded herself to buy the same style showerhead for their new home.

She felt herself up as the water worked its magic. Within minutes she was erupting in a full-body orgasm. It was difficult to hold the showerhead, and even more difficult not to let out an earth-shattering scream. She finally lost control of her body and lay convulsing in the tub, water spraying everywhere.

After the convulsions stopped, she was freezing. She stood up, lathered herself quickly, adjusted the water flow to something gentler, and rinsed herself off. She exited the bathroom wrapped in a towel and decided to sleep naked, worried that even a little cotton between her legs would set her off again. She crawled into bed and snuggled up to an already-sleeping Holden.

Just as Paige closed her eyes, Holden's cell phone rang. It was an alarm he had set before their nap. She saw the time and couldn't believe she had actually been asleep for three hours.

Holden said he was going to have a shower and rolled out of bed. She stayed put and watched him walk by. She particularly watched his muscular calves flex as he walked. She caught a glimpse of his ass too before he disappeared into the bathroom. She loved how the boxer briefs cupped his firm ass cheeks. She also loved that the cotton was starting to separate from the elastic waistband. She was going to have to buy him new underwear and take care of him. It made the seemingly independent and strong Holden appear a little vulnerable, and that made her feel needed.

When Holden got out of the shower, he was amazed at the speed with which Paige had gotten ready. She wore pigtails that made her curly hair seem very thick. She had applied a thin trace of black eyeliner and brushed on several colours of eye shadow. It came to a point in the corners of her eyes like cat's eyes. It was very discreetly applied, so it didn't jump right out.

She wore a black blouse, buttoned up so as not to show much cleavage but to accentuate her breasts. Below was a red plaid skirt that was cut just above her knees, and a thick black belt with big silver buckles on the front. On her feet she wore white knee-high socks and black boots that came up mid-calf. They had the same buckles as her belt.

"No fair," Holden said, referencing their vow of celibacy.

She glanced down at him and nodded at his growing penis. "Same to you."

He hadn't noticed his towel had slipped off. He looked down, laughed, and got dressed.

She told him she had intended to wear her fishnet nylons and fishnet gloves, but figured that would be too much. Holden told her she should have gone for it, and to keep it in mind for next time.

Holden put on a clean, newer pair of boxer briefs, slid into designer jeans, added a T-shirt from a retro rock band, and threw a dress shirt over top, which he left open and untucked. Paige watched him intently as he dressed, wishing she could unwrap his pretty package. Holden knew she was watching, so he made his moves more deliberate, flexing whenever possible without being too obvious.

He pulled out a pair of black Tommy socks and pulled them over his feet. He looked up at her, and she giggled and applauded him. He was a bit embarrassed but flattered he could hold her attention. A warm wave hit him as he realized he was falling that much more in love with her. The uncertainty of their relationship was slowly being replaced with confidence that they were doing the right thing. At that moment, all doubt vanished. He knew he couldn't have done the move without her. He wanted to tell her how much he loved her. He wanted to kiss her.

Instead he got control of his runaway emotions and went to put on cologne.

The phone rang. His buddy Mike was on the other end. "Hey, you guys ready?"

"Yeah. What time you getting here?"

"I'm down in the lobby. I'm on my way up. I thought I'd give you a chance to, um, clean up. We'll have a beer and head out to the restaurant."

Holden said that he didn't have any beer in the room. "No worries" was the reply, followed by the click of the line going dead. Holden barely had time to realize he had been hung up on before there came a knock at the door. He rushed to answer it, excited to see his friend.

Paige was nervous. She doubted her clothing choice and wondered if she would fit in with his friends.

Holden swung open the door and had to dodge a flying beer cap. He looked behind him to see where it landed, then up at his buddy. Mike was holding most of a twelve-pack in one hand and an opened bottle in the other. "For you, my friend," he said.

Holden politely took the bottle and took a long drink. He invited Mike in and made introductions.

Mike froze when his eyes met Paige's. He pushed the rest of the beer at Holden, who dug into the box and pulled out two more bottles. Mike extended his hand to Paige. She was beginning to feel more comfortable after watching his comical entrance. She took Mike's hand, and they shook. Still staring at her, he said, "Oh my God, you are beautiful. Good job, Holden. Seriously, Paige, how'd you end up with a bum like this?"

"Oh, you know, he got me drunk and knocked up. Now I'm stuck with him."

The expression on Mike's face changed to panic. "You're *pregnant*? Holden, what did you do?"

Paige and Holden almost collapsed with laughter. "No, you dopey bastard, she was kidding," Holden mocked. "Have a beer."

"Oh, I get it," Mike said, laughing nervously. "Paige, you remind me a lot of my girlfriend. She is a hopeful on SuicideGirls. As a matter of fact a few hopefuls, models, and members are having a gathering tonight. We'll have to join up with them later."

"I would love to," Paige answered.

Holden handed Mike and Paige their beers, and they sat and talked. Holden told Mike about the drive, Mike told Holden the ins and outs of the office, who to watch out for, and who was a good person.

Mike eventually checked at his watch and said they should go. They decided to walk so that no one had to worry about drinking and driving. The restaurant wasn't far away, but Paige and Holden stopped to look at everything. Mike could only laugh at "the tourists".

The restaurant was nearly full, but they had a reservation and the other two members of the party were already seated. Judging by the empty beer bottles around them, they had been there for a while. The two men hooted and hollered when they saw Mike. They stood up and said, "This must be the young man we hired sight unseen. Mike told us what a great guy you are."

"Hello, sir. I'm Holden, and this is my girlfriend, Paige."

"Enough with the 'sir' shit. I'm Charlie and this is Steve."

They exchanged pleasantries and took their seats. The waitress appeared as if on cue. She took their orders, and the night blossomed from their first toast.

Halfway through the evening, Charlie told Holden and Paige that the moving company had called the office that day. Because of a big job in Vancouver, they needed the moving truck and wondered if they could drop off the furniture sooner than they had quoted – in two days, not a week.

Paige and Holden were ecstatic at the news. Charlie handed them the keys to their new place. They hugged each other in excitement at the chance to see their home early. Holden ordered another round.

Several hours passed. They ate until they were stuffed and drank until they could barely walk.

Mike jumped up, getting the attention of everyone at the table. He fumbled in his pocket, pulled out his cell phone, and shouted "Hello? Hello?" into the phone.

Holden took his cell from him and pushed the green button. "Hello, you have reached Mike's phone. I'm sorry he is too stupid to answer his own cell phone. This is Holden. How may I help you?"

The voice on the other end shouted back. She sounded like she was as drunk as Mike and Holden. "Holden? This Tamara, Mike's girlfriend. Welcome to BC! I can't wait to meet you. Is Mike around?"

"Yeah, he's right here. Hold on. Dingus, it's for you. It's Tamara."

"No shit it's for me; it's my phone," Mike said and took it from Holden.

The group went on with their own conversation, ignoring Mike. Occasionally Steve or Charlie would throw a leftover fry at him. Not being one to waste food, Mike snatched up the ones he could and ate them. They all had a laugh at drunk Mike.

Finally Mike pushed the button to disconnect. He turned to Holden and Paige and said the SuicideGirls group was at a dance club called

Heaven. It was across town, and the line was likely to be long, but if they told the bouncers they were with the group, they could cut the line.

The three looked at Steve and Charlie as if to invite them along. The two older men said they would pass; they were calling it a night because their wives would be wondering where they were. They sat for another half hour, finishing their drinks and waiting for the checks. When the waitress brought the tabs, Charlie, the senior executive at the table, reached for them all. Holden tried to object, but Charlie said it was a business dinner. He couldn't in good conscience let his newest employee pay for his first dinner in town. Everyone graciously accepted his offer, and they all chipped in for the tip.

Charlie and Steve headed out in the first available cab. The remaining three waited for only a couple of minutes before getting a taxi of their own. Mike sat in the front, letting Paige and Holden cuddle in the backseat. He engaged the cab driver in conversation, asking him about the wildest thing he had ever seen and other questions about being a cabbie. The driver was only too happy to tell tales of the road.

The long drive passed quickly, and soon they were at the front door of Heaven. There was indeed a huge line, and the threesome hoped that Tamara was right.

Mike strutted up to the bouncer and said he was there with the SuicideGirls group. The bouncer eyed Paige and nodded to let them in. They made their way through the packed bar. Mike knew the general area where Tamara was sitting. They headed in that direction. Finally, through the crowd, Mike noticed pink hair bopping up and down. He recognized it as the wig Tamara had been wearing earlier.

Mike grabbed Paige's hand. She in turn took Holden's. Like a linebacker, Mike pushed his way through the crowd until he got right up behind Tamara. She didn't know it was him as he put his arms around her. He put one palm slightly under her short-cut shirt, the other well below the belt on her skirt. He pushed up as close to her as possible and ground into her.

Tamara rested her head on his shoulder, closed her eyes, and whispered, "Let's go, sailor, but make it fast. My boyfriend will be here any minute." She then spun around and hugged him and smothered him with kisses. "It's about time you got here," she said to the three newcomers. She led them over to the group and introduced them.

Paige and Tamara started talking. They complimented one another on their clothes. As Mike and Holden watched, they realized that Tamara was pretty much a blonde version of Paige. The two girls clicked right away. Paige, albeit drunk, was happy to make a friend on her first night in town.

When the waitress came over, they placed their drink order. The song changed to something the girls apparently liked. They let out shrieks. Tamara clutched Paige's hand and they both ran off to the dance floor. They stayed within eyesight of the men as they strutted their stuff, moving erotically to the music.

The drinks came, and Holden bought the first round. The guys clinked glasses as they watched their girls on the floor. Paige wrapped her arms around Tamara and danced close to her, Tamara reciprocated, and they ground into each other.

Others besides Holden and Mike noticed the display. Eventually every guy in the bar – and most of the girls – were watching. Holden was used to having his girl be the centre of attention, but despite Tamara's incredibly good looks, Mike wasn't as comfortable with it. He began getting upset.

Holden asked him if he trusted Tamara. He said, "Of course." Holden told him to sit back and enjoy the show, and reap the benefits of it later.

As the next song came on, the girls tamed their moves. The guys took seats with the SG group. When the third song started, the house lights also brightened. Holden checked the time: three o'clock. "Fuck, it's late," he said to no one in particular. Mike nodded in agreement.

Most of the bar's patrons were heading for the door. The girls staggered toward the guys. The guys overheard Tamara say that she would love to help them move in. She slapped the back of her hand against a half-asleep Mike. "Right, Mike?"

"Huh? Yeah, whatever, honey," he replied.

Tamara dug through her purse and pulled out her cell phone. She fumbled with it for a minute before dropping it on the floor. She giggled and picked it up. "OK, what's your number?"

Paige gave it to her, but told her it would be changing soon. Paige got Tamara's number as well. They hugged and kissed each other on the cheek. That got Mike's attention. He jumped up and hugged Holden and pretended to kiss him on the cheek before Holden pushed him away. "Get away from me!" Holden said, laughing.

"Peace out, brother," Mike slurred. He took Tamara by the hand and she pranced behind him, showing way too much energy for a girl as drunk as she was.

Holden and Paige walked out of the bar, Paige clinging to Holden's arm. He was happy to have everyone see him with her, because he was very proud of Paige.

The doormen nodded at Holden. It was clear they had seen Paige dancing earlier and were giving an "atta boy" nod.

Holden got Paige into a cab. He searched through his pockets until he found the business card of their hotel. He told the cabbie the name, and then they were on their way back.

They both reflected on their night and were relieved it had been a success. Paige was happy she'd met a friend, and Holden felt more at ease at the prospect of showing up at work. Charlie and Steve had invited them for a tour after their furniture and effects arrived. The happy couple poured themselves into their hotel room and undressed as much as they could before they passed out.

—m—

The next day, Holden was the first to move. He opened his eyelids and felt a sharp pain in his temples. He lay still, staring at the ceiling, then mumbled to himself that he needed water.

Paige, barely moving herself, said, "Not so loud. Some of us are hung-over."

Holden tried to laugh, but the mere thought caused too much pain.

They stayed perfectly still for another hour or so before Paige gathered the courage to get out of bed. She slowly moved to the sink, poured herself a glass of water, drank it, took a couple of aspirin, and then drank another glass. She brought Holden a glass of water and a couple of aspirin too. They tried to talk while they waited for the pain to subside, but neither was very successful.

The aspirin didn't take long to kick in. Soon they felt well enough to go out of the hotel. They decided the first thing they had to do was get fast food. Nothing cured a hangover like greasy burgers.

After that they did a walking tour of Vancouver, spending the bulk of their time by the waterfront. Paige went into shop after shop. Holden, although pretending to be put out, secretly enjoyed shopping with Paige. He intentionally picked out clothes that were a size too small when she was in the changing room, so he could see how great she looked in the extra-tight clothing.

After they had shopped and walked for hours, they decided to go for dinner, then head over to their condo to see what needed to be done before the movers arrived.

They found an oceanside restaurant that had a very comfortable feel to it. They made a note of the name and decided to go back frequently. They walked to their condo, saying hi to everyone they passed. At the lobby door, Holden dug in his pockets to find the keys he'd got the night before. Sliding it in and giving it a turn, they were in.

Paige reached for Holden's hand and squeezed. She was very excited, as was Holden, but he was doing his best to contain it. They jumped in the elevator. Paige pushed the 10 button. The elevator gave them a smooth, quick ride to their floor. The bell dinged, the doors opened, and Paige burst through. Holden laughed and moved much slower. Impatiently, she playfully pulled him. "Come on!"

They finally got to their condo. Holden fiddled with his key chain again, trying to find the door key. Paige kept urging Holden to hurry; Holden told her he was going as fast as he could. At last he found the right key and opened the door.

Paige was about to race through, but Holden grabbed her by the back of her pants. "What are you *doing*?" she asked.

He picked her up in his strong arms and carried her over the threshold. She threw her arms around him and gave him a kiss on the lips before he had a chance to put her down. He held her tighter. Her small frame was nothing in his muscular arms; he could have held her like that all night.

They explored the condo hand in hand. They opened every door. They planned how they were going to arrange furniture, who was going to get which closet, and what art they needed to bring the walls alive. The place had been cleaned by professionals after the previous tenants moved, so that was one less thing they had to worry about.

They were so excited about arranging the condo that they didn't really notice the view. Then, as Holden was planning what he would put on the mantle, something shiny caught his eye. He looked over and had his first glimpse of the breathtaking view. He called Paige over and she stopped in her tracks.

The shiny object that had originally caught Holden's eye was a floatplane taking off. The view showed them a small bay, and on the other side of the bay were the Rocky Mountains. The locals were used to the mountains, but to Holden and Paige, they were very impressive. A bald eagle soared past their window and floated majestically floated in an air current, seeking prey. They watched it for several minutes. Then Holden scanned the bay, hoping to see the famous black fin of an orca, but they weren't that lucky.

―ᴍ―

The next morning came early. The moving company had told them they would be there around eight, so Paige and Holden got there just after six to make sure things were ready. Mike and Tamara, in keeping with Tamara's drunken promise, called and said they would be there by ten.

The movers arrived, and Holden went downstairs to meet them, rig the door to stay open, and escort them to the right condo. He got excited when they opened the truck doors and he saw his furniture. As the movers carried up the couple's things, he didn't remember owning so much.

The living room filled up with boxes. Paige directed the movers to the appropriate location for each box, making sure as many were put in the right rooms as possible.

Mike and Tamara appeared out of nowhere. Mike sneaked up behind Holden, gave him a small shove, and yelled, "Boo!" Holden jumped a foot, much to the amusement of Tamara and Mike. "Hey, man, sorry we didn't knock, but the doors were open and we thought you'd be busy."

"No worries. Thanks for coming," Holden said.

"Here, we brought you something," Tamara added. She showed Holden four Tim Horton's coffee cups. Holden yelled for Paige to come out from the bathroom, where she was emptying boxes. She gave Tamara a hug and said hello to Mike. Holden passed her a coffee. "Oh, thank you! You're a life saver," Paige said.

As the bigger furniture was brought up, the four tried to help the movers. They shifted boxes out of the way, and Holden and Mike helped position the furniture. Once the sofa and coffee table were set up, Holden and Mike stacked boxes on both to make more room.

Next to come up was Holden's queen-sized bed. Holden and Mike put the bed frame together as Paige and Tamara went into the bathroom to finish what Paige had started. When the bed was together and all the big furniture was in its place, there were only boxes left to unpack.

Holden and Mike worked on hooking up the home theatre. Mike was impressed by Holden's fifty-inch HDTV with surround sound. He couldn't wait to see its capabilities. Tamara said that they would have to get a TV as big or bigger. Paige said that if they did get a bigger TV, Holden would have to get an even bigger one. They shared a laugh at the guys' expense and continued working.

The movers came up with only two boxes on a cart. "This is the last of them," the lead mover said. "Do you want the packers to come in tomorrow to unpack?"

The four friends did a quick inspection of what was important to Holden and Paige. Satisfied nothing had been damaged, Holden signed the declaration saying everything was accounted for and refused the packers' assistance.

Holden looked at the clock to make sure the time written on the forms was right. It was only three in the afternoon; he'd thought the movers would take much longer. There was still lots to do in terms of unpacking boxes, but for now, everyone was hungry. They put the work on hold and walked down to the nearest fast food joint.

After lunch, the girls said they had an errand to run and would meet the guys back at the condo. Holden and Mike went back to continue working. Holden went to offer Mike a beer and realized he hadn't planned ahead and stocked the fridge. He apologized, then had the bright idea of calling Paige to see if she could pick up some beer while they were out.

Holden picked up his cell phone. Just as he hit call, he heard the muffled sound of "Punk Rock Girl" playing. The guys searched for the source. Holden found it on the kitchen countertop under a pile of clothes: Paige's cell phone. Holden hung up his phone. "Damn."

Mike said that Tamara didn't have her cell phone. They were shit out of luck. They decided they would wait to let the girls in, then go on a beer run.

In the meantime, Mike played with the entertainment system. He programmed in local radio stations and tested the PS4 to see if it worked right. He found the box that held the CD collection and put in the first Billy Talent album. The subwoofer had the condo shaking, Mike was very impressed. Holden turned down the amplifier, saying he didn't want a noise complaint on his first day.

The PS4 games were in the same box with the CDs. Mike thumbed through them, saying that they would have to plan a gaming night. Holden agreed and said they could send the girls out clubbing or something. Mike said Tamara liked playing video games too, so she would be happy to stay if they got "girlie" games to play. Holden thought a double-date gaming night would be fun and promised to ask Paige.

Mike flipped through the TV channels and settled on a sports highlight program before the two of them went back to unpacking. The buzzer from the front door went off; it was the two girls. Holden buzzed them in. "Surprise!" they announced as they held up a two-four of Bud and two big bottles of wine.

Holden searched through the boxes in the kitchen to find the wine glasses, and Paige searched through another box trying to find a corkscrew. Paige was successful, Holden not so much. He found a novelty glass shaped like the CN Tower and another odd glass. Paige and Tamara said they weren't too proud to drink wine from non-wine glasses.

Holden opened the wine as Paige gave Holden a beer and tossed another to Mike. Mike was sitting on the floor, leaning against the wall. Holden told him to take the couch, but Mike said he was fine. Once Tamara had her glass of wine, she settled beside him, laying her head in his lap as he ran his fingers through her hair. Paige and Holden sat on the couch.

Mike proposed a toast: "To Paige and Holden, to your new condo and your new lives." They all raised their glasses. When the first drops of alcohol touched their tongues, they knew their work was done for the day. Paige and Holden planned to tinker around later in the evening, but the important things had been set up.

Holden proposed a toast of his own: "To Mike and Tamara, our only friends in BC. Thanks for all your help in getting us here and moved." Again they raised their glasses and took a drink.

The next few hours passed in conversation, watching TV, and, of course, more drinks. Mike finally said, "Well, I think we should be going." It was eight o'clock, and the four were drunk and tired.

Holden and Paige thanked Mike and Tamara again and escorted them to the door. They made plans to hang out on the weekend.

After they left, Holden closed the door behind them and turned to Paige. "Welcome home," he said. They hugged and kissed.

Paige broke the embrace and went into the kitchen to get more unpacking done. Holden watched her for a minute and finally couldn't take any more. Using his arm, he cleared off the remaining boxes on the counter. One landed with a breaking sound. "Oops, I think I found those wine glasses."

"What are you doing?" Paige asked.

Without speaking, he picked her up and put her on the counter he had cleared off. Her breasts were at eye level, and he couldn't wait to touch them. "We're living in our new home. Vow over." He pulled at her shirt, and she helped him get it off. He reached under her sports bra and guided it over her head. He took her right breast in his mouth.

Paige leaned her head back. She was amazed how great his warm breath and mouth felt on her body after going so long without it. His tongue danced all around her erect nipple. One hand supported him on the countertop; the other was firmly on her back, so she could relax and he could easily reach her perfect tits.

He loved the feel of her breasts in his mouth. They were so firm. He knew she was self-conscious about the size of them, so he tried to reassure her every chance he got. He legitimately loved the size of them. He loved how they looked. He loved how they felt. He particularly loved the reaction he got when he touched them. She was the only girl he was able to give an orgasm to by simply caressing her breasts the right way.

Giving her that kind of orgasm crossed his mind, but after spending the last couple of weeks without being inside of her, that idea was too much for him to resist. He moved the hand off her back, forcing her to lean on her own hands. The other hand gently ran over a perky breast. The whisper of his touch was a huge tease. She wanted him to squeeze her breast, twist it, do something substantial. He could feel her wanting more. He refused to give it to her.

As he teased one tit, his teeth found the other nipple, and he bit. The unexpected pain kept Paige guessing. It was that randomness she loved. It kept her mind in suspense, never knowing what was going to happen next.

He moved the hand running over her tit to the middle of her chest. He gently pushed her back until she took the hint and lay down. Holden kept his mouth on her chest, sliding his tongue down her ribs and over her hard stomach until it reached the elastic band of her grey track pants. Not missing a beat, he grabbed her waistband and pulled. She helped him by putting her weight on her shoulder blades and lifting her bum off the counter. She was already very wet with anticipation.

Holden quickly got her pants off and was happy to see plain white cotton panties underneath. He loved unusual lingerie, but he also loved more traditional things. He left her quarter-cut socks on. He kissed her ankle, then slid his tongue up her calf. He kissed her knee and kept kissing up her thigh while his hands were firmly on her waist. He pulled her closer to him and she slid easily on the counter.

Finally his mouth was less than an inch from her wet pussy. The only thing standing in his way was a thin layer of cotton. His fingers danced around her stomach and the waistband of her panties. She reached down to take them off, but his hands stopped her. She took the hint and moved her hands behind her head for support against the hard counter.

Holden, satisfied she was going to behave, took off his T-shirt. Both of them were sweaty from a hard day's work, but neither seemed to care.

He moved her legs so that they were resting on his broad shoulders. He brought his mouth against her panties, feeling how moist she was through the cotton. He let out a warm breath. The extra heat on her hungry pussy made her fidget with anticipation. She was yearning to be filled.

His hands ran across her stomach and ribcage. She used her legs to pull Holden closer and deeper. He used his tongue to move her panties out of the way. They only moved so far, allowing him to barely get a lick of her clit and to penetrate her by a millimetre. That wasn't nearly deep enough for either of them. From the first taste, Holden couldn't play the teasing game anymore. He wanted to taste every last drop out of her. He loved her pussy and could lick her for hours, given the chance.

He groped at her waistband, and she moved her legs off his shoulders. In a fluid movement, he pulled her panties off and threw them to the ground. He stared at her for a second before going in for another taste. She had a little stubble growing from not having shaved while they travelled, but it was still very soft and smooth looking. Her legs were spread which pulled her lips apart. He could see her glistening in the light.

Apparently he was taking too long. "Lick me," Paige moaned.

Holden obliged. He put his hands behind her knees and pushed them to her chest, exposing even more of her cunt. His tongue took one long lick of her pussy and then he pulled away. A string of her juices hung off his lips, connecting him to her. He used his finger and collected it as one would a dangling piece of cheese from a slice of pizza. He brought it to his lips and licked it all off. She tasted great.

His mouth went back to work – not teasing her clit but penetrating her. It had been too long coming to play around. He had a job to do, and he was going to do it.

His tongue moved deep inside her. She placed her hands behind her knees to free Holden's hands. He ran his fingers up and down the backs of her legs as he continued to eat her. She pulled her legs back even further, allowing him to get deeper inside her. Holden slid his tongue in every direction inside her.

He moved his hands to her ass, raising it off the counter a bit and pulling her cheeks apart. He withdrew his tongue from her pussy and slid it down to her ass. His tongue made small circles there. She loved the sensation. She also loved that Holden would do that to her. A lot of people wouldn't dream of it, but it felt great.

His tongue worked deeper in her tight ass. She moved her hips to give him a better angle. His nose was buried in her pussy as he continued to lick her asshole. He took one hand off her cheek. He put a finger in her pussy to get it nice and wet, then slid it very slowly into her ass. He could feel her muscles contract around it. He moved in a "come here" motion. The movement was very soft. She was so tight that he couldn't make a big curve, but it was enough to get a response from her.

His tongue then went back up to her clit and rolled it around. As his mouth worked over her pussy, his tongue seemed be everywhere at once. The attention Paige was getting after such a long drought was like heaven to her. She lay back, relaxed all her muscles, and gave in to Holden, knowing she would have an orgasm.

Holden could feel Paige's body relax. He knew that was a sign she was ready to come. He took pride in being able to get her off so quickly, though he knew lack of sex was playing a role.

He slid three fingers into her pussy and fucked her with them very hard. His tongue continued to play with her clit, occasionally taking a very gentle bite of it to keep her guessing. She moaned. Her fingers sought a grip on the countertop, with no luck. She slammed her hands down hard, making loud slapping sounds. She needed something to hold on to, some resistance. She finally grabbed Holden's hair and pulled hard.

Holden knew she was about to orgasm, so he fucked her harder with both hands. The fingers in her pussy moved in as many directions as possible as he forced them in deep. The sudden hard jolt did the trick. Any resistance Paige had left was shocked away, and she began to orgasm. She let out a very loud "Fuck yeah" and flooded Holden's fingers.

Holden quickly slid his finger out of her ass, causing the muscles to relax, which added to her orgasm. When he took his fingers out of her pussy, her come chased them out. He pushed his head between her legs and licked up as much of her as he could. His nose accidentally touched her clit and made her jump. She was still holding his hair, and with the jump, she pushed his head away. She could see his lips and cheeks glistening with her pussy juices.

She sat up and slid herself to the edge of the counter, so she was face-to-face with Holden. She ran her fingers through his messy hair. She kissed his lips and tasted herself. Then she used her tongue to lick every last drop of herself off his face.

Holden was very turned on. They kissed a bit longer. Paige gave him that mischievous look of hers. She disappeared from the countertop, kneeling to face the bulge in his pants. She quickly unclasped his belt, button, and fly. She pulled his pants down and his large penis slapped her in the face. With no hesitation, she put her lips on his shaft, kissing it. She slid her lips up to his head, again giving it a kiss before taking the full length in her mouth. She bobbed her head, pleasuring Holden with just the right amount of pressure.

He felt her lips breaking their seal as they slid by his piercings. He could feel her breath on his testicles. She let the cock fall out of her mouth as she took his length in her small hand and stroked it. He looked down and couldn't believe how sexy she was. She kept stroking him as her free hand cupped his balls. She gently blew all over his pubic area. She grasped his cock and jerked him.

Holden spread his legs, getting into a more secure stance so he wouldn't lose his balance in the heat of the moment. He let her continue for several minutes before telling her to stop. He was dangerously close to coming. She wanted him to finish in her mouth, but he had other plans.

He helped her to her feet, then kissed her and turned her around. She bent over the countertop, resting on her elbows. His eyes focused on her heart-shaped ass. Her head dropped below her arms, and her long hair swayed as Holden touched her.

He gripped the base of his cock and slowly guided his length into her waiting pussy. She could feel all the piercings touching her lips as they passed by. Once he was in nice and deep, he stopped to let her feel him inside. She was already worked up from her orgasm, and he was close to coming from the oral he'd received. He slowly pulled his hard cock out of her so the head was just touching her waiting hole. He clenched her hips as he slid his length in again.

Her pussy contracted around him as he fucked her. She moved one hand between her legs and rubbed her clit, letting the occasional finger wander so it could graze his testicles and asshole. Holden wrapped a hand in her hair and gave her a hard pull, causing her head to rear back as she played with herself. The force started her second orgasm. She let out another moan and convulsed.

That was too much for Holden. He exploded inside her, his cock twitching in unison with her pussy as come flushed out of him. He let go of her hair, and once again her head dropped below her arms. She could feel him coming inside her, which kept her orgasm going.

Satisfied, he pulled out of her. She turned around with come oozing down her leg. They hugged and kissed like it was their first kiss.

They decided they needed a shower – their first shower together in their new place. Holden went into the bathroom and brushed his teeth. Paige came in, sat on the toilet, and began to pee. He'd never had a girlfriend pee in front him before. She saw the surprise in his eyes. "I hope you don't mind."

"Not at all." He was happy about the comfort she displayed around him.

After she was done, she started the shower and disappeared behind the curtain she and Tamara put up earlier. Holden told her he would be right in.

CHAPTER 7

Several weeks had passed since Holden and Paige first moved into their BC condo. Both had started their new jobs and Holden was really enjoying his, mostly because he hit it off with his co-workers. The puck hadn't even dropped on the next season, and already they were planning the championship party. Holden had more than his fair share of work; he was actually quite busy, but he loved it. He loved being able to contribute in such a substantial way, making decisions to improve the team instead of just doing the paperwork.

Paige was enjoying work as well. The other office assistants made her feel right at home. She had never held down a nine-to-five job before, and though the work wasn't challenging, the early hours were hard to adjust to. She made the best of it and never complained to Holden. She knew she was working as hard for herself as she was for their combined future. She knew how happy he was. He was also worried about her being homesick, and she didn't want to do anything to add to his worry.

Any free time they had, they spent working on the condo. Paige did all the interior decorating. On weekends, they combed through stores for the perfect things to tie their condo together and make it theirs. Holden liked what Paige had done with the place, and he enjoyed trying to find ways to improve their home.

Paige had been showing signs of stress because of the move, the new job, and all the work they had been putting into the condo. Holden wanted to surprise her with something big. She had given up so much to be there with him.

He talked to Mike and others at the office, and they came up with a wonderful plan – a weekend getaway. Holden planned everything and made the arrangements. He was able to do so without Paige getting even the slightest hint of what he had in store.

The weekend finally arrived. Holden was sitting in the condo with his bags packed, waiting for Paige to get home from work. They were heading up the mountain. Holden had been anticipating this escape for what seemed like an unbearable length of time. He'd wanted to tell Paige several times, but he managed to keep it a secret. A surprise would make her happier.

It was going to be perfect. He had a cabin with a hot tub reserved from Friday night until Sunday morning. He had been listening to the weather reports all week. The forecast wasn't promising for Friday, but if Paige got off work early enough, he was hoping they could beat the bad weather. He wasn't as worried about the weather once they were on the mountain. He'd packed plenty of wine, and the hot tub would still be hot regardless of the amount of snow that fell. The thought of being stuck in the cabin, alone with Paige for the night, was more than OK. He didn't plan on leaving it the first night anyway. It was the drive up he was worried about.

The rain started just before he heard Paige's key hit the front door. She was soaking wet and complained about the bad weather until she saw the packed bags by the door. She looked quizzically at Holden. Bursting at the seams, Holden was finally able to tell her his secret. She cried as she hugged him. She couldn't believe he would do something like that for her. She admitted that she was feeling a bit overwhelmed and could use the break.

Paige changed quickly and told Holden she was ready to go. She pulled him towards the door. Badly as he wanted to go, he decided to call the ski lodge's weather report. He dialled the seven digits. After the first ring, an automated voice answered. "Due to excessive snow, all runs have been cancelled and the mountain trail has been closed."

Holden's face dropped. By his expression, she knew it was bad news. She sat down, her energy was deflated. Holden hung up the phone, sat next to her, and put his arm around her. "It's OK. We can try again tomorrow. Tonight we'll cuddle up, sheltered from the rain, and make the best of it."

Paige choked back her tears, smiled, and agreed. Holden said he would get the bags so they could have toiletries for the night. "Don't touch the small black bag," she yelled. Holden rifled through the bags he had so carefully packed and saw a little black bag beside their luggage. Even though he was curious about its contents, he respected Paige's wishes and left it alone, taking only bathroom necessities from the larger bags.

He went back into the living room and slapped Paige's knee as he sat down on to the couch. "So, what do you want to do? Wanna rent a movie?"

"No, it's too wet out. Let's watch one we have here."

"OK, pick whatever you want."

Paige flipped through Holden's movies and picked *Phantom of the Opera*, the 2004 Andrew Lloyd Webber version. She knew it was one of Holden's favourite movies and thought it would be fun to relive their first date. Holden slid it into the DVD player, threw a bag of popcorn into the microwave, and cracked a bottle of wine from the fridge.

Smiling, Paige said it was getting cold. She grabbed a blanket – *all of the blanket* – and snuggled in. Holden took the hint. He handed her a glass of wine and dutifully went to the fireplace to make a fire. Paige had her trademark devilish grin on her face, the expression she wore when Holden was catering to her every whim.

The fire flamed up fast. The microwave dinged. The wine was cold. *OK, it's not a cabin overlooking a ski mountain. But it is a quiet night with Paige, so it's perfect*, Holden thought. He poured the popcorn into a bowl, picked up his glass of wine, and took his place next to his girlfriend on the couch.

Paige commented on how much harder it was raining as she cuddled up next to him. Not even halfway through the movie, the lightning was fierce. Since lightning was rare in Vancouver, Holden opened up the curtains to the balcony so they could watch the show. When he sat back down, Paige reached for his arm and held him closer. He told her it was all right and she should enjoy the beauty of it.

As he spoke his last word, lightning cracked and lit up the sky, showing the mountain range. It was fantastic. The movie became merely background noise as their attention was directed outside their window.

The storm moved closer to their place. Rain poured down even harder, and the lightning became more frequent. With one very close strike, the power flickered and the room went black. The hope for a short-term outage faded after a couple of minutes. In the glow of the fire, Holden could see disappointment in Paige's eyes for the second time that evening.

She gave Holden a "what are we going to do now" look. He wanted this weekend to be perfect; he refused to give up.

Suddenly he got a brilliant brain wave. He lit candles and handed one to Paige. He told her to go into the bedroom, change into something super comfortable, and not come out until he called for her. She asked him why, and with a smile he said, "Just do it." She hesitantly left the room.

Holden quickly ran to the hallway closet and the spare bedroom. He gathered all the blankets he could find and took them to the living room, where he started rearranging the furniture. Paige heard the commotion and asked if everything was OK.

"Fine, honey!" he yelled back.

Several minutes later he went to the bedroom and opened the door. Unfortunately Paige was already changed; Holden had missed the opportunity to catch her in the act. That disappointment turned quickly to arousal when he saw what she was wearing. She had found an old pair of sweatpants he had forgotten he owned, and one of his roller hockey jerseys. Her hair was in pigtails. Lit up by candlelight, she had never been sexier.

She could tell by his open-mouthed stare that he was happy. She walked over to him. The candle flickered on top of their antique dresser. She hugged him and whispered, "I hope you don't mind me wearing one of your precious jerseys."

The reference was to one of their first nights together at his place. She had gone through his closet to check out what he owned. When she picked up one of his jerseys, he passionately talked about his playing days and mentioned how he would love to see a significant other wear one of his jerseys someday.

This jersey was white with small perforations in it. Even in the candlelight, he could see through them well enough to tell she wasn't wearing a bra. As tempting as it was to throw her on the bed and ravish her right then and there, he instead reached for her hand and led her into the living room.

She saw the furniture moved around and blankets all over the place. At first it wasn't clear what was going on. Holden took her to where the fire lit up the area, and she recognized the arrangement. "Oh my God, it's a little fort!"

Holden smiled and followed her into the fort. He had placed the cushions from the couch and love seat on the floor, with a sleeping bag spread over the top. The pair sat down and looked at each other. No words were spoken. They leaned in and kissed. The fire, candles, and lightning created a romantic background.

They lay back on the cushions and stopped fondling each other to enjoy the lightning show that had created the situation. It really was beautiful. Every flash silhouetted the mountains. Holden placed his arm gently under her back, wanting to be as close to her as possible.

They weren't sure how long they sat in silence, watching the weather. Eventually they started talking – nothing too serious, just life in general. Holden then said he had another idea. He crawled out of the comfy fort and returned with his favourite book. He lay as close to Paige as he could and opened the book to a random chapter. He read it aloud to her.

When the chapter ended, Holden closed the book. Paige bit her lip. It was her turn to disappear out of the fort. She came back holding books of her own, but hers weren't novels. They were yearbooks. Holden had never seen them before. Paige said she kept them in a small suitcase along with other mementos from her childhood. He asked if he could see what else was in the suitcase, and she simply said, "Maybe someday."

Holden flipped through her yearbooks. He first tried to find her posed photos, then searched for candids. He read all the quotations her classmates had written her. Twice she had to point out her portrait, as he wasn't able to pick them out in the early books. She had definitely changed over the years.

The quotations were as equally funny as her pictures. Holden read the ones that were legible. Paige shared stories of high school, telling him who the people were and the meanings of the inside jokes.

She got really excited by her trip down memory lane. Holden wasn't sure if the books were going to fuel her feelings of homesickness or if they were just what she needed. Regardless, he enjoyed hearing her stories and loved seeing her pictures.

The last book she handed him had a pink cover. He flipped through the first few pages. He stopped on page 20; his eyes were drawn to the bottom third of the page. The last girl in the row was stunning. He couldn't stop staring at her. He finally let his eyes drift over to the left-hand column to read the name. It was Paige. She looked different. Her hair was long and its natural colour, and she had big bangs. But he could definitely see the resemblance between the girl in the picture and the girl sitting by his side.

She pointed out other people and showed him the candid pictures of her and her friends. She had by all appearances been a tomboy, seeming to hide her femininity under clothes that were too big for her. The generic jeans and T-shirts were better suited to an awkward teenage boy, not the beautiful woman she had become. She was, however, still wearing her familiar Chuck Taylors.

Paige shuddered at every new picture, laughing at the memories and her self-described horrible style. Holden was happy she had shared this with him. He felt they had grown closer over the past couple of hours. He wondered, had the weather allowed them to go up the mountain, if they would have had the same bonding experience.

Paige yawned and Holden followed suit. He closed up the books. Their eyes met. Holden said it was time for them to go to sleep because they had a long day ahead of them. Paige agreed. They shared another kiss, embraced, and fell asleep in their living room fort.

The sun beaming through the balcony doors woke up Holden first. He checked to see if Paige was awake yet and she wasn't. She was sleeping so peacefully, he almost hated to wake her. Almost. Then he put his arm on her shoulder, shook her hard, and yelled, "Hey, wake up!"

She jumped to the roof of the blanket fort and let out a scream. She looked around, realized what was going on, and slapped Holden playfully. "Ass."

He laughed and said they had to get going. A quick brush of the teeth and a joint shower, and they were headed out to the car. She made a point of bringing her black bag, which made him even more curious as to its contents. She threw the bag in the trunk as Holden started up the engine, and they were on their way.

The sun was shining and it was warm, with not a sign of the terrible storm the night before. Even the weather report from the ski hill described ideal conditions. Their route began in scenes of lush green grass, but twenty minutes up the hill, snow banks appeared on the shoulders of the road. Paige reached for the climate control and turned up the heat.

In no time, the two arrived at the ski lodge. Because of the storm, everything had a thick, clean, white coat of snow. They checked in but decided not to go out to their cabin right away. Instead, they took snowboarding lessons. Both were already decent skiers. With their helmets and suits of armour on, they went off to find their class.

After the lessons they were exhausted, sore, and bruised. They decided to hit the lodge for a bite to eat, because they knew if they went to their cabin, they would be in for the night. The dining room was beautiful: oak trim, a roaring fireplace, and a lot of happy people who'd left their cares at the base of the hill. The meal was fantastic.

After charging it to their room, they headed off to finally see their cabin. The drive led to the top of a hill. The view was increasingly spectacular with every turn, and the cabins seemed like small homes. The couple's anticipation built. After a couple of wrong turns, they found their number, pulled in to the lane, and grabbed the bags.

Holden took the key out of his pocket and slid it into the lock. Paige saw the excitement in his eyes as he looked over at her. She dropped her bags, put her hands on either side of his head, and kissed him. The intensity caused him to drop his bags too. They fell into the cabin, and she landed on top of a laughing Holden.

He realized he was still holding the key – or, at least, part of the key. Paige looked at his hand, then back at him, trying to gauge his reaction. He laughed. Paige hugged him and kissed him on the cheek. "Oops."

When they stopped laughing, they explored the room. "Wow" was the only thing they managed to say. Holden tossed Paige lovingly off him so he could roll over and see the room better. She landed with a thud and gave him a kick. He smirked back at her.

Holden was the first to get to his feet and walk the room. Paige followed, leaving the bags outside the door. The cabin was huge. It featured a very large bed, a 46-inch TV with DVD player, and a fireplace. The large glass patio doors showed them the most amazing view of the mountain. The yard had fences on the two sides, blocking out the neighbours, but it was open to the hill. A couple hundred feet of forest on a very sharp drop lay between them and the uppermost ski run allowing them to see down the entire hill.

They walked through the freshly fallen snow to the hot tub. Holden removed the cover and started it up so that it would be nice and hot later. They walked back inside, and Paige said she was going to have a quick shower because they were still sweaty from their day of snowboarding.

Holden said OK. They gave each other a quick peck on the lips. Holden went to sweep off the deck so they wouldn't have to walk through a lot of snow later. It only took him ten minutes or so to clean off it off, get their things from outside the door, and unpack. He carefully avoided the mysterious black bag Paige was so set on. He put the wine in to chill and heard the water shut off.

Paige came out wearing a large white housecoat that appeared as comfortable as being wrapped in a hundred bunnies. She was drying her hair with a towel. "My turn," Holden said.

He undressed before hitting the bathroom. He closed the door behind him and looked around. The tub was huge and Jacuzzi style. That brought a smile to his face. He thought of the endless possibilities the night held. The mirror took up the wall in front of the sink, which had gold plated faucets. The countertop appeared to be marble. He almost felt guilty dirtying up the place, but he did it anyway.

The shower was hot and the water pressure was strong. It was the kind of shower he didn't want to get out of but he knew he had a hot girl waiting on the other side of the door. He turned the taps off, opened the shower curtain, and reached for a towel. He dried himself off, then wrapped the towel around his waist and walked into the living area.

He stopped dead when he saw a tall, very well-built blonde girl standing in the middle of the room. Her pure white outfit clung to her hard body. She had a couple of buttons undone to show off her ample cleavage, and her white skirt barely hid the top of her thigh highs. Holden wondered what was going on.

He also saw a man almost a foot taller than himself, wearing a very tight, thin, white T-shirt that showed off every muscle in his perfectly formed body, as well as amplified his golden tan. His biceps flexed as he dug his powerful hands into a nearly naked Paige.

Paige was lying on a portable massage table, wearing only a tiny towel over her ass. From the angle Holden had, he could see underneath it but he knew the tall stranger couldn't – for the moment anyway.

The girl said, "You must be Holden. Come lie down."

Holden, trying to hide the tent he was pitching under his towel, awkwardly walked over to the massage table and lay down.

Paige looked over at Holden. "Surprise! I thought it would be a nice treat for you after snowboarding. I wanted to do something for you for arranging this weekend."

The girl flicked her long blonde hair off her shoulders as she took her spot beside Holden. Paige and Holden were positioned so they could see each other. Holden felt weird watching his naked girlfriend get touched in such a pleasurable way by a total stranger, especially one as hot as the guy working her over. He mostly felt weird because he was enjoying the show so much.

It was hard for him to focus on Paige once his blonde angel began massaging him. Her tiny hands were much stronger than he imagined as they danced over his sore body. Holden began to fade away.

He was brought to reality by a moan Paige let out. Holden watched the guy run his hands all over her. Paige was enjoying the Swedish masseuse rubbing Holden too, and he caught her sneaking a peek at the masseuse's cleavage. The woman didn't seem to mind though; she even seemed to encourage it.

Taking Paige's cue, the blonde girl took every opportunity to sneak a peek at Paige and Holden as well. Holden was not in a very good position to check out his masseuse. He settled for watching Paige get pleasured by her tall, dark stranger.

As the two professionals kneaded, rubbed, and stretched the couple, Holden could only think of the nasty things he was planning for Paige later that evening. Paige wondered if a happy ending was included in the massage. If it wasn't, she wondered how to approach the subject of inviting the masseuses to stay after for a drink and possibly more fun. She wasn't sure how Holden would react to a three- or foursome.

The thought of Holden fucking his masseuse on her massage table while Paige watched intrigued her so much, she found herself getting wet. She couldn't help but wonder what the muscular guy rubbing her was packing. Her imagination was working overtime as her masseuse ran his hands up her legs, close to her ass. She imagined Holden's cock between the other woman's perfectly round tits as her own masseuse fed Paige his gigantic cock.

Holden's masseuse told him to turn over so she could rub his chest and legs. Hesitantly, he rolled over, making sure the towel was covering him. Much to his embarrassment, the weight of the towel wasn't enough to counter the force of his erection.

The masseuse looked down at the large bulge in the towel. "Impressive," she said.

Paige was already on her back, her small but firm tits exposed to everyone in the room. She met a glance from the female masseuse, who was checking out her tits. Holden caught the glance, knowing what was going on.

He continued to watch the male masseuse as the man touched his girlfriend. He rubbed her shoulders and her stomach. Then he gave her lymph nodes a massage. His strong hands dug deep into Paige's tits. She reacted positively, letting out frequent moans of pleasure. The man moved down her stomach towards her legs.

Holden's masseuse was working on Holden's limbs, which made him feel very relaxed. It was just the thing he needed after such a long day. He resisted the urge to fall asleep so that he could watch the show on the next table.

The masseuse had reached Paige's legs. He worked down her thighs and down each calf before rubbing her feet. Holden knew he could see under Paige's towel now, but neither Paige nor Holden cared.

Holden glanced up at the male masseuse, and their eyes met. Unexpectedly, the guy raised his eyebrows twice in an "I'm the man" kind of way. Then with his eyes he directed Holden's gaze downwards. Obediently, Holden dropped his eyes to the masseuse's groin. He could see the massive bulge in his pants. To Holden's shock, the guy reached down and pulled out his massive cock. It was fully erect and looked very angry. It was a foot long and very thick.

Holden was impressed. He was so captivated with it that he wanted to touch it himself. He had never seen a cock so big before.

Before Holden could formulate an objection, the guy grabbed Paige's legs and pulled until her ass was on the edge of the table. She appeared tiny next to him. The man forced the monster into her. She winced but didn't do anything to stop him.

Holden felt helpless. He sat there watching his girlfriend wrap her ankles around the masseuse's muscular thighs. She raised her hands over her head, grasping the sides of the table. The female masseuse too was getting worked up as she watched the python penetrate Paige. Holden lay still. He was paralyzed by fear, anger, and – mostly – curiosity. He couldn't stop this man from violating his girlfriend.

Paige moaned like a whore as the man thrust into her over and over again. Holden felt his towel fly off as the blonde masseuse jumped up on the table. She pulled her skirt up, exposing a white, sheer thong. She pulled it aside and lined up with Holden. He could see the landing strip shaved in her pubic area. She reached down to Holden's hard rod, wrapped her fingers around his length, and guided it into her wet, willing pussy.

As soon as it was seated as deeply as possible, she met Holden's gaze. Putting her fingers between the buttons of her white blouse, she yanked with passion and force. Buttons flew everywhere. She ground her hips hard onto Holden; she was tight and wet.

Holden resisted the urge to come early. It was difficult because this was the first pussy he'd been in, other than Paige's, for almost a year.

The subtle differences were enough to set him off, but he fought it with every ounce of strength he had.

Paige didn't seem to see or care that Holden was being fucked. She was concentrating too hard on her own pleasure. The vein in the man's forehead throbbed as he let out a moan. Holden could tell the signs of an imminent orgasm. He was still mad at himself for letting this happen but was helpless to stop it.

Finally, the man freed his cock from Paige's tight hole and scrambled to her side, squeezing the tip closed. He slapped the baby elephant's trunk down onto Paige's chest and began to come. His load was thick and ample. Paige released the table from her clutches and rubbed her tits, smearing his come all over. Holden found the sight too much to take. He was about to come himself.

Just before he released his load inside the gorgeous blonde masseuse, he heard Paige's voice. "Holden!"

He jumped.

"Holden!"

Holden came to and looked around. He saw Paige sitting on the side of the massage table in her housecoat. The two masseuses had their jackets on. "You were snoring," Paige said, laughing. She gestured to make Holden aware that everyone could see his hard-on.

Self-consciously, Holden covered up and leaped from the table so the two masseuses could pack up and be on their way. He was embarrassed yet amazed that his dream had felt so real. He was even more ashamed that he almost had a wet dream at the thought of his girlfriend being violated by another man.

Paige and Holden thanked the pair for their work and tipped them generously. As the door closed, Holden turned to Paige and blushed. Paige asked him what had him so worked up but he avoided the question by promising to tell her about his dream another time.

Paige moved to the bed and lay down. Holden, still feeling playful, pretended he didn't notice her eyes burning into him. He got dressed. Paige, with a laugh in her voice, said, "What was the point of that? You're not going to be in them long anyway." Her housecoat fell open. Holden put a hand on her hip, leaned in, and kissed her.

"You wish!" Paige jumped off the bed.

He was left lying on the bed, staring at her with frustration and confusion. She laughed at him and took one of her bags. She dug out some clothes and tantalized him further by slowly dressing. "Tease!" Holden yelled.

She threw the panties she was about to put on at him. "A little something to tide you over until later," she said.

"What?" Holden said. Paige's taunting worked perfectly.

It was now around suppertime, but since they'd had a late lunch, neither of them was hungry. Holden poured them each a glass of wine. They sat on the leather couch that was directed towards the fireplace, but also had a lovely view of the mountain. The fireplace was gas, and Holden had turned it on while Paige was showering. They left the TV on for background noise.

Holden placed his arm around Paige's shoulder and she snuggled up tight into him. When their glasses of wine were empty, the sun was setting. "So, your masseuse was hot," Holden said.

"Yup, I'd do him," Paige shot back. "I would have done the girl who was massaging you, too."

"Yup, me too."

"Too bad neither are coming back."

"Too bad. Hot tub?"

"Yes."

With that they popped up. Holden picked up a couple of bottles of wine and headed for the hot tub. Paige said she was going to take a quick pee and would join him in a second. "Better now than in the tub," Holden quipped.

The tub had heated up nicely. Holden filled their glasses, placed the bottles into the snow built up around the edges of the tub, and slid into the water. It was too hot at first, especially compared to the frosty mountain air. He enjoyed the view, anxious for Paige to join him.

He heard music playing and looked around to see where it was coming from. Voices were audible over the music. The cabin next door was having a party, and it sounded like a bunch of teenagers. He was upset at first, thinking that the unwanted distraction might take away from their own weekend, but then decided nothing could ruin the amazing time they were having. Eavesdropping on their conversation gave Holden a couple of laughs. *Oh, those crazy teens*, he thought.

His attention was drawn back to his own cabin by the sound of the patio door opening. Whatever he had been thinking vanished as his eyes and thoughts trained on Paige.

She walked towards him, wearing the robe she'd had on earlier. She'd left it open. She got to the stairs and noticed Holden's robe on the patio. She smiled and let hers drop.

As it hit the ground, they could hear the boys next door make a commotion and bang against the fence. A series of "shhhs" then filled the air. Paige blushed and laughed.

She didn't hurry into the tub. Between the low light, the angle of the fence, and the steam, the teens weren't going to see much, so Paige decided to work it. She bent to pick up her wine and spilled some on her bare breast. She made a production of wiping it off herself. She scooped handfuls of water from the tub and used her fingers to wipe her tender skin.

Finally, she lowered herself into the water and leaned against the back of the tub. She took the mandatory couple of seconds to adjust to the water before taking a drink of her wine. After a sip, she immediately felt relaxed. It had been an adventure getting there, but now they were right where they wanted to be. Not saying a word, they sipped their wine, taking in the sights, aware that there were no doubt horny teen boys still watching their every move.

The sun had set, but it wasn't dark yet. Three big spotlights flickered on, lighting up the big resort sign near the top of the hill. The lights were soft enough not to ruin the view nor distract them.

Paige slid around to be next to Holden. Her beautiful tits were just below the water, and he could see them magnified under the waterline. She put her hand on his lap and gently caressed his leg. Holden put his arm around her and leaned in to kiss her neck and ear. Since there were no noises from the peanut gallery, they assumed their spectators had moved on to something else.

Paige's hand slid further up Holden's leg to his cock. "What do we have here?" she said with an innocent smile.

Holden grabbed a handful of Paige's hair and moved her head so she was looking at him. He kissed her. Her hand gripped his cock and softly stroked it under the hot, bubbling water. Holden moved to her cheek, her ear, her neck. He continued pulling her hair because he knew Paige loved the feeling. The pressure distracted her from other sensations, allowing them to heighten and eventually give her a more powerful orgasm. In a small way, it let her fill the submissive role, one she enjoyed playing.

Holden's other hand reached over to her wet tits and slowly rubbed. He pushed and squeezed her. Paige's grip got tighter on his cock. Without warning, she stopped stroking. She didn't say a word. She straddled his lap and guided his throbbing cock into her pussy.

She rode him without consideration for his satisfaction; she went to town on him like he wasn't even there. Holden realized he wasn't the only one getting lost in the weekend. It was the right thing to relieve the stress of the move and their new jobs.

Paige took both Holden's hands and forced them to her tits. "Fuck me," she kept saying over and over again. He stared deep into her eyes. He loved watching her fuck him: her face, the way her tits moved. It was all very intense. She seemed possessed, lost in the mood, unaware of her surroundings. She was taking in all the sensations as best she could.

The heat from the hot tub was wearing Holden out. He didn't want to stop. Paige seemed to be enjoying herself way too much. Apparently though, the heat was affecting her as well. She collapsed beside Holden. She mumbled, "This isn't over by a long shot."

She reached for her glass of wine. Holden took his, and they slammed back the remaining drops, poured another glass, and quickly drank that too. They were breathing so hard they didn't even notice the moonlit night had turned to snow. It wasn't a blizzard, but the flakes were large and puffy. They attempted to catch the crystals with their tongues, but the heat from the tub melted the snow before it got to the couple.

They caught their breaths and finished yet another glass of wine. Paige suggested they head inside. Holden agreed. On the way, Paige said she had to pee again. Holden turned off the tub and noticed that the party next door had died down, so he felt comfortable walking around naked. He got into the cabin and closed the door behind him. The room was still warm from the fireplace, so he lay naked on the bed. He noticed the mysterious black bag Paige had been so concerned about was gone.

The bathroom door opened. Even without seeing her, the anticipation started his blood flowing. Paige walked around the corner from the bathroom and left Holden speechless. The woman he loved stood in front of him wearing a pink bustier that exposed her tits, pink thigh-highs attached to the bustier by garters, and no panties. Her hair was in her trademark pigtails.

She saw his reaction, and any hesitation she'd felt about whether Holden would like the outfit was gone. "You weren't the only one who had something special planned for the weekend. I guess great minds think alike," she said. She walked to the bed, crawled over Holden, and said, "Now then, where were we"?

A series of babbles was all the response he was capable of.

"Right about here, I think." She straddled him and guided his cock into her pussy.

"Yup, that feels right," Holden said.

She rode him again. This time she pinned his arms above his head. He chose to be helpless as she fucked him. Her breasts bounced only slightly, held in place by the bustier. He didn't know how much longer he could take Paige's attention, but he was holding on as best he could.

Paige leaned down. Her hips moved more slowly as she felt every inch of Holden's pierced cock inside her. He could tell he was about to come and wasn't ready to let that happen. She pulled herself off him, letting his cock fall out of her and slap against his stomach. He stared at her, amazed at how fantastic she looked in her new outfit.

She wriggled further up his body. He felt her wet pussy drag against his abs and pecs. She knelt over his face and let him taste her. Her thigh-highs scratched the sides of his face as he licked her, getting his tongue deep inside her. He took long strokes up her pussy to her clit. She ground into his face, moving faster and harder. Her pussy splashed on him, and the sensation got him harder. He wanted to make her come so badly.

He licked her faster, harder, and deeper. Paige clenched her own tits as she rode Holden's face. Her moans grew louder and her hips moved more spasmodically, as if she wasn't totally in control anymore.

Fair is fair, Holden thought. Before he gave her satisfaction, he threw her off of him. She had a bewildered expression as he moved her onto her hands and knees. He positioned himself behind her and gripped her hips firmly before sliding his hard cock into her pussy. He pulled on her pigtails as he slowly fucked her.

They found their rhythm and moved their bodies in unison. Holden pulled her hair harder and ran fingernails down her spine. Her back arched and her pussy tightened. He thrust very hard and deep. He felt her legs tremble as his own orgasm was mounting.

Paige surprised him again by wiggling away and jumped up out of bed. "Don't you dare move," she said. Again, he was left wondering what the fuck had just happened.

She ran over to the table, picked up his glass of wine, and returned. *A hell of a fine time for a drink,* Holden thought.

Paige positioned her pussy beside his head. "Finish me," she ordered.

"OK," Holden replied. He slid his fingers inside her, and with the other hand he teased her clit. As great as sex normally was with her, he thought the bustier outfit amplified the perfection of the weekend.

Paige was getting further worked up as his fingers danced around inside her. She took his cock in her mouth and worked him over. One hand held the wine glass; the other played with his balls and ass.

As she felt her orgasm growing again, she made him move his mouth. She grabbed his cock and jerked it off incredibly fast and hard. Holden rubbed her clit just as fast. Her orgasm ran like wave through her. The sight and sensation of her coming finished off Holden.

Paige put the wine glass over the tip of his cock and continued to jerk him off hard. The first squirts of come exploded into the glass. That didn't stop her; she kept beating him harder and faster as long as he continued coming. Holden had the most intense orgasm of his life.

Breathless, he lay back. She knelt next to him. She held the glass half filled with wine and come to her lips and poured it all down her throat. When it was empty, she threw the glass over her shoulder, letting it crash to the ground. "I saw that in a porno once." She giggled and collapsed next to Holden.

"I love you," Holden whispered. Paige said it back. The two lovers slept entangled in each other's arms for the night.

CHAPTER 8

Holden slid his key in the lock and walked into the condo. He was happy to be home. As much as he loved his new job, one of the downfalls was the constant traveling. Paige had never said anything, but Holden didn't like being away from her so much. He wasn't worried about her being alone; Paige and Tamara had become very close and spent a lot of time together. He did, however, know that Paige was nervous being in the condo alone at night.

He left his suitcase in the hallway and walked towards the living room to find his love. Paige popped around a corner. She had her headset on and was selecting a song from her MP3 player. She clearly hadn't heard him come in.

He didn't make his presence immediately known. Instead, he watched her for a while. She was wearing white running shoes and black yoga pants that fit her tightly. The lines of her sports bra were clearly visible under her white shirt. It compressed her tits to appear like two perfectly round peaches. Her hair was tied back in a ponytail that ran through the back of a black hat.

She walked closer to Holden. Just as she was about to run into him, she looked up. She let out a scream and jumped, which caused her to fall to the floor. Holden tried not to laugh despite her comical reaction. He knelt beside her, put his hand under her head, and asked if she was OK. She slapped his arm, embarrassed. She then reached around and gave him a hug. "I missed you," she said.

He hugged her back and squeezed her real tight. "I missed you too, honey." He leaned in and kissed her. Her heart was still racing from the fright.

Holden lay down beside her as she snuggled close to him. He had only been gone a week, but to Paige it felt like a lifetime. They continued to embrace and kiss deeply. Between kisses, they talked about what had happened during the past week, even though they'd already talked on the phone every night.

Holden was being sent away more and more, and the frequency of the trips wasn't making them easier to deal with. The lack of intimacy was hard on them. Holden had the Internet to tide him over, and Paige had her tickle trunk of toys to relieve her stress, but neither of those was as good as the real thing.

Holden moved his hands all around Paige's back, then down to her ass. He gave her a good squeeze. Paige's fingers ran through Holden's hair as their lips locked. He rolled onto her as she wrapped her legs around his. She could feel the familiar sensation of Holden's erection against her. Even through her yoga pants and his jeans, she could feel it, and she yearned for it to be inside her.

Holden thrust his hips, trying to fuck her through their clothes. Paige did the same. Their hands were moving all over each other's bodies. He ran his hands over her firm tits, then down her ribs and stomach to her pants. He awkwardly slid his hands under her waistband and tried to get his fingers inside her, but their body positions made it impossible.

She reached into Holden's pants and squeezed his ass. He leaned to one side and rolled Paige over so she was on her stomach. He unzipped his pants with one hand and drew out his thick meat with the other. Then he pulled Paige's stretchy pants over her ass. She was wearing a very small G string that he pulled to one side, exposing her pussy. He straddled her waist, leaned forward, and slid his cock inside her.

She let out a soft moan as she finally got to feel his piercings again. He plunged deep inside her and fucked her on the hallway floor. Holden could feel the waistband of her pants sliding up her ass and rubbing against his cock. The foreign sensation heightened his sensitivity, and the random passionate act brought him to the brink of orgasm in record time.

Paige was feeling the same. The adrenaline rush she had experienced earlier from the scare Holden gave her made the blood rush directly to her pussy. She too was turned on by the spontaneity of their lovemaking.

Holden began to come hard, filling her pussy. The semen sprayed inside her with such force that it made Paige orgasm as well. Within minutes of their first embrace, the pair were lying on the carpeted floor, in need of a cigarette.

Paige was the first to move. She adjusted her pants and underwear and stood up. Holden lay on his back, looking up at her. "I'm going for a run," she said. "I'll be back in half an hour." Putting in her earphones, she turned on her MP3 player went into the bathroom to clean up before heading out the door.

Holden tucked his flaccid cock away, grabbed his suitcase, and unpacked, happy to be home. He connected his laptop to speakers in the bathroom and cranked a playlist, knowing Paige wouldn't be disturbed. As the songs played, he sang at the top of his lungs. If *Canadian Idol* were being held in his shower, he would have won easily. Feeling his fingers and toes wrinkle, he decided it was time to get out and make himself pretty for Paige before she got home.

He turned off the water, opened the curtain, and dried himself. Over the music, he heard a faint "Holden!" He turned down his speakers. Sure enough, Paige was yelling for him.

Leaving the bathroom and wearing only a towel, he followed her voice, which led him to their spare bedroom. He opened the door to see Paige standing by the head of the bed, wearing fishnet thigh-highs and the same knee-high boots she'd worn to the park on their third date. She also wore an open-bust lace teddy and crotchless panties. Her arms were accessorized with fishnet loop gloves, and in her hand was a riding crop.

Holden stopped dead in the doorway. "Nice singing," Paige said with a smile. He was embarrassed but quickly got over it.

Paige used the riding crop to point to the bed. "Lie down," she commanded. She tapped the towel with her crop. "Good boy," she said, acknowledging his erection.

He walked towards the bed and noticed four ropes, one on each corner. At her feet was her tickle trunk of toys and lotions. The tickle trunk always intrigued him. He was forbidden to go near it without her presence.

He took his spot on the bed. She grabbed his towel and pulled hard, like she was doing a magic trick. In an instant he was completely naked – and at Syn's mercy.

She held the feathery tip of the crop over his body so it lightly brushed him. She dragged it up and down his body, teasing his balls and cock each time. Once it was up by his ears, she raised it high in the air and slapped it down hard against his cock. It didn't hurt as much as he anticipated, which he figured was the point. It grazed his sac, and that sent a wave of discomfort up his body. He assumed there was a lot more of that in store for him.

She gripped his shaft and squeezed. Kneeling, she leaned over his body. Her tits pressed against him as she reached for the rope meant for his left arm. She tried tying it but was unsuccessful. Holden couldn't help but laugh.

She decided to try the rope closest to her. As she struggled, Holden said he would show her how to tie the proper knot. Using his free arm, he took the rope and made a quick loop. Before Paige realized it, her own wrist was tied to the bedpost.

Holden squirmed out from under her and jumped off the bed. He used his body mass to push her over so she lay on the bed. She could feel his bare cock pressing into her waist as he quickly tied her other arm. He then moved to her feet, where he secured ropes over her boots. Bound to the bed was not at all the position she had been expecting.

Once she was tied up to his satisfaction, he stood at the foot of the bed, staring at her. As much as she had been anticipating making Holden her slave, the helplessness and vulnerability she was feeling made her enjoy the role reversal.

"Well, well, well. What do we have here?" Holden asked. He picked up her riding crop and played the same trick she had. Starting at her knees, he ran it over her thigh and forced it into the open slit in her panties. Then it moved up her stomach, over each nipple, and on to her chest and neck. He put the tip against her lips and kissed the other side.

Standing up again, he raised the crop as she had done and abruptly brought it down hard against her pussy. The bristles made a loud snapping sound against her panties. He dropped the crop on the bed beside her, stood up, and left the room. Paige yelled as he left.

He was gone for several minutes – not because he was doing anything, but because he wanted to create uncertainty in her mind. He re-entered carrying his digital camera and tripod.

Paige melted at the sight of the camera. She had never been taped before, but they had discussed how erotic it would be to perform for the camera. She certainly trusted Holden enough to allow him to record her.

Holden extended the legs on the tripod, peered through the viewfinder, and angled the camera to get the best possible view of his slut tied to the bed. She became very wet when she saw the red light come on. That very little addition to their lovemaking made everything different.

Holden felt it too. It was like they were strangers in a porno. He walked around the bed until he was beside her tickle trunk. "What's all this, then?" He picked up the trunk and emptied it out beside her.

Inside were several vibrators and dildos of all shapes and sizes, more bondage gear, anal beads, clit stimulators, and long, thin metal rods that Holden could only assume were urethral sounds. Holden had never experienced them before but was very intrigued.

The toy that stood out was a huge dildo. It was two feet long and very wide. Paige laughed when Holden picked it up. "What? That one was a gag gift for my birthday. I have been too scared to use it."

"No shit," Holden said. He dropped it to the side. He methodically picked up each toy, examined it, and turned the vibrating ones on so Paige could hear them. All this built anticipation in the restrained Paige. She made a sound. "Shut up, whore, or you'll get this!" he said, holding up a ball gag and blindfold. He had never talked to her like that before. She really liked the idea of being his whore.

The trunk contained a small plastic bag. Holden dumped out its contents to find several clothespins. "Hmm" was all he said as he picked up one one of the pins. He closed it over the fleshy web between his thumb and forefinger. He let out another "hmm" as his eyes widened.

Paige knew what he was thinking. She tried to squirm, but the ropes did their job keeping her in place. She wanted to object, but her lips remained sealed.

He took the clothespin off his hand, squeezing it open and closed as he brought it to her body. He pushed the hard wood into her flesh. She could feel the rough texture against her soft skin, causing goose bumps as she anticipated the pain that he was about to inflicted upon her.

Holden dragged the clothespin to her ear and attached it. She felt a pinch, but it didn't hurt as much as she expected. He clipped another to her other ear. She assumed that because of the number of piercings she had in her ears, they were desensitized to pain.

He reached into the plastic bag and pulled out two more pins. He stared at her nipples, and she knew what he was thinking. She braced herself. Helpless, she could only watch as the jaws of the wooden clothespin clamped down onto her nipple.

Again, the pain wasn't as much as she thought it would be. As a matter of fact, it was just a slight pressure, no real pain at all. With a second pin clamped down on her other erect nipple, Holden dug through the tickle trunk toys again, this time pulling out a small clit stimulator. He turned it on and sat beside her with his head on her stomach. Aware of the camera, he positioned himself so it would catch everything he was doing.

He smiled at the lens as he extended his tongue and teased her clit. The hum of the vibrator filled the air. Holden left it on the bed. As he rolled around, the toy rolled against Paige's ass cheek. The surprise sensation made her jump. Holden knew what had happened and elected to keep the vibrator where it was.

His fingers buried themselves deep in her calves as he did his best to lick her. Paige wanted to reach down and play with his hair or touch his cock, but all she could do was lie bound, allowing him to use her body like his personal playground.

Holden finally picked up the toy. He pressed it hard against her clit, causing Paige to jerk. She moved her hips around to fuck the toy. Holden dragged the riding crop across her face. "No!" he ordered.

The theatrics of being dominated were driving her crazy. Holden left the clit stimulator in place, changing the speed and pressure, trying to be as unpredictable as possible. After several minutes of pure clit teasing, he clamped another clothespin to her swollen clit. He was surprised when Paige didn't seem to notice.

Happy he hadn't hurt her, he found a long silicone vibrator with a small attachment on the bottom. He wasn't sure if the attachment was intended for her clit or her ass, but he did know what he was going to use it for. Using lube from her tickle trunk, he poured a generous amount into his hand and stroked the toy. Paige's pussy was already wet, but he wanted to make sure the long vibrator would fit smoothly.

When he was satisfied the toy was sufficiently lubed, he put his hand in Paige, ensuring she too was well lubricated. She jumped when his finger slipped inside her bum. She really didn't like not knowing what was happening to her, but she couldn't stop him. Nor would she if she could have; she was enjoying the overall experience way too much.

He pressed the tip of the toy against her pussy. Gently and gradually, he slid the length inside her. He loved watching her pussy spread to take the foreign object, the way her labia wrapped around the toy as if she were hugging it.

Paige felt the penetration. It was wide, and it was going in deep, filling her to the max. The surprise happened when the attachment poked at her ass. It, too, easily penetrated her.

Holden adjusted the vibration setting to random pulsing, a pulsing that worked its way through her core. Holden stuffed the toy in as deep as he could. Confident her tight pussy wasn't going to force it out, he took his hands off it.

He went back to the bag of clothespins and placed one on her labia. Again, she didn't acknowledge the pin, so he continued to line them around her pussy. He managed to get five on each side. Appreciating his work, he laughed when he realized her pussy looked like an evil jaw with straggly teeth devouring the vibrator.

As he had clipped, he accidentally pushed hard on the top of the toy, forcing it deeper into her pussy. Paige jumped and moaned; the unanticipated movement seemed to increase her pleasure. Holden elected to get rougher with her. He escalated his aggression slowly to see how she would respond. He gingerly stepped outside his comfort zone by calling her names and slapping her well-padded areas.

Certain her pussy was taken care of for now, he focused on Paige's face. Their eyes met. Paige gaze was fogged. Holden shouted, "You like that, you fucking bitch?"

"Yes, sir," she responded.

"I like that *sir*. From now on, you call me *sir*. You got that, whore?"

"Yes, sir."

Holden crawled up the bed putting his hands on her cheeks. He squeezed them together. "You fucking got that?"

"Yes, sir!"

Momentarily, Holden broke character. He leaned in and gave her quick peck on the lips. That simple act of tenderness made Paige smile.

The vibrator continued to work away inside Paige. She still hadn't mentioned the clothespins. Holden thought about what he could do next. He removed a pin dangling from her earlobe. Paige twitched. "Ow."

Holden, again breaking character, asked if she was OK. She said that the clothespin numbed the area. It didn't hurt when it was attached, but the tingling sensation of the blood flowing back into her ear stung a bit.

Holden thought about the pins lining her pussy. There was nothing he could do about that now. Shrugging it off, he whispered in Paige's ear, "You want my cock?"

"Yes, sir."

"You want to fuck me like the whore you are?"

"Yes, sir."

"You want to feel my come on your face? On your tits? Inside you?"

"Yes, sir."

"Well, which is it, bitch?"

"On my tits, sir."

"Your face it is. Unless, of course, you have a problem with that."

"No, sir. Anywhere you wish, sir."

"Damn right."

Holden knelt beside Paige. He fucked her with the vibrator that was still alive inside her. Every time he pulled the toy out, it hit the clothespins, giving her a hint of the sensation that was to come.

Paige couldn't understand the burning she was feeling in her pussy. It wasn't constant; but it was enough for her to notice. She eventually connected it to the sensation she had experienced in her ear, amplified. She realized what Holden had done.

Holden, oblivious, continued to work the toy forcefully in and out of her. He was fascinated watching the way her pussy changed shape to accommodate it. He used care to ensure the attachment in her ass didn't hurt.

Paige moaned, and Holden looked at her face. "I didn't tell you that you could make a noise, did I?"

"No, sir."

"Then shut up."

"Yes, sir. Sorry, sir."

Holden let go of the toy. He reached up and put his strong hand across Paige's throat, squeezing it to cut off her air. She tilted her head back, mouth open, eyes wide. She wanted to grab his hand and move it, but her own hands were bound too tightly. She wanted to tell him to stop, but his grip was too tight.

Holden leaned in and put his mouth over her open mouth. He licked her lips as he continued to deprive her of oxygen. Then, careful not to hurt her, he released his grasp. He had limited experience with asphyxiation, so he erred on the side of caution and only choked her for only a couple of seconds. It had felt like an eternity to Paige, whose experience with asphyxiation was even less than Holden's.

As Holden's clutch weakened, Paige gasped for air. The oxygen filled her blood and rushed through her body, which heightened all her sensations. She was now very aware of the clamps on her pussy and the toy in her ass. "Oh, fuck me!" she yelled as she fought to get her breath back.

Holden asked her if she'd liked that. "Oh, fuck, yes," she replied.

He gave her an open-palm slap across the face, making a loud noise but again not hurting her. "Oh, fuck, yes, what, bitch?"

"Yes, sir."

"That's better."

Holden found another small clit stimulator that attached to a fingertip. He slipped it on his right hand. With his left, he removed the clothespin attached to her clit. Paige jerked and thrust her hips as the blood rushed to the area. It felt like a thousand needles were running through her clit.

Holden gave her a couple of seconds to get over the pain. Then he turned on the fingertip device and pressed it hard against her swollen clitoris. He moved it around as he would if he were simply fingering her. The bigger toy inside her continued to do its thing. He felt the familiar signs of her orgasm growing.

She wanted him to fuck her, but knew she was helpless to do anything about it. The vibrators were a tease at best. Despite her building orgasm, she knew they wouldn't be enough.

Holden fingered her faster. He reached up and choked her again. Paige went silent as she fought for air. He knew she was close. He took his hand off her clit and reached for the vibrator inside her, twisting it so she felt it hit every wall of her pussy. Then he yanked it out of her, knocking two clothespins off in the process. At the same time, he let go of her throat. The many feelings rushing through her body cumulated into her second orgasm of the day.

Holden, proud of himself, lay down with his face near hers. He hugged her. Though she wanted to reciprocate, she wasn't able to. He kissed her and she kissed him back just as hard. "I love you," they said at the same time.

Holden positioned himself between her legs again and removed the clothespins one after another. Each one made Paige jump. She was in awe at the number of clips that were attached to her. She felt a weird rush come over her as Holden continued to remove the pins. After getting the last one off her pussy, he removed the two remaining pins from her nipples.

Paige let out a deep moan and trembled as a smaller orgasm rushed through her body. It surprised them both. Paige giggled. Holden was surprised by her reaction to derogatory talk and pain. It was information he would keep in his back pocket for another day.

Holden untied Paige, starting with her feet. She wanted to be untied and he was taking a painfully long time. He was looking back at her, so she was well aware of his action. Finally he released her last hand. Unexpectedly, Paige pulled his hair, forcing him to the bed. She jumped on him, legs straddled. She leaned in and passionately kissed him: lips, cheeks, face, and ear. "How long did you think I was going to let you get away without fucking me?"

"As long as I had you tied up?"

"Well, I'm untied now. Wait a minute …"

She dragged Holden into the position she had been lying in, grabbed the ropes, and, learning from Holden, quickly had all four of his limbs secured. "Now, what am I going to do with you?" she asked as she stood up, "I think someone needs a lesson in manners, tying me up like that." She picked up her riding crop. "This is more like it."

She whipped him across the face. Again, it was all sound and theatrics, but the very slight sting did arouse him. She straddled him again. His cock felt the leather of her crotchless panties and a hint of heat radiating from her pussy. She guided his cock towards the slit. At the last second, she pushed it away. "You wish."

Reaching between her legs, she let her fingers slide up her wet cunt. She raised them to Holden's lips. "See what you're missing?"

Holden gladly licked her fingers. She tasted great. He really wanted to bury his face in her, but he was at her mercy.

"What to do with you?" She contemplated. Holden intently watched her. "What're you looking at?" she asked him. He remained silent. "I have just the thing for nosey boys like you," she said. She found a blindfold and secured it to his face. She warned him that if he wasn't careful, the ball gag was next. Holden kept quiet.

Paige knelt beside Holden, thinking about what she could do. She was happy Holden had set the bar with dirty talk and aggressiveness. It was her turn to push the envelope. She had often fantasized about a day like this, when anything went and she was in complete control, but now that it was happening, she wasn't sure what to do.

Holden felt the bed shake as she moved. It bounced up when Paige jumped off. He heard the door open and close and knew she had left. After a couple of minutes, he heard the door reopen. Footsteps got closer to the bed. He heard a sound like a metal ball banging around in a tin can. He wondered if she was about to spray-paint him. He knew he wouldn't have to wait long to find out.

The next sound was the familiar *woosh* that only a can of whipped cream could make. She sprayed a heart on his chest, a line up his hard cock, and a small dab in his shaved pubic area, like the cherry on top. Holden felt the sugary topping against his skin. It slowly slid down his cock – a new sensation, one he knew he would really enjoy. He heard the can drop to the floor and felt Paige's weight shift as she searched for a comfortable position.

Paige looked down at Holden, wondering where to start. The whipped cream sliding off his cock decided for her; that was as good a place as any. She lay down between his legs, making sure the camera could watch her suck him like a porn star. She put her tongue on the base of his cock and ran it up the full length, licking up as much of the whipped cream as possible.

When she got to the tip of his cock, she swallowed the mouthful of cream, then she put her lips around his head and took his length in her mouth. She let her tongue dance on his shaft, getting all the sticky cream off of him. Holden reacted positively to Paige's hot mouth on his cock.

Satisfied his cock was as clean as she was going to get it, she let it slide out of her mouth. She kept it under control so it wouldn't slap against his stomach and ruin the dab of whipped cream on his pubic area. Her hand stroked his cock a couple of times. She couldn't help herself; she loved it and didn't want to let it go. She wanted to touch it, lick it, and fuck it. She knew that she could at any time, but there was a long way to go before she would let herself.

She knelt beside Holden and licked the heart off his chest, loving the way he responded to her touch. Even though she wasn't touching anything one would consider sexual, it was an intensely erotic moment. It took her several minutes to get the heart off him.

She thought she'd share the whipped topping with Holden. She grabbed the can and lay down, ensuring the camera had a good view of her spreading legs. She sprayed a small line of cream on her pussy. She carefully positioned herself over Holden's head until she could feel his breath on her, and then gave him the order to lick.

Holden tilted his head back, stuck out his tongue, and lapped up every bit of the whipped cream. He really wanted to squeeze her ass and force her hips onto his face so he could get deep inside her, but he was unable. The frustration was part of the build-up and something he had to endure.

Paige wanted to sit back and let him lick her, but she knew she had to seek her revenge. She gripped his cock by the base and squeezed firmly as she moved it out of her way. Leaning down, she opened her mouth and put her lips around the gob of cream, taking most of it in her mouth. She licked the whole area clean, not letting go of his cock. She forced his member around as roughly as she could, abusing and punishing it. Holden could feel the force on his cock. He was happy she'd stopped treating it like a china doll, but he was too involved in licking Paige's cunt to fully focus on what she was doing to him.

After Holden was licked clean, she sat up, stared at the camera, and gave her clit a quick tickle. Confident that Holden had cleaned her off well, she raised her left leg and swung it over his head. Holden wasn't nearly done tasting his lover, but again the situation was beyond his control.

Paige figured it was time for another exploration of the contents of the tickle trunk. She wasn't sure what she wanted to use on him. She finally decided that her focus was going to be his ass, so she selected a thick lube, pressed the tube against his ass, and squeezed.

Holden jumped as he felt her finger penetrate him. Her fingernail scratched him a bit, but remembering the ball gag threat, he remained silent.

Paige brought out a long cord of anal beads. She pressed the first and smallest ball against his hole and forced it into him. She was fascinated as she watched them disappear inside him. Bead after bead went in. Each was bigger than the last, making the final beads difficult to press into him. Holden wondered how much more he could take. She pushed as hard as she could until all that remained outside him was a string with a finger loop on the end. "Do you like that?"

"Oh yeah," Holden said.

"What did I say about you talking?" Paige said sternly. She picked up the ball gag, forced it into Holden's mouth, and tied it behind his head. "That's what you get, slut."

Holden loved the way she was talking to him. It was so out of character for what he knew of her. It was as if he were with a different girl. Since he couldn't see her, she very well could have been.

Paige wondered what else she could do. She saw the bag of clothespins and figured he should experience them as well. She placed them on each of his nipples. She clipped one on each of his penis piercings. They didn't cause him pain, but the slight pinch made him well aware of what she was doing.

Holden could feel Paige moving around again. She took the camera off the tripod and started filming his bound ankles. She moved the camera up his body, a couple of inches off his skin. She made sure his cock, the clothespins, the blindfold, and ball gag were all captured. "This is what happens when you don't listen to me," she said into the microphone.

She then rested her head by his penis. Putting the camera on the bed, she used the covers to angle it up to her face. She talked to the camera in a whisper so Holden would only be able to hear what she had said during the playback.

After she was done speaking, she kissed his head and put the camera back on the tripod, ensuring it was repositioned to see everything she was doing. She lay down so her head was by his waist, her leg resting against his arm. He could feel the rough texture of her boot and knew her pussy and ass were close, yet so far away.

Paige grabbed the same finger-mounted clit stimulator Holden had used on her and turned it on high. She slid it onto her middle finger and wrapped her fingers around his cock. Each finger fit perfectly around the well-spaced clothespins.

She jerked him off. Her grip was firm, and the jaws of the clothespins pulled at his skin. Holden loved the vibrator on his cock. Every time he moved, the anal beads rubbed his prostate, heightening all sensations.

Paige stopped, which disappointed Holden. He really wanted to come. She sensed he was close, so she kissed the tip of his cock, licking all the pre-come dripping from him. She selected a urethral sound, the skinniest one she had. She turned off the vibrator and took it from her finger. She seductively coated the sound in lube before she very slowly, she slid the sound inside him.

Holden had always wanted to experience a sound, but until that moment, he never had. It felt much better than he expected. Paige said, "We don't want you making a mess, now, do we?" She pressed the sound as deeply into him as she could comfortably get it. Since she had no experience with sounds either, she asked, "Is that OK? If it is, nod yes."

Holden nodded.

"Does it hurt at all?"

Holden shook his head.

"Good." She turned her focus back to his cock. She put the fingertip vibrator on her left hand this time. Instead of pressing it against his shaft, she pressed it hard against his scrotum, between his testicles. The vibration radiated through the beads in his ass and directly to his prostate. To increase the intensity, Paige jerked him off with so much force that it felt like she was going to rip his cock off. She used the tip of her tongue to push the sound back into him each time it slid out.

Although Holden was incapable of talking, his body thrashed. She felt his balls tighten and knew he was seconds from orgasm. She put her lips over the head of his cock and used her tongue to keep the sound in place. The finger loop still protruding from his ass. *Should I?* she wondered. Not having much time, she decided to go for it.

She put her index finger in the loop and pulled hard, like she was starting a lawnmower. The overstimulation of his prostate was enough to start Holden's orgasm. She kept her mouth over his cock, amazed and disappointed that she didn't taste even a drop. Once his orgasm subsided, she unwrapped her lips and turned the vibrator off. Not sure what to expect, she slid the sound out of his still-erect cock.

Nothing happened. The only evidence of his orgasm was a small trace of come at the end of the tool. She brought it to her mouth and licked it like a thin Popsicle. She gripped his cock again, giving it a couple of tugs, wondering where the come had gone.

Giving up the search, she turned around and removed the ball gag and blindfold. She left his arms and legs restrained. "Where's your come?"

"I don't know. I thought you had it." He laughed. They both looked at his cock like it was going to give them the answer.

"Well, there is only one way to find out." Paige swung her leg over Holden's head, allowing him to see her perfect ass. He wanted to bite it or spank it, but he couldn't. She stopped so her pussy was pressed against his chest, just out of tongue reach. She unclipped the clothespins from his nipples and from his cock.

Holden realized what Paige had talked about: the blood returning to his flesh tickled, burned, and stung. All in all, it was very uncomfortable, yet he didn't dislike it.

Paige was happy to see Holden was still hard, because she was on a mission to find out where his come was. She lowered herself on him in a reverse cowgirl position. She grabbed the finger vibrator and turned it back on. As she began to fuck Holden, making sure the camera could see his entire length penetrating her, she pressed the vibrator against her clit. Sometimes she moved it between herself and Holden's cock and balls.

Holden responded well to the toy. He was happy he could see now, because he loved watching her fuck him, especially in that position. He could see his cock disappear and reappear, driving him wild.

Paige too was sexually overcharged. Having the camera watch her fuck felt like a voyeur watching them from the shadows. She was ready to orgasm yet again.

Holden was also ready to explode. He was overfilled with come and needed to release it upon the world.

Paige leaned back, which caused her hair to tickle his chest. She fought to keep the vibrator on her clit as long as possible before she began to orgasm. She collapsed onto Holden. Her pussy contracting in the new body position forced his cock to slip out of her. Since the gears of orgasm were already set in motion, Holden came with all the pressure of a fountain. A long, thick stream of come splattered up her entire body, contrasting against her black teddy. "Oh, there's that come we were looking for."

"And then some," he added.

Paige remained motionless for several minutes. "Wow" was all she could mutter. Holden remained quiet. "Oh crap," Paige said and spun around. As she lay flat on him, the come that had been solely on her teddy was smeared against his chest. She stared directly into his eyes and smiled, as she so often did.

"Nice," he said.

She untied his arms and legs, then stood up to and turned off the camera. She took off her bulky boots. Holden watched intently as she slowly slid the fishnet stockings off her long, well-defined legs. Bending to tease him, she showed him her ass as she pulled the stockings off her feet. She gazed deep into Holden's eyes as her fishnetted arms reached up to the satin bows of her teddy, slowly untying each. Pushing the come-soaked fabric and crotchless panties to the floor, she declared that she needed a shower.

Holden thought that was a great idea. He said he was going to clean up the room and would join her in the shower. She happily agreed.

While Paige was in the shower, Holden thoroughly cleaned all the toys then put them back into Paige's not so forbidden tickle trunk, took the camera off the tripod, and put the tripod back in the closet. He took the camera to their big-screen TV and connected it via the video ports. Once it was ready to be watched, he paused the playback and joined Paige in the shower.

Exhausted as they were from their afternoon sexcapades, the shower was uneventful. Paige helped wash Holden to make sure all the whipped cream was gone. Holden rubbed his soapy hands all over Paige's breasts and ass. But mostly they got down to the business of cleaning themselves.

With the shower off, the pair towelled dry and dressed in their comfiest clothes. In the living room, Paige laughed as she saw herself naked on the bed and Holden's back facing the camera. "Wait, I'll make popcorn."

She threw the bag into the microwave, took a couple of beers from the fridge, dumped the popcorn into a bowl, and joined Holden on the couch. He accepted his beer, and they touched the long necks together to toast their porn debut. He hit Play.

For the next two hours, they watched themselves on the big screen in surround sound. They laughed at how funny they were. At the time they'd thought they were as good as professional porn stars, but the replay showed quite a different story.

Paige watched in amazement as Holden clipped all the clothespins on her. It hadn't hurt at the time, but watching it made Paige shudder with retroactive pain. Holden gave her a glance when he saw the heart on his chest. Paige smiled back at him and snuggled closer. Holden put his arm around her. Beer in hand, he reflected on how happy he was and how much he loved Paige.

Holden turned away in embarrassment as he watched the camera run up his body. He was suitably impressed at how big his manhood appeared when Paige held the camera between his legs. They watched her suck him. He finally heard what Paige had whispered to the camera: "I love his cock. Don't tell him this, but I can't get enough of it. I could suck it all day every day if he would let me." Paige put her hands over her face, trying to hide her embarrassment.

"Is that right?" Holden teased.

"Shut up and watch the TV," she responded.

Finally the screen went black. They each took a drink of beer and laughed. "We'll keep that for a cold, rainy day," Holden said.

"OK, but don't be having your little friends here watching it without me."

"Never."

"Yeah, right." She laughed.

They watched a bit more TV before Paige said she had to go to bed. She had to get up early for her first day back to university. She also was going to continue to work for the roller hockey team. To get evening hours, she would have to change departments. Holden felt bad for her, but it was her choice to continue working.

—m—

The alarm went off, telling them both it was time to get up and start their day. Holden drove his university girl to school. He was a bit disappointed she wasn't wearing the traditional schoolgirl uniform. She said she would for him another time.

When Holden made it home from work, he knew Paige would just be getting out of school and heading to work. He felt bad for her as he sank into the couch, turned on his video games and cracked a beer. It would be a couple of hours before she got home.

Holden finally heard her keys hit the door. Paige looked tired as Holden greeted her and gave her a hug and a kiss. He told her he had a surprise for her. Paige objected, saying she'd had a long, hard day and wanted to veg on the couch.

But Holden stopped her from going into the living room. Instead, he guided her to the bathroom, where he had a hot bubble bath waiting for her. He kissed her and gave her time to get undressed.

He returned a couple of minutes later with a glass of wine. Paige was already fully submerged in the tub, almost invisible among the bubbles that were overflowing the sides. Holden reached into the tub, which caused water to soak his sleeve. He leaned in and kissed her deeply as he handed her the glass of wine.

Paige gratefully accepted the drink. She leaned her head back into the water. She had the most beautiful smile on her face, which made Holden extremely happy. She sipped her wine and drifted off into her own world. Holden told her to relax and take her time; dinner would be ready in an hour.

Paige closed her eyes as he left the bathroom. She didn't notice the amazingly comfortable new bathrobe hanging behind the bathroom door. Nor did she notice that Holden took all her clothes, with the exception of her panties, with him when he left.

An hour passed. Paige came out of the bathroom, wearing the thick white bathrobe. Her hair was slicked back and still wet. With a smile she asked Holden what had happened to her clothes. Holden casually said he had put them in the wash and told her to take a seat at the table because dinner was ready. "Oh, the table, like grownups." Paige laughed. Their normal dinners consisted of sitting at a fold-up living room table while they watched TV.

Paige took a seat at the large dinner table, which was almost never used except for mail, keys, and other odd household items. Holden had bought a beautiful flower arrangement on his way home from work, which he used as the centrepiece. He also had two very large candles lit on the table.

Paige sat down with one foot on the chair. She innocently gave Holden a quick glimpse of her panties. Holden was getting aroused but controlled himself while they ate. Paige told Holden about her classes, professors, classmates, and new job. Holden told her about his day and about the video games he'd played after work.

After dinner, they moved to the couch. Holden sat on one end. Paige lay down and put her feet up on Holden as they started to watch a movie Holden had rented. He rubbed her feet and found he was looking at Paige more than he was watching the movie. Her robe gapped open, and he could see the outline of her breast. Once again he had to control the passion he was feeling for her at that moment. His self-control was getting harder and harder to maintain.

Paige complained about tension in her shoulders. Taking the hint, Holden sat on the back of the couch. She settled between his legs and lowered the robe to her waist. Holden gave her a deep massage, which caused Paige to get aroused as well. She twisted her head around to kiss Holden, but he gently pushed her chin forward, telling her, "Not yet."

After a very long shoulder massage, Holden asked Paige if she wanted a full-body massage. Without answering him, she jumped up, grabbed Holden by the hand, and led him to the bedroom. She dived on the bed and in one quick motion ripped off her panties. She playfully threw them at Holden as he ran through the open door.

Holden reached into the nightstand drawer, where they kept some of their toys. "Oh, what you gonna do?" Paige asked hopefully. Holden pulled out the baby oil and said he was only going to give her a massage. She huffed and rolled over on her stomach.

Holden straddled her bum and poured the oil over her back. She tensed as the cold oil hit her warm skin. Holden's hands slid magically over her body, touching her in all the right places. He adjusted the pressure and intensity before he slid two fingers down her spine. His thumbs dug deeply into the small of her back. His body was positioned just below her gorgeous ass. He leaned over, and she could feel his chest on her ass. She tried to spread her legs, but his legs stopped her.

Holden took off his T-shirt and leaned even further down. He rubbed her back, shoulders, and arms right down to her wrists. She could feel his naked chest on her back. He kissed Paige's ear, and she told him she wanted him inside her. Holden again told her not yet. He worked his way down her body. His oily hands slid down her ass cheeks and rubbed each leg. Paige spread her legs slightly, and he could see her glistening pussy. He fought the urge to lean in and taste her. He thoroughly rubbed each leg, thigh, calf, and foot.

Finally Paige rolled over and commanded him to kiss her. Holden slowly slid his body up hers. His hand grazed her pussy and tits as he did. Holden then placed one hand behind her neck, firmly but gently gripped it, leaned in, and kissed her passionately. With the previous day's events still very fresh in their minds, they both were already close to orgasm.

Paige forced Holden on his back, fumbled at his belt buckle, and pulled his pants off, leaving his boxers on. Paige rubbed her hand over his boxers. Then she did something Holden loved. She slowly folded his boxers down, exposing his dick. He felt vulnerable, but not in the same way as the day before.

Paige took one hard lick up his shaft. Before she had a chance to take him deep into her mouth, Holden reached for her hair and pulled her back up to him. "No," he said, "today is all about you."

He kissed her, then slowly twisted around until he settled on top of her. He paused so she could feel the head of his cock just touching her pussy. She wanted him inside her so badly. Holden wanted to be inside her as well, but paused to build anticipation, making her want it even more. Seeing the eagerness in her eyes, Holden slid his cock inside her. She could feel every millimetre. It seemed to take forever, but Holden was very careful not to go fast.

Finally his whole length penetrated her. He paused again to feel her pussy contract. He kissed her neck and gently squeezed her breast. Then he slowly pulled his cock out again. She felt each piercing touching the walls of her pussy and lips as they slid out of her. She had felt it many times before, but never this slowly or with such clarity.

She wanted him to fuck her fast and hard, but Holden refused. He repeated the move several times; it took five minutes to get three full thrusts into her. He made sure he forced his cock in as deeply as possible. They were both getting worked up. He fucked her faster – only slightly faster though. Her nails dug deep into his back as she dragged them down his flesh, trying to force him to fuck her faster. He could tell the sensation of his cock slowly penetrating her was driving her wild, just as wild as it was making him.

With a quick, hard bite of her neck, Holden thrust his cock deep. Her nails dug more harshly into his back, drawing blood as she felt his come shoot inside her. The sensations were enough for Paige. Her orgasm shuddered through her body.

Holden collapsed onto Paige, his sweaty body pressed firmly against hers. They kissed passionately as Holden ran his fingers through her hair and looked into her eyes. He was falling deeper in love with her with every passing day.

She could feel his once-mighty cock get smaller as the blood rushed out of it into other vital organs. Holden's hand ran up her thigh and over her soaked pussy. He grazed her clit with just enough force to make her jump. He continued to pull his hand over her belly, her breast, and her lips. Paige kissed the finger that was on her mouth. She used her tongue to taste what he had tasted.

Holden pulled the comforter over them as they fell asleep. They woke up to the alarm the next morning, holding each other tightly.

CHAPTER 9

The wind blew through the car as Holden manoeuvred it down the road. It was a perfect Sunday for a lazy drive up the coast. Holden threw the GPS in the backseat. Paige plugged in her MP3 player. They decided to drive up the highway for a few hours to explore as many side roads as they could.

The BMW twisted and turned down the highway as Holden and Paige took in the sights. Paige reached deep into her purse and pulled out a couple of soft drinks and a bag of chips. They snacked and talked, mostly about passing motorists and the brilliant scenery. "It's like we're living in a postcard," Paige remarked. Holden agreed with her.

The mountains were still snow-covered, but the rain and chilly BC winter had finally passed. Spring was in the air, and the couple wanted to take advantage of the beautiful weekend weather. Holden was going away on yet another business trip that coming Monday morning, so they wanted to spend as much time together as possible. Paige was sad but she was getting used to having him gone so often.

The kilometres clicked by on the odometer, and the hours clicked by on the clock. Holden and Paige found themselves far up the coast. The city was well in their rear-view mirror. Only the odd gas station indicated signs of life in that remote part of the province.

They decided it was a good time to veer off the highway and go exploring on back roads. Holden flipped the blinker and turned off the main highway, heading west on a secondary road. They weren't sure where they were or where they were going; all they knew was the ocean was west.

As Holden drove the car around corner after corner, he picked up speed. After not seeing another car or house for twenty minutes, he felt it was safe enough, even though he wasn't familiar with the roads.

As the roar of the engine's RPMs vibrated through the car, Paige's heart raced. She swayed with each corner. The trees became a blur as they whizzed past. Holden went faster and faster. The tires squealed as they struggled to grip the pavement.

Holden was motivated by Paige's excitement for speed. He downshifted and turned the car to the right around a sharp corner, upshifting on the roll-out and accelerating. The car caught air over a bump, giving them a floating sensation in their stomachs.

The road opened up to a long, straight stretch. The forest also broke and turned into fields on either side. Holden took advantage of the open road and quickly upshifted, pushing the classic car's engine to the limit. Paige grabbed the holy-shit handle on the door as she braced herself against the opposing force of the car.

Before Holden entered the corner at the end of the straight stretch, he caught a glimpse of headlights floating over the same bump he had just passed over. Worried it might be a cop, he throttled back a bit. Paige was unaware of the company and didn't really notice the car slowing. She was drinking in as much of the passing scenery as possible, as well as reading signs of upcoming tourist spots.

As Holden continued to drive, he kept his eye on the rear-view mirror to see if he could catch another glimpse of the trailing car. If he didn't see it after a few more turns, he would feel confident the car wasn't chasing him and could again speed up. Just as he exited the next turn, he got a mirrorful of headlights. He squinted to get a better look at the car that was now on his bumper. It was a new convertible Mustang. The driver was a young man. Like Holden, he had a beautiful young woman in the passenger seat.

Holden saw the driver's frustration when he pulled up on the slower Holden. Relieved it wasn't the police, Holden put his foot to the floor. The Mustang kept pace with him through every turn. Confident his BMW could easily outmanoeuvre the much newer North American car, Holden toyed with his young challenger. He let his car roll out of the corners before accelerating, allowing the less agile Mustang to keep on his tail.

Paige clued in to what was happening and cheered Holden on. She acted as his spotter. Holden's heart started racing only after seeing Paige's intense reaction to the car race. The girl in the passenger's seat of the other car was equally excited. The drivers did their best to remain focused.

Holden easily kept the Mustang at bay in the tight corners, but as the road opened up for another lengthy straight stretch, the Mustang got a jump on Holden and pulled up beside him. The roar of the powerful American engine drowned out the quieter but just as powerful BMW engine. Even Holden had to admit the sound of raw power got his blood flowing.

Paige leaned forward, staring into the car next to theirs. The female passenger looked back. The two drivers glanced over at each other as well, but remained focused on keeping their cars on the road. Paige licked her lips seductively at the girl. The girl countered Paige's taunting by kneeling in her seat and flashing Paige.

Holden nearly lost control of his car when he caught a glimpse of the bare breasts next to him. His momentary lapse almost allowed the Mustang to overtake him, but he managed to stay door to door as they entered a gentle left turn. Because the turn was to the left, it gave Holden's opponent the inside lane. But the BMW's greater cornering ability still gave Holden the edge through the turn.

As the Mustang's driver let off on the gas to hold the car on the inside, Holden kept his foot pressed to the floor and roared past. Paige, completely wrapped up in the moment, gave the female in the other car the finger as they passed. The girl reciprocated.

As the cars exited the corner, Holden caught a glimpse of a van coming towards them. The Mustang's driver had quick reflexes and powered his car inches behind Holden's bumper, allowing the van to safely pass, its horn blaring. Holden felt his legs tingle with the close call, and Paige yelled with excitement. They could only imagine that the other two were as jacked up, if not more so.

The other driver wasn't happy on Holden's bumper. He pulled out to pass again before they entered a tighter right-hand turn. Both drivers underestimated the turn. The Mustang driver knew he had no chance on the outside of the European sports car, so he pulled in behind Holden again.

Through the centre of the turn, Holden felt the back end of the car slide out after losing traction on sand. Worried that the Mustang, which was only inches off his bumper, wouldn't be able to react quickly enough to avoid a collision, Holden kept his foot on the gas as he drifted through the turn. All four tires squealed, and smoke poured out of the rear wheel wells.

As the car straightened out, Holden checked his mirrors. Not only had he gained on the Mustang, but it was drifting through the corner as well. Holden had to resist watching. All he heard was Paige next to him, her eyes fixed on the passenger-side mirror. "That was fucking cool!"

Her fingers were still clenching the holy-shit handle. Her leg bounced as her nerves got the best of her. She was quite confident in Holden's driving abilities, but she was scared of the unpredictable road conditions. She wasn't going to tell Holden to slow down, because her adrenaline had taken over her and she wanted more. She liked to be scared. It awakened senses in her that were rarely touched.

Holden shucked off the most recent close call and kept his foot on the gas. He had a big lead on the Mustang, but that hard charger was pushing his car to its limits in an attempt to catch the BMW and impress his girlfriend. Holden ducked into yet another corner and had to hit the brakes hard for a much slower car in his lane. When it was as safe – or as safe as possible on the windy road – he downshifted and easily passed the obstruction.

The Mustang's timing was perfect as it came around the corner. The driver noticed the slower car, saw Holden passing it, and kept on the gas, easily following Holden around the car. He was again only inches away from Holden's bumper.

Paige's eyes were glued to the side mirror, watching the other racer. The engines continued to roar, tires were squealing, and the smell of burning rubber filled the BMW. Paige pulled up her shirt and ran her fingers over her stomach. Holden noticed but tried not to stare at Paige getting worked up.

As they drove through corner after corner, Holden opened up on the Mustang until it was almost out of sight. After yet another very tight turn, Holden shifted down to kill momentum and to get the most power out of the engine. When the car straightened out, he once again slammed on the gas and worked his way through the gears. The BMW caught some air before the end of the corner, causing it to lose traction momentarily. It regained its grip quickly when the tires once again made contact with the pavement.

The momentary loss of control spooked Holden and Paige. Holden decided that the fun was up and things were getting too dangerous. He wasn't worried about his own safety, but he would never forgive himself if anything were to happen to Paige.

As he was about to pull over and concede the race, he saw the Mustang come speeding around the corner and over the same bump, catching air in the same spot he had. But instead of an uneventful landing, the heavier Mustang's rear end had too much momentum and passed the front end. Holden and Paige could only watch in horror as the car disappeared into cloud of smoke.

Holden stopped in case the other car needed help. But when the smoke dissipated, Holden and Paige could see the headlights of the Mustang stopped in the middle of the road. The car was angled about forty-five degrees off centre. Holden stayed put as the driver of the Mustang selected a gear and slowly rolled towards the BMW. Holden and Paige were curious to meet the other couple but were nervous as well, unsure how they would react. The recent road rage horrors in the news had them uneasy.

The convertible pulled up alongside Holden. The driver yelled over, "That was intense, awesome."

"Hell yeah!" Holden shouted back. "You guys all right? That was a hell of a spin."

"Yeah, we're good. I think we're going to take it easy from here on in, though. Great driving."

"You too," Holden replied.

The young driver waved and allowed Holden to take the lead. Just as Holden released the clutch, he and Paige looked over again at the Mustang. The girl was kneeling on her seat, her shirt up over her head. This time Holden was in a much better position to see the show. He and Paige laughed as they drove off. Paige waved back, this time much more politely than the last.

"Wow, that *was* intense," Paige said.

"Yup. How are you doing? Are you OK?" Holden asked.

"Oh yeah, I'm good." Paige gently fanned herself with her hand.

As Holden drove off, the Mustang quickly disappeared from the rear-view mirror. He and Paige were once again alone on the road.

The drive turned into a lazy Sunday cruise through the countryside. As the air cooled, the smell of the ocean filled the car, and they knew they were close. They took a couple more corners and found themselves at a T intersection. They could see the ocean peeking through a patch of trees, but they didn't know the best way to get to it.

Taking a chance, Holden turned the car left. They drove less than a kilometre before they found a trail just big enough for a car. Holden cringed as he heard the sound of branches dragging along the side of his pride and joy. He continued driving forward despite the teeth-clenching sound.

After only a few minutes, the trees opened up and they found themselves in a clearing with a picnic table. They couldn't have imagined a more perfect spot. With the car parked, they popped out and unpacked their provisions. Even though there was a perfectly good picnic table, Paige spread out a red-and-white chequered tablecloth on the ground where the grass met the beach sand. Holden questioned her. Paige said that when she started the day, she had pictured sitting on the grass next to the ocean, and nothing was going to change that. Holden knew better than to question her when she had her mind made up, so he smiled and unloaded the cooler.

The night before, they had bought a precooked chicken from the grocery store, as well as a couple varieties of salads. Paige pulled out paper plates and plastic utensils as Holden grabbed the bottle of white wine and the corkscrew he had tossed into the cooler. The cork popped out. They giggled at the sudden noise. It was very apparent they were both still riding the adrenaline rush from the race.

Neither spoke much as they ate. They spent time gazing off into the ocean and staring at each other and at the clouds. The sounds of the waves crashing onto the beach mere feet from them was hypnotic.

Paige was the first to break the trance. "You never did tell me the dream you had about your masseuse that had you so worked up."

Holden laughed. "It wasn't just about her. You were very much involved." Holden said. He told her his very vivid dream.

Paige listened intently to Holden's every word as he described the fantasy in painstaking detail. She recalled the night, the room, the sounds and the smells. Paige stood up, took Holden by the shirt, and dragged him to the picnic table, listening all the while. She pushed him down on the table, and Holden adjusted himself so he was lying in the middle.

Paige opened the button on Holden's shorts, unzipped the fly, reached into his boxers, and pulled out his flaccid cock. She used her mouth to get Holden hard. He finally got to the point of the story where the female masseuse began riding him. Paige acted out the story as he spoke. She hiked up her thin sundress and placed her knees on either side of Holden's legs. Holden kept explaining his dream as Paige reached for Holden's exposed cock. She pushed his penis against her panties, which made Holden pause his story. Paige looked back up at him and smiled as she said, "Was it something like this?"

She pulled her panties to one side and wrapped her hand around his thick meat. She raised her body an inch over Holden's full length. Using her hand, she guided his cock into her well-lubricated pussy. Both sighed very pleasurable sighs as they became one again.

Holden resumed his story, and Paige continued acting it out as best she could. Instead of ripping her dress – the only clothing she had with her – she let the straps fall off her silky shoulders. She pushed the dress down over her chest and reached back to unclasp her bra before she tossed it carelessly to the side. Her breasts were highlighted in the hot spring sun.

As Paige took Holden's cock deep inside her, she gazed into the surf. She was now lost between the scenery and Holden's words as she let the sun warm her body. Her mind was torn between so many different images: the adrenaline of the race, the spectacular scenery, Holden's dream, and having the man she loved inside her as she was fucked outside, aware of the possibility that someone might catch them at any minute. She felt a very intense pleasure. She wasn't even close to orgasm, but her pussy was very sensitive. She felt a tingling sensation that was foreign to her, making her legs weaker by the minute.

Holden was now finished with his story, so he watched Paige. Paige's hips rhythmically ground onto Holden. She was still focused on the nearby ocean. She pulled her sundress over her head and carelessly tossed it on the ground by her bra. She continued to work over Holden. As during dinner, they didn't exchange any words. The normally vocal Paige remained silent.

Holden too kept his normal enthusiasm low-key because he was worried that he would ruin Paige's moment. He had never seen Paige so distant yet so focused, and he didn't want to come, not yet.

Waves from a passing cruise ship thundered into the beach. Paige synched her thrusts with the beat of the waves; as they got faster, so did she. She spread her legs to get lower onto his cock. She leaned her head back, causing her long hair to tickle his legs. She didn't move.

Holden was about to speak when he felt a deep, long shiver course through her entire body. She shook her head and refocused on Holden. "Wow" was all she said before she rolled over onto the tabletop and snuggled next to Holden. She lightly caressed his still-hard cock. "Oh, you didn't finish yet?"

"Nope," he said with a smile. "Did you?"

"I don't know what I did. It wasn't an orgasm, but it was very intense."

Holden rolled off the picnic table and stood at the end. He put his hands on Paige's thighs and twisted her around so she was lying on her stomach. Paige instinctively knew what Holden wanted, so she got up on her hands and knees. Holden grabbed the waistband of her panties and pulled them over her ass and past her knees. He then placed his strong hands firmly on her ass checks and spread them apart.

He lowered his head and gently kissed her bum, her asshole, and her freshly fucked pussy. Spreading her cheeks even wider, he extended his tongue and took a long, hard lick of her pussy. He slid his tongue up to her asshole. His tongue danced around her hole, getting deeper and deeper.

She leaned forward to rest on her shoulder. Her free hand appeared between her legs, and she violently rubbed her clit. He knew she was ready to orgasm, and he wanted to finish the job for her. He wasn't as worried about himself because he knew he could take care of that later.

Her hand worked faster and harder. Holden tried to match the pace, but his tongue was getting tired and sore from working away in her tight button. Just as he thought she was going to orgasm, he moved his mouth down to her wet pussy and licked everything that was splashing out of her. As she had earlier, she stopped and rolled over, kicking her leg over Holden's head. "Wow," she said again.

"What happened?" Holden asked.

"I don't know. I feel like I'm having an orgasm, but I don't, ya know?"

"No, no, I don't." Holden laughed. "You're fucked up."

Paige laughed. Then her eyes widened. "Let's go for a swim!"

"Not only no, but *hell* no. It'll be freezing."

"Oh, you big baby," Paige said as she jumped up and ran down the beach.

Holden couldn't do anything but shake his head as he watched as Paige run and jump into the ocean. Her head disappeared under the water and reappeared with a shriek. Holden laughed as he saw Paige run out of the water twice as fast as she had run into it. He found it incredibly sexy watching her naked body wiggle in a full sprint to the car.

He casually walked to the car and opened the door for her to dive in. He reached over her and started the ignition. He cranked the climate control to fully hot. He also clicked on her seat warmer.

After closing the car door to let his crazy girlfriend warm up, he went back to where they had their picnic set up and cleaned the area, throwing everything in the trunk. He made sure to pick up all their clothes and put them into the backseat.

Paige was shivering on the front seat, cuddled up in the foetal position. Holden covered her with the blanket they had had their picnic on. It wasn't very thick, but it was all they had. He couldn't help but giggle at his wet, naked girlfriend. She looked at him with big, sad eyes. "Told you it was cold," he reminded her. She signalled *fuck off* with her eyes, but she didn't say anything. Holden began the drive home.

They took their time. The telephone poles no longer appeared to be closely spaced picket fence. Something on the shoulder of the road caught Holden's attention. When he checked over his shoulder, he saw Paige's dress and panties on the backseat. Just the sight of her clothes made him hard.

He then looked at her asleep under the blanket, forgetting all about whatever it had been that caught his attention in the first place. He saw she was no longer shivering, so he turned down the heat and the fan. It was feeling way too much like a sauna for his liking.

Paige woke up halfway home. She too was feeling the effects of the heat, mostly because Holden had forgotten to turn off her seat warmer. She searched for her clothes in the backseat. First she pulled on her tight white panties. Then she pulled her sundress over her head, leaving her bra on the backseat.

Holden fought to keep his concentration on the road. It had been almost a year since they got together, but Holden still couldn't get enough of Paige. In his eyes, she was getting more beautiful each time he saw her.

Their day finally came to an end. They pulled into their condo parking lot and headed upstairs. The sun had set roughly an hour earlier, and Holden had packing to do. With the start of the roller hockey season only a week away, he had to go to yet another distant meeting so the teams could iron out last-minute problems.

Paige and Holden didn't talk about the upcoming trip very much, Paige knew she would be seeing less of Holden. That prospect made her sad, but she had known what she was getting into before she moved to BC with him.

After they unpacked the car, Paige shed her clothes and crawled into bed. She watched as Holden packed his bags, something he did very quickly now. When he was all done, he undressed and joined Paige in bed. The fresh air and day's activity had them both exhausted, so Holden set the alarm, rolled over, and fell asleep in his lover's arms.

The alarm sounded, which made Holden jump. He made sure the time was right, because it felt like they had just gotten to sleep. Paige let out a cute little hmmpff and told Holden to turn the alarm off and go back to sleep. Holden told her he couldn't because the cab would be there for him in forty-five minutes, and he still needed to shower.

Paige reluctantly let Holden go. As he walked out of the room, she rolled over and closed her eyes. Holden paused a moment and watched her. He then turned and stepped into the shower. He no sooner had his hair lathered than the shower curtain opened. Holden jumped and Paige let out a laugh. She stepped into the tub and put her arms around him. Holden tried to fight her off for half a second or so before he gave in to her advances.

"You thought you were going to go away for an entire week and I wouldn't say goodbye?" she demanded.

"What was I thinking?" Holden replied.

Holden grabbed Paige's ass, picked her up, and pushed her against the cold shower wall. He tilted the showerhead so it was spraying on both of them. Paige wrapped her legs around Holden's thighs as he fucked her. She wrapped her arms around Holden's broad shoulders, giving in to his powerful thrusts.

The hot water splashed over their shoulders and dripped down their bodies. Paige clutched Holden tighter. Her legs flexed, and he could feel she was getting ready to orgasm. That was a good thing, because he too was about to come and he didn't want to leave her high and dry before he left. After hearing a particularly deep moan from Paige, he released his come inside her.

Paige felt his hot semen filling her up. She felt the same deep, intense wave rush through her as she'd experienced at the beach. Again, it wasn't an orgasm.

Holden hated to run off, but the delay in the shower had him behind. He washed himself quickly, towel dried, and got dressed. He no sooner had his shirt buttoned up than his phone rang. It was the cabbie telling him that he had arrived. Holden picked up his suitcase, gave Paige a kiss on the cheek, and ran out the door.

Paige was alone in the condo again. She had a busy week of school ahead of her, and she was happy for the distraction.

Paige got home from school and fumbled through her bag for her keys. Just as she was about to place the key into the lock, she noticed the door was slightly open. It didn't seem right to her. She looked around and quickly dismissed her uncomfortable feelings as craziness. She was missing Holden and didn't like the idea of being in the condo alone.

As Paige moved around the condo, her discomfort grew. Something wasn't right. She wanted to call Holden, but she knew it was nothing more than silly paranoia. She reached for the hallway closet door. As her hand touched the knob, she took a deep breath. She flung open the door and saw nothing. She let out a loud laugh and put the weird feelings behind her once and for all.

As she hung up her jacket, she noticed one of Holden's favourite coats. *Weird, I thought he took that with him,* she thought.

Paige moved more freely about the condo with her newfound sense of security. She didn't have to work that night, so she decided to go for a jog. Stepping into the bedroom, she pulled out her jogging clothes and began to undress.

As she had her shirt over her head, she heard a sound coming from the bedroom closet. She turned quickly, her breasts exposed. She stared long and hard at the closet door, which was hanging open. Letting out a giggle and a sigh of relief, she continued changing. She was embarrassed about her ever-growing paranoia. She intended to tell Holden about her silliness that night on the phone.

She unfastened her belt, the button to her jeans, and her zipper. She reached her thumbs into the waistbands of her jeans and underwear and pulled them down. She no sooner had her pants around her ankles than she heard a much louder bang coming from the closet. Before she had a chance to turn to investigate, she felt a large force slam into her back, knocking her naked body to the ground. She was winded and fought to catch her breath. Before she could regain her composure, she felt a hand cover her mouth and breathe on her neck.

Paige struggled, causing the assailant's grip to tighten. Paige gasped for breath. She felt sharp, cold steel pressing against her throat. She began to cry but stopped, not giving the attacker the satisfaction of seeing her weak. Paige tightened her body to be strong in defiance. "Tough little whore, aren't you?" a deep voice said. "On your knees, bitch."

Paige didn't move, trying to stand her ground. She felt his hand reach into her hair. Forcefully clutching a handful, he pulled her to her knees.

Paige still refused to show any pain. She tried to twist to see what she assumed was going to be her rapist, but was met with a hard pull of her hair. "Do *not* fucking look at me!" the attacker said as he pressed the knife harder against her skin. Keeping his grip on her hair, he leaned in. "We can do this the easy way or the hard way. Which is it going to be, whore?"

Paige angled herself and spit in his direction. She felt a sharp sting across her face. "The hard way it is," the attacker said.

He shoved her head towards the floor. Paige nearly lost her balance but managed to stay on her knees. She felt a bag slide over her head. It was tied around her throat, tight enough to remain in place but loose enough to allow her to breathe, albeit in a laboured fashion. Paige realized the seriousness of her predicament. She became anxious and claustrophobic.

Paige lost her bearings as the attacker grabbed her by the hair and pulled her to her feet. She reached up to clench the man's hand so he didn't pull all her hair out. Paige struggled to get to her feet as the man pulled hard on her hair. He flung her onto the bed as if she were a rag doll.

Paige propped herself up on her knees. She heard a snap, then felt a burning sensation in her jaw. The force of the blow was enough to knock her backwards. Still dazed, she felt the man moving around her. He gripped one of her arms. She panicked as she felt the cold steel of a handcuff attaching to her wrist. He pulled her arm over her head. She heard the hinges of the handcuff again; then the man let go. She tried to move her arm and couldn't. He had apparently fastened the other end to the bedpost. He took her free arm and affixed it to the opposite bedpost.

Unable to move, Paige did her best not to give in and cry. She thought about Holden and hoped he would barge into the room and save her. Her thoughts turned to their happy times together. She did everything she could to take herself out of her current situation.

She felt the man tie rope around both her ankles and secure the ends of the rope to the bedposts. Paige was tightly bound to the bed, completely naked, legs spread. She knew she was helpless to stop the man from violating her.

As she was contemplating all the horrible things that he was about to do to her, he once again leaned in. "Pamplemousse," he said. She heard him stand up and walk out the door. Several minutes passed. Those minutes felt like an eternity. She focused on the word he had whispered to her.

Footsteps approached the door. Paige prayed he had left and a new person was her rescuer. Hope faded as she felt the weight of someone climbing on the bed. She again almost began to cry as she realized that this wasn't help, nor was help likely to come.

Paige felt a hand press against her stomach, up to her tits, and back down to her pussy. "How is it? Nice and wet for me, bitch?" Paige winced but was unable to move. "Now, now, that's a good girl," the assailant said with a laugh.

Paige was unable to see, but she could feel him moving around again. Paige held her breath as she felt something slap across her throat. It was very heavy. She recognized the texture as leather. The man walked around the bed to the opposite side. He pulled the leather strap tight, almost to the point of cutting off her air and circulation. Paige knew she was in a lot of trouble. She let out a squeak. "I can't breathe."

"Not my problem, whore."

Paige was completely helpless – unable to move, talk, or even breathe. Her heart raced even faster as she felt the sharp metal of a knife on her cheek. He moved the blade to the top of her head, then slid it down her forehead, across her eyelid, and over her cheek to her chest. The blade worked across her tits. "Kinda small, but they'll do," the man said harshly. "Let's see what the rest of you is like."

He moved his hand down her stomach to her crotch. The knife poked her thigh. She jumped, but the restraints did their job, keeping her firmly in place. He dropped the knife, but she could feel the cold metal handle against her thigh as a reminder. He moved his hand between her legs and touched her, letting a finger penetrate her. Her pussy was extra sensitive with the blood racing through her body, but there was no way she was going to let him think he was pleasuring her. As his fingers moved around her pussy, she got wetter and wetter. Her attacker felt it. "I knew you were a whore ripe for a fucking," he said. There was a sucking sound. "Tasty little fuck, aren't you? Well, it's my turn to get off now. How do you like that?"

"Fuck you!" was all Paige could muster.

The man became very angry. He took the knife and poked it into the bottom of her chin. "Why do you have to be like that? Just lie back and enjoy."

Paige remained silent. The point of the knife was close to puncturing her.

The man regained his composure and crawled off the bed. Paige could hear him taking off his clothes. She winced as she felt him crawling back onto the bed, this time at the foot, between her legs. She felt his breath on her pussy. Instinctively she tried to close her legs, but she was bound too tightly. She twisted, doing anything to stop this madman from violating her.

As she flailed uselessly, she felt a very painful slap on her chest. "Stop fucking around!" the man yelled. Paige stopped moving and wondered what had hit her. It was too sharp to be a hand, and she didn't think it felt like a knife. Could it have been a whip?

She stopped thinking about what had happened and began thinking about what was going to happen. She felt his tongue press against her pussy. "Nice. I knew you wanted me. You really are a dirty fucking whore, aren't you?"

Paige, not being able to take any more, began to cry. The assailant slide his naked body up hers. She felt his cock press against her pussy. She couldn't stop the rape that was already fully in progress. "Let's have a little fun shall we?" he said.

Paige tightened up as she felt cold steel sliding across her face and down her chest to her tits. He grabbed one and pulled it hard, making Paige wince in pain. She felt the blade slide underneath. "You call these tits? I'd be doing you a favour cutting them off." Paige felt the knife press even harder against her bare breast. Paige barely let out a whimper of no; she couldn't say anything more.

"All right, you can keep them for now," he said.

The sharp tip of the knife circled around her belly button, then down to her clit. "How wet for me are you, whore?"

The man penetrated her again, this time with several fingers. "You call that wet? Everything I'm doing for you, and that's all you got?"

The fingers that had been inside her pussy slid under the hood and touched her lips. "How do you taste, slut?" His voice was louder and angrier. Paige was becoming increasingly scared with every second.

Paige felt something slide into her. It was cold and felt like metal. *Is it steel?* She thought. As she tried to figure it out or if she felt any pain, she discovered she was becoming increasingly wet – way wetter than she should be.

After several minutes, the torture stopped. "There you go, nice and wet for my cock." The attacker rammed his cock deep into her pussy, very hard, not concerned for her comfort. It hurt at first, but as the cock worked in and out of her, she could feel an orgasm building. She hated herself for it.

The large cock violated her again and again. She fought the sensation, but the leather strap choked her to breathlessness. The rapist pulled hard on her hair. That was one sensation too many for the already overstimulated Paige. She began to have an orgasm.

She had realized on that day at the beach that the orgasms which hadn't happened were in a reservoir. They were all coming together at this moment in one mammoth orgasm. Paige hated that this man was not only getting her off, but he was getting the result of her passion and lovemaking with Holden. It almost made her physically ill.

She heard the man's voice: "I told you you were a whore." He became faster and more erratic as he fucked the unwilling Paige. "I'm going to come," he said. She felt the cock quickly exit her. A warm puddle formed on her stomach. *At least he didn't come inside me*, she thought.

She felt fingers run through the warm come. The hand once again slid under the mask. "How do I taste, bitch?" Fingers forced their way into her mouth. Paige took the fingers and licked all the come clean off. Despite the leather strap across her throat, she laughed. "What's so fucking funny, bitch?"

"I love you," Paige said. "Why didn't you leave?"

"I'm glad you remembered *pamplemousse*," Holden said as he removed her hood. "I was worried you forgot. You were getting so worked up, I almost pulled the hood off several times, but I didn't want to ruin the fantasy."

"Even without the safe word, I knew it was you from the beginning. I'd recognize your touch and scent anywhere."

"Really? You were a good actress then. You had me freaked out a couple of times. I wanted to say *pamplemousse* the second I popped out of the closet, but I also wanted to create a little bit of doubt to get your heart racing."

"I admit, I was scared a bit at first. But yeah, I didn't want to ruin the fantasy either. Thanks for doing that for me, but we don't have to do it again."

"Fair enough. I hope knowing it was me didn't ruin it for you."

"No! Knowing it was you was the only way I could have possibly enjoyed it."

Even though she had known it was him, she was still relieved to see him. After their earlier experimentation with domination, they had talked in depth about fantasies. Paige reluctantly admitted that she had a rape fantasy: to be taken by force and made to submit to her assailant. But she wanted it only under very controlled circumstances with someone she loved and trusted. They decided on the safety word *pamplemousse* because it wasn't something they would normally say. Even if they used a ball gag, the number of syllables meant the word could easily be identified.

Holden quickly unfastened all her restraints. He smiled sheepishly and pulled out a new steel vibrator she had never seen before. "I bought it for you before I left. I was going to call you tonight and tell you where I hid it."

"Is that the steel I felt? How'd you get me so wet?" Paige asked.

Holden reached to the side of the bed and pulled out a bottle of baby oil. "About half a bottle of this," he said with a laugh.

Exhausted, Paige collapsed against Holden. "You're an ass, but I'm glad you're home. Thanks again." She draped her arms around his neck. Holden leaned in and kissed his love. He returned her embrace, and they fell asleep in each other's arms for a much-deserved mid-afternoon nap.

CHAPTER 10

Paige was standing at the bus stop for what seemed like an eternity before she finally saw the number 3 round the corner. She gathered her things and walked to the curb to await her chariot. The airbrakes hissed and the door opened, and Paige climbed aboard. She was the only one waiting at the stop, so as soon as she was clear of the doors, the bus was on the move.

Paige found her seat and turned up her MP3 player to drown out the city sounds. At the next stop, a young woman boarded. Paige stared at her. She thought she was incredibly beautiful. She couldn't pinpoint what it was about her, but Paige couldn't turn away.

The young woman put down her bag and took a seat across from Paige. The woman glanced over and smiled, and Paige smiled back. Just then, she noticed the girl's firm, round belly. She was pregnant.

"It's kicking. Do you want to feel it?" the girl asked, noticing that Paige was staring at her belly.

Paige hesitantly reached over and put her hand on the beautiful woman's belly. Paige giggled as she felt the tiny life under the skin.

The two talked for several blocks, until the conversation was interrupted by Paige's ringing cell phone. She excused herself and answered the phone. "Hello? ... Just riding on the bus ... Shut up ... Shut up ... Oh my God, that is fucking awesome ... Yeah, definitely ... talk to you later."

Paige hung up the phone and looked over at the pregnant girl. She smiled and dialled her phone. "Holden?"

"Yeah, what's up?" he answered.

"Tamara called. Guess what."

"What?"

"She told me Mike proposed last night, and they are getting married in two weeks."

"Oh yeah, that. Didn't I tell you he was going to do that?" Holden asked with mock sincerity.

"No, you did *not*. How long have you known?"

"About a month or so. You sure I didn't mention it before?"

"Uh, yeah, I'm pretty sure. Anyway, that's awesome. Her stagette is Saturday night."

"Yeah, Mike's bachelor party is Saturday as well. We'll have to make sure we don't go to the same places."

"We'll shop for a gift after work."

"Sounds good. I have to run, honey. Love you."

"Love you too."

Paige hung up her phone. She hadn't realized the pregnant girl had got up and moved to the door. As the bus stopped, she turned and waved goodbye to Paige. Then she disappeared down the stairs.

Paige spent the rest of the bus ride thinking about how happy the pregnant girl had appeared and how happy Tamara had sounded when she was telling Paige about her engagement.

She saw her stop, rang the bell, then grabbed her bag and got off the bus in front of her school. Her day was pretty much a waste as she daydreamed about being pregnant and about walking towards Holden at the altar.

She called Holden at lunch, and they agreed to meet up at the end of the day so they could go shopping. Holden asked Mike where they were registered, and Mike said the beer store. When Holden pried further, he found out that they were having a very low-key, intimate wedding. They weren't expecting a lot of people nor did they want a lot of gifts. Neither of them were religious. Mike explained it was more of a party to celebrate their love. Holden laughed and asked how he was managing to get away with that. Mike said it had been mostly Tamara's idea, and that the subliminal tapes he played her at night seemed to work.

Even though Holden knew Paige wasn't going to be happy with "they aren't registered anywhere and they don't want a fuss made", he dropped his line of questioning.

Holden and Paige spent several hours after work going from porn store to porn store, trying to find the right gifts for the upcoming bachelor and bachelorette parties. They spent most of the time adding to their own wish lists and laughing at the inventory.

Finally, they were confident they had found just the right things, so they moved on to the mall to find outfits for the wedding. Paige tried on clothes. Holden spent most of the time bringing Paige clothes that were one size too small so he could see her in the overtight garments. They both enjoyed themselves. After carefully selecting a returnable gift for Mike and Tamara, they went home.

Saturday rolled around, and they were woken up by a ringing doorbell. Holden had an idea who was at the door. Paige had no clue. Holden did his best to keep the surprise visitors just that, a surprise.

Holden climbed out of bed, threw on pants and an old T-shirt, and ran to the door. He opened it up to see Pete, Andrew, and Jeff standing in the entrance. Andrew handed Holden a beer and smiled. Holden looked at the beer. "Dude, it's nine o'clock in the morning."

"It's noon in Toronto. Don't you ever forget where you came from."

"Fair enough. Come in," Holden said. He took the beer and showed his guests into the living room. They all made sure to poke their heads in the bedroom to say hi to Paige, who was still in bed.

Taking the hint, she got out of bed and dressed, then joined the boys in the living room, where they were exchanging war stories. Pete had amazing stories from his adventures on the police force. Andrew told stories of his conquests at the resort. Jeff simply said the law firm was busy representing clients in suits against Pete.

Holden and Paige told them how great life in BC was. Holden told them embarrassing stories about Mike. They were excited to meet his bride-to-be.

They all asked Paige if she had met any single friends yet. She told them there was no one she would subject them to. Pete said that was probably a wise choice.

Several more beers went downrange as Holden and Paige took turns showering. When they were both ready, the guys decided they wanted to go for lunch. Holden kept looking at his watch and stalling. As he was about to lose the battle to stay put, the doorbell rang once again. "Paige, honey, could you get that?" Holden asked.

"Yes, sir, anything you wish," Paige said playfully.

Holden smiled. The guys asked who it was. "Just wait and see," he told them.

Then they heard a shriek come from the front door. Holden could only laugh. Two sets of footsteps ran down the hall. It was Paige's old roommate, "Sunshine" Mel. Jeff froze as he stared at his past crush. He shot Holden a dirty glance for not warning him.

They all talked as Holden took Mel's bags and put them in the spare room. He offered her a beer. Pete spoke up and said he would buy her one at the restaurant, but they had to go because he was starving.

Over lunch, they continued sharing humorous stories. Jeff was disappointed to hear that Mel was only in town for the bachelorette party. Tamara had invited Mel because she knew Paige didn't really know any of the other girls who would be attending. She wanted Paige to have a close friend there too. The guys were staying for the entire week so they could attend the wedding as well.

Andrew pushed Jeff to make a move on Mel while he had the chance. He reminded Jeff that Mel lived in the same city. Jeff took a drink to contemplate his options.

Paige checked at her watch and said they had to go get ready, so they paid their bills and headed back to the condo.

The boys sat in the living room, watching TV, while the girls took over the bedroom and bathroom. They took the better part of the afternoon getting ready, but the time turned out to have been worthwhile. According to the guys, they were stunning when they were done.

Inside of thirty minutes, all fur guys were showered and dressed. They looked the same as they had before the showers; they just smelt a little better.

The taxis arrived. Paige and Holden locked up and reminded each other that both parties had hotel rooms, so neither would be back at the condo that night.

Paige and Mel headed for an extravagant hotel in downtown Vancouver. The girls had all chipped in and got Tamara a suite for her party. When they arrived, all the other girls were there with the exception of Tamara. Paige put her party gifts in the corner with the rest of the gifts as one of the girls' phone rang. On the other end was the girl assigned to the task of not only distracting Tamara for the day, but figuring out a way to get her to the hotel.

The girl who received the call said Tamara was on her way up. The girls got excited. They pulled out Tamara's outfit for the night. There was a knock at the door, and Mel answered it. They had chosen Mel because she was the only girl in the room Tamara didn't know. They thought it would be a good way to confuse her further. Even the girl escorting Tamara was a bit confused when the door opened. She looked at the room number written down on her key card, then back up to the door. Finally she verbally confirmed that she did indeed have the right room.

Mel opened the door wider to let them in. The girls yelled, "Surprise!" Tamara walked in to hug all her guests and thank them for the effort. Before she could finish, one of the girls handed her a glass of wine. Tamara quickly drank that glass and asked for another.

As the girl topped up Tamara's glass, another girl grabbed Tamara by the arm and escorted her to a chair they had put in the front of the room. They arranged a couch and other chairs around the seat of honour. Tamara quickly sank into her chair as she felt the warmth of the first glass of wine rush through her.

One of the girls ran to the freezer and brought out a tray of penis-shaped ice cubes. She splashed a couple in Tamara's glass, then passed the tray around to the other girls. Once all the girls had a drink, they brought forward their gifts and laid them around Tamara. Before she could start opening them, Paige brought over a cheap wedding veil and put it on Tamara's head, instructing her that she couldn't take it off for the rest of the night.

Tamara reached into the first bag and pulled out an oversized dildo. She held it up for everyone to see and moved it around so the head flopped. They all laughed. Tamara put it on a table beside her. The next gift was a Chippendales calendar. It was passed from girl to girl for them to ogle the buff men on each page. The girls found their birthday months and declared their own months were hotter than the other girls'.

Next was a card with a man on the cover, equally as buff as the men in the calendar. Inside was a coupon for DVD rentals at an adult store. The rest of the gifts were similar: novelty gifts from various adult stores.

Tamara said she needed another drink, so two girls got up and went to the fridge. They pulled out a glass that was shaped like a foot-long penis with a white curly straw coming out the urethra. Tamara fought them, saying she wouldn't drink out of it, but the girls told her that her only other option was not to drink at all. Tamara put her lips on the straw, took a big gulp of the alcohol inside, and said "Mm-mm good," to the amusement of the girls.

They continued to laugh. Someone turned up the music. There was a knock at the door. Paige opened it, to be met by a police officer. He said there had been complaints and they would have to keep the noise down. Paige apologized, but the cop ignored her and peeked around the door. "What's going on in here?" he asked.

Paige told him it was a stagette and they would keep the noise down. The cop asked if there were any drugs in the room. He radioed something into his walkie-talkie, and very quickly he was joined by two more cops. All three were tall, ripped men in tight uniforms. One was a light-skinned black man. Paige thought he was particularly hot because of his steel-grey eyes.

The cop who had first knocked on the door asked if they could come in to look around. Paige said she would rather they didn't, but the cop forced his way through the door, almost knocking Paige down. "I'm sorry, ma'am. I insist. We had a call, and we have to do our duty."

The three men stormed in and surrounded the girls. Everyone was silent. Only the music broke the tension. One of the girls went to turn off the tunes. The black man told her not to move. The girls all turned to each other, puzzled.

A police officer walked over to Tamara. "Is this your party?" he asked very professionally.

"Yes, sir," she said in a broken voice.

"I'm going to have to place you under arrest."

With that, he pulled her arms behind her back and put handcuffs on her. He pushed her into her chair. None of the girls noticed that one cop slipped a CD into the player.

Just as Tamara fell into her chair, the music turned from rock to a dance beat. The cop who had cuffed Tamara turned to his partners. "Frisk 'em, boys."

In unison, the cops ripped open their shirts to the cheers of the girls. Only two had known about their special guests, and they were very impressed with the guys' performance. They were hoping to be even more impressed very soon.

The star of the show kept his focus on Tamara while the other two men entertained the rest of the girls. Each girl had an opportunity to run their fingers down the men's six-packs. Mel pulled on one guy's waistband and tried to sneak a peek, but he backed away from her, wagging his finger in a no-no motion. The other girls laughed at her failed attempt. Mel playfully pouted and sat back, taking a sip of her drink as she waited for the rest of the show.

As the first song ended, the men gathered in a line, facing Tamara. Another song started. Their police belts fell to the floor. They ripped their Velcroed pants off and tossed them. They were each wearing the same style of thong, only in different colours.

The girls on the couch and chairs behind only had a view of the men's perfect asses. Tamara, on the other hand, had an unobstructed view of three very generous endowments. Giving her ample time to spectate, they spun around, causing their mighty cocks to fly straight out and slap against their thighs. All the girls were suitably impressed.

Mel, taking a sip from a drink that was getting stronger with each refill, simply said, "Now *that's* what I'm talkin' about." The other girls applauded.

The star of the show gave Tamara a lap dance. The other two walked up and down the line of ladies, letting them all see what the men had to offer. Each girl reached out, some to touch their abs again. One or two slapped their tight butts. Mel, sitting pretty much in the middle, waited until the guys were standing beside each other. She placed her hand under their cocks and bounced them as if comparing them for weight, size, and balance. "Hmm" was the only sound Mel made.

Paige laughed because she was always amused by Mel's antics. The other girls were also finding Mel quite humorous. The guys took an immediate liking to her too, almost as if they sensed one of their own.

The two guys kept up their feeble attempts to dance, which mostly consisted of them shaking their asses and walking back and forth. The star was still focused on Tamara. He put his feet on either side of her chair and raised himself so her face was lined up with his waist. He met her eyes and then directed them to his crotch. He told her to take off his thong. She said she would like to but she couldn't, glancing at her shackled hands. The guy looked back at her and made a biting motion. Taking the hint, Tamara leaned forward and took the waistband in her mouth. The guy did the rest. He continued to lean over her head until the thong slipped off his ass. He then backed away, letting his thong fall to the floor.

The other dancers took their cue. They turned their backs on the women and pulled their thongs off, letting the girls see their asses, which received a round of applause. They were impressed when the guys turned around again. Each man had a hammer almost a foot long.

The guys again walked back and forth in front of the girls, allowing each one to poke, prod, and lick whatever they wanted. The girls couldn't resist. Tamara tried not to do anything too inappropriate, electing just to stare. She was unable to touch anything anyway.

The guy servicing Tamara moved behind her. He whispered in her ear as he lowered his cock until it was touching her hand. Tamara opened her palm, allowing the cock to slide until she gripped it firmly. "Very nice," she said.

"Thanks."

He spun around to the front of the chair and danced a couple of paces in front of her. The other guys gathered in front of Mel again.

"Don't be shy," Paige said, grabbing one of the mighty cocks and pressed the head against Mel's cheek. Another guy took Paige's cue, gripping his own cock, and brought it to Mel's face. She kissed the tip of each one before suddenly taking the black guy's cock in her mouth. The girls intently looked on as Mel performed oral sex on the man. They were very impressed she could make the foot-long disappear. "Oh, I see you've had your tonsils removed," he joked.

The other guy still had his cock against Mel's face. Paige had her hand on the back of Mel's head forcing it even further onto the cock. Mel finally pulled away, letting the cock fall to his knee. She turned to the other cock and offered it to Paige. Paige politely declined, saying it was very nice but Holden's was enough for her.

"Whatever, more for me," Mel responded, and then she laughed. Looking around at the other girls, she asked "Anyone else care for a taste?"

Mel could see that a couple of girls wanted to, but they were too shy to act on it or too embarrassed to follow Mel's expert deep throating. Mel, not wanting to make the poor guy feel neglected, put her hand at the base of the dancer's cock and took him deep. Paige cheered her on. Even Tamara struggled to watch Mel's performance.

The star giving Tamara his attention turned to her and whispered, "Wow, girl's got skills."

"No shit," Tamara replied.

"You know you could—"

"Nice try. Not a chance."

"Can't blame a guy for trying."

"Nope. I couldn't top that anyway."

The star continued dancing, which meant rubbing his cock all over Tamara's chest and lap, then dragging it up her bare knees to just under her skirt. Tamara took the antics in stride. She was having a lot of fun and was mildly curious what a huge cock like that felt like.

Mel let the cock slide out of her mouth and reached up to her lips, wiping the spit off with the back of her hand. "OK, that was fun. Now what we going to do?"

The girls checked the time, as did the dancers. The dancers informed the girls that their hour was up. If they wanted the men to stay, it would cost extra.

The girls agreed the hour was enough and thanked them for their time. Each girl slipped cash into the guys' pants and told them where they'd be later in the night if the men cared to join them. With that the guys left and closed the door behind them.

Tamara, now free from her cuffs, gave slaps on the shoulder to the two girls responsible for the strippers. "Bitches," she said with a laugh.

The girls gathered up their things. Tamara was forced to put on a white T-shirt that each girl had written something dirty on. Paige had drawn two large nipples. They gave Tamara a black marker and instructed her to get one hundred names on the shirt before the end of the night.

Confident they had everything, the girls headed out for a night of drunken mayhem. The bridesmaid called ahead to ten different places, letting them know the girls would be coming so they could get priority in line. Bars, always eager to have drunken women in their establishments, gladly obliged their requests.

The first place had a huge line, but the girls walked right past it to the doorman. He waved them in and congratulated the bride-to-be as she passed by. The DJ saw the group enter and made an announcement over the microphone: "Ladies and gentlemen, I would like to congratulate Tamara on her upcoming wedding. If I could give you some advice ... *run*. I kid, I kid. If any of you nice people would like to wish the bride-to-be well, I'm sure she is taking gifts in the form of free drinks."

Tamara was embarrassed at the attention, but his words worked. A wave of guys rushed to the bar and bought the party drinks. Each guy hoped to cash in on the girls' decreased inhibitions. Each girl found a guy and danced for a couple of songs.

Mel pushed her guy away as he got too frisky. She grabbed Paige, stealing her from her dancing partner. "Mind if I cut in?" she said to no one in particular as she didn't care to hear a response.

Mel got the room's attention as she squeezed Paige's ass and pulled Paige into her thigh. They ground into each other. Mel breathed heavily onto Paige's neck.

Tamara, feeling left out, joined the two girls and pulled up her skirt, allowing her legs more flexibility. She entangled her legs with Paige's and Mel's, and they all danced. Every guy in the place watched with dropped jaws.

The maid of honour announced to the party that it was time to move on to the next bar. Half the guys in the place wanted to know their schedule so they could meet up later, but none of the girls would tell them.

The girls went to bar after bar, getting drunker. Tamara continued to collect names at each stop while drinking from her penis cup. Although the original plan had been to head back early to the hotel for more drinks and partying, the later the night went on, the drunker everyone got. The last bar was close to Paige's condo, so she and Mel decided to walk back there at the end of the night. The place would be empty, so they had all kinds of room to sleep.

Mike's gang met for pre-drinks at a hotel. The room wasn't nearly as luxurious as the girls'. The groomsman took a lot of flak from the guys for getting such a seedy room. "Don't worry, guys. You won't be complaining for long," he told them.

As if on cue, there was a knock on the door. "Gentlemen, the entertainment has arrived." The best man rushed to the door and opened it for their guest. He was startled to see a woman in her fifties, escorted by a very large man with no neck.

The man spoke up first. "This the Mike bachelor party?"

"Yes."

"Two hundred dollars for the hour," the man with no neck said.

Once the best man paid the bodyguard, the woman took her spot at centre stage. The guys glanced at each other, assuming this was a joke before the real entertainment arrived. The dancer called up Mike as she pulled out a wooden chair for him to sit on. Once he was seated, she straddled him. The guys all felt uncomfortable for Mike.

As the music played, the woman shed her clothes. She first exposed her aged breasts, which sagged down to her belly button. "Do you want to touch them?" she asked Mike.

"Oh no, I'm good, thanks. My fiancée would kill me."

"Oh, she isn't here and I won't tell." She flashed Mike a smile with several teeth missing. Mike did his best to not cringe but he had never felt more uncomfortable.

Next she pulled off her jeans, and then her control-top panties. She lay on the floor, put her fingers on either side of her pussy, and spread it apart. Mike could only relate the experience to watching someone spread open a grilled cheese sandwich. The guys fought to hold back their laughter.

The dancer stood up and tried to do a dance routine. Her loose skin flew uncontrollably in every direction. The straw that broke the camel's back was when she tried to do the splits. She made it about a quarter of the way to the floor and fell over. Not only did she try once and fail; she tried over and over again without success.

Finally, she stopped and nodded to her security, then disappeared into a side room. "OK, guys. For fifty dollars each, you can get a private dance with the lady."

The guys awkwardly looked at each other. Pete, acting as the spokesman, said, "I think we're good, but thank you for the offer." The guys couldn't restrain their laughs.

The security guy tried to intimidate them into forking over more money. Pete finally had enough. He pulled out his badge and told him firmly that they were good. The woman hurriedly gathered her things and barely got dressed before the two scrambled out of the room.

The guys turned on the best man. "What the *hell* were you thinking? *Never* go to discount escorts for a stag party, you dopey bastard." They teased him relentlessly, giving him idle threats that the night had to get much better or he was in trouble.

They cut their losses and headed to a gentlemen's club. They told every girl who would listen that it was Mike's bachelor party, and each one sat and chatted with him. The odd girl even gave him a free dance. Even the headliner called Mike out of the audience and sat him down onstage. She tied his arms behind his back and his feet to the legs of the chair. She proceeded to give him the lap dance he had been looking forward to in the hotel.

Her large implants rubbed over his body, which made him hard. She noticed his erection and rubbed her tits over his jeans. She turned and sat on his lap, grinding her prefect ass into his crotch. The song ended, marking the end of the show, but before she left she called every girl onto the stage. They came up one by one and rubbed their tits on his head.

It was very apparent Mike was in his glory onstage. He was sad as the last girl moved on. The headliner turned to Holden. "Come get your guy off the stage."

Holden laughed and contemplated leaving him up there, but Mike begged for rescue with his eyes. Holden finally gave in and went up onstage, enduring the catcalls of all the other guys in the audience. He untied Mike, turned to the crowd, and took a bow to even more applause.

They watched a couple more sets and bought Mike a couple more lap dances. He told every girl that he talked to about the horrid stripper from the hotel. Most volunteered to come by after for a private show.

Getting all worked up, the guys decided it was a good time to head to the bar. The old married guys abandoned the party as the group moved to actual dance bars.

The bridesmaid and the best man had made sure they booked reservations at separate bars so they wouldn't have to worry about running into each other. The bars the best man got were all seedy dives full of cougars. The night slowly made a turn for the worse.

The last place on the list was a decent dance bar, but it was close to the end of the night and it was starting to clear out. Pete, Andrew, and Jeff were frustrated they hadn't had a chance to pick up. The guys reminded Jeff he still had Mel, whom they were meeting for breakfast.

As the lights of the bar turned on, the guys decided to go home instead of back to their seedy hotel. Assuming Holden's place was empty, they knew that between the spare room, the couch, and the air mattress, there was more than enough room for all the guys.

Holden opened the door to the condo, and the remaining guys followed him in. Holden grabbed them each a beer.

Pete claimed the spare room. He opened the door and was startled to see a naked Mel sleeping on the bed. She peered up at him. "Taken."

"Can't we share? I don't bite," Pete said playfully.

Mel got up, walked past Pete, entered Paige's room, and slammed the door behind her.

The guys could hear the girls talking. Pete came back into the living room and told Holden what had happened. Holden was surprised the girls were home. He went into the bedroom to talk to Paige. He saw Mel cuddled up next to Paige, who was also sleeping sans clothes. He temporarily had some very bad thoughts run through his head. "Hey, honey, what's up?" Paige asked.

"Just got home. What you doing here? How was your night?"

"Good. We'll talk in the morning. Can you make room for the guys?"

"Yeah. Pete can have the spare room, I'll take the couch, and Andrew and Jeff can share the inflatable bed. You two can stay put in here."

"Cool. Night."

As Holden closed the door, Mel leaned closer to Paige. "I like him. He's a good guy."

"Yeah, he's great. I love him to death," Paige said.

"Are you ready to settle down? You are so different from who you were in Ontario."

"Yeah, I'm happy," Paige said, not giving a second thought to Mel's hand on her stomach.

"I miss the old you."

"Yeah, sometimes I miss the old me too," Paige said sadly.

"I love you."

"I love you too," Paige reciprocated.

"No, I *really* love you," Mel said, leaning in to kiss Paige. Paige kissed her back.

Mel moved her hands up Paige's stomach to her ribs, finally putting her delicate palm on Paige's breast. Paige didn't stop her. Instead she put her arms around Mel and pulled her closer. Mel pressed her breast firmly against Paige's. The two continued to kiss passionately.

Mel tried to push the envelope by moving her hand down Paige's body to her pussy. She rubbed Paige's clit a couple of times before sinking her fingers inside. Paige let out a moan as Mel's thin, long fingers went deep. Mel used her free hand to pull on Paige's hair, tilting Paige's head back. Mel kissed Paige's exposed neck as her fingers danced around inside Paige's pussy.

Paige loved the way another woman touched her. She felt that not only were girls softer and gentler, but they had more experience with the equipment.

Mel slipped her fingers out of Paige and brought them to her throat. They both could smell Paige's pussy on her fingers, which heightened the experience. Mel firmly gripped Paige's throat, cutting off her oxygen. She then straddled Paige's leg to rub her pussy on Paige's thigh. As Paige fought for air, she felt Mel's soft skin against hers.

Mel gave Paige her air back, and as Paige took a deep breath, Mel gripped Paige's tit and squeezed hard, simultaneously biting her neck. Paige finally stopped Mel. "As great as this feels, we can't do this. It's not right."

"Whatever," Mel said and rolled over, putting her back to Paige.

A couple of minutes passed. Mel rolled back over. "I need to get laid." She crawled out of bed and walked into the living room.

She saw two guys on the inflatable bed and Holden on the couch. Knowing Holden wasn't an option, she kicked the mattress, waking the two up. "I need to get laid. Who's going to fuck me?"

"You're up, slugger," Andrew said to Jeff.

Jeff cautiously stood up and took Mel's hand. She escorted him to the master bedroom. Mel lay down and spread her legs. "Fuck me."

Not wasting time, Jeff undressed and crawled into the bed. He was about to slide his cock inside Mel, but she stopped him. "We need a rubber," she said. Jeff agreed.

Mel woke up Paige. "Do you have condoms?"

"What do you think you're doing?"

"Something you wouldn't."

She reached over Paige to open the drawer in the nightstand Paige motioned to. As she opened it up, she felt Jeff move in behind her. She collapsed onto Paige. Jeff could see Paige undressed on the bed with his crush lying naked on top of her. He couldn't resist. He put his hands on her ass and fucked her as she continued to lie on Paige. Mel, forgetting about the condom, let him continue.

"Get off me," Paige ordered.

Jeff let Mel up. She sat with her legs crossed, reached for Jeff's hard, wet cock, and slipped the condom on. "OK, where were we?" she asked. She lay on her back and wrapped her legs around Jeff as he thrust into her. She got increasingly loud, making Paige cover her head with a pillow to drown out the noise.

Jeff, being drunk and horny, didn't last long. Paige could hear him grunting as his final moments approached. He collapsed onto Mel as he came in his condom. "How was that?"

"It will do, I guess. Now get out of here. I'm going to sleep."

His ego shattered, Jeff took comfort in having had the opportunity to fuck his long-time crush. He went back into the living room, where he received a round of applause from Andrew. Jeff shared his experience in great detail before passing out.

Holden was the first to wake in the living room the next morning. He turned on the TV and heard stirring in one of the bedrooms. Pete strolled out of the spare room in his boxers and a T-shirt, showing signs of the rough night. He walked to the fridge, opened it, picked up a couple of beers, walked to the couch, and sat beside Holden. "'Mornin'," he said, handing Holden a beer.

Holden took the beer. "Mornin'."

No other words were spoken. They watched TV and slowly sipped their beers.

Disturbed by the TV, Andrew and Jeff woke up. Neither immediately told Holden that Jeff had nailed Mel across his naked girlfriend. They figured they'd wait until the perfect time, that being when they were safely back in Ontario.

Andrew followed Pete's example and went to the fridge to grab a couple of beers, hoping it would be just the thing to cure his headache.

The four sat watching TV and reminiscing about the bachelor party and what a mess it had turned out to be.

Paige finally woke up and came into the living room, wearing a cut-off T-shirt and tiny cotton shorts. She sat on the couch and cuddled up next to Holden. She told them about the girls' night, leaving out crucial details.

Mel slept for another few hours before Paige told Jeff to go wake her up. She winked at him. Not needing much urging, Jeff went into the bedroom, where he stayed for over half an hour. No one heard any commotion.

Then Mel and Jeff walked into the living room. Mel looked very rough. Her long blonde hair was messed up, her shirt hung off her small frame like it was three sizes too big, and under the shirt she was only wearing boy-cut briefs.

After everyone got showered and dressed, they went for lunch and a walk around Vancouver. Mel had a late-night flight home, and she wanted to see as much of the city as she could.

After the tour, it was time to take Mel to the airport. Jeff and the boys volunteered to accompany Holden, Paige, and Mel. Holden could see right through Jeff's offer, but he wasn't about to cock block him.

Jeff escorted Mel to the security gate. Before she disappeared into the line, she reached into her pocket and handed Jeff a piece of paper. He slipped the note into his pocket and gave her a hug.

After they left the airport, Holden and Paige dropped the three guys off at the hotel they had booked for the rest of the week. It was the same hotel where Paige and Holden had stayed for their first few nights in the city. Holden had taken the week off to act as their tour guide. Paige was happy that she had a busy week of classes ahead, because she didn't want to spend the week in and out of Hooters and various strip clubs.

The week sailed by. The four guys spent every day out and about, seeing the sights and touring the bars. The day of the wedding finally arrived. The three Ontarioians planned to head home the next day. As sad as Holden would be to see them go, his liver couldn't wait.

—ɯ—

Holden got dressed in his suit. Paige was taking her time in the bathroom. She yelled to Holden that she would be a few minutes, and told him to go into the living room and have a beer. Not needing further incentive, Holden strolled into the kitchen to get a beer. Then he turned on the TV. Nothing special was on, but it did the trick to kill time.

After about twenty minutes, Holden heard Paige walk down the hallway. He saw his angel dressed up. She was wearing fishnet nylons under a very sexy, short black dress that showed a hint of cleavage. He wanted her very badly.

Paige smiled, reading Holden's thoughts. She looked into his eyes and said, "Not yet, tiger."

Before they left, Holden put on his dress shoes, which were black leather Chuck Taylors. Paige laughed at the contrast between the expensive suit and his trademark Chucks. As Holden was putting on his shoes, Paige moved close to him and bent at the waist to put on her Mary Janes. Her skirt rode up her thigh – completely unintentionally, she claimed. Holden could see that the fishnets she was wearing were thigh-highs attached to a garter. She knew that was his kryptonite. She smiled a coy little smile as she caught him in her peripheral vision. Holden was frozen, staring at her exposed leg and garter belt.

Paige finally stood up with a devilish grin and asked, "Something wrong?"

Holden snapped out of his trance. He grabbed Paige and threw her against the wall. He lifted her skirt to expose her panties.

Paige reached down and rubbed his throbbing cock through his dress pants as they kissed passionately. Paige then turned and threw Holden against the wall, still rubbing his cock. Then she pushed him away and said, "Not now, slugger. We're going to be late." She walked out the door, giggling. Holden gathered himself and quickly joined Paige outside.

The wedding was very small and intimate. Andrew, Jeff, and Pete sat next to Holden and Paige. Holden caught all of his friends checking out Paige. It made him proud. He knew she looked hotter than hot. They also made fun of Mike standing up in front of the justice of the peace.

The organ played "Here Comes the Bride" and Pete yelled, "Run!"

Mike laughed, and Andrew hit him across the chest. "Shut up."

As Tamara walked by, she glanced over at Pete. "Ass. If anyone's running, it's me," she said.

The group broke out in laughter. Mike, who had missed the exchange, turned to Holden. "What?" he mouthed. Holden shrugged his shoulders.

Tamara finally reached Mike, and the JP started the ceremony. Paige gripped Holden's hand tightly and put her head on his shoulder. Holden even caught Paige shedding a tear.

The JP finished, and the newly married couple kissed to the cheers of the crowd. Everyone in attendance left the building and headed to the dance hall, where they were expecting a much bigger gathering.

At the reception, Paige and Holden found seats and talked to the few mutual friends they shared with Mike and Tamara. Andrew, Pete, and Jeff took seats near the bar, where a couple of attractive young waitresses were working.

Holden slid his hand into Paige's, which was demurely folded on her lap. He casually rubbed her garter to remind her that he remembered what she was wearing and that she still owed him for her quick exit earlier. She stood up, kissed Holden on the cheek, and excused herself from the table. She came back as one of their favourite songs started to play. She reached out to grab Holden's hand and said, "Let's dance."

Holden took her hand, and he quickly realized it wasn't empty. He looked down as she shoved her hand in his pocket. Curious, he reached in to see what she'd slipped him. Whatever it was, it was damp. It didn't take him long to realize she'd slipped him her panties.

Laughing, she took him by the hand and led him to the dance floor. The lights were almost off except for a single mirrored ball. Holden held Paige close, close enough that even air couldn't get between them. Holden ran his hand up her back and squeezed her even closer. She responded by burying her head into his shoulder. His free hand gently caressed her neck and hair.

As if by magic, the packed dance floor seemed to have emptied. Paige and Holden felt as if they were alone in the room. As the song ended, he hugged her tight. Neither of them wanted the song to end.

Holden peered deep into Paige's eyes. "I love you," he said. The words had never meant more to him.

Paige smiled a very sweet smile and pushed her hips into his hardening cock, teasing him once again before they returned to their seats.

More songs played. Holden danced with Tamara, congratulating the bride. Paige danced with Mike. Pete, Andrew, and Jeff each had a dance with Tamara and Paige. Pete even danced with each of the waitresses.

The night wound down, and Paige and Holden said their goodbyes to the newlyweds. They asked the three guys what their plans were for the night. They said they had been invited to an after-party that the wait staff were attending.

Holden wished them luck. He and Paige headed out. Holden couldn't get home fast enough.

They held hands in the cab on the entire way home. Each of them drifted off into their own little worlds. Holden was thinking about what he would do to Paige. Paige thought about the wedding. She imagined her own wedding, then thought about the pregnant girl she'd met on the bus.

She thought about what Mel had said to her about her past. A thousand thoughts a minute raced through her mind. She thought about Holden and how badly she wanted him.

The cab stopped. Holden threw a handful of money at the driver. Paige pushed Holden out of the car. As she did, her skirt rode up, giving the cab driver an unexpected peek at her perfect ass and her garter.

They finally got inside. She was in his arms. They kissed. His tie came off. She ripped open his shirt, and buttons flew everywhere. Paige stared at Holden's muscular chest and ran her fingers down his abs. She bit her lip as she backed away. "Can I get you a drink?" she asked.

"Uh, I thought we were in the middle of something?"

"In time." She went to the kitchen and poured them each a glass of wine. "Here, drink up," Paige instructed Holden. "I'm going to change into something more comfortable." With her own wine glass in hand, she ran into the bedroom.

Holden sat on the couch and turned on the TV. He flipped through his DVDs to see which would be the best one to watch when Paige finally returned.

Several minutes later, Holden heard Paige yell urgently, "Holden, come here a minute!" Holden ran into the bedroom. He saw that Paige had lit several candles all around the room. Classical piano was playing on their CD player. She lay on the bed, seductively wearing only her fishnet nylons and garter belt. On her chest, in edible sex paint, she had written *I love you*. The shape of a heart had been substituted for the word *love*, and a *U* replaced *you*. The *U* was in her pubic area.

Holden paused for a moment, taking in the sights and smells. Paige looked gorgeous lit up by the flickering candles. Paige tapped the bed beside her. "Come here, big boy," she said in a whisper.

Holden scrambled out of his suit as fast as humanly possible and joined Paige on the bed. He reached under her chin and put his hand on her ear. They leaned into each other and kissed. Paige rolled over carefully, trying not to smudge her artwork. Their kiss was long, deep, and passionate.

After the kiss, they talked. They told each other how much they loved each other; they talked about the wedding and fantasized about the possibility of their own. Paige brought up the pregnant girl on the bus and how beautiful she was. They also talked about their future hopes and dreams.

When there was a pause in the conversation, Holden kissed Paige's luscious lips, then moved down her cheek and kissed her ear. After kissing it and softly blowing in it for some time, he whispered, "I love you." He put his finger on the edge of the heart and brought the sticky strawberry candy to his tongue. "Yummy," he said.

Paige smiled at how playful Holden was being. "Well, there is more where that came from," she said, looking down at her body.

Holden rolled his eyes. "Oh, OK, if I must," he said with a big smile. He repositioned himself between her legs, up far enough that his chest was pressing against her pussy and his face was directly above the *U*.

With small flicks of his tongue, he licked the candy paint off her freshly shaven mound. Each touch drove Paige crazy. She wanted him inside her badly, but it was her game and she was going to see it through to the end.

Holden was in wonderland, He had his two favourite things: candy and a naked Paige. Both of them were just a tongue stroke away.

With the *U* gone, Holden slid up Paige's body so his stomach was firmly between her legs. He could feel the fishnets rubbing his sides. He started at the bottom of the heart. With one long lick, he traced it to the top. He left a sticky trail behind, one he was only too happy to clean up. His fingers dug firmly into Paige's hips.

Paige put her hands over her head to grip the headboard, ensuring Holden had complete access to her body. Holden's tongue flickered and danced its way up her hard abs, tickling Paige along the way. Satisfied that half of the heart was cleaned up, he repositioned himself once again. This time he was lying perpendicular to her body. His hand reached under her thigh so the side of his palm could occasionally graze her pussy. His chest rested in the sticky mess that used to be half of the heart.

This time Holden used small kisses to pull the candy gel off her chest. His full lips softly caressed her stomach. She wanted to grab his cock and massage it until she could feel his own candy treat in her hand, but she resisted, knowing it would be hers very shortly.

He slowly moved up her stomach. The small kisses did their job, and all the gel from the heart was gone. When he was finished, he leaned back to stare into Paige's eyes and lick his lips. "Delicious," he said.

He shifted again to lie parallel to Paige. She was flat on her back and he was on his side, tucked in tight against her. She could feel his cock pressed against her hips. He reached across her stomach to the side of her left breast. He used his chest and hand to push her tits together. They both looked down at her cleavage. "Very nice," Holden said.

"Yeah. If only you could follow me around all day, holding them like that, I might do better at school." She laughed.

"I wish" was Holden's reply.

"You wish I was doing better in school?"

"No! I wish I could— *Hey*," Holden said as he saw the smirk on Paige's face.

He turned his attention to the *I* between her breasts. His squeezing had left residue on each breast. Holden used his tongue to quickly clean them off, making sure he gave each nipple a kiss in the process. He then lay back and used his right index finger to collect any remaining candy.

As the red, gooey substance dripped from his finger, he slowly brought it Paige's lips. She dutifully opened her mouth to accept the candy treat and let out a very long, seductive "mmm" as she sucked Holden's finger. Once she was willing to give his finger back to him, he crawled on top of his princess. She could feel the head of his cock pressing against her; it was very close to penetrating her. She wanted him to give it to her hard, but she didn't want to spoil the anticipation for either of them.

Holden rested on his elbows so he didn't crush her. He put his hands by her ears and brushed the hair off them as he gently kissed them. He purposely pushed his chest into Paige's because he loved the feel of her small breasts against his skin. Still leaning into Paige's ear, he let out a small cat purr. She laughed because the vibration tickled her ear and the sound was unexpected. "Oh, you're an animal," Paige said between her laughs.

Holden enjoyed being called an animal, so he let out a small roar. He sounded less like the king of the jungle and more like a baby Simba. Paige laughed even louder. She used the distraction to roll over so she was lying on top of Holden. It was her turn to lean in and kiss him. She gave him a series of small pecks on the lips before straddling his stomach. She leaned over to the bedside table and picked up the paint. "Your turn."

Paige dipped her finger into the paint and brought a dollop to her extended tongue. With a curl of wet flesh, she lapped up the oozing mess.

She then painted Holden. She dabbed a small amount on each nipple and drew an arrow down to his cock. With a big fingerful, she ran her digit between the beads of his piercings. She gently bit one nipple and pulled the candy paint off. She wrapped her mouth around the other nipple and sucked until the candy was all gone. Then, copying Holden, she used small kisses at the top of the arrow until she got halfway. She slid down his body and used her tongue to finish licking up the arrow.

With only the two points left, she put her tongue flat against his hard body and dragged it across his stomach until the gel was gone. Proud of her job, she was very happy knowing that she could concentrate on the only remaining paint, which was on his penis.

She lay between his legs. Her face was only an inch from his cock. Her hand reached around his leg and gripped the base of his penis. She did the same trick as she'd done with the ends of the arrows: she flattened her tongue on his cock and licked up. Although she got a good mouthful of paint, there was some remaining. She opened her mouth and lowered it around his shaft. Once she had the entire length in her mouth, she used her tongue to clean him off.

Her tongue was like magic to him. He didn't know how much he could take. He soon found out.

She popped up so that she was kneeling between his legs. She used her finger to collect the spit and paint that had formed at the corners of her lips. "All done, nice and clean," she said with a smile. "I'm going to shower to get this stickiness off me." She crawled off the bed and walked towards the bathroom.

Looking down at his cock, he asked, "What the hell?"

Holden heard the shower start. After a couple of seconds, he heard Paige yell for him once again: "Care to join me?" Without hesitation, he ran into the bathroom.

She was standing in the tub with water running down her body. The curtain was wide open. She was still wearing the garter and thigh-highs. She grabbed the soap and slowly lathered herself up. Her eyes never once left Holden's.

Holden watched intently, not saying a word. Once Paige had lathered her body, she rubbed the soap in, concentrating on her tits and pussy. Confident she was clean, she turned around, causing water to spray everywhere. It made a big puddle on the bathroom floor. It was a small price to pay, Holden thought.

Paige lathered up her ass. Bending at the waist, she worked a hand between her legs. Her fingers moved in and around her pussy, causing the view to become very obscured by bubbles.

With teasing phase two complete, she turned around and slowly unclasped the thigh-highs, pulling each stocking down her leg and tossing the wet garments at Holden. They hit him with a slapping sound. Holden let the first one fall to the floor. The second one hung over his shoulder.

She removed her garter and tossed it with much more care towards Holden. She was worried the straps and buckles would take out an eye or knock out a tooth. The garter fell well short of him.

Paige, naked, closed the shower curtain. She extended her hand and gave Holden the come-hither signal with her finger.

Holden paused, trying to create doubt in Paige's mind as to whether he was going to join her. Of course he did. Paige wrapped her arms around his neck and kissed him. "I love you so much," she said.

Holden, gripping her hips, squeezed her tightly against him. "I know, baby. I love you too."

Paige jumped up and wrapped her legs around Holden as Holden slammed her against the shower wall. He slowly slide his very worked-up cock inside her. As he thrust, she pulled the showerhead off the holder and positioned it under her leg. She focused the stream of water onto them. The spray of warm water against Holden's balls and ass put him over the top. He came hard inside her.

Paige felt him filling her up. She moved the showerhead between their stomachs so the stream struck her clit.

Holden, realizing Paige wasn't done yet, did his best to keep his cock hard and continued to fuck her. He bit her neck. Paige pressed the showerhead hard against her clit and set off her orgasm. She dropped the showerhead. It swung back and forth, spraying water everywhere.

Paige reached around, sunk her fingers into Holden's muscular ass and pulled it tight to her, hoping to get his flaccid cock further inside her – to no avail. Holden lowered Paige until her bare toes touched the porcelain. Their grip on each other loosened as they kissed each other deeply.

All the while, Holden's boys were coursing deeper inside Paige.

Holden replaced the showerhead in its bracket, and they began to really wash themselves off. Satisfied they were actually clean, they climbed out of the shower and towelled dry. Feeling a cold draft, Paige ran naked into the bedroom and dived under the sheets. She held open the covers on Holden's side. Holden quickly blew out the candles so they wouldn't burn down the condo, then joined Paige in bed.

CHAPTER 11

As their one-year anniversary approached, Holden teased Paige with hints of his special plans for the evening. Paige's mind wandered. Although it had only been one year, they had gone through a lot as a couple. The excitement of Tamara and Mike's last-minute wedding made Paige think about her own wedding. She convinced herself Holden was going to propose on their anniversary. She even told her mom and Tamara what she was thinking. Everyone was excited for her.

She dressed up in a black, form-fitting dress and her Mary Jane shoes. Holden put on a nice shirt and tie under a fun sport coat he'd purchased earlier in the week. They arrived at a restaurant neither had been to before. It had the reputation of being the nicest in town. Holden had had to use some recently made connections to even get a reservation.

If first impressions meant anything, the establishment appeared well worth its reputation. Behind the large, solid oak doors was a lobby complete with a wall fountain. A handsome man in a tuxedo stood behind a small podium. Classical music played softly in the background. The maître d' greeted them and asked their names. After verifying the reservation, he turned and showed them to their table.

Holden and Paige became giddy as they got caught up in the ambiance of the classy establishment. They tried to hide their excitement and pretend they were well accustomed to such places. Holden held out his elbow so Paige could slide her arm through his. They followed the maître d'.

He finally stopped at a very beautiful and private corner table that overlooked the ocean. He pulled out Paige's chair and gently pushed it in as she took her seat. He then turned to the already seated Holden. Unfolding a napkin, he laid it in Holden's lap, much to Holden's surprise. Paige laughed at Holden's expression.

Once they were settled, Paige searched all over the table for anything that might be out of the ordinary. Seeing nothing that might contain a diamond, Paige convinced herself that the surprise would come with dessert.

Over the next couple of hours, the two enjoyed their dinner and several glasses of wine. Their eyes left one another only to look out at the tremendous view. It was a beautiful night. The waves crashed against the beach. The hypnotic sounds of the ocean held their attention for some time.

When the last of the wine was drunk, the waiter brought them coffee and a dessert menu. Holden took his time ordering. The anticipation was killing Paige. What was the big surprise Holden had in store for her?

Finally, Holden ordered something for the two of them to share. Paige's legs became weak with nerves. The dessert was delivered and they began to eat. After it was gone, there was still nothing.

The waiter came around and asked if they would like anything else. Not wanting to leave right away, Holden ordered two glasses of champagne. He made a point of mentioning that they were celebrating their anniversary. Paige's hopes rose again.

When the drinks arrived, the waiter informed them that the champagne was on the house with their compliments. Holden and Paige thanked him, then tapped glasses to toast their year together.

Holden was amused when he caught Paige staring hard into her glass. Her expression of disappointment wasn't lost on him. As the last drop was downed, Holden gave the waiter his credit card. He signed the slip and the pair was off.

Paige, despite the fantastic meal and the great ambiance, felt the dinner had been a bit anticlimactic. On the way to their car, she suggested that they go to a movie. Holden told her he was too tired and that they should head back to the condo. Reluctantly, Paige agreed. Then it struck her that maybe the surprise was waiting for her at the condo. She didn't even wait for the car to be turned off before she bounced out and headed for the door.

Holden purposely took his time walking to the door. He asked her what her problem was. Did she have to pee?

Paige told him to shut up and open the door.

Not being one to argue, Holden obliged. Paige ran into the condo to look around. She didn't see anything out of the ordinary. Nor did she notice that Holden disappeared into the bedroom for a minute before joining her.

Holden stood behind Paige, wrapped his arms around her waist, and kissed her neck. She leaned back against him and thanked him for a wonderful dinner and a wonderful year. Holden squeezed her tightly and returned the sentiment.

Holden then asked Paige if she was ready for her surprise. Paige tried to turn around to face him, but his grip tightened to hold her securely in place.

Paige wasn't sure what the surprise could be, but she was sure there was nothing in the living room for her. Holden reached into his pocket and pulled out a mask, which he slipped over her head. Paige was really becoming unsure of what he had in store.

Holden asked Paige if she trusted him. She, of course, said she did. Leading her by the hand, he escorted her into the bedroom. She felt the bed at her knee. She started to lower herself, but Holden stopped her.

Holden slowly unzipped her dress, then slid it off her shoulders and down her body to the floor. Paige hadn't wanted to show any lines under her tight dress, so she had elected not to wear a bra or panties to dinner. She was now blindfolded and completely naked.

Holden wrapped his arm around her waist. He kissed her shoulder and asked if she was OK. Paige smiled and gave him a nod. Holden slid his hand down her tight stomach, which sent shivers through her. Holden carefully guided her to the bed. Then he paused to look at his beautiful girlfriend.

Paige wasn't sure where Holden was. Her mind wandered as she thought of him staring at her. She anticipated what he was going to do to her, what part of her body his eyes were looking at, and what he was currently doing. She could hear him fumbling with something across the room. She wasn't sure what it was until she felt the fibres of a rope slide over her hand and wrist. Her arm was restrained above her head. She could hear him walking around the bed to work on her other arm.

After her arms were secured, she felt him pull on her legs, tying them up one at a time so they were spread open. Once the last knot was tied and Holden was satisfied she couldn't move, he stood to appreciate his work. She couldn't hear him, nor could she feel him. She definitely couldn't see him. But she could feel his eyes burning into her naked, vulnerable body.

She heard sounds of what she guessed to be Holden taking off his clothes, but that was mere speculation. Paige was eager to have Holden touch her in a way only he could.

Holden moved around the bed. She felt only small grazes of his touch. His fingers ever so softly ran up her thigh and caressed her stomach. They moved to her heaving breasts. At the same time, she felt his breath on her neck. It moved down her body. She felt the touch of his tongue on her pussy. She didn't know when or where the next touch would be, but she wanted it soon. She was already very wet and in need of release.

Paige tensed as Holden's tongue met her clit. Holden took one, maybe two very hard licks of her pussy. Paige begged him to fuck her, "In time," Holden responded.

She felt his body slide up hers. His nipple ring slide past her own nipple at the same time she felt his cock pressing against her pussy. She was helpless to guide it into her. She didn't say anything, but she moved around as best she could to get him inside her. He wasn't cooperating. Holden whispered that he was in control. Paige took the hint and stopped moving.

She felt his hand move towards his cock to aid it in penetrating her. First his head slipped inside her. Then she felt the familiar piercings.

Just as Holden started to get a good rhythm going, the doorbell rang. At first Paige was upset by the unwelcome intrusion. But Holden stopped fucking her and whispered, "Right on time." He got up. She heard him put on some clothes. Then she heard Holden say, "Don't go anywhere."

Footsteps ran down the hall. Paige was nervous but still very worked up. She could hear Holden outside the bedroom, talking to an unfamiliar voice. The bedroom door opened. Panic set in as she realized there was now a third person in the room. She moved to cover herself, to no avail.

Holden obviously saw the discomfort in her face. He sat down next to her and whispered, "Do you trust me?"

Paige hesitated to answer.

He said, "This is for you. I want you to enjoy it. But if you aren't comfortable, tell me and we can stop it right now."

They had talked about threesomes before but it had always been more of a fantasy thing than something they expected to take place. She was upset that Holden hadn't consulted her first. But she did have the fantasy regularly and she also really needed to be satisfied. Since she trusted Holden completely, she nodded, giving him the OK to proceed.

Her mind spun as she worked herself up at the endless possibilities the evening had in store. Who was the third person? She was pretty confident it was a guy, but did she know him?

The questions running around her head disappeared when she felt the first set of hands touch her body. She wasn't sure if they were Holden's, but they were definitely male hands. They worked from her knee to her thigh to her pussy. Music started, and it was a bit loud. Paige could barely hear what was going on in the room, but she could definitely feel it.

She felt the weight of a person on the bed beside her head, which startled her. When a cock touched her lips, she could feel the piercings, so she knew it was Holden in her mouth. Because the other set of hands never left her body, she guessed that that meant the hands on her pussy had to belong to the stranger.

Paige opened her mouth and accepted Holden's very hard cock into it. She sucked him while he played with her tits and the stranger explored inside her. Over the music, she could barely make out Holden saying, "Beautiful pussy, isn't it?" She couldn't hear the stranger's response, but by the more energetic fingering, she knew he agreed.

Holden pulled his cock out of her mouth and twisted around as the mystery man pulled his hand out of her pussy. Holden kissed her lips. "I love you, OK?"

Paige, still very hesitant, let her imagination and curiosity get the best of her. "I love you too."

Holden crawled off the bed. Paige heard a commotion in the background. The thought of two men staring at her helpless, naked body, both waiting to fuck her, was eating her up. She wanted to be ravished.

Then she felt knees on the other side of her head. A cock pressed against her lips. She wasn't sure what to do until she heard Holden reassure her that it was going to be great. She opened her lips, hoping to once again feel the metal on Holden's cock. But as it went deeper, she felt no piercings.

She felt guilty initially because it was the first cock other than Holden's that she had tasted since they started dating. All doubt was removed when she felt Holden's cock sink inside her, very quickly and very forcefully. She was surprised because she didn't feel Holden move between her legs. The extra intensity told her he was enjoying watching her suck someone else's dick, which in turn made her put more effort into pleasuring the cock in her mouth.

Holden fucked her harder and harder, which brought Paige closer to orgasm. She felt him pull out of her and come across her stomach as she continued to suck the stranger's cock. She knew Holden was watching her, and she wanted to put on a good show for him. She also knew that watching her was what had made him come more quickly than normal.

Even though she was flattered, she was also annoyed. She still needed to get off. Holden knew he hadn't make her come. She could hear him tell the other man it was his turn to fuck her. Paige was reluctant to let the stranger penetrate her, but she had no time to object before he was between her legs and fucking her hard.

Paige enjoyed the feeling of the other man's cock inside her. She liked the helpless feeling of being tied up, and fucking two guys at once made her feel so dirty. She liked exploring her dirty side, and she loved that Holden encouraged her to do so. But she felt guilty regardless.

She felt two hands grab her tits. She wasn't sure whose they were until she heard Holden speak. "Do you like his cock? Does it feel good? Tell him how good his cock is." Paige let out a guilty moan. She was about to come. She didn't want to. She didn't want to come for the stranger. She wanted to save it for Holden, but she had no choice. She couldn't hold back.

She felt Holden's teeth gently clench her nipple as he bit into her. The unexpected pain allowed her mind to clear, and she began to orgasm. She vibrated and came hard, very hard.

The man inside her didn't lose a beat. He continued to pound her, making her orgasm that much more intense. Once she was done, she heard a moan. She felt the strange cock inside her release, filling her pussy with come.

As the adrenaline subsided, she felt even guiltier. All kinds of bad thoughts ran through her mind. What if this guy had something? What if he made her pregnant? She was mad at him for thinking he had permission to come inside her.

Holden leaned in and hugged her. He told her he loved her and thanked her for keeping such an open mind. He slowly untied her – legs first, then arms.

Once she had a free arm, she tried to rip off her blindfold but Holden stopped her. "Wait. Are you ready to meet the guy who was nice enough to join us on our special occasion?"

Feeling embarrassed but curious, she really wanted to meet the mystery man who had just pleasured her so wonderfully.

Holden removed her blindfold. Shyly, she glanced around the room. She didn't see anyone. She wondered where he had gone, because she knew he hadn't had time to leave. She looked at Holden in bewilderment. "Where is he?"

Holden smiled and pulled out a dildo she had never seen before. It was a replica of Holden's cock, complete with piercings. She was still confused. Holden explained that he had played her a recording of some voices he'd made earlier in the week. She asked who had been at door. Holden told her there was a pizza waiting in the kitchen if she was hungry. He directed her eyes to the nightstand, where she could see his three piercings, removed to change the feel of his real cock.

He then filled in the rest: how the blindfold and music were designed to disorient her, how he had planted a couple of small details and let her assume everything else. Paige loved the effort Holden had put into her surprise. She also had to laugh at the thought of Holden making the replica toy.

The two went into the living room, snuggled up naked in front of the TV, and watched an old Marx Brothers movie. They woke up the next morning, spooning each other on the couch. Neither of them was feeling too great from the wine and champagne at dinner, so they stayed on the couch until lunchtime.

Paige was the first to move. She rolled off the couch and barely avoided falling on the floor. Holden wanted to laugh, but the urge to not move was greater. Paige stood up, and Holden stared at her naked body. She didn't say anything to him. She walked to the bathroom and jumped in the shower.

Over the next few days, Holden noticed a change in Paige. She became more distant. He tried to talk to her about it, but she brushed him off, saying it was nothing. Holden asked if she wanted to go home for a visit or if she wanted her family to come visit them. She said having her sister there would be fun.

Holden knew she was getting stressed with school and had been homesick all along. Having her sister there might be the thing to cheer her. He called Paige's parents and set everything up. With school getting out for the summer, the timing was perfect. Holden even discussed the possibility of her sister Chelsea working at the rink, selling tickets or something.

Paige, even though she loved her sister, thought that much time together would be too much. Holden didn't argue. Paige's mom thought the visit was a great idea. Holden knew she liked the notion of having a spy to check up on everything. She also told Holden that Chelsea's birthday was coming up in a week, so this trip would be a wonderful gift.

Holden bought the ticket, and before they knew it, they were at the airport waiting for Chelsea's flight. The two sisters greeted each other with a hug. Holden simply said, "Hey." Since Chelsea had never been out west before, Holden took the girls for a drive around town. They showed Chelsea the main tourist sites and the arena they both worked at. They also drove Chelsea by Paige's university before they finally made it back to the condo.

Holden carried Chelsea's bags into their home. They were heavy. He wondered exactly how long she planned to stay. Paige informed Holden that a woman needed to pack outfits for all possibilities, plus accessorize for those outfits.

Holden had to work during the whole week Chelsea was scheduled to stay, since he had taken a week off for Mike's wedding. Paige had recently finished a gruelling semester, so she took the week off to entertain her sister. Tamara had to work most of the week, but she managed to scam that Friday off. Paige made reservations for Thursday night. They were going to go out and cut loose with the girls.

Paige showed Chelsea around the condo while Holden fired up the barbecue. When Holden looked back into the condo from his smoke-filled balcony, he saw that the drinking had already begun. Chelsea was holding a beer and Paige was sitting next to her, drinking what appeared to be a rum and Coke. Holden stayed out on the balcony, watching the meat and enjoying the view.

After a few minutes of girl talk, they joined Holden out on the balcony. Paige handed him a beer, for which Holden was grateful. Chelsea admired the view. It was a beautiful night with not a cloud in the sky. The sun was setting behind the farthest mountain range.

Holden ran into the condo and brought out a third chair so all of them could sit down as their supper cooked. Chelsea told them about her new boyfriend, one her mother didn't know about. Holden and Paige laughed at the fact she was worried to tell her mom. Then Chelsea dropped the bomb that she wasn't sure her mom would like her dating one of her teachers. Holden offhandedly said that was one way to get good grades. Paige hit him across the chest. "Chelsea, *what* are you thinking? Is he married? How old is he?"

"He isn't married. He's only 28, and hot."

"You're only 18—"

"I'm 19 in two days," Chelsea interrupted.

"So? He's still ten years older than you."

"Yeah, but he's great in bed."

"I don't want to hear that."

"Here, this is his picture."

"Oh, he is hot," Paige said reluctantly. She handed the picture to Holden.

Holden didn't want the picture. But he took it anyway and said, "Well, damn, he *is* hot. I'd do him." He passed the picture back to Paige and took another gulp of his beer as he tried not to laugh.

Paige glanced at him. "You're not helping."

"Not trying to. Seriously, what's the big deal? She's graduated, so technically he isn't her teacher any more. He has a job. Things could be worse – he could be a drummer."

"Yeah, true. Well, whatever. As long as you're happy," Paige said.

"Thank you," Chelsea said, looking appreciatively at Holden.

Dinner was cooked to perfection. After dinner, Holden didn't want to waste a beautiful night, so they drove Chelsea to the waterfront. They walked on the boardwalk. It seemed everyone in Vancouver had had the same idea, because the boardwalk was full of activity.

There was a young man leaning up against a tree, playing the saxophone. They all stopped and watched. He played amazingly well. Holden gladly tipped him ten dollars. The man, not missing a note, nodded before they turned and moved on.

There were also carnival-style games lined up on the boardwalk, complete with the hustlers trying to bait Holden into spending his money to win cheap prizes. Holden resisted, despite being teased by Paige and Chelsea for being scared. He instead led them to an ice cream truck, where they all got vanilla soft serve.

After he paid, he turned and ran into the Witch Doctors' goalie. He was taking a late-night skate along the boardwalk. Holden introduced him to Chelsea; Paige and he had already met on several occasions. The goalie was only 20. Despite being a remarkable player, he was social awkward. Normally a clown in the dressing room, he clammed right up when he saw Chelsea.

Holden and Paige continued to talk to him as Chelsea quietly ate her ice cream. Holden tried to get Kurt into a conversation with Chelsea, but he didn't take the bait. Finally he bashfully looked at Chelsea, and their eyes met. Kurt put his finger to his lip and told her she had ice cream there. Chelsea, being Paige's sister, stared hard back into his eyes. Deliberately, she licked the vanilla from her lips.

Paige laughed at her sister's antics. Kurt blushed harder and stopped talking. Finally Holden let him off the hook and told him that they should move on. He invited Kurt to join them but knew he wouldn't. Kurt told them he was just about done his skate and was heading home. Holden couldn't wait to get back to work to let the team in on the story.

They walked around the boardwalk and neighbouring park for another hour before they decided to head back to the condo. Once they got there, the two girls went out to the balcony. Holden joined them with three beers. Paige turned him down, so Holden and Chelsea gave her a hard time.

Holden put the extra beer beside him and told Chelsea it was up for grabs for the first one done. Taking him up on the challenge, she raised her bottle, and they had a chugging contest. Paige acted as the unbiased judge. Holden won hands down but still tossed the beer to the runner-up for her valiant effort.

Holden turned on the entertainment system and cranked some tunes while he went in for another beer. He asked Paige if she was OK when she requested a can of Coke. Holden asked if she wanted rye in her Coke, but again Paige turned him down. He shrugged and went for the drinks.

Holden turned in early because he had to get up for work, but the two girls sat on the balcony well into the morning. Holden could occasionally hear them giggling over the music playing in the living room. He still managed to sleep over all the noise.

The next day while Holden was hard at work, the girls went downtown, leaving no mall unturned. They went to a patio bar for lunch and enjoyed the ocean spray in the warm summer sun.

Holden had left work and was walking to the parking garage when he heard the sound of thunder coming up behind him. Before he could turn and get out of the way, he was tackled by two hyper sisters, both of whom were carrying their weight in shopping bags. They looked helplessly at Holden as they begged for a ride home.

Holden contemplated whether to let the girls in the car with him. Chelsea tackled him, securing his arms behind his back while Paige dived into his pockets to swipe the car keys. She dangled them in the air. "You don't have a choice now. Chelsea, should we let him come home with us or should he take the bus?"

The timing couldn't have been better. Mike walked behind Paige and ripped the keys out of her hand. He tossed them back to Holden. "There ya go, man. I suggest the bus for them and their little bags too."

"Hey, no fair!" Paige yelled.

Mike yelled back, "Losing is never fair!" He got into his car and drove away.

Chelsea and Paige walked towards Holden. "You don't have anyone to help you now," Paige said. Holden slowly walked backwards towards the car. Once he got up against it, he jumped over the hood and into the driver's side, leaving the passenger side locked.

The two girls ran to the car and tried to open the door. Holden sat in the leather seat and pointed and laughed at them. Paige, after looking around, pulled up her shirt and pressed her tits against the glass. Chelsea laughed. Holden popped the locks so they could get in.

Paige buckled into the front seat, then leaned over and kissed Holden. "I knew you'd let us in." Holden laughed. He brought the car to life and headed for home.

Paige and Chelsea filled Holden in on their day. In turn, Holden told them what he'd done all day, to the exaggerated yawns from the peanut gallery in the backseat. Holden brushed her off and kept talking in amazingly graphic detail about every piece of paper he'd printed, every inane conversation he'd had, how many coffees he'd drunk, and what he ate for lunch. Paige laughed because she knew he was exaggerating the mundaneness of his job for Chelsea's benefit.

Having enough, Chelsea interrupted and asked what the plan for dinner was. They asked Chelsea what she wanted to do, and she said that while she was online, she'd seen a cool little dinner theatre she would like to go to. Paige and Holden thought it was an excellent idea and wondered if they could get tickets. They drove by the restaurant, and Paige called them from her cell. Luckily they had tickets for the eight o'clock show, which gave them enough time to run home and change.

The dinner theatre wasn't what Chelsea had anticipated. She expected better acting and better food. But it wasn't a complete letdown. She had a great story, and she even managed to order drinks without getting carded. Although she was three years younger than Paige, Chelsea appeared five years older. She too had long hair, but hers was straight, and she was a couple of inches taller than Paige. Though she was very far from fat, she had more mass than Paige and much bigger tits, which she did not hesitate to accentuate.

The night ended fairly early. Holden turned in as the girls went back onto the balcony. Paige got drinks, and Chelsea and she talked. Chelsea noticed Paige didn't mix alcohol into her drink nor had she drunk all through dinner. Chelsea asked her what was up. Paige sat in silence as Chelsea waited for her sister's response.

Finally Paige swallowed hard and looked Chelsea straight in her eyes. "I think I'm pregnant."

"Whoa!" Chelsea said. "How do you feel about that? Does Holden know?"

"No, and I'm not sure how I feel about it. I don't know if I'm ready to be a wife, let alone a mom."

"Bummer, dude. But seriously, that is awesome. You'll make a great mom, and Holden is great. You're done school now. What is your problem?"

"I don't know, dude. I'm just worried it's a big step. I don't know how Holden will take it, and he hasn't even asked me to marry him."

"Seriously, relax. It's not that bad. This is good news. Mom is going to be so happy."

"It is good news, isn't it?" Paige reiterated.

Chelsea let out a shriek. "I'm going to be an aunt!"

"Shut up. Holden will hear you."

Paige, feeling more energetic and positive about her possible state, called it a night. For the next hour, Chelsea tried to watch TV, but she had to turn up the volume to drown out the sound of her sister getting nailed in the next room. Holden wasn't sure what had inspired Paige, but he wasn't about to question it.

The next day, the girls went out shopping again. This time they left the ransacked malls alone. They concentrated on the downtown core, stopping in almost every little shop. Chelsea, wrapped up in the aunty thing, kept pulling out baby accessories. She told Paige all the stuff she was going to buy the baby. She also spent the better part of the day telling Paige why naming the baby after her was the only choice. Paige, sinking into the hype, nevertheless reminded Chelsea she wasn't positive. She was going to wait a couple of days, then get a home test.

Once Holden got home, the girls were waiting for him. They decided they were going to have another barbecue for supper, but first they needed to run out and get some things. Chelsea said she was going to miss the outing so she could talk to her boyfriend online. The happy couple ribbed Chelsea for a bit before they left for the store.

Holden got down to the parking garage before he realized he'd forgotten his wallet. He took the elevator back up to the condo and apparently entered very quietly. He overheard Chelsea say, "Yeah, they went to the store. Yes, I got it. Yes, I'm using it. OK, I'll turn it on, but it has to be fast. They won't be long."

Holden was curious about the conversation. He cautiously walked towards the living room, where he'd left his wallet. He heard a humming sound. As he peeked around the corner, there was Chelsea, completely naked, a webcam positioned on the table to record her entire body.

Holden was amazed. She had an incredible, muscular body. Her large breasts, which he'd wanted to see on more than one occasion, were so very firm that they didn't move as she fucked herself with a vibrator. Apparently her boyfriend had bought it for her before she went on the trip.

Holden sat behind the wall, trying to figure out the best way to approach the situation. He had to move fast because the moans from his girlfriend's sister and her Internet lover were arousing him.

Finally he walked in. "Don't mind me," he said as he grabbed his wallet.

Chelsea struggled to find a cover-up, but Holden was gone before she could. She heard him yell, "Very nice, by the way." Embarrassed, she cut the session short with her boyfriend and went out to the balcony for a drink. Neither Holden nor Chelsea brought up the subject again.

On Thursday night, Tamara showed up for ladies' night. Tamara bugged Paige about not drinking. Holden too was beginning to wonder what was up, but he figured she would tell him soon enough.

Over the course of the night, Paige, with the prodding of Chelsea, told Tamara her suspicions. The drunk Tamara screamed and stood up on a table. "Get me a drink over here! I'm drinking for two!" She jumped off the table and hugged Paige.

Paige reminded them both not to get excited yet, but they ignored her. The night continued like that. Paige realized that going to the bar sober was painful, but she toughed it out for her little sister.

Last call was announced, and it was time to head home. Paige pried the girls off the dance floor and away from the two prospects who had been buying them drinks all night, much to the guys' chagrin. Before they parted ways, Paige made Tamara promise not to tell Mike until after she had a chance to tell Holden. Tamara agreed and told Paige she'd be there for her if she needed anything. Paige hugged her and thanked her, and they jumped into separate cabs.

Paige and Chelsea crawled into their beds. Paige tried her best to not wake up Holden, but it was too late. Holden was curious about the evening, so Paige filled him in on everything. She told him about the hot girls at the bar, and described one in detail: her hair, her make-up, and her outfit right down to her shoes. It aroused Holden, which was Paige's intent.

She slowly slid her hand beneath the covers and below the waistband of his boxers. She squeezed his stiffening cock and firmly stroked it. Holden sat back and visualized the girl. Paige went on to tell him what she wanted to do to him as she stroked him faster and harder. Her lips were against his ear as she spoke. He tried to twist over to fuck her, but she refused to let him. She wanted to make him come her way.

She lay on her back and changed hands so she could comfortably explore her own pussy. Holden enjoyed the experience. He wanted to do more to aid Paige, but it was obvious she had something specific in mind. Her hand was slow but firm on his cock. The steady tugs built him up slowly, making the sensation that much greater.

Paige turned herself on with her story. She was always able to click her mouse just right to get herself off fast. As she was about to make herself come, she slid down the bed so her mouth could take Holden's cock. She moved her hand to the base of his cock as her mouth took over the slow, steady pace she had created. The extra warmth and the moans from Paige pushed Holden over the edge.

He told Paige he was about to come so he wouldn't surprise her by exploding in her mouth. She didn't pull away. Instead she pushed her head down further on his shaft and let him fill her mouth. She simultaneously made herself orgasm.

Holden relaxed. The unexpected sexcapades were going to make him sleep well, he thought. Paige swallowed the massive, gooey load, then kissed her way up Holden's chest to his mouth. Holden, without hesitation, kissed her back.

She pulled away. With a tear in her eye, she told Holden how much she loved him and how she couldn't imagine life without him.

Holden wasn't sure what had brought on this unexpected sincerity, but he reciprocated the sentiment and hugged Paige. She began to cry, which was completely out of character. "What's wrong, sweetheart?"

"Holden, I love you."

"I know, baby. What's wrong?"

"I think I'm pregnant."

CHAPTER 12

Holden didn't move when he heard the news. His eyes widened as he absorbed the information, but he remained speechless.

Paige looked at Holden for signs of hope that everything was going to be OK. The still-shocked Holden met her stare. "What? How'd this happen? What are we going to do?" he asked.

Paige fought back more tears. She questioned herself. Should she have waited to tell Holden until she was sure? She was beginning to regret her decision. "What do you mean, what are we going to do? And as far as how it happened, I'm pretty sure you were there every time."

"I know, but I thought we were protected. What are we going to do?"

"Nothing is a hundred per cent. I don't know what we're going to do," Paige replied.

Holden tried to let the information sink in. He leaned back in the bed, putting his hands on his forehead. "*Fuck*."

"Nice, Holden." Paige got up to leave the room.

"Where you going?"

"In to sleep with Chelsea. I can't be around you right now." Her tears began to flow. She needed Holden to be strong for her. His reaction was the exact opposite of what she'd been hoping for.

"Wait, Paige. We need to talk about this, figure something out."

Paige ignored him as she firmly closed the door behind her.

Holden remained in bed for several seconds. Thoughts ran through his mind. He regretted his initial reaction, but it was too late to do anything about it. He could only try to apologize to Paige and hoped she understood.

Holden got out of bed. Because he was concerned about his girlfriend, he forgot to get dressed. He tried to talk to Paige through the thin door of the spare bedroom. Finally the door opened, but it wasn't Paige behind it – it was a very tired Chelsea. She exited the room and closed the door behind her. She ignored the fact that Holden was naked; she herself was wearing only a T-shirt that barely hung below her waist.

"You're an ass." she said.

"Tell me something I don't know." Holden hung his head in shame.

"Look, she knows you love her. She is upset and confused. This has been bothering her for days now, and she needed you to be more supportive."

"I know, but that's just it. She's had several days to let it sink in. I had two minutes. It's a lot to take in, ya know?"

"I know. Go sleep on it. I'll talk to her and try to calm her down. Things will be fine in the morning, I promise."

Chelsea turned to go back into her bedroom. Being so tired, she stumbled and reached out to Holden for support. She missed. She crashed onto her knees in front of the naked Holden. She again reached out for support, and her hands landed on his thighs. Her face smacked into his thigh, causing him to let out a small moan.

"Fuck me," Chelsea cursed, startled by her trip.

Seconds after the thump, the bedroom door opened again. Paige came out to see what was happening. She saw her sister's face inches from Holden's naked waist. "Nice," she said. She turned and slammed the door, locking it behind her.

Chelsea, at eye level with Holden's cock, thought, *Nice indeed*, but she dared not say anything.

They had to laugh at the misunderstanding. It felt very *Three's Company*. Chelsea climbed to her feet and pounded on the door in an attempt to explain to Paige. Paige wasn't in the mood to hear any explanations.

Holden ran into his room and put on a pair of shorts before he joined Chelsea in trying to explain the situation. Tearfully, Paige finally swung open the door. "Fuck you both. You want him, he's yours!" Then she slammed the door again.

Holden heard her crying in the room. He felt helpless. He wanted to support his love, but he couldn't. He finally told Chelsea she could have the master bedroom. He would stay outside the spare bedroom in hopes that Paige would eventually be willing to talk.

Chelsea fell asleep in the master bedroom. Holden, his back to the bedroom door, finally heard Paige's sobs stop. Several minutes later, he too fell asleep. It felt like he had just closed his eyes when he heard the alarm going off in the master bedroom.

He scrambled to his feet, the events of the night before still very fresh in his mind. He ran into the room to turn off the alarm. Forgetting about Chelsea, he dived across the bed to avoid waking anyone. When he crashed onto Chelsea, she sprang to life. "What the fuck?"

"Oh shit, sorry. I forgot you were in here," Holden said.

She rolled over, and the blankets fell off her naked body. As Holden struggled to get to his feet, he realized he was inadvertently using one of her tits as leverage. He could see her exposed ass. He thought great asses must run in the family. He became guilty when he realized that he was getting hard looking at Paige's sister.

He finally rolled off the bed. The entire interaction had only taken about five seconds, but he was happy it was over. He was also glad she was going home that day, because she was getting dangerous to be around.

Holden showered and got ready for work, avoiding the master bedroom at all cost. Before he left the condo, he gently knocked on the door to the spare room. "I love you with all my heart, Paige. Together we can get through anything." He then left for the office.

All day he couldn't concentrate, and it was noticed at work. Mike asked him if everything was all right. Holden took him into his office and explained what had happened. "That's heavy. So you're going to be a daddy, eh?" Mike asked.

"I guess so."

"How do you feel about that?"

"I don't know, man. It's weird. I know I love her, and I want to be with her, and we talked about kids. But, you know, all our lives, hearing those words 'I'm pregnant' has been a very bad thing. It's hard to wrap my head around the idea that we're grown-ups and it's not necessarily a bad thing anymore."

"Grown-ups," Mike said, laughing. "Dude, I'm married and I still don't feel like a grown-up." Holden nodded at him in agreement.

During the day, Holden tried calling Paige. He also sent several text messages without getting an answer. He couldn't wait for the end of the day. Once he was finally done, he scurried home, not sure what to expect.

When he got to the condo, he unlocked the door and headed in. He was surprised to see that the place was empty. He was upset that she wasn't there because he was anxious to talk to her again, but he assumed she was out with her sister.

Holden went into the bedroom and changed out of his work attire into something more comfortable. He then went to the fridge to grab a soda. He noticed a note on the kitchen counter.

Holden—
I'm sorry about last night, I know nothing happened between my sister and you, but I need time to think. I'm not going to be home for a couple of days.
Paige

Holden's heart sank. He reread the note several times, then took a seat on the floor. He pulled his cell phone out of his pocket and called her number. He didn't get an answer, so he left a message expressing his concern for her and asked her to call him back. He thought it would be unlikely, but he needed to know she was safe. He also wanted to tell her he was excited to start a family with her, but he didn't feel comfortable leaving that as a voicemail. He was worried she might think he was saying it just to win her back.

Over the next few hours, he tried his best not to obsess about it. He knew she would call him soon. But the harder he tried to put it out of his mind, the more he thought about her.

Finally he called Tamara to see if she had heard from Paige. She said she hadn't, and sent Mike over to calm Holden down.

Holden and Mike watched a roller hockey game on TV and had a couple of beers. Neither spoke much, but Holden was appreciative of his friend being there for him in his time of need. Even with Mike there, he couldn't stop worrying about Paige and wondering if she was OK.

Hours passed before Holden's cell rang. It was Tamara. She said that Paige was there, that she was OK, and that she was going to stay with Tamara for a couple of days. Holden thanked her for telling him and for taking care of Paige. He also asked her to work on Paige to get her to talk to him, and to tell her he loved her. Tamara said she'd try her best.

Holden spent the next few days reflecting on his relationship, what his life had become, and how much Paige meant to him. Paige did the same. Since Mel's visit, she had been doing that a lot, and even more so after she found out she was pregnant. She felt lost and lonely. Her sister reassured her that she was doing the right thing, but Paige wasn't so sure she was ready to settle down. She felt too young and wanted to do more things, like travel, before she became a mother. She loved Holden; she knew that much, but things were moving way too fast for her. Tamara tried to help her, but she knew only Paige could decide what was best for her.

Holden, not wanting to be at home alone, spent more and more time at the office. His office had a view of the arena, so he could watch the practices and games. When there was nothing going on, he would stare at the empty rubber surface and think about his love.

This was one of those nights. His MP3 player played music through his laptop. The lights were low in his office. His feet were up on a table beside the window to the arena. He was lost, staring blankly out the window.

He heard a knock at the door. Turning in that direction, he saw Paige standing in the doorway, bags in her hands, looking at him. "Mike told me you'd be here. I'm sorry. Can I come back now?" she asked sheepishly.

Holden scrambled to his feet and ran to her as Paige dropped her bags and jumped into his strong arms. She kissed Holden all over his face. "I love you so much. I'm so sorry for overreacting," she said.

"I'm sorry for being an ass. I should have been more supportive. I was caught off guard," Holden said.

"I know, baby. It's OK. I love you."

"I love you too," Holden said, holding Paige in his arms. All the worry and stress over the past week evaporated in that single moment. He had his love back, and he swore he'd never let her go again.

Paige also felt relief in Holden's arms. She knew things would be OK as long as she was with him.

Holden carried her to his desk, supporting her with one arm as he cleared his desk with the other. She was kissing his neck the entire time. He put her down on the desk. Their hands were running all over each other. The passion was like it had been on their first date.

Holden had often fantasized about taking Paige in his office. He saw the empty surface below and had a brilliant idea. He climbed off Paige and grabbed her by the hand. She had tears running down her face. He brought her close to him, used his index finger to wipe away her tears, kissed her, and told her everything was OK.

He led her into the depths of the arena. It was dark, so Holden had to use a flashlight to navigate the tunnels of the basement. He finally led her up a ramp to the home team's bench. He sat her down on the bench, then ran out to his car. He had a bag with their inline skates in the trunk.

Before he brought them in to Paige, he ran to the announcer's booth and turned on his MP3 player, filling the arena with music. He set the lights on low so there was just enough glow to see. Shadows were cast all over the empty arena. It spooked Paige until Holden rejoined her.

They put their skates on and slowly skated. They talked about the last week and how much they had missed each other. They held hands as they mindlessly skated around the rink.

As the song "Pump It" by the Black Eyed Peas played, Holden sprinted ahead of Paige to show off his skating skills. She clapped and cheered at his antics. He sped around behind her and skated as hard as he could towards her. Then he put his hands on her shoulders and jumped over her. She wasn't a strong skater, and she worried he would knock her over, but he barely touched her as he made the leap. She was suitably impressed.

After "Pump It", a slower song came on. Holden put his arm around Paige and led her to centre arena, then spun her around. She almost lost her balance. Holden caught her and gently guided her to the floor. As he kissed her, she tried to dig her heels into the surface but the wheels of her skates kept rolling away. Instead, she used her arms to pull Holden tight against her. She kept repeating that she loved him over and over again.

Holden could feel the intensity in Paige. He was happy she had missed him so much. Holden shared Paige's passion. He reached under her shirt, and in one fluid movement pulled her shirt and bra off. He rolled them up into a pillow for her. She pulled his shirt off, popping buttons in the process.

Holden stopped to look at his girlfriend. At one point during the week, he hadn't been sure if he would get to touch her again. He wasn't about to pass up this moment. His hand ran all over her bare skin, feeling every inch of her as he took in her soft texture and her warmth.

Paige welcomed Holden's tenderness. She became very submissive, letting Holden explore her body as if it were their first time. She ate up how he looked at her and how he touched her.

He knelt beside Paige as he unclasped their skates – first hers, then his. Once the skates were off, Holden stood up and undressed. Paige stayed on the floor, topless, not making an effort to take off any of her clothes. She didn't want to miss Holden revealing his well-sculpted body. He noticed Paige's eyes burning through him, so he took off his clothes as deliberately as possible.

When he got down to his tight boxer briefs, he slowly pulled the elastic band down, showing Paige his shaved pubic area. He slid it further, down his shaft, until it slid over the head. His hard cock sprang to life with enough force to slap him in the stomach.

Cock exposed, he let his boxers fall to the floor. She reached up to touch the cock she had been longing for, but Holden moved just out of her reach. Paige let out a cute noise. Holden laughed at her.

He bent and crawled to Paige. He undid her belt and her zipper and pulled off her jeans, revealing she wasn't wearing any panties. She had a freshly shaved landing strip. Although it was barely more than stubble, Holden had never seen her with anything less than a completely bare pussy. He ran his fingers through the coarse hair. "What do you think?" Paige asked.

"I like it. Why the change?"

"I thought I'd try something new," Paige said, blushing.

Holden smiled his approval. He put his mouth on her hair and gave her a kiss. Then he licked both sides of the patch with his tongue. Paige again tried digging her heels into the floor for support, and this time they held.

Holden rubbed his penis on her thigh. She felt the piercings graze her skin and she couldn't wait to feel them inside her again. She wanted to scream at the top of her lungs *Fuck me*, but she restrained herself.

Holden gently put his hand on Paige's ear and gazed deep into her eyes. "I love you." His voice crackled as he said it. He sank his cock deep inside her. She embraced him tightly as he gently made love to her. Her fingers dug into his back, leaving long scratch marks. His shaft penetrated her over and over again. Neither said a word, and their eyes never broke lock.

Holden had made love to Paige many times before, but never with this shared passion. It was also the longest they'd gone without sex since they first began a physical relationship.

Paige's fingers continued to clutch Holden's back as he methodically thrust into her. Her pussy, starving for attention, accepted his cock and formed firmly around his shaft. His piercings tickled her lips with every movement. Everything that was inside them – the sadness, the love, the intensity – combined to make one big culmination of emotions that released between them at the same time.

Holden began to come without warning, so much so that it even caught him by surprise. The sudden commotion inside Paige triggered her to orgasm. They forced themselves closer to each other.

After they were both done, neither moved. Holden brushed Paige's hair behind her ear. "Welcome home. I love you," Holden said.

Paige grabbed Holden and hugged him tight. She could feel his flaccid cock still inside her and his come slowly leaking out of her. "I love you too. Don't ever leave me," she begged

"I won't."

Several songs played as they lay there. Eventually they released their embrace and got dressed. Holden ensured there was no residue left on the arena – it would be hard to explain why one of his players injured himself slipping in a puddle of come.

On the drive back to their condo, Holden asked Paige if she would like to go camping on the weekend. He'd found several sites that he wanted to check out. Paige told him she'd love to. So they checked out BC campsites online and picked the perfect one. They hoped that it would be theirs alone for the weekend.

Saturday morning finally arrived. Holden and Paige packed the BMW with everything they would need for a night of camping, then went to the grocery store for some last-minute food ideas. They packed the cooler with meats, buns, and wine and hit the road.

The road they took went in the same direction as the one they had taken for their oceanside picnic. But instead of turning west off the main highway, Holden kept heading north for a couple more hours. They figured the farther away from the city they got, the more likely they would be alone at the campsite.

Paige tried to read the map while Holden navigated from the GPS. When the voice told him to turn, he turned. The voice successfully led them to their ideal spot. It was a secluded area that the BC foresters had made as a condition for their forestry license. It was barely big enough for two tents, but it had a picnic table, a small beach, and an incredible view.

The beach was on a small freshwater lake that got its water from the melting snow on neighbouring mountain. They were in a valley; peaks surrounded them except for an opening to the west. The mountains seemed to part for them, giving them a most incredible view of the ocean. They looked down on it like royalty peering out over their kingdom.

Paige unpacked their car while Holden set up the two-man pup tent. He told Paige horror stories of going camping with his family when he was young. The tent they had used was a large canvas tent that required at least two people to set up. It had several metal poles to be screwed into each other, plus there was a centre post, larger than the others, that was easy to mistake for a corner post. He had dreaded setting up that tent.

Paige said it was lucky for them the hardware store sold foolproof tents. "No doubt," Holden responded.

After the campsite was set up to their liking, Holden started a fire in the designated pit. They got the fire roaring and gathered enough wood to keep them warm throughout the night.

Paige decided to take some pictures. She stood by the car and put Holden and the fire in the foreground, the mountains and beach in the background. She then walked over to a ledge and looked down at the ocean, getting several shots from that angle.

When she'd gotten enough photos to satisfy her, they sat on the picnic table. Holden was going to turn up the car stereo, but Paige asked him to wait. She wanted to listen to nature for a while. Holden thought that was a good idea. They sat in silence for a bit. Despite the higher elevation and the snow-capped peaks, the air was warm.

Paige jumped up and took off her clothes as she walked to the beach. Holden thought she should have learned her lesson from their oceanside picnic, so he let her go. By the time her toes hit the cold mountain lake, she was completely naked. She casually walked in. When the water reached her waist, she dived in, disappearing under the water. She quickly resurfaced, gasping for air. She snapped her head back, causing her long hair to spray water in an arc as it flipped over her head.

Holden had Paige's camera. He snapped pictures of her entire swim. Paige saw him and posed like swimsuit model, sans swimsuit. She positioned herself in all kinds of poses. Then she crawled up the sandy beach and rolled around, covering herself with sand as Holden continued taking pictures. "Work it, work it," was all he kept saying, making Paige laugh.

Once she was completely covered in sand, she crept back into the water to clean off. She swam around and Holden continued to take pictures. Her hair floated free in the water, and her bare ass occasionally peeked out of the watery depths.

She swam back to Holden until her feet touched the bottom and she could walk out of the lake. The scene reminded him of the pool scene from *Fast Times at Ridgemont High*. Her toes left impressions in the sand as she proceeded towards the tent. Holden watched the water cascaded off her body.

She reached into the tent to get a towel. Once she was dry, she pulled her summer dress out of her bag and pulled it over her head, then took a seat by the fire. Holden saw that she was still shivering, so he went to the trunk of the car and pulled out a sleeping blanket. He put it over Paige's shoulders. She grabbed it and pulled it more tightly around herself.

Holden put hot chocolate in a metal container and let it cook in the fire. He then went to the car and turned up the stereo. He'd made a CD for this occasion. It played quietly in the background.

Holden joined Paige on the log. They waited for their hot chocolate to heat up. He asked her how the water was, and she told him that it was much warmer than she had anticipated. She teased Holden for being too chicken to join her. Holden assured her that he would take a swim with her later.

The hot chocolate was ready. Paige warmed up quickly once Holden served her.

The sun was setting behind the mountains. Holden went to the trunk and pulled out a rod and reel. Paige asked what he was doing. Holden said he was going to catch them some dinner. Paige laughed at him and watched as Holden stood as close to the lake as he could. He cast his lure into the lake and sat patiently for quite a while. Eventually, he reeled in his line. He told Paige that it was the spot that was to blame for his lack of results.

He walked further up the lake. Paige could still see him, but barely. He stood on a log, casting his line. As Holden continued to fish, Paige slapped hamburgers on the firepit grill. By the time he returned, admitting defeat, the burgers were done. Paige had also slipped into a cotton sweater and jogging pants.

Moving to the picnic table, they dressed their burgers and quietly ate. "Mm, I do love fresh fish," Paige teased as she bit into her hamburger. "What were you going to do with it once you caught it? Do you know how to clean a fish or even how to cook one?"

Holden looked back at her as seriously as he could. "I didn't think that far ahead. In all the movies I've seen on the subject, the guy caught the fish and the woman cleaned it. I assumed it was one of those girl things."

"You think all girls know how clean fish?"

"Yeah, sure. Is that wrong?" Holden asked with a smirk. Paige rolled her eyes.

The sky was getting red. It slowly faded, making the night air much cooler. After they finished eating, Holden began cleaning up. Paige stopped him by undressing again, "Let's go for a swim before it's completely dark."

"Are you nuts? It's cold."

"At least we know there aren't any fish in the lake to attack us," she said. She ran into the water. Completely submerged, only her head peeking out, she teased Holden relentlessly until he took off his clothes. He slowly walked to the water's edge. Small waves tickled his toes, and he withdrew to the sandy shore. "Wimp!" Paige yelled.

Holden decided to approach it like a Band-Aid. He yelled his war cry and charged into the water, tripping as the water reached his knees. He stumbled to his feet, but once the air hit his wet body, he figured he'd be warmer in the water. He dived in and grabbed Paige from the murky depths. She let out a playful shriek.

Paige and Holden splashed each other in the water for a bit. She then swam seductively over to Holden and wrapped her arms around his broad shoulders. He put his hands on her waist as she wrapped her legs around him, and they kissed. The sunset was brilliant orange and red and was low on the horizon.

Paige moved around until Holden was inside her. They watched the sun disappear into the Pacific Ocean. Once it was gone, only the fire and a crescent moon provided light. The dancing flame cast shadows all over their campsite.

Paige refocused on the cock inside her. She was impressed that Holden was able to stay so big and hard in the cold water. Holden moved his hands from her waist to her ass. She used her legs to fuck him. They weren't kissing, but their mouths were open and very close to each other. They could hear each other's subtle moans as they fucked.

The cold water was taking its toll on Holden in another way; his thigh muscles began to cramp. So he carried Paige to the beach. He lay down on his back. His cock never left Paige. She assisted Holden until she was on top of him. Once they were supported by the ground, Paige became more aggressive in her thrusting. Leaning back, she moved her legs so her feet were beside Holden's head. He put his arms on the outside of her legs. It was a position they'd never tried before. The trick was that all their moves had to be very smooth or he would fall out of her. She leaned until her back was almost in the water, allowing the tiny waves to wash over her shoulders as she fucked Holden. He tilted his head and kissed Paige's ankles.

As he watched his penis penetrate her, he thought that the best thing about this new position was the view. Watching was increasingly hot in his mind. He became worried he was going to come before she even started. To slow things down, he got Paige to change positions again. She stayed on top but got on her knees and spun around. Holden shimmied up the beach a bit so Paige wouldn't be deep in the water. With her back to him, she lowered herself on his still-hard cock. She did all the work. Her ass bobbed up and down on his cock, and he watched her pussy swallow his length as she fucked him faster and harder.

The moonlight silhouetted the mountain range and cast light on the water. Paige could watch her reflection as she rode Holden. They were both getting colder, but neither was about to stop.

Paige spun around, leaned in, and kissed Holden. Holden hugged her and easily flipped her onto her back. She clenched her legs tighter around Holden so he wouldn't slip out of her. Holden fucked Paige with increasing speed as the waves splashed against them. Paige's hands ran through Holden's hair, covering it with beach sand.

Holden was now pounding Paige hard. She loosened her legs from around his hips and put her feet flat on the sand, spreading her legs wide, allowing Holden to penetrate her deeper. Paige dug her fingers in, hoping for resistance. She came up with handfuls of mud. Her eyes broke from Holden's as they rolled back in her head. Holden took that as a good sign.

Trying to get his knees firmly in the ground for more leverage, he slipped awkwardly around inside her. The unpredictable movements helped Paige not to fall into a rhythm. Instead, every thrust penetrated her differently, helping her orgasm heighten. With one hard, deep thrust, Paige released her orgasm on Holden.

Holden was getting closer himself. Hearing her come, the moans and the extra force with which she was fucking him, certainly helped. Paige's orgasm subsided, but she knew Holden had yet to release. She turned her attention on him, scratching his back, moaning, talking dirty, and flexing her pussy muscles.

Holden was no match for her. "Oh yeah, that's it, fuck me hard" was enough to finish him off. Once again he filled her pussy with come.

They lingered only briefly in their embrace because, as their adrenaline wore off, they grew much colder. They decided to take another quick dip to wash the sand off. Hand in hand, they dived under the water. Holden, confident the sand was out of all of his crevices, walked towards the tent. He glanced back at Paige. "You coming, honey?"

"Give me a minute. I have sand *everywhere*."

Holden left the water, went to the tent, and found them both towels. Paige took her time splashing around in the water. Holden watched her. The way the moon lit her up, he thought she looked exquisite.

Holden slowly dressed, then stirred up the fire, throwing on a bigger log. Paige joined him by the roaring flames. He offered her another cup of hot chocolate, and she gladly accepted it. She held the tin cup with both hands. The tips of her fingers were barely visible because she had most of her hand hidden in the sleeves of her heavy sweater. Holden was captivated by her fingers holding the cup. At that moment they appeared so tiny and frail. Then he imagined them wrapped around his cock.

They exchanged ghost stories. As if on cue, a wolf howled in the distance. Holden took a break to clean up the campsite. He put their food in a plastic bag, which they put in a net and hung on the other side of the clearing to prevent any unwelcome visitors. Holden elected not to put the food in the car, in case curious bears decided to try for it. That would not only ruin their chance to escape, but also damage his pride and joy.

As Holden was securing the food, Paige made s'mores on the campfire. Holden came back proud of his outdoorsy ability, and Paige gave him a s'more for his efforts. After a few more scary stories, they crawled into the tent. Although they each had their own sleeping blankets, they elected to share one, falling asleep embracing each other.

The next morning, Paige was the first to wake. She carefully crawled out of bed so she didn't disturb Holden. She opened the flap to the tent and crawled out, getting dressed outside in the fresh morning air. The fire had died down but had not gone out during the night. She stirred it up and fed it another log. In no time the flames were roaring again.

Holden woke and crawled out of the tent. He saw Paige sitting quietly by the fire. The sun was rising. Mist was on the lake. He could see the marks in the beach sand from the night before.

Paige was again wearing a bulky sweater. The arms covered all but her fingertips. She was hunched over by the fire, trying to get warm. Holden watched her for a minute before letting her know he was awake. She turned and smiled and offered him a cup of hot chocolate. Holden told her he would be back for it in a minute.

He walked over to the car. On the way, he saw fresh prints in the dirt. He imagined they belonged to a bear. He decided that not telling Paige would be the best thing. He dug through his glove compartment, found what he was searching for, and walked back to Paige.

She looked at him and tried to figure out what he had on his mind. He appeared unusually focused for having just woken up. She held up his hot chocolate again, Holden reached for it and took a sip. Then he told Paige to get ready for a hike, because he wanted to walk up the trail to watch the sunrise.

Paige thought that was an excellent idea. She changed her socks and put on her running shoes. Since she was getting warmer, she changed from her sweat suit into the sundress she had been wearing the night before. Holden took her by the hand and they headed up the hill. Holden didn't tell Paige about the fresh bear tracks, but he kept them in mind.

The trail was very narrow. Holden broke the way but was careful not to let any wayward branches hit Paige in the face. She appreciated his extra effort.

Holden froze. Paige, not paying attention, crashed into his back, causing him to stumble. "What's up?" Paige asked. Holden ushered her in front of him and mimed for her to be quiet. She peeked through some branches and found herself just a couple of feet from a family of deer. The biggest of the bunch, Paige assumed, was the male. He was so close she could reach out and touch him. Holden put his hand on her back as he tried to see the deer as well. Behind the male were two smaller deer with the white and black spots on their backs. The humans watched for as long as they could before Holden suggested they keep moving so they didn't completely miss the sunrise. Paige agreed. With her first step, she broke a twig, causing the deer family to scatter.

She looked back at Holden to apologize, but he didn't give her the chance. Her brown eyes were huge with excitement; she had a smile like a schoolgirl on Christmas Eve. She was excited, hopeful, and very pure. He grabbed her, pulled her into him, and kissed her. She could tell by Holden's intensity that she was in for more than just a kiss.

He picked her up in his arms, as he'd done when he guided her over the threshold of their condominium. He carried her only a few feet deeper into the woods, where he found a large, flat rock. He sat her down, stood up quickly, and undressed. She watched him and laughed at his haste.

Once he was naked, he focused on Paige. He gently pushed her back so she was resting on the palms of her hands. He knelt before his princess and ever so carefully leaned into her knees, using his hands to guide her dress over his head. She looked down at the bulge under her skirt and imagined how she would look pregnant. That thought disappeared quickly when she felt his tongue pressing against her panties and over her clit. She felt his mouth making her panties hot and wet.

He finally pulled at her underwear; she took the hint and raised her bum off the hard rock so he could free her pussy from the cotton confines. He pulled them down her thighs, over her knees, and to her ankles. He then slipped one of her feet out. As he was about to pull them completely off, she told him to stop. She wanted them hanging around her ankle so she could find them again when they were done. Holden thought that was a good idea, so he left them where they were and went back to work under her dress.

His fingers reached under her thighs, digging deep into her flesh. She was angled awkwardly for him to penetrate her, so he settled for kissing and licking her clit and labia. As Holden licked her, Paige closed her eyes. Visions of the past few days flashed in her mind. Trying to not lose the mood, she opened her eyes and took in the sights of the surrounding forest. She had always loved making love outdoors. She imagined people watching her; the feeling that she was being watched or even filmed was often enough to bring her to orgasm with very little effort from her partner.

As she was in the height of her fantasy, she heard a twig snap. A shadow moved in her peripheral vision. She tried to jump, but Holden's grip on her thighs was too tight. Looking in the direction of the shadow, she saw nothing. She imagined a man hiding, watching her getting eaten out. In her mind's eye she could see him reaching into his pants and pulling out his long, hard cock. He stroked it as she put on a show for him. Her moans were loud and exaggerated.

Holden didn't know what he was doing differently. He assumed she really enjoyed the fresh air. Her movements and moans kept him motivated to please her.

Paige kept staring off into the empty forest as she gently opened her mouth, inviting the stranger in. She reached into the air, trying to pull the figure towards her as Holden's tongue danced deep inside her. She'd had enough. She could feel her juices running down her leg. But she still wanted the stranger's cock.

Her desire was too much to control. She tapped Holden on his head. He pulled the dress back and peeked at her over the material. "You knocked?" he asked.

She stood up without saying a word. She was still looking into the shadows as she pulled her dress over her ass, then lay on her stomach over the rock. Her legs spread as wide as they could possibly go, inviting Holden to move in behind her.

Flexing his knees, he guided his firm cock into her waiting pussy. He barely had time to slide his entire length into her before she started moaning and thrusting her hips. Her clit searched for something to rub against. Despite how violently her body moved, it came up short every time.

She continued to fuck Holden for the pleasure of the imaginary stranger. She reached back for Holden's hand and pulled it to her mouth, causing him to lose his balance and penetrate her deeper. She sucked his fingers as she wanted to do to another cock. She didn't understand why she was as horny as she was, but at that moment one cock wasn't enough for her. Making the best of what she had, she forced his fingers deep down her throat, causing her to gag.

Holden didn't know what was possessing Paige. He just knew he wanted to please her. He grabbed her hair. As he pulled hard, he pushed his cock and fingers deep inside her. She let out a cough and spit out his fingers as she orgasmed.

Instantly, she stood up. Holden saw the stream of her fluids running over the once-dry rock. Even though she just had an orgasm, she was still very focused. Without talking, she repositioned him so he was sitting on the rock. He gladly sat, wondering what she had in store for him.

She knelt on all fours. She dropped with enough force that her dress blew halfway up her back, exposing her ass to the wilderness and her imaginary friend. With her hands on the forest floor, she used her mouth to take his cock. At first, her outstretched tongue was at the base of his cock; then she slid it up his shaft. Once she got to the tip, she used her tongue to scoop up all his pre-come before sinking her lips around his manhood. She took his length entirely in her mouth. She could feel the head sliding deep down her throat. She kept her eyes open in hopes of getting a glimpse of the man in the shadows.

Paige had no desire to tease or toy with Holden. She was using his cock as a tool to satisfy her own needs. She sucked him off methodically to put on a good show. Feeling the invisible eyes burning into her exposed body, she reached between her legs and frantically rubbed her clit. Finally, she let Holden's cock fall from her mouth. She took it in her left hand as her right hand abused her clit. Keeping his member pressed against her cheek, she stroked him, long, deliberate strokes, making sure Holden could feel every inch being satisfied.

Holden couldn't take much more of it. With her scent still fresh on his lips, he took a lick. Paige looked more like Syn as she was caught up in the moment. Her hair cascaded over his legs, and his cock was pressed into the flesh of her cheek. The scent, taste, and visual combined into one massive overload. Holden came across Paige's cheek; she stroked him faster and harder as she felt him splash against her skin. Her fingers ravaged her pussy as she imagined herself in porn, performing for the man in the woods.

Her imagination caused her to have yet another orgasm. Upon completion, she let out a loud sigh, then collapsed on the forest floor.

"Wow. What was that all about?" Holden asked.

"Wow is right. Yeah, I don't know, but it was great, wasn't it?"

Holden couldn't argue.

They stayed where they were for a few more minutes before standing up, Holden cleaned the leaves out of her hair and then turned his attention to the mess he'd made on her face. Using his finger, he wiped as much come off her as he could. He pulled off his shirt and finished cleaning her up.

Holden elected to hold on to his shirt instead of putting the soiled garment back on. Paige smiled. Not only had he sacrificed his shirt for her, but his chest appeared more muscular than normal in the morning light. She glanced over her shoulder to see if she could catch another glimpse of her voyeur. She found nothing, as she expected. She smiled a bit bigger at her dirty little secret.

Paige and Holden walked another half an hour until they reached a cliff edge facing east. The sun had already risen, but the sky still retained morning colours of yellow and red, and the view was spectacular. They could see deep into the valley for miles and miles. Behind them, they could see the ocean, but their private lake was completely hidden from view.

Holden took Paige by the hand as he fumbled in his pocket. She looked curiously at him. He began to speak. "Paige, since I first laid eyes on you, I knew you were special—"

"Oh my God."

"This past year has been the most amazing in my life. Today is a perfect example. Having you gone the last week made me realize I didn't want to live another second without you."

He took a deep breath and dropped to one knee. "Paige, will you marry me?"

CHAPTER 13

Paige looked down at the kneeling Holden. Her eyes began to swell. Holden jumped to his feet to embrace his girlfriend and potential fiancée. His heart was beating so fast, he thought he was going to pass out. He felt Paige's tears against his cheek. He thought it was odd when he felt her body shaking as if she was outright crying. He expected her to be emotional, but he didn't expect the response she was showing.

He pushed her to arm's length so he could see her. He realized she wasn't crying tears of joy but tears of sadness. The excitement drained out of Holden. His legs grew weak.

Paige stared him in the eyes. "Sit down. We need to talk."

Holden wasn't sure what Paige was about to say, but he knew it wasn't going to be good. He sat on the ledge overlooking the valley. Paige sat next to him and took his hand. Their feet dangled several hundred feet above the valley floor. She talked to him through tear-filled eyes. "Holden, are you only asking me to marry you because you think I'm pregnant? Because I'm not. I found out while I was at Tamara's. I don't know why my period was so late. I think it was my new birth control. I know I should have told you that night at the arena. I'm sorry." Her voice was guilt-ridden, as if she were confessing to something she'd done wrong.

Holden returned her gaze through swollen red eyes as he fought back tears. "I was surprised when you told me you were pregnant. I wondered if we – if I was ready for a baby, but I wanted to be with you.

I wanted to be there for the baby. I proposed to you because I love you. I can't imagine a second without you, whether you're pregnant or you're not. We have the rest of our lives to have babies. What I want is the rest of my life with you."

He wept. Paige wiped his tears away, leaving hers on her cheek. Holden repeated, "Will you marry me?"

Paige paused. She turned her eyes down at the ground, then raised her eyes to Holden's. "Holden, you know I love you …"

"But?"

"But I can't marry you, not now. I have something to tell you."

She paused, waiting for Holden to say something, but he remained speechless. She took a deep breath. "Over the past couple of weeks, so many things happened. Mike and Tamara got married, I thought I was going to be a mom and a wife, Mel and Chelsea came to visit. Holden, I don't know who I am anymore or what I want. Everything is moving too fast. I need time."

"Time? What do you mean?" Holden was completely lost.

She squeezed Holden's hands tight. "I sincerely thought you were going to propose to me on our anniversary. I really thought I was going to be a mother. I really thought I was going to settle down in a house in the suburbs with a white picket fence. Holden, I really wanted it. But when none of it came true, I thought about Mel and I thought about Chelsea. I loved my life as a dancer. Don't get me wrong; I love my life with you. But I have to know for sure if I'm ready to settle down.

"I know I want to be with you, but I'm going home for a few weeks to clear my head. I've booked my tickets. I'm leaving next weekend. I hope you're not too upset."

Holden sat motionless, struggling to take in all that Paige had told him. He couldn't speak.

"I can't ask you to wait, but I truly hope you do. I love you. I *will* be back." She went to hug Holden.

He pulled away and looked into the valley. "You can't ask me to wait? How long are you going to be gone for?"

"I don't know."

Holden sat, tears freely running down his face. In the last five minutes, he had lost everything. He was no longer going to be a father, and the love of his life was leaving. Paige did her best to reassure him, but he wasn't able to hear her. She repeated that she loved him and that she'd be back. Holden wanted to believe her so badly. She was convincing. However, he knew the next several weeks were going to be very hard. Perhaps when that time was over, he would know if they were meant to be together.

They slowly walked off the hill to their campsite, packed up their things, and got in the car. The drive back was quiet. Holden tried to put the news out of his mind. He focused on driving.

Paige sat turned towards the door, staring out the window, crying. Holden occasionally looked over at her. His heart sank, but what could he do? He wasn't pushing her away, and he certainly didn't want her to go. It was all her decision.

Over the next week, he tried to show Paige how much he loved her and subtly tell her he didn't want her to go. But he knew ultimately the decision was hers and hers alone.

Neither of them told Mike or Tamara the news, but Paige told her family. They tried to talk her out of leaving by reminding her of everything she had to lose. Her stepdad got mad and said he'd known she would find a way to blow it.

Holden thought that was unfair, but he didn't entirely disagree. Holden wasn't vain enough to think he was Paige's saviour. If anything, she had saved him. But he thought that together, they had a perfect life, and he couldn't understand Paige's willingness to let it go.

They tried to keep living life like nothing was happening, but her departure day was looming. Holden had to leave the condo as Paige packed. Since she was flying, she was going to leave most of her belongings in the condo. She would send money to have them shipped if she decided not to come back. Holden found it too hard to watch.

He struggled at work. Everyone noticed how distracted he was. Mike knew Holden had intended to propose, so he asked how the camping trip went. Holden didn't answer. Mike continued trying to figure out what was wrong. Holden told him he would explain everything later. Mike reluctantly let it go at that.

Friday came around quicker than Holden had hoped. He'd hoped it wouldn't come around at all. On Saturday, Paige would leave him.

As Paige was out taking care of last-minute details, Holden assured her he would take care of everything at home while she was gone. He decided to make Paige a special dinner of all of her favourites. He even considered drugging the food so she would pass out and miss her flight, but he knew that wasn't realistic.

Paige came home and found Holden behind the stove. He had chopped up fresh vegetables, fried chicken, and cooked sticky rice – all the ingredients to make a delicious stir-fry. Paige pulled two big bottles of red wine out of a bag. She knew it was going to be a rough night, and the wine couldn't hurt.

Once dinner was ready, Holden popped a CD into his CD player and turned it up. It was a CD he'd made for her. He'd put the same playlist on her MP3 player so she could listen to it on the plane if she wanted to.

"Hey hey, momma, said the way you move, gonna make you sweat, gonna make you groove" rumbled through the surround sound. Paige stared at Holden. She didn't want to cry for the entire night, although she knew it was going to be hard. The fact that Holden remembered the song that had played when they first saw each other was enough to set her off on an emotional roller coaster.

She didn't move towards Holden; she just looked at him. The love in her eyes ran deep, which made her decision to leave even harder for Holden to understand.

He dished out the sticky rice and covered each plate with a generous portion of the teriyaki stir-fry. He carried the plates to the table, which he'd painstakingly set with perfect detail, a fact that wasn't missed by Paige. They quietly ate dinner while the songs continued playing. Each one was a sentimental favourite of Holden's. They were songs he listened to when he was feeling sad or depressed.

Halfway through dinner, "Somebody" by Depeche Mode played. Holden put down his chopsticks, walked over to Paige, and extended his hand. She smiled as best she could, given the circumstances, and reached out for his hand. They danced for three carefree moments, forgetting about the problems of the past week and the inevitable time apart.

Then the words of the song sank into Paige. By the end, tears were streaming down her cheeks. Holden apologized and said his intent wasn't to make her upset but to give her a reminder of how much he loved her, so she would never forget while she was away. She said she loved the CD but didn't need a reminder because she could never forget.

Holden wasn't sure what the future had in store for them, but it made him feel better to know she really did intend to come back.

After the song ended, they sat back down and continued eating. Paige drank several glasses of wine. Holden hoped she'd drink enough to sleep through her early-morning flight, but again, he knew that wasn't realistic.

When supper was done, Holden cleared the dishes and reached into the fridge to get dessert. He pulled out a match, lit the two dishes, and brought Paige crêpe Suzette. Paige clapped at the flaming dessert. "How elegant!"

They made idle chit-chat. The mood lightened as Paige made fun of Holden's song choices. Holden laughed along with her, knowing some were unnecessarily sappy.

When dessert was done, Holden again cleared the table. He blew out the candles, and they walked to the couch. Holden turned on the fireplace, even though it was warm in the condo, because he was trying to set a mood.

Holden went to turn off the CD, but Paige stopped him. She snuggled in tightly and wrapped her arms around him. She told him she wanted to sit and listen with him for a bit.

Holden was happy with that.

She put her feet up on the couch and assumed a foetal position. Holden put his arm around her shoulder. Paige talked about her trip and how nervous she was about going. She was worried that he would easily replace her. Maybe she was making the biggest mistake of her life. She was scared to leave him, and she also repeated that she was coming back.

Holden didn't say much. He listened to her nervous ramblings. He tried to reassure her, but he couldn't do so with confidence because he was too uncertain about their future.

The song "Save Tonight" by Eagle Eye Cherry played. They stopped listening to the lyrics and squeezed each other as tightly as they could. Then, at the same time, they leaned forward and took a sip of wine. Falling back into the couch, Paige let out a sigh. Holden leaned his head back and closed his eyes.

He dreamed that he was fucking Paige. His cock got hard. The dream felt very real. He soaked in it for as long as he could. He woke up, worried he was about to have a wet dream, and saw Paige's head in his lap. She was sucking his cock.

She returned his stare. "Good morning," she said, then took his cock in her mouth again.

"Umm, good morning," he said. He looked at his watch. It was seven o'clock in the morning. He was pissed he'd fallen asleep on their last night together.

Paige put extra effort into rubbing him and sucking him. Her hands glided up and down his shaft, following the movements of her mouth. Holden cautioned her that he was about to come. She told him it was OK and to make it good, because it had to last him awhile.

"What about you?" he asked.

"I have your anniversary present to hold me over until I get back."

She continued to stroke his cock. Her grip was firm but gentle as it caressed his penis. Her warm, wet touch felt great. Holden tried to block out the thought it might be the last time he felt her touch in that manner.

Her lips stroked him up and down, and he twitched and came. She swallowed as much of it as she could. The rest seeped from her lips and down her chin. She knelt up beside him and used her tongue to clean up the overflowing come.

Once she'd done her best to clean out her mouth, she kissed Holden, deep and passionate. She straddled his waist. Her arms embraced him tightly.

She finally stood up and looked at Holden's watch. "I guess I should shower; it's getting late." She undressed in the living room and walked into the bathroom.

Holden heard the water running and couldn't resist. He walked in to brush his teeth, but really he wanted to see Paige's wet, naked body under the showerhead. He took his time brushing while watching her silhouette.

Paige knew he was in the room, and she knew he was watching her. She made her movements very deliberate to put on a show for him.

Holden took a seat on the toilet to be as close to Paige as he could. She climbed out of the shower. As he watched her dry off, he knew his time with her was dwindling to mere hours. Paige didn't mind him being there, since she didn't want to be alone either.

Holden followed Paige into their bedroom as she dressed. He fought back tears. Paige too was trying to be strong.

Once she was ready, Holden picked up her bags, which were full of her necessities for a prolonged absence from home. He carried them down to the car and threw them in the trunk. Then he hurried to the passenger side to open her door for her. "A gentleman right up to the end," Paige joked.

The end. Those words haunted Holden, but he didn't say anything to her about it.

They stopped for a coffee on the way to the airport. They quietly sipped through downtown traffic while listening to the song "Think of Me" from the *Phantom of the Opera* soundtrack. He knew it was one of Paige's favourite songs from the play. He also knew, of all the songs he'd put on the CD, it had the most meaning.

After Holden parked his car, Paige ran and found a luggage cart. Holden loaded it up and pushed it to departures. The line was long, but luckily Paige had printed her boarding pass at home. The baggage drop-off line was considerably shorter – short enough that when she was ready, she just walked up to the counter.

She and Holden walked to security. Holden walked as slowly as he possibly could to prolong his time with Paige. He couldn't believe she was really leaving. Since he found out, he had hoped against all hope that she would change her mind. She hadn't; she had stayed strong.

It was time for her to go through security. They stopped to look at each other. Holden hugged her, and she eagerly hugged him back. She began to cry. Holden felt tears running down his cheeks as well, but he did his best to keep them under control. He didn't want to have to walk through the busy terminal, crying all the way back to his car. As they shared their embrace, the words to "Leaving on a Jet Plane" ran through his head.

Paige finally pulled herself away from Holden to give him a kiss on the cheek. She then grabbed her carry-on and turned towards the security gate. Just before crossing through the doors, she turned to Holden one last time. She raised her fingers to her lips and blew him a kiss. Then she walked through the doors and was gone.

Holden waited for a minute, hoping she would come running back to him. She didn't. He turned and headed to the parking lot. The automatic doors opened wide, allowing him to exit. When the doors closed behind him, he felt a raindrop land on his forehead.

He looked up at the sky. The clouds were turning black. They opened up in torrential downpour. Holden then turned his eyes to the ground. He slowly walked to his car, avoiding all the other pedestrians who were running for shelter.

Printed in the United States
By Bookmasters